"This extraordinary collection reminds us just how profound the influence of families is on all of us. Highly recommended."
—*Library Journal*

"A moving experience . . . While *A Member of the Family* reminds us that not everything is perfect, it also shows us that we aren't so different from each other after all."
—*Northwest Gay and Lesbian Reader*

"EXCELLENT . . . some stories are touching, while others charm the reader with memories of childhood; all of them captivate the imagination." —Dr. Charles Silverstein, author of *The New Joy of Gay Sex*

"BEAUTIFUL . . . A FEAST OF HUMANITY. BOOKS THIS ELOQUENT AND LOVING ARE FEW AND FAR BETWEEN. . . . A wonderful collection of memoirs on the transitions by which the writers became spiritually integrated with their kin, and their kin with them." —*Arizona Daily Star*

"POIGNANTLY ELABORATES ON THE NOTION OF 'FAMILY VALUES' WHEN SOME MEMBERS OF THE FAMILY HAPPEN TO BE GAY." —*Lambda Book Report*

"Juxtaposes humor with compassion, anger and all the poignant contradictions that compose any American family."
—*Casco Bay Weekly*

JOHN PRESTON has published over thirty-five books, among them several important volumes of gay literature, including *Hometowns: Gay Men Write About Where They Belong*, *The Big Gay Book*, *Flesh and the Word* (all available in Plume editions) and *Personal Dispatches: Writers Confront AIDS*. He is the former editor of *The Advocate* magazine. His articles have appeared in *Harper's* and *Interview*, and he writes a regular column for *Lambda Book Report*. He lives in Portland, Maine.

other books by john preston

fiction:

Franny, the Queen of Provincetown, 1983.
Mr. Benson, 1983, 1992.
*I Once Had a Master and Other Tales of Erotic
    Love*, 1984.

"The Mission of Alex Kane"
Volume I: *Sweet Dreams*, 1984, 1992
Volume II: *Golden Years*, 1984, 1992
Volume III: *Deadly Lies*, 1985, 1992
Volume IV: *Stolen Moments*, 1986, 1993
Volume V: *Secret Dangers*, 1986, 1993
Volume VI: *Lethal Secrets*, 1987, 1993

Entertainment for a Master, 1986
Love of a Master, 1987
The Heir, 1988, 1992
In Search of a Master, 1989
The King, 1992
Tales from the Dark Lord, 1992 (short stories)
The Arena, 1993

edited:

Hot Living: Erotic Stories About Safer Sex, 1985
Flesh and the Word: And Erotic Anthology, 1992

nonfiction:

*The Big Gay Book: A Man's Survival Guide for
    the Nineties*, 1991
The Art of Being a Hustler, 1993

with frederick brandt:

*Classified Affairs: The Gay Men's Guide to the
    Personals*, 1984

with glenn swann:

Safe Sex: The Ultimate Erotic Guide, 1987

edited:

Personal Dispatches: Writers Confront AIDS,
    1989
*Hometowns: Gay Men Write About Where They
    Belong*, 1991
*Flesh and the Word 2: An Anthology of Erotic
    Writing*, 1993

edited and with an introduction
by john preston

a member of the family

gay men write

about their

families

A PLUME BOOK

PLUME
Published by the Penguin Group
Penguin Books USA Inc., 375 Hudson Street, New York, New York 10014, U.S.A.
Penguin Books Ltd, 27 Wrights Lane, London W8 5TZ, England
Penguin Books Australia Ltd, Ringwood, Victoria, Australia
Penguin Books Canada Ltd, 10 Alcorn Avenue, Toronto, Ontario, Canada M4V 3B2
Penguin Books (N.Z.) Ltd, 182–190 Wairau Road, Auckland 10, New Zealand

Penguin Books Ltd, Registered Offices: Harmondsworth, Middlesex, England

Published by Plume, an imprint of Dutton Signet, a division of Penguin Books USA Inc.
Previously published in a Dutton edition.

First Plume Printing, February, 1994
10 9 8 7 6 5 4 3 2 1

 REGISTERED TRADEMARK—MARCA REGISTRADA

LIBRARY OF CONGRESS CATALOGING-IN-PUBLICATION DATA
A Member of the family : gay men write about their families / edited
    and with an introduction by John Preston.
        p.   cm.
    Originally published : New York, N.Y., U.S.A. : Dutton, c1992.
    ISBN 0-452-27032-4
    1. Gay men—United States—Family relationships.   I. Preston,
John.
HQ76.2.U5M46   1994
306.874—dc20
                                        93–30305
                                        CIP

Printed in the United States of America
Set in Garamond No. 3
Designed by Steven N. Stathakis

For my sisters Linda and Elizabeth and my brother Kurt, who also have their own stories about our family and me.

acknowledgments

One of the great pleasures in doing this volume was working once again with my editor at NAL/Dutton, Matthew Sartwell. As always, Peter Borland provided extraordinary support and nurture at NAL/Dutton as well.

My agent Peter Ginsberg performed his usual supporting role with his usual aplomb. Tom Hagerty once again set up the files and did the proofreading. Robert Riger dispensed the necessary succor.

This is the fifth anthology I've edited. Once again I've been amazed by the goodwill and helpful response that the contributors have shown as we've worked putting this book together. I thank them all for their hard work and great understanding.

contents

john preston

introduction
my brother and the letter

I had to leave my family to be gay.

I tried not to. I had just graduated from college and had moved back to Massachusetts. It was the late sixties, before the Stonewall riots that would date the beginning of a widely organized gay movement. I'd watched other young men commit suicide because of their anguish over sexuality. I'd met other graduates of the elite college I'd attended who'd settled for clerking positions in department stores because they were so convinced they couldn't have one of the careers to which we'd been taught to aspire in school. I watched healthy young men destroy their lives with drugs and alcohol in a dark expression of their self-hatred.

My family had prepared me for more than this. I was determined that those weren't going to be my stories. The fact of my homosexuality wasn't an issue; that had been revealed long ago and my parents had dealt with it as best they could. The actual problem was that we didn't have a vocabulary to discuss homosexuality. We didn't know the words or the symbols that could take this powerful, but almost always hidden, force and bring it into the light.

The most my parents could do—and it was as much as any parents could really be expected to do back then—was express concern. My mother thought I would be unhappy. My father thought I would never be successful. They couldn't move beyond that because we didn't know any alternatives. We knew of no words being spoken or written that could change the discourse.

I was infuriated by the frustration that overcame me when my parents couldn't talk to me about what was happening. I dismissed their reactions as bourgeois; there had to be a way out and they weren't going to help me.

I decided to leave. I would go and discover my own life. One day I left a letter at home on my parents' bureau and announced my anger and my sense of defeat over what had gone on between us. I wasn't even going to tell them where I was going. I'd had enough. I expected they had as well.

I moved to Minneapolis. I chose it because it had one of the earliest and strongest gay communities in the country. Most recent histories are about the early movement in New York or San Francisco, assuming that those hearts of hedonism and escape were the birthplace of the political and cultural efforts for gay identity that seem to be taken for granted today. In fact, Minnesota was another of the centers of gay liberation, and much of the community building and social action that took place there was more sophisticated than what was happening on the coasts.

I had determined to do this coming out business in a big way. I was not going to just enter into a social world of other gay men— I'd had that for years in Chicago and Boston—I was going to take the political and organizational skills I'd learned in the civil rights movements and other social change organizations and give them to my own kind. Within a year, I became one of the cofounders of the gay community center in the Twin Cities. I was on television; I gave newspaper interviews; I wrote polemics.

The issue of my family didn't disappear just because I became an activist and a community leader. When I gave speeches or talked to reporters the most frequently asked question still was simply: "What do your parents think?" Stonewall had happened by then, there was an articulated ideology and worldview of what it meant to be a gay man, and the idea that my parents would be my highest concern—not my community, not my lovers, not my new world, but the old one—seemed senseless.

Because others were so focused on the issue of parents and their gay children, almost no one understood the real point about me and my family. Yes, there had been a breach between my father and my mother and myself, but that wasn't the real family dynamic that was going on in my move to Minnesota. Hardly anyone asked why I chose to go there to do this gay work and why I hadn't stayed in New England, or at least Illinois, where I'd gone to college. The real motivation for my move had been my brothers.

I have two sisters, five and ten years younger than I am. I loved them deeply, but I also felt they were approaching the world in a way that meant they could handle my being publicly known as a gay man. But my brothers were fifteen and seventeen years younger than I was. I had no compunction about staying in the Boston area and being public about my homosexuality—it wouldn't have bothered me if it had embarrassed my parents at that point. But as I thought of myself becoming a gay activist, I imagined how my brothers would react, how their schoolmates would taunt them, how they would be shamed.

I was actually shocked by my response and its intensity. Of course I loved the boys, just as I loved my sisters. Still they were simply young things who often seemed in the way when I'd come home for college vacations. Changing their diapers had hardly been my favorite diversion when I was in the house for Christmas. Yet here they were, dictating a major factor in my life.

Many things changed over the next ten years. I did find that new life of my own. I went from being an activist to becoming a counselor and, eventually, a writer and editor. When I was asked why I worked so hard at gay liberation, I said I did it so there would be more healthy men to love, and I meant it. The ghosts of those lost lives and lost careers that had haunted me after college were being exorcised by the new communities that were being built and the relationships that were developing within them. We had images of an army of loving brothers coming together, and it seemed attainable.

As I developed my own strength, I was also able to allow a reconciliation with my family. It wasn't a powerful one—great distances still remained—but I began to communicate with them again. I remember once when I was living in California I found myself in Boston on business. I decided, with some apprehension, to call my parents and ask them to dinner in the city. My schedule was grueling and I had a plane to catch, it would have to be an early meal. Because I wasn't so familiar with Boston restaurants anymore, I suggested meeting at Locke-Ober, a restaurant I could remember, a city landmark, and an expensive one. My mother and father showed up, we had a pleasant meal, and then I had to rush off. I picked up the check and put it on my expense account, more out of a desire to be on my way than anything else. That gesture has become part of the family lore: the night John took Jack and Nancy to Locke-Ober. Years later I can now understand that it erased, in its way, one of my father's great concerns: would I ever be successful? Well, I was successful enough to buy him dinner in a good restaurant and that counted for a great deal, it turned out.

There were other events that brought us back together. I began to return for visits to a lakeside camp my parents had in New Hampshire, often bringing my friends along. My family never made an issue of that, though the introduction of gay friends and lovers is often very stressful in other families. It probably helped that it was also never an issue for me. I never felt I was using those introductions to do anything to my family; these were simply the people in my life and they went where I went.

There were phone calls home to Massachusetts as I continued to move around the country; there were even occasional letters. I was not nearly so obsessed with finding acceptance from my parents as other people appeared to be, but I was happy we had reached an accommodation. And, of course, there were my siblings.

My sister Betsy had lived in San Francisco part of the time I'd been there; we saw each other and talked on the phone often. My sister Linda had gone to college in Ohio and we never had the chance to become as close, but we were in touch with each other.

The boys seemed so far removed from my life that I seldom even thought of them. I heard all the stories and talked to them when I was with them in New Hampshire or Massachusetts, but the age gap seemed so great I didn't pursue any real relationships with them.

My sisters and I at least shared academic goals. We were all moving in similar directions as far as education was concerned. The schools we attended read like a litany of liberal arts havens in those days. The boys weren't on the same track. They were much more interested in athletics and were much more, well, *normal* than the rest of us. They were much more just some of the guys.

Whatever responsibility I had felt toward them when they'd been young had disappeared. As far as I was concerned, they were a couple of jocks having a good time, famous for their vigorous sports activities and their enormous size—both began lifting weights in high school—and they seemed to have little connection with the gay activist-writer's life I had constructed.

By the time Marvin, the older of the two, was in junior college (a soccer scholarship had gotten him in—no matter how lousy his academic grades were, he was a mean goalie), I was living in New York. I was working at *Mandate*, one of the new gay magazines more famous for its nude male layouts than any literary content, when I got a phone call from my mother. Marvin had left school and had joined the marine corps. That only made sense, in its own way, we agreed. He was old enough and the school he'd gone to wasn't working out. What was strange, my mother said, was that he wanted to come visit me.

My parents had told him that he could have a weekend wherever he wanted just before going to boot camp. They'd assumed he'd pick something like a wild weekend in Florida or some such place. Marvin had a propensity for beer at that time and for roughneck socializing. We could see him at Fort Lauderdale picking up the girls, crashing into bars. But he'd surprised them. He was adamant. He wanted to come see me.

I had him pegged from the beginning. I was sure he only wanted to visit me because he wanted to do up the town. He wanted to party in New York—which still allowed eighteen-year-olds to drink in bars—and his big brother had an apartment in Manhattan.

Of course he could come, I told my mother. It didn't make any difference to me. He'd be gone the whole time. I told her to send him on down. We made train reservations for him, and I gave him instructions on how to take a cab to SoHo, where I worked.

Now, you must picture this. I was sitting in my office at *Mandate* when the receptionist called me. There was a breathlessness to his voice I'd never heard. He told me my brother was waiting for me at the desk. I walked out front to greet Marvin and then I realized what I'd done, so very unconsciously.

There, looking like a recruiting poster for the marine corps, was my eighteen-year-old, blond, blue-eyed jock brother with his short-cut hair, bulging muscles, quick smile, and perfect complexion. Standing around him, looking stupid as they ran imaginary errands that would take them closer to him, were the rest of the staff, staring at Marvin with ill-hidden awe. (This was not an easily impressed audience. After all, we constantly had would-be centerfolds coming into the office for interviews.)

I stopped all the foolishness and took my brother and his bag out of there. We went to a bistro and ordered drinks. So, I told him, you're here to party?

No, he replied. He obviously had something pent up inside him; he was nervous and uncomfortable. He told me he had come to see me with a specific purpose. He was upbeat about entering the marine corps. This was something he really wanted to do and he knew he wasn't going to make it in college. This was also a chance for him to start over, in his own way. He wanted the challenge of the corps and he wanted to prove himself as an independent person. But, if he was going to move into this new chapter in his life, he had to clear up some old business, and the old business was me.

I wasn't at all prepared for what he was saying, nor how he was saying it. His boyishness might still be there in his appearance, but along with it was the staunch demeanor of an adolescent announcing that he demanded to be taken seriously. I had used part of my memory to dismiss much of who he was to me. Now, seeing him across the table, I remembered more, I remembered those things that had once made me so protective of him that I moved just in order to shelter him. I flashed back to the times I had spent with him when he was so little, such a small boy who was a bit too rambunctious. The kid brother who'd been a pain was, I discovered, overwhelmed with memories of climbing into my bed in the mornings during my vacations and telling me secrets, or sitting with me doing something as simple as watching television and having me look over and see that expression on his face, half-puzzled, but quite pleased, an expression that told me that I was his big brother and that meant a lot to him.

Even while these strong feelings surged through me, I couldn't understand what his business with me could possibly be about. What could have happened that he wanted to talk about with me now? Then he explained that he had been the one who'd found the letter I'd left on our parents' bureau years before. He'd found it and read it. All he'd known was that something had been upsetting the family and he hadn't understood what was going on. He was more than idly curious when he saw the envelope. He'd opened it and discovered that I was leaving.

The words had been horrible. My anger had been directed at my parents, but he read it as though he had done something wrong. If he had been a better boy, maybe I wouldn't have left. He had also taken it as a moment of supreme abandonment. As much as I had been unable to talk to my family about my sexuality, he had conceived of me as that big brother he looked up to, the one who did have a language that could speak to him. In the midst of all the troubles that our family went through, he had seen me as his strength, the fallback, the one he could count on. The small notes or phone conversations that had seemed so trivial to me had been supremely important to him.

He described the romance of being an eight-year-old with a brother who was in college, of the excitement and anticipation of my vacations, of how exotic my postcards and letters had seemed when I'd gone to the South to do civil rights work and to New Mexico to explore the Navajo reservation. Those were the dreams a big brother gave, he told me. And those were the dreams I had taken away when I'd written that letter he'd found on our parents' bureau.

I was crushed. I felt one of the great sorrows of my life. It was similar to that moment with a lover when one realizes that things aren't so simple after all, that there really are two sides to the story. I had had to leave my family, I knew that, and I had accomplished the goals that required that break with my past. I had become a success and I was happy. My friends and lovers were no longer the victims of society but were striving to new aspirations and purposes. I had been part of a group of people who were changing history. I was proud of it all, but I was devastated that it had come at the expense of this hurt that Marvin felt.

It was too ironic that one of the reasons I had left Massachusetts a decade earlier had been to save him from difficulty. I had wanted him to be able to escape the stigma of having a gay brother, at least of having many people know that. Now he was telling me that the price he'd paid—the price of losing his big brother for so long—had been too high. I had misunderstood where the pain really would be.

But did I *want* a brother now? That's one of the answers he wanted from me. Because, he assured me, he wanted his brother back in his life. Oh, yes, I did!, I told him, and I meant it. Even if he became a marine, he asked with a smirk? Even if he was a marine, I smiled back. But I would have to deal with him as an adult now. He was going into the service. He was becoming a man. He didn't want to be treated like a child. It was time to do that, right now. There were no bars in Times Square during the next couple days. There weren't any other people involved in our time with each other. Marvin and I talked, and we talked more. It was as though we were satiating some enormous thirst, one that had been so great we hadn't even been able to acknowledge how parched we'd been for ten years. Some vital connection had never been severed and now it demanded to be fortified with more information, more details, more of whom we had each become.

That was nearly fifteen years ago. That weekend is still one of the most important events in my emotional life. The details are clear in my memory. I remember the passions that I felt as we talked about what it meant to be brothers. I remember the sadness of hearing his hurt, and I remember just as clearly the way he felt so badly that I had felt hurt as well.

Pledges were made that weekend, and they were kept. My brother wrote me from boot camp, he called me from his assigned bases around the country. Spending time together became one of our priorities, and one that we were able to fulfill more often than not.

I got many pleasures from my brother over the next years. One of the most exciting was to watch him grow older. I have always been told that my eyes were my most striking feature. A favorable comment about them was a too-often-repeated line in bars or at parties. Disparagement of the way they looked was an easy way for someone to let me know that I, myself, wasn't approved of either. I had never understood why people responded so strongly to my eyes. I never saw anything special about them when I looked in a mirror. But a mirror is a weak reflection compared to watching my own eyes come to life as Marvin matured. I could sit and look at him and understand how others could read what they wanted to in eyes like these, light irises surrounded by shadowy skin. If you wanted to see craziness, it was there, but so was intense attraction and sensuality.

It wasn't that we only shared physical attributes. Being with my brother has shown me some of the ways I approach the world, both good and bad. I can see in him my own stubbornness—no small thing. And I can see the way that we become silent when angry, how we close down, still not in command of all the language that we need to talk to the world. I can also see the tenderness with which we treat children and animals. I can see the patience we display when teaching others. I can see how we really do approach being men in similar ways, wanting to be strong and forceful, yet never wanting to misuse our power.

The idea that a marine and a gay activist could be as close as Marvin and I became over those years always attracted attention. How could it be, people wanted to know, when you seem to be diametrically opposed in every way. It's true, most of our political arguments seemed to end with Marvin sternly pronouncing, "People like you couldn't express your opinions if people like me weren't willing to defend your right to do it!"

It's also true that we used to try to force our lifestyles on each other too much. He wanted me to go to singles' bars with him; I would insist that he be politically correct and go to gay bars if he wanted to have a drink with me. In the end, we just agreed that the discomfort we each felt in the other's world was too difficult; instead, we decided to go to neutral places, quiet lounges in hotels, places where we could talk without defenses or unease, because, after all, the talk is what we wanted more than anything else.

In the end, when someone asked Marvin how we could possibly get along, he came up with the best answer: "Given the way the world's going to hell, being a gay writer and being a marine are the two best options I know of." No one ever did come up with a response to that one.

I did wonder what it had meant to him to have a gay brother, and what it had meant to Kurt, the youngest of the siblings. I finally got to talk to both of them about it once. It really hadn't been a big thing, they insisted. They might not have talked about it very much when they were younger—they had known that the stigma I'd feared was real—but it hadn't really bothered them. It certainly made a difference, they told me, that they never *discovered* my sexuality. It had simply been a given in their lives. John brings home men, other big brothers bring home women; that's just the way it was and they hadn't known anything different.

If anything, Marvin did admit, and Kurt agreed, he had felt it was unfair that he had to explore his own sexuality much more carefully than did any of his friends. Much more seriously than any of their peers would admit to doing, during their adolescence my brothers considered the idea that they might be gay. After all, with one gay man in the family, they might be no different. In the end, though, these reflections had also made them more comfortable with sexuality in general.

I was astonished when they told me of the times they had stood up for me. Even though our individual relationships had deepened, I had never heard any stories about my brothers as supporters of me as a gay man, or of gay rights. Kurt had also gone to state college for a couple years. It turned out that he would stand up and walk out of any classroom—psychology or political science or any other—where the professor talked about homosexuality as "deviant behavior." "No one was going to talk about my brother that way," he announced stolidly. (To this day I wonder about those professors and what they thought of this hulking jock stalking out of their rooms. "If they asked me, I told them," Kurt said. "If they didn't, to hell with them.")

My renewed relationship with Marvin coincided with my move to Maine and, with the closer proximity, even more time spent with the rest of my family. Marvin's and my special connection was something of which the others were very aware. It made some of them unhappy, feeling somehow that they were left out of our secrets. We were aware of that and tried to make room for the others, but it didn't always work.

When Marvin was about to get married, he made a surprisingly formal journey to Maine with his fiancée. They wanted, in a sort of anachronistic manner, my blessing, and, once given, they wanted me to be the best man at the ceremony. Of course, I agreed.

Postings in the marine corps took Marvin and his new wife far away from New England for many years. They were in Asia and then in California, and it was more difficult to keep up the intimacy we'd developed. But I didn't worry about it. Nor, apparently, did he. Whenever they were on the East Coast it was assumed by everyone that he and I would have to spend time together. The cards and letters—the stuff we all use to keep a relationship in place when distance presents a barrier—were there to keep us in touch. When we did get together, the same emotional bond that we'd rediscovered in that SoHo bar was still intact—if anything, it was made stronger by time.

We both needed that strength. When I finally told Marvin that I was infected with HIV and that I was in danger of having AIDS, his response was automatic and forceful. He came east and visited, first announcing that he'd feel terrible if our physical separations had left me with any idea that he cared less about me. And when I'd assured him that I had no doubts about that, he looked at me with those eyes that we share, the ones that some people find demonic and others think are so fascinating, and he said, "I will do anything you want. I will provide everything I can. I will be here in any way you want me to be. You only have to ask."

If I ever trusted that statement from anyone, I believed it when my brother said those words to me.

Later, Marvin's marriage fell apart. He had left the marines and moved to New Hampshire, spending some time alone at the cottage where we'd each spent our boyhood summers. He called me and told me that he and Linda had separated. He wanted me to know.

I drove up as soon as I could. We sat in the living room and drank a couple beers, watched a Red Sox game, and talked to each other as honestly as ever, all about intimacy and love, failure and rejection, hope and aspiration.

My brother is, in a unique way, my best friend. I sometimes worry that I romanticize our relationship, that I have made it into a fraternal myth, good material for the writer, but impossible in reality. I have even occasionally been uncomfortable when we're about to see each other again, thinking that I've dreamed up this bond, that no one could sustain the expectations of intimacy and fondness that I had developed. But in all our years since that conversation in Manhattan, my brother has never failed me. I don't think I've failed him, either.

If that one relationship is in place, it doesn't say that the rest of my familial associations are positive. In fact, as I've grown older, I can see that many of the conflicts that I and others might have ascribed to my sexuality were much deeper than that. There are tensions that exist in our family circle that have little or nothing to do with my being a gay man. What is in place, because of Marvin, is a sense that I'm not alone. It's like having those same eyes; now I have someone to call to discuss a family dynamic and what the hell is going on. There's someone who can say, "It's not you. I've had the same experience. I know what it's like." The table turns and the younger brother becomes the nurturer, giving me support, telling me I'm not alone with my feelings of alienation or pain. I have a brother who understands who I am and what I have experienced.

That trust gives me a chance to reconcile even more deeply with the other members of my family. My sisters and I have begun to grow closer now that we are in our middle age. My parents more freely express their pleasure at how my life has turned out. After all, my mother will tell you, I have written books, and let the contents be damned! They may have gay themes, but her son is an author and, while she might not have discussed my homosexuality very lavishly in the old days, I don't think her pride in that particular achievement can be underestimated now. She attends my readings, brings her friends along, passes out photocopies of my reviews.

And so our lives go on.

Yet, even as I'm forty-six, when the interviewers come to talk to me they inevitably ask, "What do your parents think?" I wonder how many heterosexual writers my age who have written as much as I have are ever asked that question. What is it about gay men and our families that seems to make that one topic so fascinating to others and so vital to ourselves?

The topic isn't easily covered by self-help books that reduce everything to a list of pop psychology know-all. Families are complex and they are all so unique to themselves. But they are so vital to our understanding of ourselves. I needed to have a brother to see my own eyes in a way that a mirror couldn't show them to me. Examining our families and understanding what they have done to us and what we have done to them is a crucial part of our learning about how we are gay in our society.

Not wanting to get into theories or gross generalizations, I realized that the best way to look at gay men and our families was to ask writers to investigate a single relationship in their lives. How had that one person treated you? How had you treated him or her? What elements of that relationship formed you, made you look at life differently? What was there about that relationship that still lingers in your mind and your emotions?

The authors in this volume had responded with a wide variety of emotional statements. Because this was never designed to be a book to express a party line, the stories they have to tell are not always positive. There is hurt and fury in what they have to say as well as love and affection.

Something should be said about the writers who are represented in this volume. Most of us are dealing with the aging and death of our parents and grandparents at the same time we are dealing with some of us and many of our friends being ill with AIDS. An ultimate alienation and separation seems to be an unavoidable topic in some of these pieces. Yet, there is life in them all, the living affirmation of self and connection that is important to our being full persons in our world.

This book is not about being a perfect child in a perfect family. This is about life with flaws and accomplishments, hurt and nourishment. It is about being human in our world.

michael nava

abuelo

my grandfather,

raymond acuña

It was no secret in my family that I did not have a father. On weekends, my older brother, Tommy, was picked up by his father, whom my mother had divorced shortly after I was born. Though Tommy and I had the same last name, I knew I was not his father's son. My younger brothers and sisters bore the last name of my stepfather and were, indubitably, his children. I was the son of a man with whom my mother, then married, had had an affair, to the lasting shame of her Mexican-Catholic family. To preserve appearances, I was given her husband's last name but the pretense ended there.

All I knew about my natural father was his name, and I saw him only once, when I was five years old and he turned up, drunk, at our house. My stepfather drove him out of the yard, screaming invectives. After that, I never asked about him and was ashamed when my mother mentioned him to me.

This one incident aside, my stepfather showed little paternal interest in me. More often, he used my mother's infidelity to her first husband against her when they fought. Once, during a drunken argument, I heard him call her a whore, and the humiliation I felt was as much for myself as for her. Practically speaking, I was my mother's child, her favorite, she told me occasionally, and both she and her own mother indulged me. But even then, at five and six, I was aware that my mother's solicitude was due as much to pity as love, not to mention her own complicated shame. What I felt toward my mother in return was a confusion of love, guilt, and resentment. At that early age, in my innermost self, I was no one's child, and as I grew older my sense of estrangement from my family deepened. When, at eleven, I was sexually molested by an adult family member, I felt cast off completely.

Until I left home, at seventeen, the only member of my family with whom I felt any kinship beyond a shared bloodline was my grandfather, Raymond Acuña. Not only was he the nearest person I had to a father by blood, he was also a solitary, secretive man. Watching him, I could discern my potential adult self.

My grandfather was a Yaqui Indian, short and muscular, smooth skinned and dark. His face was broad and high cheeked, almost Asiatic. His black eyes were wary and intelligent. He spoke Spanish and English with equal facility when he chose to speak at all.

He and my grandmother had built a big, gloomy house in Gardenland, the Mexican barrio of Sacramento, on what had been a distant relative's farm. My grandfather lived in a small room off the kitchen in the back of the house. He slept in a narrow bed shoved up against the wall, and there was just enough room left for a nightstand and a dresser of drawers. On the nightstand were piles of magazines and paperback books, Argosy, Ellery Queen, the Perry Mason mysteries, Westerns by Louis L'Amour. He was the only person in my family, other than me, who read for pleasure.

My grandfather kept a jar full of pennies on his dresser. One day, when I was four or five, I stole into his room while he was at work and emptied out the jar. I took the pennies to the neighborhood grocery store and spent them on candy. My theft enraged him.

He beat me with his belt, and for years thereafter I lived in such fear of him that, if he entered a room, I would leave it. Looking back, I don't think it was the theft that angered him as much as the invasion of his room. Later, I would come to appreciate his mania for privacy.

He worked at Del Monte, one of the big canneries in Sacramento where most of Gardenland's residents worked. From there he brought home boxes of damaged canned goods. There was always food in the kitchen, the bills were paid on time, and the house was owned outright by my grandmother and him. These were not small accomplishments in our poor neighborhood, or even in our family, where my mother struggled for years raising her children on welfare money. Yet, although he provided for it, my grandfather seemed to take little pleasure in his family. It was a matriarchy, with my grandmother at its center. My grandfather stood apart, a scowling, silent presence whose greatest wish was to be left alone. One of my abiding memories is of him sitting in the living room watching a boxing match, drinking beer, and chain-smoking Kents.

And yet, though I loved my grandmother more than anyone else in my family, it was my grandfather to whom I was drawn. He represented a kind of masculinity from which I was not excluded by reason of my intelligence or, later, my homosexuality. It was exactly these qualities that separated me from the boisterous athletic boys who were my peers. Fat, myopic, and brainy, I escaped sissyhood only because of the aggressive gloominess I shared with my grandfather. I was like the cartoon character who walks beneath his own rain cloud, so fiercely unhappy that I deflected the taunts to which I would otherwise have been subject. By the same token, of course, I deflected any attempts at friendship, unable, in my unhappiness, to distinguish friend from foe.

In this respect, too, I was like my grandfather. His only male acquaintances were his sons, sons-in-law, and the strangers with whom he drank on Friday nights at a bar in downtown Sacramento. He never had a single visitor to his house to whom he was not related by blood or marriage.

If my grandfather sensed an affinity between us, he kept it to himself. The extent of his interest in me was to ask what I was reading if he saw me with a book. As for me, I was still too afraid of him to initiate conversation. Now I wish I had spoken to him, because perhaps he might have understood the estrangement I felt from the family over which he was the unwilling patriarch.

Certainly, this estrangement was nothing that the women who raised me could have understood, even if I had been able to tell them. I worried my mother and grandmother; resigned to ungiving marriages, their creed was to believe in God and sacrifice for the children. It was beyond their power to imagine a hurt that could not be healed by prayer, food, or the occasional five-dollar bill filched from the rent or grocery money. They had no idea what to do with me, a moody boy, precocious at one moment and withdrawn the next, who sometimes accepted their solicitude and at other times angrily rejected it. And it was beyond my power—because it was beyond my understanding—to tell them how I hurt. I could only have told them that, lying in bed at night, I prayed for time to pass, to be grown and gone. I could only have told them, though not in these words, that I was waiting for my life to begin. Sitting with my grandfather I divined, beneath his anger and loneliness, something of the pain I felt.

When I went off to college—vowing to myself never to return—the only picture I took with me of anyone in my family was a photograph of my grandfather in his World War II navy uniform. I put it in a frame and it sat on my desk the four years I was at college, including summers, though I never wrote or spoke to him during that entire time. His picture was an icon, the significance of which I did not myself completely understand, but it had something to do with self-denial and keeping secrets. "You're so evasive," one of my college teachers told me, and I took it as a compliment.

I was twenty-three when I returned to Sacramento. My grandmother had died and my grandfather had remarried. His new wife was a much younger woman whom he had met in Mexico. They had moved out of the big house in which he and my grandmother had lived to a smaller house just down the street owned by one of my uncles. Virginia, the new wife, was a fleshy, cheerful woman, far different from my tiny, perpetually worried grandmother. My grandfather looked the same as he had always looked, ageless in his Indian darkness. But, as I watched him put his arm around his wife, tease her about her girth and then kiss her, gestures I had never seen him make toward my grandmother, I knew he had changed in the six years since I had last seen him. And for the first time in my life, I felt toward my grandfather a simple, uncomplicated emotion. I was happy for him.

I lived in Sacramento for another year. It was a difficult, lonely time for me, though not in the same way that my childhood had been difficult and lonely. Childhood had been a form of imprisonment to me. Now, as a young man, it was freedom that weighed upon me; I had no purpose or aspirations, much less the means to achieve either. I worked at little jobs, lived in a studio apartment downtown, frequented the city's seedy gay bars, and waited for something to happen.

On weekends, I sometimes visited my family, making a point of stopping to see my grandfather. He was, by now, an old man, and old age made him voluble. All that I had known about his life was what I observed as a child, when he was already middle-aged. As far as I knew, he had always been married to my grandmother, always been a father, and always toiled at his monotonous job. But now, sitting on the porch of his little house, listening to him, I realized that he had once been as young as I. What's more, unlike me, his youth had not been spent buried in books looking for a way to make sense of life. He had traveled the Southwest with his brother, worked as an extra in silent movies, fought in the Pacific. I began to understand that all his silence had concealed was a middle-aged man's regrets and disappointments. Now that he was old, he had come to terms with the vagaries of life simply because he had outlasted them.

I left Sacramento at the end of that year, and I never saw my grandfather again. He died after a brief but excruciating bout with cancer. True to form, he chose cremation rather than burial with my grandmother. Virginia disappeared into Mexico after his death, taking most of his relics. The house in which they'd lived was sold, passing out of the family.

Maybe it's true that men don't become themselves until they can finally separate their identities from their fathers'. In my case, I had to recreate my grandfather's dour middle years for myself before I could let go of my belief that masculinity and self-denial are the same thing. By the time I was thirty-three, I had constructed a life so fraught with obligation that it left me no room to breathe. It wasn't until I was forced to own up to alcoholism that I began to unravel the threads in my own character to determine which were authentic and which I had taken from him. In the process, I came to see that, although I am not the same kind of man as my grandfather, I am, nonetheless, a man.

By the same token, I am finally able to see my true debt to him. There was genuine courage in my grandfather's self-abnegation. He fettered his spirit in the interests of a family which, truth be told, he probably never wanted. It isn't necessary for me to live the same kind of life because he did it for me. By his example, I have been given my freedom.

eric latzky

---

the way back home
revisiting my
grandfather

New York City, July 1990: I came home. Death? Rebirth? The end of an exile? Maybe it was just having lived outside my natural habitat for too long. After living in Los Angeles for nearly five years, I knew more about why I left the place where I was born than why I decided to return.

I took the red-eye. The flight landed at six in the morning, I dropped off my bags at my mother's apartment, nearly at the bottom of Manhattan, and went directly up to the Bronx, where I'm from. There, at Montefiore Hospital, Louis, my grandfather, was about to undergo emergency open-heart surgery. I arrived just in time to see a nurse inject a needleful of morphine into his arm. My family— my grandmother, my uncle, my mother, my brother—turned away, horrified. I watched. I think it was the first time in years Louis had felt something other than pain.

Four. I have just caught my first fish. We are at the lake near the pink bungalow in Denville, New Jersey, but down at the far end away from where the people swim, near where the trees start. It's dark inside where the trees are, it's scary, but also I wonder what's in there. It's early Sunday morning. There is no one else around, just me and Louis. I look like this: my hair is cut in bangs and I am wearing my striped overalls, rolled up past my knees so I can go in the water. It's not sunny out; it's kind of smoky. The water is calm. I have my black fishing pole that Louis got me. It is more than two times taller than me, and it has a reel that I can cast with, and a red-and-white bob. I think Louis put a worm on the hook, which is how I got the fish, a gray lake fish that I am holding up above my head, still on the hook, with my left hand. I'm holding the pole with my right. I look a little mad. Louis says I should throw it back because it's too small, but I won't do it. I stand there until he takes the picture.

Louis survived the operation. The surgeon thought it was incredible how well he did, how strong he was, considering his age.

For fifty years, Louis worked as a purveyor, buying meat out of Little West Twelfth Street wholesale meat market, an area of a few square blocks near the river, and making deliveries to his clients, restaurants in and around the city. He would go to work at four in the morning, make all his purchases—sides of beef, legs of lamb, endless provisions—by six or so, and get everything delivered by eight, before the rest of the city even got started. I used to go to work with him from the time I was very young.

I didn't know then what the strange triangle-shaped building in the middle of the market was. Not too many years later I would come to know it as the Anvil, the notoriously historic gay bar. Nor did I know, as a boy, that this area surrounding what I called simply the meat market—rows of nineteenth-century town houses, cobblestone streets, and, closer to the river, industrial warehouses and seemingly abandoned piers—had such an eloquent double meaning. I didn't know that it was actually a neighborhood with a name, the West Village, and that it was then the center of New York's gay world, a place where I would later spend a fair amount of time.

■   ■   ■

Eight. The sun is just coming up around the West Side Highway, the part of it that's still standing. I'm cold; it's not winter anymore, but it's not really spring yet either. It smells like meat. We are in the old green truck. It's bumpy because of the cobblestone streets. Joe is driving. Michael, my brother, is sitting on the crate. I'm on the seat, high up so I can see out. Louis, like always, is riding half outside the open door, wearing his cowboy hat. It's a Stetson. I know because he let me try it on once, even though it was bigger than my whole head. Louis tells Joe to pull over for a minute. He wants to run into a place to see if he can get a special cut of something a client needs. He tells us to wait. The sky is orange, streaked with clouds. Across the street, a man comes out of the triangle-shaped building and walks in the direction of the truck. When he gets close, I can see he has what looks like a diamond in his ear. It's sparkling. I look at it, then I look at the man, right into his eyes. He looks at me. When I realize that our eyes are looking directly at each other, it makes me turn away.

With no plan in mind, completely disoriented and kind of shocked, I went to live with two friends in Soho. I spent the summer on the subway, back and forth between their apartment and the Bronx—first the IRT to Jerome Avenue until Louis was discharged from the hospital there, then the Broadway local to 231st Street in Riverdale, near my grandparents' apartment. Those long, air-conditioned rides were what really, finally brought me back to New York—every site, every image of my childhood came into and then went out of focus through the windows of the elevated subway cars. They were like giant TV screens moving constantly, playing reruns of the same old show over and over.

Louis began to recover, slowly. He didn't seem to want to talk much; he seemed distant, inside himself, the opposite of the way he had always been. We sat on the terrace of my grandparents' apartment surrounded by thickly greened treetops limiting the view to a small, comfortable, familiar distance. It was quiet, breezy. We watched the summer rainstorms. Louis read the paper, did the crosswords as he had all his life. We didn't say too much to each other. Perhaps it was enough for him just to have me around.

■ ■ ■

Nine. Papa Harry, my other grandfather, died last night. My father said that means I won't ever be able to see him again, except one more time. It's early in the morning. We're at this place called Hirsch & Sons, down near the end of the Grand Concourse. All of my family, I mean everyone, is coming here. They're all being really nice to me, and to my brother, and to Marc and Scott, my cousins. I'm all dressed up, and I think people are crying, the big people, and it smells like some kind of chemical or something in here. I don't know what it is. My father comes over and says we can go see Papa Harry now and he takes us into this room. When we get up close to the box Papa Harry is lying in, I can see his face is white and his eyes are closed, but not like he's sleeping. He's wearing a suit. I don't want to keep looking, but my father says I have to, at least for a few minutes. As soon as he lets me, I go outside; Michael and Marc and Scott go too. Then—I don't know why—I start crying, really loud, and I can't breathe almost, but I can't stop. Louis comes over and he takes my hand. I tell him that I don't want to go back in there. He says I don't have to and, when everyone else goes back in, he takes me for a long walk in the neighborhood. We walk by a pet store and in the window there's a fish tank. There are no fish in it, but there's a tiny live stingray. It's amazing, the way it glides through the water, the way the tail follows. It looks like when I fly my kite, but under water. Louis asks me if I want him to buy it for me. He's still holding my hand. I tell him no, I just want to look at it.

The summer passed. By August, Louis seemed ready to leave the familiar comfort of the terrace, to begin to get back out somewhat. There were moments when it would occur to him that he could do things now that he hadn't been able to do without pain for years. We drove the car a little, we shopped for groceries, once or twice we went out for a meal.

He was cautious, unsure. The first time we drove he had me sit next to him. After just a few blocks he said that maybe I should drive. I asked how he was feeling. I thought perhaps it was too much of a strain, that turning the wheel was even too difficult. The doctors had said he would be sore for a while. I thought, maybe, he wasn't ready to be doing this. But still, he wasn't talking much, as if he wanted you to know what he was thinking. He would motion with his fingers and half expect you to understand. I said, "Louis, I don't know what it is you're trying to say." He said he was feeling all right. I said in that case I wouldn't drive.

Twelve. We are going to Florida today—Miami Beach. It's Christmas vacation. I have never flown in an airplane before. Neither has Michael. I can't believe you can be in one place now, where it's really cold and snowing, and a few hours later be in a place where it's warm enough to go to the beach, even go swimming. I want to see what a real palm tree looks like. The flight's not until four in the afternoon, but it's beginning to look like a blizzard outside and Louis is getting nervous. It's only about ten-thirty in the morning, but he says we should go to the airport now. I guess he thinks we won't be able to get there at all if we wait. Everything's packed, so we just get in the car and go. We get there quickly, maybe it takes an hour or so. The flight is leaving from this special charter terminal, and there's not a whole lot to do. Michael and I get candy, we run around, we watch these little pay TVs that are pretty cool because we can each watch what we want and for once we don't have to fight about it. Around two they make an announcement that the flight is being delayed, because of the snow I guess. They say it won't leave until seven at night. Michael and I start to kind of fight. We start out playing, but like always Michael gets mad, and then he gets really mean. He always ends up winning, which he can do because he's bigger than me—by less than two years, but still, he's bigger. I guess we're making a lot of noise or something because the next thing I know Louis is right there and we both get hit. Then we're quiet for a while. The flight takes off at about eight. When the plane starts to move fast down the runway, I can't believe it; it's not like anything I've ever felt. It's like there's a hole of air in my stomach. I smile and look at Louis. My grandfather is sitting next to me.

In Soho, we kept the air conditioner going most of the time, but every once in a while we would rough it. On those nights, I would lie in bed, sleepless, late into the night, sweating, naked, wondering what would happen. To my grandfather. To me, my new life back in New York. I wondered what I would do. Not constantly, but sometimes, I would think, maybe this is it. Maybe I've lost the ability to live. Maybe, now that I've made it back home, this is the end after all.

One Sunday, like many others, I took the subway up to the Bronx for a visit. But there was no answer when I rang the buzzer. I rang it again. Nothing. It's strange, I thought, that they would go somewhere without me, without at least telling me. Especially because they knew I was coming. I went to a diner around the corner, drank coffee, ate breakfast, tried to figure it out. I called down to Soho to see if there was a message, I called the hospital, I sat there. I wondered. After about an hour, I tried the hospital again—the emergency room this time. That was it. When I got there, half my family had reconvened. It wasn't catastrophic; the doctor wasn't sure what it was, and by four Louis had been discharged and we all went home.

My family dispersed, my grandmother relaxed a bit, Louis and I sat on the terrace. Louis seemed to be talking more about death than anything else. It didn't seem strange though, perhaps because it seemed natural to me that one would want to contemplate the subject. Somehow we began to talk about my cousin Harold who had died of AIDS about a year and a half earlier.

I think Louis was trying to say something to me that afternoon, something, perhaps, he thought I could understand better than the others. Louis and I never had the language to discuss big things directly. As his friends began to die throughout the eighties, he would tell me of the deaths but never what it was like, what it meant to lose someone you knew, cared about.

He became quiet for a while. We sat there on the terrace, surrounded by the trees, into the evening. I think that Louis was cherishing the summer. He never turned to me, didn't look at me directly when he spoke. "It's a shame," he said quietly, almost like his thoughts were dreams, "all these handsome, talented men dying so young."

Twenty. It's Thanksgiving. I'm packing. Tomorrow I'm leaving for Europe. Actually I'm going to travel through Italy and Switzerland, then on to Austria. In Vienna I'll get a train into the Ukraine, and then on to Moscow. My other grandmother, Dora, still has family there; I'm going

*to meet them for the first time. I have plans to go to Leningrad also.
Eventually I'll head back through Berlin, maybe some other places, Amsterdam or wherever, and at some point I'll land in Paris. At this moment I
have no plans to return to the States. On the outside, Louis has been saying
things that make me think he doesn't want me to go, that maybe I won't
make it, that's the way he puts it. Make it, he says, as if I haven't. Those
words keep running through my mind. I've been out on my own since I was
eighteen, and out of the closet since I was fifteen, but I guess he hasn't seen
too much of that. I guess I haven't let him. After dinner we sit down on
a couch together. Louis has an old photo album in his hand that he wants
me to see. He doesn't say much; we just sit together and he turns the pages,
telling me where each photo was taken and when. First there are a few in
New York. He is wearing a long beaver coat and he has his foot up on
the runner of a Stutz Bearcat Roadster—I think that was the name of it.
It has no top. He says the car was his and he kind of starts to smile when
he says it but just a little. Then there are a whole series of photographs
taken in South America: Rio de Janeiro, Buenos Aires, a bunch of different
places. He says he sailed there on a steamship from New York. He is so
handsome and cool-looking in the photos. He looks like a gangster, like that
old movie star that played gangsters—George Raft. When he closes the photo
album he doesn't look at me, but he tells me he was exactly my age when
he took that trip.*

Louis's health fluctuated. Some days he felt all right, other days
not so well. He continued to move further and further inside himself. He sat on the terrace, he read the paper, we talked a little but
not too much. Overall, it appeared as though he was getting better.

September came, the weather moved into that teasing period
where the hint of fall is always in the air and somehow, still, it
feels as hot and unpleasant as it had for the last three months. Gilda,
my mother, had been talking to my great-aunt Rose, Louis's sister,
about throwing a birthday party for Louis, to celebrate his health,
but perhaps even more to help him see that life goes on, that he'd
be okay. That was the thing he had the most trouble believing. A
party would be something he could look forward to. It would suggest that he could begin to make plans again, to continue his life
on more than just a moment-to-moment basis.

Gilda and Rose decided to go ahead. It was to be about fifteen
of us. At first they thought it would be better to have a private
room, someplace where it would be just us, but in the end they
booked a huge table at a large, busy, well-known restaurant uptown,
on the east side. I think they wanted people to see us celebrate, to
see us be happy, as if in doing so it would confirm that we were,
in fact, and that everything here was just fine.

Gilda and Michael and I decided to get Louis a gift together.
We sent away to New Mexico for a kachina, a Hopi doll. Louis had
talked, for some time, about wanting to own one. The doll arrived,
full of complicated detail, as did the date. Michael flew in from Los
Angeles yet one more time. Everyone dressed as if it were a wedding:
suits, dresses, jewels, shiny shoes. Despite all the difficulties—endless feuds, ancient stalemates, serious health questions, absent members—we looked like a family. We sat together, we laughed, we
toasted, we feasted, we put our differences aside and spent an evening together celebrating Louis's birthday. He was happy that night,
as was my grandmother, Claire, everyone really, even if we weren't
necessarily happy together.

Was it one week or two, or only a matter of days after the
birthday party? I don't remember exactly, though if I looked at a
calendar I could pinpoint the date, that I know. It was Yom Kippur,
the most religious day of the year for Jews, if you're religious. The
call came at two that Saturday morning. I was sleeping but woke
up instantly; the moment the phone rang, I jumped right off the
futon in my friends' place in Soho. The moment the phone rang, I
knew it was the end. I knew it before I even picked it up. "I'm
sorry to wake you," my mother's voice was shaking, scared. "Louis
died tonight."

Things happened quickly. It was only a matter of moments
before I was dressed and in a taxi with Gilda and her brother Harold.
Very shortly, we were in the Bronx, my grandmother was crying,
people were being called, arrangements were being made. Jews don't
wait; they bury the dead immediately. Which isn't easy on a holiday
when, according to the religion, you're not even supposed to turn
on a light.

The following morning, little more than twenty-four hours later, a limousine arrived. We climbed in wearing dark clothing, silent except for crying and breaths, and drove across the Bronx to the old neighborhood, the place where Louis and Claire had spent half their lives, where they had raised Gilda and Harold, where they had grown older, more comfortable, until they moved to Riverdale, to the apartment with the terrace that Louis loved so much.

The funeral parlor on the Grand Concourse was covered in graffiti, the parking lot surrounded by barbed wire. But if it weren't for these outward signs, it could've been a moment from any number of days in my childhood. Rooms full of people arrived, people who had known Louis forever.

The immediate family was called in to view the body. My beating heart was in my throat as I walked through the door, but I made myself be strong. I made myself stand up and do it. How many deaths had I been present at in the last decade, I asked myself. Why was this one any different? I walked up to the casket and there was Louis, my grandfather, lying still, in a burial shroud. He looked small, angelic. How could it be? He looked like a young man, like the gangster, the man in the photo with his foot up on the car. I remember the rabbi saying that for the father to die on such a day, on Yom Kippur, that it was surely a mitzvah, a blessing for the whole family.

I took a breath, put my hand first on the side of the casket and let it rest there for a minute. I closed my eyes, let out the breath, opened my eyes, and then I did it. I put my hand to Louis's cheek and kept it there, the cheek that I had kissed so many times in his life, in mine, the same cheek that boy had kissed—the boy in bangs with a fishing pole refusing to throw back a too-small fish; the boy in his grandfather's Stetson hat; the boy about to fly in an airplane for the very first time; the boy who cried after seeing his grandfather dead in a box.

mother

Yes, well. Faggots and their mothers.

"Close-binding," emasculating. Warping the twig.

"My mother made me a homosexual." (If I get her the wool, will she make me one too?)

Middle-aged men and old ladies, unnaturally symbiotic.

Jokes, humiliations. Farces of oppression.

A paragraph from something I wrote:

"After the funeral, the house was full of relatives. I walked out and drove to the grave, paced beside it in my gray suit, getting the cuffs muddy, talking out loud. 'Whatever you had to go through,' I told her, 'you didn't have to go through this. So just shut up.' And, 'Look,' I said, 'I used to go to the baths all the time, and get fucked in the ass by strangers.' So there. Bitch. Almost screaming this. Cold and drizzle. Funeral wreaths on a patch of mud."

(It's five years now. I stop at the grave when I'm back there; when Dad dies and the house is sold, nobody will go again.)

Symbiotic indeed. Real tangle, there.

As R was dying, he was reconciled with (his phrase) "my Nazi mother." Hold me, Mom, I'm scared.

■   ■   ■

We were an air force family, military chattels, camp to camp.
Bride on rebound, only child, postwar.

I wasn't liked, much. Sissy bookworm, fat, glasses.

Mama's boy, sure. Choosing her dresses, stories of her beaus,
ganging up on Dad. Lullabies. Very you-and-her, no question, on
the road.

Eleven or twelve. Little photo magazines: young men in posing
straps. (Oddly enough, I found the first one at the PX.) I didn't know
how to hide; she got the idea. (Later, the *Stars and Stripes* listed publications "appealing to the prurient interest of homosexuals." Oh.)

Tension ever after, between us. (But not *said*.) Wanting it
back, knowing you can't.

In my teens she started pushing therapy; never said why. Late
high school, early college I had (cover) girlfriends.

At twenty, I fell in love. He was straight. Afterward, I saw
some shrink with a pipe a few times.

I was long gone from her. Professors' pet, academic trainee; then
sixties blitz, drugs, protest, to Berkeley, grad-school dropout, Haight-
Ashbury, turned in draft card, hit the road, very long hair. Etc.

She was in Virginia, terrified. (Dad said later, "We thought
we'd lost you.")

The last utopian moment, crash-and-burn. Black hole. Early
seventies. I lived in Berkeley, delivered mail in East Oakland. They
came to visit once. Outside, a dopers' carnival, riot of styles. I told
her, "It's an asylum, but I'm crazy too. There's nowhere to go."
(Also I said, "I miss you." She said, "I miss you too.")

When the post office fired me for being gay, I finally wound
up telling them. Needless to say, it was no surprise; not even, at
the time, my most pressing deviation.

Another visit to Berkeley, when I was living with Barbara,
failing to go straight. Barbara on the family dynamics: "It's obvious
how she feels about you."

1972. Coming out to stay. Gay lib, leafletting and speaking,
passionate espousal. Boyfriend I never quite got home to Mother. I

only remember one thing she said. A sort of biting-the-bullet look,
and, "Well, it's not something I would have chosen."

No indeed.

As it happened, my life was not a success. Gay lib guttered
out. Didn't work and play well with others, achieved no distinction,
made no money. Years passed, no boyfriends to try and bring.

Ugly little scene, one visit. In my bag a leather strap that came
with a Walkman, she took it for a harness or something. Funny I
guess; not at the time.

Once or twice, back there, I tricked overnight. Dad actually
asked me about the guys; she of course didn't. That or anything
related.

After a while, why-bring-it-up.

Later, she was on chemo, begged me to come live there. (They
were in Oklahoma by then.) I thought, can't you see? Gay, *here*? I
said no. No indeed.

Then she was dying. Stoic, kept up forms, constant pain. Dad
getting crazier. I'd go back every month. Near the end, a stretch
of weeks. She hung on, I cracked, flew back west. That day, she
went into a coma. Overnight flight back. She woke and knew me,
a minute; under again. By the bed, in tears: "How can you go and
leave me with these awful people?"

Something else I wrote: "After she died, I lay in the spare
room till morning with my Walkman, listening to hymns. Will the
circle be unbroken? I am a poor wayfaring stranger. Farther along."

Two months later, I volunteered for the AIDS hotline. The
training was on Mother's Day.

Slowly, it's turned around. There's stuff I'm proud of. (Boyfriends still sparse, however.)

I don't know that there's much to be said. Though she took
pride in teaching till she had to retire, her tradition was prefeminist:
self-sacrificing, conventional, all that. Like her sisters, like the
women she knew.

Our betrayals were mutual and, all things considered, unavoidable. She was who she was, Christian, Republican, a little philistine. Not the kind of thing that bothers you as a kid. Later, a pretty common gap.

I saw how lonely she was, and if I owed anyone, she was it. But you can't go home, and lonely is pretty common too. (Hold me, I'm scared.)

Once at twenty-two, teetering on the abyss, I was home for the weekend; Dad was disowning me, she was hysterical. Then somehow, in the front hall, he came up and hugged me and said, "It's all right. Whatever you do, we'll stand by you." And she was fixing dinner, talking mostly to herself: about when she was first married, it was wartime, they lived in Washington and went out to clubs, had fun, she worked at the British admiralty; exciting days, and still she felt a lack. And then she had me and looked at me and: "I knew. I knew then what it was for."

I'm not sure I've established, quite, what it's for. It appears I won't have a family of, as they say, my own. (I went to a reunion once; a cousin I'd never met said, "Where's your family?" I pointed to Mother and Dad. "Yeah," he said, "but where's your *family?*")

I miss her. I'm sorry her life wasn't happier. Whatever she made me, she could have done worse.

b r i a n
k i r k p a t r i c k

---

the lost umbilical cord
my mother

The facts about my past are scarce, so scarce that when I assemble a picture of my parents, I must include the words of an astrologer and the images from a dream. The only direct link I have with the two people who fucked and produced me is my middle name. When I was given up for adoption, someone, my mother presumably, asked that I be called James. The couple who adopted me had already settled on Brian. No one, of course, asked me. I was six months old.

I can go for months or years without thinking about the adoption, or for that matter, months without remembering that I was adopted into a dysfunctional family. In my mind, I was dropped onto the planet. Then, I'll be sitting in a doctor's office with a form on a clipboard, and I'll panic. Diseases—if I inherited them—are buried in me like snakes in a camouflaged pit.

Some years ago, I worked with a brilliant Jungian analyst. His Cambridge office was three blocks away. I would come and go, work steadily for months, reach a plateau, and then, with his help, steady myself for the reentry into the working world. During those terms,

I was not able to create fiction and so I was always anxious to dive quickly into my psyche to make whatever repairs I could. But I remember the time when I started one therapy term and I announced—with some defiance—that I planned to work until I had regained my memory.

He looked at me from his rocking chair and said, "It'll destroy you." Tears had glazed his eyes. I knew then, as I knew whenever I saw tears in his eyes, that I had stumbled over a disguised truth. Usually, it meant that, in either retelling a dream or describing an event, I had reached a numb area that had once been painful. That afternoon he explained that the very mechanism that produced the numbness had been acquired so early and was so deep I would risk suicide.

I cried. More than anything else, I wanted to remember emotions, to remember precisely people from my past, my exlovers, my old friends, my parents, and what the time with them was like. My mind could paint vague pictures of people, maybe even a few of the events, but not the reasons I had been with them.

My analyst told me, that day, *he* would have to be my memory.

I am not sure, but I suspect that I lost the ability to log my emotions during my first six months, the time between my birth and the signing of papers. I craved to be picked up. This feeling, perhaps the only one I recovered in years of therapy with three different men and several emergency diagnoses, this craving lasted as long as I could tolerate it, then I stifled it. From then through my early twenties, I did not trust anyone who wanted to touch me. I think of myself back in the orphanage, in a room with a vaulted ceiling, in one of many cribs made of wicker. I am not aware of the other babies nor of sounds. I seem to wait for a shadow over me.

A Boston astrologer, in the first minute of a reading fifteen years ago, looked down at the chart she had previously studied and told me I came into the world hating my father. "Even in the womb," she said.

This startled me. Hatred I knew, though I carried it for my biological mother. I assumed she had been the last one on the scene, the one who had deposited me in the Catholic orphanage.

In the sessions with my analyst, I learned to reenter my dreams like a farmer who returns to a field and kicks the clods for a few more potatoes. So, too, I can fly back through time for an image of my mother. She is always twenty years old. Her youth frozen. I sit here, my forties ticking away, and I am unable to move her past that age. She has dirty blond hair. Green eyes. But her hair is cut and she is dressed like the women I see at the malls in southern California in 1991. Her pregnancy is a current problem—not something she has escaped.

Whether the astrologer was correct or not, I incorporated her suggestion—the rage in the womb—into my birth story. It did make me wonder, though, where the name James came from because, if the astrologer were right, then I must have absorbed the negative feelings toward the horny devil from my mother—no doubt abandoned herself. So, then, would she have wanted me to bear his name? Or was sticking me with the name, James, her way of getting even with the world? I have never been comfortable with it; I associate James with the stooped posture I had through high school.

My brother in the new family was also adopted though not from the same mother. He was ten months younger. That fact, when it was revealed during our years in school, led people to click their tongues, and one or the other of us would feel compelled to add that we had both been adopted. This knowledge was part of our childhoods, and it wasn't any more or less important to us than the fact that I had blond hair and he had brown.

"Aren't you curious about your real parents?" people asked.

"No," I would answer, puzzled, and at times guilty, feeling that I should be curious.

I never knew blood relatives, never held in me the thick knots of emotions my friends had toward the people who produced them. Nor have I ever figured out why my gay friends are so solemn or wistful about being the end of a bloodline. I never felt the species' urge to procreate or the familial pressures focused on bachelor sons. Children, to me, are strange creatures; I don't understand why people plan them. Accidents, on the other hand, I know by instinct, being one myself.

I lack cultural traditions and a sense of ethnicity. This empti-
ness, as far as I can tell, is not the same as the urge by so many in
this country to assimilate—to lose themselves in suburbia and to
deny grandparents. Rather, I compare myself to the Woody Allen
character Zelig, a chameleonlike man, an empty vessel, who in the
pseudodocumentary film is discovered to have been part of a bizarre
mix of ethnic and social groups in the 1920s.

Unlike Zelig, I do not participate as a member; I do, however,
project myself well beyond my probable Anglo-Irish-Scots background, and I find links to my past with Italians, Arabs, Australian
aborigines, Jews, American Indians, Asian Indians, Pacific Islanders,
as well as back through time to European pagans in the Middle
Ages and non-Christian Roman farmers. At times, it's a very physical sensation—my heart beats a little faster, tears start to accumu-
late—as if I am approaching home.

As a fiction writer, this floating identity is helpful—this putting myself in other people's bodies and minds. The one constant,
the core of me that remains stable as granite, is my being gay.

I have had the rare pleasure, twice, of loving men who were
also adopted, and through them I learned that my experience was
not unique. Adopting parents frequently can and do reject children
as if they were incompatible organ transplants. The sexual attraction
with both men was intense, but we spent as much time spilling out
our adoption stories during our first lovemaking sessions as we did
stroking cocks. By morning, we were convinced that we had broken
the incest taboo. It felt good.

With these two men, I was sure I had found biological brothers. I felt obligations already in place. There was not a sense of
newness I have experienced at other times with men—the excitement
of the first attraction, the strangeness, the slow peeling away.
Rather, it was a reunion, and if we had not come from the same
womb or the same supply of sperm, we came from the same planet.

So I have felt family ties.

The dream, which I mentioned above, the one with evidence
of my biological parents, occurred this winter. I woke up around

three a.m., and I was so struck by the images I jumped out of bed and stumbled to the next room for my dream notebook. It had been six years since my last entry.

The next morning I felt queasy. The details, the intrusion of religion, of Catholicism in particular, produced the same shiver in me that the name James had always done. I had been proud of the way I had repelled religion, kept it at arm's length through my childhood, as if, somehow, I had dipped my soul in silicon. Emerson dismissed the problem of original sin as "the soul's mumps and measles" and when I read that, I felt the same way about religion— a transitory illness, something unavoidable, an irritation, an affliction to recover from.

And yet, now, I wonder if I had put Catholicism—the faith of my adopting parents and the faith, presumably, of my biological mother—on trial. It owed me something. After twenty years, I can't explain why I went to a Catholic college. At the time, I had this vague sense that I needed a quiet, paternal atmosphere, a not-too-competitive place.

This is what I recorded from the dream:

I'm confused as to why people avoid me and make me feel iso-lated—I'm told to go see a man who knows all. I trudge along a gravel road that runs parallel to a freeway. I find a tiny house—wonder why {the} occupants live so close to noise; inside, on {the} left in {the} one-room house is Dr. Albert Einstein, whom I've come to ask, and on a chair to the right, his assistant. I apologize for not having {an} appointment. They seem taken aback that I enter without knocking and just appear in their doorway. The assistant tells me I'll be allowed one problem to be solved. That's all I want. After I talk, Einstein, before answering, puts me down for having stayed so close to facts. Typical of an American, he says. He talks of flowers; then quickly moves to {the} problem. With a Polaroid camera, Ein-stein takes two pictures of a woman, a severe plain person with a nun's habit on. I feel a flash of recognition that she was my mother—that she was in a convent where she gave birth to me and where the other nuns ignored me because they didn't want

*to be contaminated by this sin. The woman registers no emotion
in either of the pictures.*

What struck me in the weeks following the dream was the
unrelatedness to anything I had thought of or experienced. I couldn't
remember the last time I had mentioned biological parents. It had
been seven years since the last of my adoptive parents had died.

When I reentered the dream, as I had done so many times for
my analyst, I located my father. He was not twenty—as my mother
is in my mind's picture—but rather fifty. A priest, if not her confes-
sor, someone with authority over her. My conception, it seems, was
forced, an act of submission.

Do I literally believe these fragments—the request for the name
James; the primordial hatred; the plain, abandoned nun? Maybe.
Truth, when it tangles with sex, can stretch the limits of what we
think predictable and normal and comfortable. As I mentioned, I
was never curious about my parents. I neither asked questions nor
spent any conscious hours figuring out how I was conceived. The
fragments, themselves, came to me over a thirty-five-year period.

Still, I have the urge to commit what I know to paper, and
by doing that I can touch the past. My birth certificate, like an old
Soviet textbook, reflects not what happened nor does it name the
characters involved. . . . Rather, it brashly reinvents me. It lies. It
proclaims my adopting parents as the source of my life. No doubt
this was done to avoid embarrassment—for my own good and for
the protection of squeamish adults. Now, by committing the truth
to paper, I can add an important footnote. My mother existed.

larry duplechan

she's my mother

I have my mother's eyes: a rather pedestrian shade of brown but almond shaped, with a slightly Oriental slant. Also her high, prominent cheekbones, courtesy of one of her great-grandfathers, who was a full-blooded something-or-other Indian. My skin—coffee-with-Coffee-Mate medium brown in color with the occasional chocolate chip of a mole here and there—comes from her family, the Andrus side, rather than the more high-yellow Louisiana Creole Duplechans (whose café au lait complexion and greenish eyes were inherited by my brother Lonnie). The older I get, the more my own face reminds me of my mother's; and the older I get, the more I see her in my own personality. What I don't see, Greg—my life partner—often does. I have inherited from the former Margie Nell Andrus—among other things—her taste for pinto beans (she claims to have consumed great bowlfuls of them while pregnant with me), her Fourth of July firecracker of a temper (flash, bang, sputter, and it's all over), and her penchant for eyebrow-singeing sarcasm combined with an incongruously thin skin: we can both dish it out, but we can't really take it. I have also been saddled with a reasonable facsimile of her smooth mid-alto speaking voice.

Oh, I'm definitely my father's son. Much as I've wished from time to time that I *had* been sired by Harry Belafonte, James Baldwin, or the Fullerbrush man, the fact is I'm going through life wearing Lawrence Duplechan, Sr.'s first and last names, his flat EE-width feet, his naturally straight, even teeth, and a scaled-down version of his high-waisted, big-bicepped amateur-boxer physique. But the hand-to-hip weight-shift stance even my best friends have grown to dread, the sidelong "Have you lost your last sense?" glance, the mean-spirited yet all-too-accurate remark muttered out of the corner of the mouth—all vintage Margie Nell.

Shortly after she met Greg—my lover, a man and a *white* man, to boot—my mother said to me, "I can't help wishing you had picked somebody a little more like me." She had taken it as a personal affront that I hadn't wanted a girl just like the girl that married dear old Dad. What she obviously didn't understand—and what I hadn't the wherewithal at the time to explain to her—is that while I hadn't chosen to sleep with someone like her, I had paid her a compliment at least as great: I had largely *become* her.

At the risk of lending credence to a particularly tired myth, the fact is I didn't see much of my father when I was a little boy. Dad worked hard at fulfilling what I assume was his notion of what it meant to be a good father; that is, to be a good provider. Larry Sr. began working at Lockheed Aircraft in Burbank before I was born, fresh from the infantry during the Korean War, washing helicopters during the day while finishing high school at night. By the time I was old enough to want to know, he was still at Lockheed, now an electronics liaison engineer. And no, I haven't the first idea what an electronics liaison engineer does. What I do know is that Dad worked hard and worked well. He was the first colored man employed in his division, then the first Negro engineer at the Burbank plant, still later the first black man at Lockheed to—well, to do something or other. Anyway, you get the picture. Lawrence Duplechan Sr. was a man determined to better himself; a man dedicated to making a better life for himself and for his wife and children in southern California than he had known growing up in rural southwestern Louisiana; a man who had bought into the American Dream in a big way, and was making it work. Generally speaking, pulling

one's self up by one's muddy bootstraps tends to be a time-consum-
ing endeavor. So for several years, Dad seemed to be away more
than he was at home. There were stretches of time when he'd work
in one town while we lived in another—we'd see Dad on weekends.
My most vivid childhood memories of Dad are as the subject of an
oft-repeated threat from Mom—"Wait till your daddy gets
home!"—and as a brawny, belt-wielding arm once he did in fact
get home.

Which left me and Mom.

The relationship between my mother and me was special from
the beginning. *Before* the beginning. Mom began exerting conscious
influence on me while I was little more than a hormonal shift and
a craving for strawberry ice cream. Mom tells of visiting art museums and galleries, of buying and listening to recordings of classical
music (the *Nutcracker* Suite and *Peter and the Wolf* and hodgepodge
starter-kit classical collections), of reading good books while pregnant with me, her first child, in the hopes that her unborn child
might somehow begin absorbing culture in utero. As her belly bal-
looned and the dimples in her increasingly chubby cheeks deepened,
she talked to the imminent arrival that was me. And she sang to
it: lullabies and spirituals, Mahalia Jackson gospel and Ray Charles
blues. The songs she sang to accompany herself while cooking a pot
of rice and stirring dark brown roux for gravy or pushing a hot
steam iron across her husband's shirts, Margie Nell sang—a little
softer and in a general downward direction—for me. Following my
arrival into the world, a world of Eisenhower and Elvis, of Milton
Berle on the black-and-white TV and Sam Cooke on the transistor
radio and ladies in white gloves and veiled hats for church on Sunday
morning, Mom was just as likely to lullaby her firstborn son (named
after her husband despite her preference for the name Stephen, nick-
named Sandy for a head of incongruous sandy-blond hair) with "Who
wears short-shorts" as with "Rock-a-bye baby in the treetop."

And I'm here to tell ya, Mom could *sing*. She had, and has,
one of those strange and wonderful singing voices that's more than
merely pretty. In my first novel, *Eight Days a Week*, when a character
is described as having "one of those voices that can bring a tear to
your eye just singing *Oh*," it's Margie Nell's voice I was writing

about. Mom's voice has an ache in it, a tiny heartbreak, the audible residue of all the trouble she's seen that nobody knows but Jesus, the bone-marrow-deep racial memory of enslaved foremothers, and maybe some Karmic nettles from a few previous lifetimes thrown in (though Lord knows Margie Nell doesn't believe in reincarnation and would no doubt roll her eyes and shake her head in motherly exasperation at the thought that I do).

I remember her singing in our living room with her brothers, Jim and Sherman, and her sister Orelia, all of whom lived nearby during my childhood and all of whom sang. (I consider myself quite lucky to have inherited some of this Andrus musicality—my father is tone-deaf.) They'd stand in a little square, facing inward, singing along with some gospel group wailing from the hi-fi, singing, "My Lord's getting us ready for that great day" with the Staple Singers or "Lord you've been so good to me" with the Original Five Blind Boys of Alabama. I can still close my eyes and see my mother, thirty years younger (younger than I am today), her hair a cap of patent-leather curls, eyelids lightly shut, gold-hoop earrings swinging softly as she moves her head from side to side with the rhythm of the music and the power of the Holy Ghost. I started singing along with my mother only shortly after gaining the power of speech, long before I understood much of the songs I was singing. Sunday mornings before church, Mom cooked breakfast to the accompaniment of Radio KGFJ's broadcasts of gospel-music programs sponsored by Conner-Johnson Funeral Home ("where the best costs no more"). Mom, two- or three-year-old me and any number of black Baptist choirs would awaken my father with the smell of frying bacon and the sound of our soul-stirring (and not exactly quiet) renditions of "Gonna ride that glory train" and "I been runnin' for Jesus for a long time, but I'm not tired yet."

As a child, I was my mother's very pride and joy—good-looking, well behaved, and uncommonly bright. I knew the ABCs, my address and phone number at two, read at three, and at the age of five, my first IQ test revealed the intellect of an eight-year-old. It was about this time—I was about six years old—that Mom caught me in my first (but not my last) experiment in crossdressing when she happened upon me and my three-year-old brother Lloyd in her bedroom playing dress-up: both faces liberally smeared with her lipstick, little boy bodies spritzed with her ersatz Chanel No. 5, necks and arms a-clatter with her costume jewelry. As I recall, Mom didn't wait for Dad to get home, but administered the spankings herself.

When I was a little boy (lo these many years ago), growing up in the San Fernando Valley town of Pacoima, there was an expression adults used to describe certain boys: the term was "all boy." I don't know if this term is still in vogue (I don't have that many friends with small children), but back in the early sixties, it seems to have been used quite a lot. Though *never* about me. My school friend, Kelvin, was "all boy"—I once heard his mother say so to my mother. Kelvin was husky where I was delicate, with a speaking voice deeper at the age of seven than mine is now. He was a cowboys-and-Indians player, a tree climber, a run-run-run, slide into home base and tear holes in the knees of his blue jeans kind of boy. And he could throw a baseball, which I couldn't do at seven (actually, I threw like a girl—ask anybody), and which I still couldn't do at seventeen, at which age I finally gave up the attempt. My cousin Butch—I swear, that was his real name, though he wasn't really my cousin, just the firstborn son of my mom's then-buddy, Thelma, my godmother—Butch was "all boy." I once heard my mother say so to Thelma. Butch was a prizewinning swimmer with a mantle full of trophies by the age of eight, at which point my idea of a great time was spending the afternoon with my cousin Vivian, playing with her truly impressive collection of dolls. Upon finding me in Vivian's room and company, teasing Chatty Cathy's blond nylon hair into a rather professional-looking bouffant (and yes, Chatty Cathy was blond—they didn't have black dolls in those days), Mom planted hand into hip, looked at me with an expression somewhere near the corner of amusement and disgust, and said, "Well, maybe we should just send *you* to beauty school." I'm not sure what she thought of my reaction—my little face lit up like the light bulb in my Give-a-Show Projector and my voice jumped up into piccolo range as I squeaked, "Really?" She turned heel and left the room without another word.

As I grew up, Mom remained my champion, my harshest taskmaster, and my biggest fan. She closely monitored my schooling, rewarded As with praise and sometimes cash. She never missed parent-teacher night, and when my fifth-grade teacher, Mrs. Byrne, informed Mom that she found it odd that, at ten years old, my best friend was a girl—Jacqueline Honoré, with whom I hopscotched, drew crayon pictures of elves and dragons, and coauthored a one-act play in imperfect iambic heptameter about the origin of the Easter Bunny—Mom claims to have shrugged and said, "How's he doing in spelling?" She helped me with my homework in arithmetic—always my weakest subject—though her characteristic lack of patience made her somewhat less than the ideal tutor: I still remember her eye-rolling look of exasperation as she howled, "It's three with a remainder of two! Can't you *see* that? Plain as the nose on your face!" When I was eight years old, she somehow found the money for weekly flute lessons and an instrument of my own and for the ensuing decade, she saw to it that I practiced at least half an hour every day and attended my every performance until I put the flute aside my senior year in high school. By then, we'd moved to Lancaster, in the Antelope Valley, some eighty-five miles northeast of Los Angeles in the high Mohave Desert.

I didn't have many friends in high school: I was hiding something from my peers, and I feared that if I got too close to someone, he might see it. Besides, I knew I wouldn't be staying in Lancaster once I graduated and saw no reason to cultivate any deep relationships. And I didn't date much—I just wasn't interested. I spent my evenings at home in my room listening to records or face down in a book or watching television. I spent my summer days around the house with Mom, helping her dust and vacuum, learning to cook her specialties and improving upon some of them—my chicken enchiladas are considerably better than hers—and watching the soaps, or as Mom called them, "my stories," as in "Girl, I gotta get off the phone, it's time to watch my stories." All summer long, Mom and I sipped cups of percolated Yuban, pale with Pet evaporated milk and candy sweet with sugar, and followed *General Hospital, Another World*, and especially *As the World Turns*, which had been part of Mom's daily ritual since before I was born. I shall never forget the time Mom had left the room during a commercial break to warm up her coffee or something, and I called her back, "Mom, hurry up! Lenore had a miscarriage!" She rushed back into the room, only to stop dead in her tracks just a few feet away from me, staring at me with an odd, equivocal look on her face. I didn't understand at the time what the problem was—it crossed my mind that perhaps she was surprised I knew what a miscarriage was. It occurred to me years later that the thought had probably hit her like a frozen flounder upside the head that she had inadvertently allowed her firstborn son to become one of her best girlfriends.

It was shortly thereafter (at least, as I recall) that Mom attempted to fix me up with the daughter of a friend of hers from church. The friend's name was Viola (accent on the second syllable, as in "pay-O-la"). "Vi" for short. "Why aren't you seeing some nice girl?" Mom asked. "Someone like Vi's daughter. You ought to call Vi's daughter," she said. I didn't know Vi, and I didn't know Vi's daughter. I looked up her picture in the school yearbook. Vi's daughter was—to be kind—not pretty. My brother Lloyd—who is two and a half years younger than I, who is not gay, who in fact *had* a girlfriend when I had none, and who was at that time unaware that his big brother was gay—peered over my shoulder at the picture of a homely black girl with a gardenia perched Billie Holiday–style in her coarse hornets' nest of straightened hair. He grinned and said, "You ought to call Vi's daughter."

I hoped the whole Vi's-daughter-thing would just go away if I ignored it, but neither Mom nor Lloyd would allow that, at least not right away. Either Mom would glance up from the basketful of laundry she was folding and say, "Have you called Vi's daughter?," or Lloyd would send one of those grins of his across the dinner table at me and say, "Say—have you called Vi's daughter?" Strangely, I don't recall anyone ever calling Vi's daughter by name—only Vi's daughter.

At any rate, I never did call Vi's daughter. And after a time—in my memory, it seems like weeks and weeks—Mom finally let it drop. And I don't recall her ever bringing up another girl. Maybe it occurred to her that I just wasn't interested in Vi's daughter or *anybody's* daughter. But then I did take up with a girl named Cherie, just long enough to throw Mom off the scent. Not because of Mom or Vi's daughter or any of that, but because I liked her. Cherie and I hung around school together and went out a couple of times. But I got as far as kissing Cherie's overly full lips and fondling her large, pillowy breasts before I realized I had no real desire for any of her body parts and backed away from the possibility of going any further with the relationship.

It was during my first year at UCLA that my mother found out I was gay. I'd told my father about a year earlier, but he had simply prayed over me, asking God to remove these wild ideas from my mind, and considered the case closed. How the news was broken this time is a story unto itself, which I won't recount here. What's important is my parents' respective reactions: my father, big and muscular and handsome, wept openly as I hadn't seen him weep before, refusing to look at my face; my mother stared directly at me, her glare hard and accusatory. "It's like hearing you'd been killed in a car crash," she said. I don't suppose I really have to mention how much that hurt.

At that time, I wouldn't have believed I would ever feel warmly toward my mother again, or have even a cordial relationship with her. I'm happy to say I was wrong.

Currently, when Greg and I visit my parents in Lancaster, which we do two or three times a year, Mom greets me at the door with a hug and a kiss, and she greets Greg the same way. If she calls on the telephone and I'm not around, she'll chat with Greg for a minute or two. We've come a long way since the day I first introduced Greg to my family, when, in addition to the "someone more like me" statement, Mom also took me aside, wagged a disapproving forefinger in my face, and said, "And I don't even want to hear about two young men calling yourselves *courtin'*. 'Cause that's *crap*."

I didn't visit, call, or write to my mother or father for a year or more after that. I don't remember who made the first move, Mom or me, but after a time we spoke again. And Greg and I visited again. And years went by. And at some point, it was just understood that Greg would probably be with me when I came home to Thanksgiving dinner or at Christmastime.

Which is not to say my current relationship with Mom is marked

by her full and unconditional acceptance of my gayness. Not nearly.
In fact, my mother has yet to set foot in my house, which I've owned
for seven years, and for which she loaned me one thousand dollars of
her own money to help cover closing costs. She will actually go so far
as to come to Los Angeles to visit friends and not drop by, if only to
see where her money went. I extended a few invitations—for dinner,
for coffee, for a few minutes—but it was always "maybe some other
time." A couple of Novembers ago, I pushed the issue.

Mom called to ask if I was, quote, coming home for Thanksgiving, end of quote. I don't know, maybe a person can only take so
much hurt for so long before something's gotta give, or maybe she
just caught me in one of those moods. Anyway, I said (taking a
snooty, snotty tone I know she hates), "Mother, I *am* home. And
I've already made plans to have Thanksgiving with friends." Fact
was, Greg and I were planning to spend Thanksgiving with a good
friend with AIDS whom we didn't expect to live to see another
November—and we were right. Well, from there the conversation
grew long, convoluted, and increasingly ugly. Here's a particularly
pertinent snippet:

MOM: I don't know why you never seem to want to come
over anymore.
ME: Mom, you've *never* been to *my* house.
MOM: I don't have to play you-come-to-my-house-then-I-
come-to-your-house. I'm your mother.

[Mom still uses that one quite a lot. Sort of a corollary to that
old favorite, "Because I said so." I don't think she realizes this sort
of *ex cathedra* pronouncement just doesn't have the punch it used to
back when she was taller than her children.]

ME: I know who you are. You've still never been to my
house.
MOM: Well, I'm just not quite comfortable with your
lifestyle.
ME: I don't have a life*style*—I have a *life*!

It's a Neil Simon line. From *Plaza Suite*. I've never been above
borrowing a good retort. Anyway, now it was out: my mother
couldn't bring herself to come to my house because she wasn't quite
comfortable with my lifestyle. Mom and I parried and thrusted,
bantered and bitched, traded snide remarks and tore scabs off each
other's old wounds as only loved ones can do for a good twenty
minutes more, the result being that not only would I not be "coming
home" for Thanksgiving, but it would likely be a cold day in blazes
before Margie Nell Duplechan set eyes upon her firstborn son again.

In a flurry of hurt, anger, and indignation, I fired off a five-
page typewritten letter to Mom reiterating some of my more pertinent points from our conversation and repeating my promise-dash-
threat that if she couldn't bear the thought of coming to my house,
then maybe it might not be so easy for me to find my way to hers.
[Please note that my father was conspicuously silent through all this.
He probably knew better than to step between these two bitches.]

Greg read my letter, agreed that it was quite the fiery little
epistle and said, "Of course you don't intend to *mail* it." Oh, didn't
I?

I'll let you in on a little secret. Once your mother has compared
your gayness to death on the highway and dismissed the great love
of your life as "crap," you're rendered mighty-nigh invincible. You
have nothing to lose. I mean, what could she say to me?

I mailed the letter.

About a week later, I received in the mail an envelope addressed
to me in my mother's inimitable wide-looped handwriting. Inside
was my letter to her, tucked back into its original envelope, upon
which Mom had written these words:

"I'm praying for you. Love, Mom."

I laughed, cried, groaned, crumpled the letter and both envelopes into a raggedy little ball and tossed it across my living room,
all in the space of a few seconds. I know when I'm licked. Never
underestimate the power of the statement, "I'm your mother."

I made the ninety-minute drive to Lancaster the day after
Christmas, pointedly without Greg. Mom greeted me at the front
door with her usual hug and kiss. Upon ascertaining that I'd come

alone, she did the old hand-to-hip and said, "I *hope* Greg doesn't think he's not welcome here."

"I'm sure he doesn't think that," I said, taking as equivocal a tone as I could muster. We looked into each other's eyes for a moment. Mom removed hand from hip and applied it to my shoulder. Her face softened a little.

"I like Greg," she said softly. "He's a sweetheart. I just wish you weren't sleeping with him."

So that's the way it is. And you know, I have to respect that. Sure, I'd love to have one of those families (and I know some) where the gay child and his same-sex partner are accepted as first-class citizens, treated as a married couple, included in the family gift exchange and called Uncle So-and-So by the nieces and nephews. But I haven't. What I have is a couple of middle-aged, black, foursquare Southern Baptists who truly believe their firstborn son is destined to spend eternity in perpetual hellfire unless they can pray him into heterosexuality before it's too late. Who can't quite bring themselves to my doorstep for fear of—of what? Of being struck down by a lightning bolt from the forefinger of Jehovah as they step over my gay threshold? Of finding a naked sex slave dangling in a sling from my living room ceiling? Or maybe just fear of the obvious implications of a house with two men and only one large bed in it? Hell if I know.

And yet. And yet, my mother greets my white male lover-friend-life partner at her door with hugs and kisses. And gives him a gift at Christmas. And says, "Tell Greg I said hi" at the end of our phone conversations. It isn't Shangri-la. But it could be a lot worse. Hell, it's *been* a lot worse.

A couple of months ago, my father retired after thirty-five years with Lockheed Aircraft. Mom tossed him quite a wing-ding—huge cake, lots of presents, and a houseful of friends and extended family that all but broke fire laws and who had about as much fun as humanly possible without the aid of alcohol. At one point in the proceedings, Mom introduced me to one of the deacons from her church, a huge, bald-headed, effervescent gentleman in a shiny ill-fitting suit. "This little lady," he said, tucking my mother beneath one arm, "she's been my sweetheart for a long time."

Taking my mother's hand in mine, I smiled and said, "She's been *my* sweetheart for even longer than that." Mom smiled from one end of the house to the other, freed herself from the big man's embrace, reached up and hugged me around the neck. "My baby," she murmured.

Seems we're stuck with each other. I'm her baby. She's my mother.

r . n i k o l a u s
m e r r e l l

---

mother, isaac,
and horses

"When you were young," mother said,

Two thousand feet above, the weather is harsh, but down here,
in the valley, it is milder. Up there, the forest and its meadows are
full of wild, carnivorous animals—bears, cougars, rumors of
wolves—but down here all the animals are safe, tame—dogs, cattle,
and horses. Above, the forest stretches for hundreds of miles, and
people disappear, are lost, are never found. But here below, there
is a town, two Indian villages, and scattered cabins.

My mother likes the isolation of the valley, how the valley
forces its people into self-reliance, how by denying them the security
and comfort of urban institutions, it makes all of its people stronger,
braver.

Except for the fog, it is a good place to be a child. The valley
is open, mostly unfenced, and there are many well-trodden paths
and a myriad of secret openings through the pines and thorns. All
the paths and openings lead up to the forest, but two thousand feet
is too much of a climb for a child. Unless he has a horse.

My mother and father had horses. Late at night I could hear
them ride, I could hear their bodies slapping against saddles, the
creak of leather, the tickle of spurs, the delighted moans of a completed leap.

When Isaac and I met, we were eight: too young for horses.
We walked. Sometimes alone, sometimes with others, but most
often with each other. We explored the hillsides, found hidden
places, views we were convinced no one had seen, hillocks and prom-
ontories we believed no one had touched. And he told me his secret:
he didn't belong to the tribe in the valley, but he, too, was "part
Indian."

I defended him. Behind his back, people guessed the truth. In
years past, missionaries had named Indians from the Old Testament,
doubtful that the newly converted were strong enough to bear a
fully Christian name such as Robert or Alice or William. Isaac's
name descended from that time.

And people criticized him for other reasons: his cockiness, the
way he poured too much oil on his hair, and the fact that often, in
spite of being freshly bathed, he carried a sharp scent that suggested
he had not wiped himself clean.

I defended him: told everyone he had no Indian blood, tried
to imitate his cockiness, poured too much oil on my hair, and as I
drew close so I could breathe his private scent, denied I could smell
a thing.

We grew older and closer, and often, at night, we slept together. We climbed closer to the top of the hillside. Then one night
he got his horse. I held him while he grew rigid, leapt over the
top, broke through the forest, charged across the meadows.

Two months later, I got mine.

"kids didn't know about sex.

Others had tried to tell me, and I understood it to be much
like taking a piss, only better. But how can anyone explain? To be
the first boy-man to leap onto the back of a horse, to straddle its
back, to feel the power of a thousand pounds clasped tightly between
his legs, to hang on, as beneath, the horse surges upward, its power

flowing into his legs, into the depths of his loins, coursing up his spine, arching his neck, clinching his teeth, as he strains to open his jaws, to breathe, to scream, then beneath, the horse surging, insane—bucks, circles, rears—and in a last lunge for freedom, charges out of control, galloping, bounding, leaping across the meadows, while high above, the man-boy becomes one with his horse and soars, transformed in glory, as free as an eagle, as fast as the wind.

Bonded together by our horses, our friendship, and the excitement of adventure, we rode into the depths of the untouched forest and explored its wild canyons and windy peaks. More hair sprouted and we grew close to the animals, imitated them, shed our clothes, leapt, bit, wrestled, howled.

I thought it would go on forever, that eventually we would ride up out of the valley, enter the forest, and never return. Perhaps I should have guessed, for there had been signs. Often he was reluctant to venture farther and balked against exploring the next mountain, always hinting of some terrible but allusive danger, insisting instead that we return to the valley.

I remember that day your father called you into his library

Sometimes, though, the valley becomes dangerous. From the river, creeks, and grasses, fog rises, unexpected, heavy and thick, and veils the paths, hides all the secret openings. The lights of the town, villages, and cabins disappear, and children are lost, step through the willows and fall into the creeks, are swept to the river, and are seen no more.

They are searched for: from atop the fire station a siren howls its long, wailing, missing-child alert and the people of the valley gather. All those old enough for a horse go into the fog to search.

A breed of horses is native to the valley—Appaloosa. They are grayish-white, their flanks and behinds discolored, mottled with specks and spots that, in the fog, give an illusion of depth, that are seen as only dark spaces, that camouflage the horses as they move.

They are born of the fog. Rugged and surefooted, they move slowly through the deepest fog, lifting their legs, testing the ground before they set each hoof. Their nostrils flare, their ears stand; they smell and listen for what is not seen.

and told you about Isaac

Like a native horse, my dark, blue-eyed father knew things he couldn't see. He knew I had a horse and rode it. He ordered me into his library, told me in which drawer he kept his condoms, and how I was to use them. Then he told me why.

Others had told me, the same ones who said he was too cocky, put too much oil on his hair, carried a smell, had Indian blood. I defended him, as I had before, turned away, refused to listen to their words. Never mind that we had not been riding for the last five months, that we had not touched, that I had ridden alone, thinking only of him, knowing that his occasional smile and nod meant everything, that the girl he walked with meant nothing.

There were other times when we had been apart. In the summer, when school was out, my family traveled or camped near other towns. Each time we returned, he seemed almost a stranger, for he had grown closer to others, further from me, but after a few days, he would always leave them and come back to me.

and his girlfriend.

Father continued his lecture about Isaac: how he would have to quit school and work full-time changing tires and pumping gas. And how he would never have a chance for anything better because anything better requires a high school diploma.

I turned away, quit listening.

From the other side of the doors drifted the smell of apple strudel. Mother loved the grains, their magic, how the little milled seeds, mixed with a bit of water, yeast, and egg, could become, in a few hours, breads, cakes, cookies, noodles, and dumplings. Her kitchen always smelled of baking spices and cooking grains.

So did she. After school, when I was younger, I would run into the house, run to the bathroom and wash, run to her kitchen to drink a glass of milk and to snack by the warmth of her oven.

Her eyes were blue, as blue as the summer's milkweed that dotted the field behind her kitchen door, and her hair hung long and golden brown, the color of the honey she used for her cakes. Often, she would pull up her kitchen chair and sit down, cup her hair and toss it over her shoulders to make room for me. A little too plump to be called slender, she had a mother's ample bosom and a wide, welcoming lap.

Later, my younger brothers arrived, and I grew further from her, grew too old to sit on her lap. But there were occasional moments—after times of unjust punishment, the death of a favorite pet, a painful wound—when I still wasn't quite grown up, when I could no longer control the pain, when I became a baby again and cried. She would snuggle me, hold me close, warm me, and magically I would emerge again from her alive.

Father ordered me to sit up, to look him in the eye; I obeyed, listened to his begrudging praise of Isaac, praise because he was man enough, at least, to marry so the baby would have a name.

When you came out of that room,

The siren wails for a missing child, and the riders gather. They split up to search the valley, spreading through the fog, some going in groups, some in pairs, others alone. If the lost child is old enough for a horse, he is easier to find, for a horse remains by its downed rider, and a searching horse will sense the other horse's presence, will sense its trouble.

Mother always sensed those in trouble. In the days when the word cancer was whispered and others shied away from its victims, she would drop by with a gift from her kitchen, stay to give a bath, return again, until the end, to change beds and give shots.

She helped when no one else would. Up the river, ten miles, there was a whorehouse, run by a filthy-talking madam who drove a long, white Cadillac. Near the center of town, on a day with no fog, a GMC and the Cadillac collided. Mother dismissed the snickers of the neighbors, brought the madam home, served her coffee and strudel, let her rest on the couch until another car came from the whorehouse.

And on searches, too, she paid no attention to the others, rode alone into the fog, saying that alone, without distractions, she could hear better, see better.

Father finished his lecture, dismissed me.

I pulled myself up from the chair, groaned, called for Isaac, caught myself before his name escaped.

I've never seen you so shaken,

Thrown from my horse, I lay in a clearing, surrounded by thorns, barely breathing, bleeding. My horse ran on, disappeared.

The fog rolled around me. Alone. No one ever told me there was a place so alone.

The fog swirled. My horse reappeared, nosed me. Numbness shot through my legs, arms. I forced myself to stand, stumbled, leaned forward against something, something cold, brittle, weaving.

From somewhere, muffled, far away, came the wail of the missing-child siren.

To the south and east, far back in the mountains, some say there is a band of people, descended from those banished from the surrounding tribes, from those who successfully evaded their pursuers for the required three days. They are said to be a people with no pride, who eke out their existence among the mountain sheep, a people so desperate they will accept anyone who runs to them.

Again, my horse nosed me, whinnied. Already far from town, I had a headstart on three days. No one knew I was hurt, the extent of my wounds, the cause of my bleeding.

I grabbed his bridle, his mane, tried to throw myself onto his back, slammed against his side, fell, too weak, too hurt.

Among certain people, when it is time for someone wounded to die, he gathers his strength, leaves, spares the others from hearing his death rattle, spares them from watching as he bleeds away, spares them from watching his end.

you were as white as the fog.

The fog rolled over me, warmed me, covered me, hid me in

its blanket. My horse and I became invisible, for like my mother,
I am light-skinned. Mother's people came from the rainy, fogbound
Baltic coast of northern Germany, from the Duchy of Mecklenburg,
and searched across America until, in the Pacific Northwest, they
found another home at the edge of a rainy, foggy forest.

Mother liked the fog. She would leave the warmth of the
kitchen, go stand in the living room and watch through the window
while the fog rose from the grass, blurred the lights from the houses
across the street, made everything whiter, safer, more distant.

My horse pawed at my legs, snorted. I pulled at his leg, struggled to my feet, stood broken and bleeding, propped against his
side.

In the deepest of fogs a searching horse halts, listens, shudders.
There is a muffled whinny, an answer. The horses draw closer to
each other, reassure, touch.

Through the thorns, I heard mother calling. I took a step,
stood straight, listened.

But she would see my wounds, my blood. And how could I
explain? How could I explain to someone who taught me to wash
my hands after taking a piss? For I loved Isaac, loved him so much
that I'd touched his cock, kissed it, put it deep in my mouth, went
up and down until he grew rigid, galloped beneath me. And I'd
touched his forbidden, private place that no one touches except with
paper or soap and water. And I slipped mine inside, reached beneath
to stroke him until we both grew rigid, clinched our teeth against
the scream, and flew.

And those evenings when we had to separate to sleep, I went
to bed without brushing my teeth so I could still feel the marks of
his bruises, so I could fall asleep with his taste still deep in my
mouth.

I took another step, pushed aside the branches, looked through.

She sat on top of her horse, on the other side of the thorns,
peering at me through the thickening fog. Her horse flinched,
groaned, started toward me. The fog thickened, swirled, rolled.

She saw me. Relief, then a question crossed her face, and for
a moment, I thought she would dismount, push through the thorns,

discover my wounds. I smiled, reassured her that I was all right, that nothing was wrong, that I was unhurt.

Her horse stepped closer, almost too close, but she pulled back the reins, forced it to stop. The question faded from her face. She returned my smile.

You were so innocent, I was afraid I might laugh and hurt you,

The horses are well trained. They can be turned away, spurred, forced to trot, even to gallop, through the deepest of fogs.

I tried to shout, but nothing came from my throat. She turned and rode away.

so I put on my coat and went to the grocery store.

Camouflaged in the swirl of fog around me, I led my horse down through the willows, washed off my blood, followed the trail back to town. I covered my wounds and never explained my disappearance. And I learned to tell no one, to be a man.

Occasionally, when things hurt too bad, and the smell of baking grains and spices drifted from her kitchen, I was tempted to tell her, to have her hold me, so that I could emerge again from her alive. But I never did.

As for Isaac, he discovered alcohol and his life descended from tragedy to tragedy; as for me, one day I followed the river down to the Snake, to the Columbia, to the ocean, followed the coast down to California; and as for mother, she still lives in the valley.

steven saylor

my mother's ghost

1

The ghost of my mother lives on in her children. I know, because I just felt her shade pass through me.

I was twenty-three and living in Austin when I came out to my mother. This was in 1980. Rick and I had been together for almost five years. It was my second summer after college graduation, August, a prime month to get away from the Texas heat. Rick and I were planning a repeat of the previous summer's weeklong trip to San Francisco—to see the redwoods, visit the baths, do the Castro Street Fair, exult in being young and gay.

I don't recall the exact circumstances that caused her to write the letter. Perhaps it was a phone conversation. Or perhaps she had driven down from our little home town of Amethyst on a Saturday to shop and visit her children (we were all living in Austin then, my little sister Gwyn in college, my older brother Ronny married and working). Something was said or left unsaid. Possibly she'd heard that I'd sold an article and had asked me about it, and I'd rebuffed her, acting as if she was being nosy, because I didn't want to tell her what the article was about or where it would be appearing. Anyway, I got a letter from her:

Steven,

I've thought about it quite a lot and I don't know
what I've done—but I've known for a long while that you
don't want to share even a little of your life with me. I'll
try not to intrude—you were really too rude to me
today—and that's about all I can take—I'm not that
tough. So have fun in California—You can call me
sometime.   Mom

The letter is in blue ballpoint on yellow legal paper, written
in her casually elegant hand, a cross between printing and writing.
As a child I thought it was the most beautiful handwriting in the
world, especially when she signed the looping capital L in her first
name, Lucy. When I grew up I tried to emulate it.

I can't recall the rudeness she referred to, but I do remember
the pall of evasion that had hung over my life as long as I tried to
keep my sexuality secret from her. I had cautiously skirted the
topic before. Once at a Christmas gathering in Dallas I had posed a
hypothetical question about lesbianism involving a girl we both
knew. Wouldn't the parents want to know? No, she had said, "it
would just kill them." I think we both knew what was really being
discussed—my own secret—and her message was clear: keep silent.
I think I fumbled on with some humanistic argument, and she
stopped me cold by saying that homosexuality was a "sin against
God." My mother was not a very religious woman, but she knew
how to bring out the big guns. I didn't bring up the subject again.

Evasion was nothing new in our family. When dealing with
our mother, I suspect that my brother and sister had never been
entirely forthcoming about their sex lives, either, and we certainly
didn't discuss all the details of drug use, alcohol, pornography, VD,
and various other forbidden topics. The lines were implicitly drawn
and enforced by my mother's invisible tools of guilt and disapproval.
We did argue about politics and religion. In a poor Republican
household headed by a divorced woman during the Vietnam-to-
Watergate years, shortly after the Death of God, there was plenty
to argue about besides the things that really mattered, like sex.

The evasions were special in my case, because I was gay. Not that I was dishonest—I never went out of my way to hide the fact, once I made up my mind about it at the age of nineteen. I never pretended to have a girlfriend, no matter how often well-meaning relatives and acquaintances queried me about it. I quickly found a lover, and we moved in together; our little student apartments always had one bedroom and one double bed. I did put my gay magazines into a bedside drawer when my mother visited, just as I hid the marijuana. I brought Rick home to meet my mother, but I didn't introduce him as my lover. I wasn't ready for that, and neither was she.

Until she wrote the letter. It was her way of asking me to tell her.

My Xerox copy of the letter I mailed to her runs to five pages in longhand. It's stapled at the upper left corner and shows faintly the holes and rules of the notebook paper I used. It was the third or fourth draft of a coming out letter I had first written a year before. For years I've kept my copy stuck away in a drawer, occasionally coming across it when looking for something else, realizing with a start what it is and as quickly shunting it away among the other cards and letters. I avoided it even more after my mother died.

Rereading it now is not as embarrassing as I had thought it would be.

Dear Mother,

I am sorry I have hurt your feelings. You are right. I have been evasive with you, and that is not fair.

Of course there is a large reason why I have been secretive about my life and my work. It is a fear of rejection, tied to a larger overall "secret." One which you may already know or suspect—or may not; I have never been able to tell from your reactions.

As you know, I have been living with Rick for almost five years. We have always shared everything. We are not roommates, but lovers, in the complete sense of the word.

Which is another way of saying that I am gay. I use that word because it is the closest thing to a neutral term

that our culture has come up with. I want to be honest
with you.

Why have I not told you before? Mainly for fear of
your rejection. Perhaps this was unfair of me. I know that
you love me, and care about me, but I've always feared
that knowing the whole truth about me could change your
feelings. I hope I am wrong.

Also, I have evaded this issue because I did not want
to hurt you with it. You once told me in a conversation
(perhaps you have forgotten) that you believed homosexuality was a sin against God, and that finding it out about
a child would "kill" a parent. Knowing you felt that way,
it has not been easy finding a way to share this basic truth
about myself. Your religious objections are outside my
understanding, and I cannot change them. I know it will
bother you—just how much I can't be sure.

I don't think I have ever lied when asked a direct
question. But I am guilty of being secretive and closed
with you. That has caused its own problems. I don't like
the distance it has created, and I know you don't. It has
been a long-running problem for me, one I have always
tried to push into the background. I have even had dreams
about telling you. Sometimes you react coldly; other times
you just said, "Well, I knew that."

There are practical things you will want to know.
Who knows about me? I have known since I was eleven
or twelve, in gradual phases. It was something that took
me years to come to terms with. I don't expect you to
accept it overnight.

Ronny knows. I told him when I was nineteen. Gwyn
figured it out and asked Ronny. Theresa [a cousin], who
of course has a gay son of her own, knows through [her
daughter] Becky. Judy [my mother's half-sister] also put
two and two together, and asked Ronny.

I realize the above list may make you feel left out.
It should not. My relationship with you is far more com-

plex than with any of these others. The stakes are higher
for me.

As for my private life: Rick supports me financially
on and off. I have essentially done the same for him in
the past. My relationship with him is loving and secure.
I have problems, as we all do, but I am content. I need
no one to feel sorry for me—I think you can sympathize
with that. [My mother had divorced when I was quite
young, and, despite the hardships of working full-time
and raising three children, had never wanted anyone's
pity.]

Most of my writing has been for gay magazines. Book
reviews, articles—I have not shared this with you because
of their content. I will now, if you wish.

I know there are a thousand questions that arise; I
have been dealing with them since I was twelve, and some
remain unanswered. It is something I have come to see as
a natural, if mysterious, part of human life—but no more
mysterious than any other part of life.

This letter can't begin to answer everything. I've
wanted to be honest with you for a long time, and now
I have. It is something you deserve. I hope it will work
out for the best. I love you.   Steven

A few days later I received her reply:

Steven,

Yes. I knew. I had suspected for some time—but
was sure when I was in your apartment last and saw your
pins on the board in the kitchen. I guess you had been
demonstrating and I reject that completely. Yes—I love
you—no matter what you are or what you do. But I don't
know when, if ever, I can discuss this with you or with
anyone else. I would give my life if it were not true—I
hurt—I feel responsible—I can't allow myself to think
about it long enough to reach a conclusion about anything.
I hyperventilate and my legs get too weak to hold me.

This is not to make you feel guilty—it's just the way it is. I know that you are still you—but it's like I never knew you at all. I never understood anything. My mind rejects it completely. I feel you are so vulnerable and there's nothing I can do to protect you. No—I don't think I could bear to read what you have written—not yet. I don't know what else to say. I know this is not satisfactory—but I've had to force this—it's like if I ignore it, it will go away. I just didn't want you to have to wonder—Please take care. More later—love,

Mom.

But there was no "more later," not really. August passed, and September and October; that Thanksgiving in Amethyst, I remember exchanging a few desultory words on the subject while I helped my mother dry dishes. The tone was the same as our letters: me, reasoning, distant, dispassionate; her, perplexed, emotional, repressed ("I just don't understand how it can be like that between two men. . . ."). That December, our heads agog with the possibilities of endless sexual liberation, Rick and I moved to San Francisco. Driving a U-Haul truck with a Datsun and two cats in tow, we spent a last night with my mother and grandmother in Amethyst, opening Christmas presents early. Rick was welcomed in the house, as he already had been for years. My mother could accommodate, even if she could not accept.

I didn't try to convince, convert, or change her. I didn't know how. Also, a part of me resented the idea of having to justify or explain who and what I was. Once I had written the letter—once I had been honest—a tremendous pressure was off me. It was no longer my problem, but hers. I had struggled to come to terms with my sexuality; now she would have to come to grips with it.

We were both victims, of course; the same social stigmas that had victimized me had victimized my mother by not allowing her to accept her child and his nature without question, by placing a cruel barrier of confusion and disapproval between us. Just as I had had to overcome the lies I had been taught, she would have to

overcome the same crippling lies that she had been taught and had
passed on to me.

Perhaps I could have done more to educate her, but I was
young then, more clever than wise, and the skein of lies that bound
her seemed too tangled for me to ever penetrate them. I knew a
little about love and sex and living, but I had nothing to say about
sins I did not believe in, perpetrated against a god I didn't believe
in, either.

The family remained close, in its way. I returned to Amethyst
every Christmas. Mother's accommodation never turned into acceptance, and I never volunteered more than was asked of me. My
personal and working life remained closed to her. I was editing a
gay newspaper and writing pornography for *Drummer* magazine, I
was going to all-night dance parties and doing the baths twice a
week together with Rick. I was no more open with her than I had
been before, but at least the burden of evasion was off me; there
was no longer a secret about *why* I was secretive.

There was a great gulf between us, but the links between a
mother and child can withstand estrangement and reach across many
miles, can endure time and be stronger than death. When I decided
to write this remembrance, I knew that I would have to reread those
letters. I put it off for days and then weeks. At last I opened
the drawer. I picked out the envelopes with her casually elegant
handwriting, opened them, puzzled over forgotten messages about
long-ago holidays and faraway visits. Then I looked inside an envelope postmarked August 12, 1980, and found two pages of yellow
legal paper inside, each folded three times.

I read: *I don't know what I've done—but I've known for a long while
that you don't want to share even a little of your life with me.*

I read: *Steven. Yes. I knew. I had suspected for some time—*

I realized what they were. I scanned them quickly, afraid to
read them, afraid to remember and to summon up old feelings. I
cannot say that I hyperventilated, or that my legs became too weak
to hold me up. But the shade of my mother was with me, in me—
the shade of my dead mother *was* me, trembling and suddenly blind
with tears.

2

My brother, who among other spiritual experiences has been "born again," believes in life after death. My sister is attracted to the idea of reincarnation. Neither of these concepts has ever seemed particularly credible or even interesting to me. But I do know that the dead live on through their progeny. The ancient Chinese and Romans worshiped their own ancestors above any god, and with good reason, for who else made us, and where else did we come from?

The Romans buried or burned the remains of the dead. What they called the shades of the dead came out to walk not at midnight but in broad daylight. Rather than afterlife or rebirth, the very word "shade" suggests transposition and dispersion, a projection into the future that grows more tenuous with time and distance, and so it is that I sense the continued presence of my mother in my life. I see her manifested in a turn of phrase from my brother's lips, or in an attitude expressed by my sister. In the three of us siblings, in whom she invested so much and from whom she demanded so much, a part of her is preserved.

The values she instilled in me transcend the particular taboos that estranged us. Her demand for order and excellence, her disdain for stupidity, small-mindedness, and vulgarity, her pride, her essential decency, are parts of me that come directly from her. I have her weaknesses as well—intransigence, aloofness, a need to control, an aversion to spontaneity, a quickness to judge, a slowness to forgive, a hesitation to physically show affection. I can see her identity within my own so clearly that, even before her death, I used to joke with Rick that our partnership was like a marriage between his father and my mother.

Sometimes when I open my mouth, my mother speaks. When this happens to a person while his parent is still alive, there's often a denial, a sense of conflict, an aversion to the passed-on identity. But because my mother is dead—because she died unreconciled to my identity and while I was still young—I treasure the moments when she reappears. I let them linger, savor them, give in to them. These moments are like a running conversation between her and me and the third mind that contains us both.

A counselor once told me that I must have had a good mother, by which he meant a mother who invested me with a solid sense of self-worth at the outset of my life. I think this is true, and I consider myself luckier than many people I know whose parents seem to have given them more tangible but less durable advantages. How did my mother do this? I discover clues now and again, as when I find myself cuddling my cats and cooing the most preposterous praises at them. Modesty forbids me to reproduce baby talk verbatim, but I will say that the words "good boy," "so special," "precious," and "perfect" recur over and over. They come to my lips unbidden. They are my mother talking, and for me to reproduce them so effortlessly, I must have heard them spoken to me when I was very little and most receptive to them. The same mother who would later write "I would give my life if it were not true" and "It's like I never knew you at all" had much earlier told a certain baby that he was good, special, precious, and perfect, and the baby saw no reason not to believe every word.

My grandfather divorced my grandmother not long after she developed polio, quite a disgraceful thing to do. My grandmother returned to the little town of Amethyst, paralyzed from the waist down and using crutches, and set up a watch repair shop; my mother, who had spent her childhood in Dallas, did the rest of her growing up in Amethyst.

When I was growing up, Mother led us to believe that her teenage years were a model of impeccable behavior, but I've since heard that she was quite a wild high schooler, at least by the standards of a small town in Texas in the 1940s. With only a polio-stricken mother to control her, I think she did pretty much whatever she wanted to do.

She married my father for his looks, not for love. "I thought we'd have good-looking children," she once confessed to me in a soul-searching period of her life. The marriage lasted ten years and did produce three reasonably good-looking children. It broke up when my father had an affair with his young secretary. My mother achieved a little revenge with a whispering campaign that ruined Dad's run for the city council of Port Lavaca. After the divorce Mother took us to Dallas where her father (the one who had run out on his polio-stricken wife) put her through secretarial school.

Like her own mother, she decided to raise her children in the small-town security of Amethyst. Ronny, Gwyn, and I grew up in a succession of rented houses with my grandmother, while my mother found work first as a beautician, then as a medical secretary at the town's private hospital. We were poor, but there was a cushion of security provided by relatively well-to-do grandparents on both sides of the family. My mother was hardworking, self-sacrificing, and ingenious with money; I can't remember a Christmas when, by some miracle or other, I didn't get just about everything I wanted. She was also a very good cook, a skill that stood out even in stiff competition with the Methodist ladies who brought their best casseroles and desserts to Sunday-night covered-dish suppers at the church. We were expected to do well in school (Ronny was once deprived of TV for weeks when he made a C); academic and athletic achievements were rewarded with glowing support.

This was in the years when America was still at least the shadow of a Great Society and not just a kinder, gentler plutocracy, and there was plenty of grant and loan money to put all three kids through four years at the University of Texas. With her children finally on their own, my mother at last had the time and money to lavish a little attention on herself, which she did with a few trips. One of them was to Colorado, where she renewed a romance with her old high school sweetheart, a recent widower.

She bought new jewelry and new clothes. I noticed a sun lamp and some exercise pulleys in her room; she was getting herself toned and tanned, and it showed. My brother and sister and I held our breaths, thinking she might just remarry.

But it didn't happen. I remember a car trip I took with her from Austin to Amethyst, a year or so before I came out to her. It was one of the few occasions when she spent much time in my dented, dumpy, butt-numbing 1965 VW Bug. The self-conscious discomfort of driving my mother for two hours in my rattling wreck of a car was memorable in itself, but more than that I remember the way that she opened up to me, just a little.

Without my asking, she told me that she wasn't going to marry Doyle. "I married a man once when I wasn't really in love with him," she said, looking at the giant roadcuts and the gnarly oaks and cactus of the Hill Country, "and I won't make that mistake again." That was when she told me that she'd married my dad for his looks. She might have married Doyle for money and security, not to mention companionship, but she wasn't going to do it. I was disappointed, but I had to respect her for knowing her mind.

Then she said something that startled me. We must have gotten onto the subjects of dying and life after death. I was very much the confirmed atheist, and she knew it. But instead of arguing with me as usual, she shook her head and stared at the winding gray ribbon of asphalt ahead. "It would be so much easier if people could really know what happens after they die. A lot of people are so sure—but I don't know. . . ."

I glanced at her, a little awed and trying not to smile. *You sly fox,* I thought, *you're just like me, after all. You and I are just the same!* The wild high schooler who became an ideal mother, the divorcée who went to church to set an example for her children, the believer who had cautioned me that homosexuality was a sin against God, was a closet doubter all along. I didn't say a word, but I think I never felt closer to my mother than I did at that moment.

There was another evasion that went on between my mother and me. For years my siblings and I pressured her to stop smoking, with the kind of shrill pestering that only righteous white Protestant children can bring to bear on their repressed, guilt-ridden parents, until she finally did quit smoking—or pretended to. Meanwhile, perversely enough, I took up her habit and started smoking Camels and Luckies my freshman year in college. From then on, whenever we were together, we engaged in a strange charade—we each pretended not to smoke, and we each pretended not to know that the other smoked, all the while sneaking cigarettes the way that cocaine addicts sneak lines in public bathrooms, and with as little success at fooling anyone.

So powerful was this denial in our family that to the bitter end no one expressed the anguish and the guilt we all felt because my mother still smoked, had never really stopped smoking, and that it was the cigarettes that were killing her. The time between diagnosis of inoperable lung cancer and death can be shockingly brief; the doctors told us to expect six months, and they were accurate almost to the day.

Six months is a very short time—not long enough for my mother to see her infant grandchildren grow up, to see my sister married, to see my brother's marriage end in divorce, to see my first novel published. Not long enough for her to have a new worry about my sexuality, because what was then being called "gay cancer" was still only a vague rumor to most people. Certainly not long enough to say all the things that needed to be said, and so these things were left unspoken.

My brother did tell me that, before her diagnosis, my mother had made an appointment with her pastor to discuss some things that weighed on her; I was no doubt high on the list. After the diagnosis, she canceled the sessions, saying that those problems were no longer so important. I like to think that in her extremity she found a sense of proportion and perspective that freed her from the useless worry and guilt she felt because of me.

She was diagnosed in the fall of 1983. She was fifty-six. That Christmas, as usual, I came home to Amethyst. I'd had some portraits done and gave framed photos as gifts. Later, back in San Francisco, I mailed her a copy of *The Wicked Day*, the newest in the series of Arthurian novels by Mary Stewart that my mother loved so much.

Looking through my desk drawer, I came across the last letter I received from her, dated only "Sunday":

Dear Steven,
    Thanks for the book. I thumbed through it in a store while Christmas shopping—and really thought that was what you would give me for Christmas. Just think how

upset I would have been if everyone got a picture and I got a book. It makes a nice surprise for now. I started it last night.

I'm feeling pretty good—better than when you were here. I had a treatment on the 7th—then worked from Tuesday—was to have another treatment the 14th, but my platelet count was too low. Maybe next week. The treatments are long and unpleasant but not painful. I really get tired of the bed and am too groggy to do anything about it. I'll answer questions, honey. If there is anything you want to know—feel free to ask. Thanks for the book—I'll enjoy.   I love you,
                                                            Mom

As an afterthought, on the same line as her name, she added: *Hi to Rick*.

Within the range of the possible, we can choose the hour of our death. My mother taught me this.

In April I got a call from my brother; the doctors said the time had come. I booked a flight to Austin. On the afternoon I arrived I went to see her at the hospital. I had been afraid that her appearance would be shocking, frightening, but she only looked very weak. I helped her write some thank-you notes for flowers and candy.

My sister arrived the next day. That night she and my brother and I all gathered in the hospital room while my mother slipped into a coma. She had waited for us all to arrive, and then she slowly let go. I believe that her choice was a conscious one, to see her children gathered in one place again and then to relinquish life and pain and struggle to their inevitable end. She became reconciled to death, something I had never been able to imagine. To witness this was to be given a strange and beautiful gift.

Through the night, Ronny and Gwyn and I talked about shared memories. At one point they both left the room, and I whispered words of love in my mother's ear, perhaps some of the very things she had whispered to me as a baby. I tried to stay the night, but Ronny and I were at last too exhausted from the strain and the hours and left to get some sleep. The next morning Gwyn called to let us know that Mother had died.

The previous fall, when I first heard about Mother's cancer, Rick and I were seeing a counselor. I told the counselor about my mother, and he encouraged me to talk about my feelings. Oddly, I told him, one of the things I was feeling was that after my mother died a part of me would be set free. He told me that in some ways we don't grow up until our parents are gone, and when they die there can be a strange sense of exhilaration, of freedom from old, cumbersome expectations and restraints.

It was true; her death freed me from the evasions and guilts of childhood. It also ended my childhood, and with it my illusions of immortality. Before her death, a part of me was still innocent. To be innocent is to be untouched by death, immortal. After her death, the world was changed forever.

My physical memories of her grow dimmer with passing time. Old photographs capture aspects of her appearance, but not her animation. Old letters preserve her handwriting, but they do not show the hand that wrote them—small and slender, if I remember rightly, and etched across the back with veins, like my own. I can't quite recall the timber of her voice, though sometimes Gwyn or Ronny will call me on the phone and use a phrase I haven't heard in years, and I hear her echo. I can even go home to Amethyst now and not think about her much; then my grandmother, fixing breakfast from her wheelchair, will mistakenly call my sister Lucy instead of Gwyn, and her shade passes through the room.

harlan greene

what she gave me
my mother regina
and history

Where I come from people spend a great deal of time talking about their families. They do it easily—on porches in the long twilight evenings, at church, at the grocery store, and in the street. It is often carefree, and often something else. For family, after all, can really determine your place in Charleston, entitling you (or not) to a spot in the social hierarchy. Bring the subject up and some will laugh and say, oh, it does not matter, but oh, it does. In reverential tones people still speak about their ancestors and point to portraits with gestures as if to say, "I told you so. See?" They can recite their genealogies by heart and will show you relics—spoons and bowls buried by a slave in the war to keep from the Yankees. Then, putting up their sacred bits, they'll turn to receive your awe and envy.

I grew up right down the street from folks like that, and I listened to their stories, but it was not the same for us. No. In our little house on Ashley Avenue, history was an abyss, something you crawled over to the edge of and peered into carefully. The view down was compelling, and not a little bit frightening—for there was always the possibility that the vortex would rush out and suck you in, and you'd never get free.

But that, paradoxically, also made us similar to the families up the street; for if you look about Charleston with anything resembling an open mind, you'll come to realize that the air is tinged with the past and something akin to a biblical curse rests on the city. The sins of the parents are visited on the children: look about you and you can see what centuries of cruelty to African-Americans have wrought and you'll run smack into the smugness of the inherited aristocracy. We never had that to contend with—at home at least. But there was a different cloud hanging over our house. In it, we came up against the sins committed on our parents by Nazi Germany.

When I was young, I didn't know any of these things. I sensed we were different, but that didn't bother me. My mother was the center of my universe, and she transfixed me. So much so that I was stunned when, at about age six, I realized she did not share my every thought; I was dumbfounded to discover that we were not the same being inhabiting two bodies. I remember my astonishment and dismay when I apprehended that she did not instinctively know everything about me.

Yet after that I still thought of her all the time. At school when I was bored or in trouble I imagined her coming up the walk to pick us up at three-thirty, her dress billowing about her like the chiffon on Loretta Young Theatre on TV. I imagined her swooping down like a bird, or superwoman, to grab and rescue me from all the school kids who teased and tormented me. I was fat and wore glasses and made good grades; no one but Momma made me feel good about being me.

Before Momma told me anything about her family I had a blank, and against it I pictured her arisen like Venus from the sea. Momma—Regina—had been born awfully far away from my world—that of Charleston in the 1950s; she had been born in Warsaw, Poland, in 1920. Her first memory, she told me, was of being in the country; she was supposed to watch her grandfather, dozing in a wicker chair, but she wandered off, searching—only to find some coins in the straw of a barn. Oh, she said, remembering it and speaking of it to me in an excited child's voice, oh, those bright shiny pennies. That was the only time I heard her use that voice—a happy voice—when she talked of her history.

She was the oldest of three children. But it was not until Momma died that I saw a picture of her whole family. It is compelling. There is Regina at about sixteen, her posture stalwart and defiant and proud, her eyes agleam; she's standing there as if a captain of a ship. A breeze is blowing in her face and she looks as though she can fill the brush and thrill of destiny. Her younger sister Edith stands by coyly. And then there are her parents and younger brother. Although those three are in the forefront of the photograph, they are dark and their eyes reflect no light—as if they can see their doom already. Regina's father with his gentle eyes and long beard looks wise and knowing and smiles at the world, wanting to agree.

He treated Regina like a son, she told me. He let her bring in the tea while he was discussing politics and philosophy with his friends on Shabbos; he knew that when she left she would leave the door open a crack so she could sit outside in the hall and hear. Regina grew up into a dramatic blond-haired, blue-eyed beauty who shunned the wealthier boys of her class for the self-made men from the country, like my father. She worked as a dressmaker in Paris when she went to the Sorbonne to study math and philosophy. Going to Paris was a daring gesture for someone of her upbringing, but she would not stoop to the humiliation handed out to Jews in Poland—such as being forced to sit on a certain side of the room and not being awarded the grades she made. She loved studying but as the world situation worsened she went home to Warsaw without taking her degree.

That summer of 1939 was golden, they say, the sunlit air as rich as the ripening wheat. On June 15 of that year Regina Miedzyr-zecka Kawer married Samuel Gruenblatt. They had a few weeks. September came, and I could see her pulling back the lace curtains from the window to watch Nazi storm troopers goose-stepping up the street.

What came after that—the exact chronology—I never did get straight; I think Momma lost it too—what with all the lies, forged documents and false identities. And she made herself forget, too. I think for her to remember what she had been before the war must have been upsetting. No doubt that was why she had hidden the photograph of her family.

Momma rarely spoke to me of those times. But when she did, I could see it all happening. "September 1939" appeared before my eyes like an image on a movie screen—and there was Poppa, like all able-bodied Poles, fleeing east, right into the advancing Russian army. I could see him being marched off to a slave-labor camp in Siberia. Eventually he would escape to Tashkent and then leave Asia as the war was ending. I saw Momma taking charge of Poppa's half-sister, who could only speak Yiddish, directing her to act like a mute as they crossed enemy territory back to her family. Then there was Momma, back in Warsaw, with her Aryan looks and flawless Polish, bribing a priest for baptismal documents proving she was Catholic. I could see her with her underground compatriots blowing up trains. She would never tell them she was Jewish or they would have killed her. The Poles, her own people, were as anti-Semitic as the Nazis. She carried a cyanide capsule with her constantly. She was smuggling in food to her family, who were walled up in the Warsaw ghetto, her father dying in there. One version (and there are others—I do not know which to believe) has her family being smuggled out of the ghetto in a hay cart to their country place where they live in hiding. This version has them being sold to the Gestapo for salt; the peasants need it, what with pigs to slaughter and Easter coming.

I am not sure what really happened and probably never will be. The only fixed and sure thing is the ending: Treblinka and her mother and brother vanishing into the air, into history. Her sister Edith also passed as Catholic (she is still known today as Maria in the family) and survived as a farm laborer in Germany where she witnessed Berlin's destruction. And somewhere in there, free-floating in the darkness was this: on a dark, cloudless night in a bombed-out neighborhood, Momma crawling through a fence into a Jewish cemetery to scoop out the earth with her hands to make a shallow grave for her dead baby.

"Where was that?" I asked Momma.

"I can't remember," she answered in wonder, looking amazed that she could forget such a thing.

And then, finally, there was Momma after the war, reunited with Poppa and Maria, digging up the old china that had been passed down in her family and that we later used at Passover much to my fascination, them living in Vienna where my older brother was born, then coming to this country.

And then there was me. As I reflected on her story, I felt as I had one day when I lay flat on the doctor's table, naked, and he examined me. Momma was in the room, too, and she seemed to float above me like a Chagall angel (like her story later would), looking down on me—like a specimen, helpless and pinned. I felt cowed and tiny—paralyzed by what I had heard, by her history. And there was a shame of sorts attached to it, too, for back then no one discussed the Holocaust. That my parents had been hunted like animals and treated like vermin was humiliating—especially in such a chaste and gentle, Gentile city.

For years after her telling, I thought I would have no life of my own, for I had a mission instead: to take care of my parents— Momma especially—to shield her from any more suffering. I did what I could. I helped her around the house and did well in school; I beat all the others, and it made her happy. "You can't trust anyone but family," she told me. So I had no friends, only my siblings and parents—her especially. Regina was my soulmate, but as I grew older I stopped telling her everything.

I had to, because we were in Charleston—or I was. (Momma always seemed to live in a place distinct, in her own charged atmosphere.) But I was in Charleston and there it was conformity that mattered; there was no escape from it in the Jewish community. The kids—and my American cousins especially—made fun of my parents, for not keeping kosher, working on Saturday, and talking funny. So we were blackballed and picked on. Yet I never told Momma what was happening. It would have distressed her to know that in America kids made fun of her, and that they made fun of me.

So I suffered silently. I knew instinctively that Momma would not understand peer pressure, because she had no peers. She thought all the foolishness of the fifties just that. She worked, though no other Jewish women did; she paid her maid a decent salary; she treated black people fairly and paid no attention to the social niceties that were the sacred rites of the city. She was too bright, too intellectual, and she moved too quickly. Like a mathematician, she went at solutions and the roots of things. And, following her, I turned inward; I had no friends, no outside world, just my inner one of feelings.

In the long run I suppose it was good for me, for when I realized I was gay, coming out was easy. I was used to being alien and different, outside the mainstream. And from Momma I had gotten the message to believe in myself and to do what I thought right no matter what others said or thought about me.

I'm not sure that the other gay kids in the Hebrew day school I went to had it so easy. For they had fit in and were used to belonging; it might have been harder for them to adjust and to accept that they were an alien minority.

My father was worried for me; he is a joiner and so fit in better in America and in Charleston than my mother or I did. He was bothered when we discussed my sexuality. He knew, he said, how cruel the world could be to those who are different and had learned the hard way (as had my mother and aunt) the value of appearing to be just like everybody else. I think he was also bothered by what he had heard, what he had read about homosexuality.

But it's not like that, I told him. Imagine what you might have heard about blacks in Charleston in 1860, 1930, or what you hear today. You know, I told him, what was said about Jews by the Nazis. I told Poppa I had inherited his courage to go against the grain—and explained that gay was the same as black or Jewish—all can be victims of lies and hate and bigotry.

There was no problem at all with Momma; she was the one who brought the matter up, after all. "I think it's time to discuss things," she told me one day at lunch. So we talked and she threw her stereotypes away and started reading. Momma said she just wanted me to be happy. And I told her that there was nothing to stop me.

And there wasn't really, except for some of the attitudes I still had and some of the attitudes around me. Though all of us were named for the dead and we were supposed to go on living for them, Momma never stressed it as much as many Holocaust survivors. She did not carry on about us marrying and having children. She welcomed anyone we brought home; she and my lover Olin and I got along wonderfully. We would go out to eat once a week and talk about everything under the sun. Together we were happy, and I wonder now if she did not, in a way, hand me over to Olin. She could not have failed to see the light he brought to my life nor fail to notice how I was finally alive, no longer just an adjunct to her history. It cost her a lot when Olin's psychiatric residency took us from Charleston. In her heart, she did not want me to leave, but she encouraged us to, for she knew she and Charleston were no longer enough for me.

I called her all the time, though she never demanded it. She did not sit on her laurels or trade off her past; she never expected compassion or even understanding from anybody. Whenever the survivors of the Holocaust were gathering, she never went; when I asked her why, she said because holocausts are still happening all over the world and we should channel our efforts into stopping them instead of just remembering one of the most recent ones. Momma, I'd brag to the new people I was meeting, could stand up to anything.

Except history—or at least its repeating.

Soon after I left Charleston Hurricane Hugo descended on the city like a blitzkrieg. It was in September of 1989, almost fifty years to the day after the Germans occupied Warsaw. I don't know why she did not leave. I was talking to her on the phone from my home in Chapel Hill when the lines went down; I was in Charleston with bottled water and plastic and food and batteries and a generator the morning following the storm.

They compared it to a war-torn landscape and it *was* frightening; once in town it took me forever to get up the street. Our house

had holes in the roof; huge craters exposed by pulled-up roots were
filled with water and the trees had no tops. There was no water, no
food, no electricity. And people were acting oddly—some walking
around dazed—many staring in disbelief. It affected Momma badly.
She started hoarding food again, as she had in our childhood; eating
secretly; telling us that there was no one out there who would help.
There was just family. It was Momma I had been thinking about
when I drove to Charleston; but it was Olin who was worrying me
when I left. When we could get a phone line through, I found out
he had persistent fever and was coughing.

Olin was working hard in his residency and was not getting
better—but he couldn't be getting sick, I told myself. He couldn't
have *it*. (I couldn't say the word AIDS to myself then. It was too
frightening.) He is so young, I told myself, so pure; there is no
chance he could be sick. The world couldn't be that cruel. No, no,
we were both screaming to ourselves as the world tilted and the hole
in history yawned open. When he went to the hospital—it was Yom
Kippur—he could barely breathe; and then one night, he went into
intensive care suddenly. . . .

Olin was hospitalized for weeks; and while I was there with
him, running between the house and work and pretending to the
outside world that nothing was happening, it was really Momma's
secret world I was inhabiting. I was in her twilight world of horror
she had given me glimpses of—as if preparing me. There were
streetcars in the Warsaw ghetto, she had told me; the Poles rode
through not seeing the suffering, the bodies on the street, the children dying. Olin's being in the hospital made me realize that it is
the same in this country with the AIDS epidemic. We are a lower
form of life most folks see dying. In the weeks and months following, some of our family and friends withdrew or acted oddly, as if
it did not concern them. But not Momma. Once we told her, she
rallied immediately.

When Momma and Olin finally saw each other, they nodded,
communicating silently. They may have known each other well before, but now, I saw, they were peers, each a victim of cruelty.

We had a few months of peace. But Momma went into the
hospital in the spring. The cancer she had fought and thought she

had defeated years before came back suddenly. In the hospital, she never complained; she tried to be cheerful for us; she apologized for being a drain, for being weak. She had no patience for dallying and rushed things. Olin and I were in her room with her when she died; it was one of the rare times I felt the place was holy.

It has been two years since then; I feel Momma's absence, but not her lack; I feel Regina with me. It's funny: I do not think about the woman who worked and scrubbed pots as if possessed, and pushed food, or even of how we discussed articles in the *New Republic* and what we were reading. For Momma to me is more of what she personified—she is as deathless as her honor, honesty, and her liberality of spirit, summed up by her love and dignity. These are some of the things she gave me. And she was right about holocausts, I see; they are still happening. It is as if Momma went through the darkness even before I was born, to light the way to grief for me. She made it possible not just for me to love and to give, but to look beyond betrayal and horror and cruelty, and hope to persevere.

Because of her—and because of Olin, for whom she prepared me—I myself am prepared. I know that, despite the cruelty, there have been kind souls here who are good and wise and loving. I know what I owe the dead and that I owe the living. Regina and Olin are with me—I, their witness, and they my testimony.

The rest is unimportant, is history only.

darrell g. h. schramm

father's sorrow, father's joy

Weep not, my wanton, smile upon my knee;
When thou art old there's grief enough for thee.
Mother's wag, pretty boy,
Father's sorrow, father's joy.

—Robert Greene

"Sephestia's Song"

I remember nothing of my early years with him, nothing that concerned me directly for the first six years anyway. The one incident in which I can still see him, he did not see me. I'd been playing in our North Dakota barnyard when he attempted to chase one of our stubborn horses from the corral. Picking up a sharp stick, he tossed it toward but not at the horse. The stick glanced off the side of the barn, arched, and struck the horse, piercing its eye. Wild with pain, the animal screamed; its neighing ripped the air as it reared several times in bloody agony.

It was not so much a violence done inside me, crawling into silence, as it was the silence of my father's restraint that jarred me then. What did he feel? He showed nothing. What he did immediately after the horse had been blinded, I don't recall. I remember only my feeling of dismay and bafflement as I observed him from a corner of the barn. There were no cries, no calls for help, no curses. It was the beginning of my realization that some things don't die; they go underground.

Years later as an adult I once studied a photograph of him standing beside me when I was perhaps four years old. His smile is a pencil line, his arms straight—they are close to but not touching me as I stand on the running board of a 1940s Packard.

It was a winter morning when the photo was taken, the sun having melted the nightfrost or the thin lick of snow that skirts a Midwestern house like a ruffle even when the rest of the ground is free of any precipitation. My little fist is clenched; it must have been cold.

Studying that picture, I thought, "He could have held my hand." But he didn't. We stood smiling pleasantly for a camera's eye, unmoved by anything but the social obedience that demands a subject stand still for a photograph. "He could have held my hand. In all those years of growing up, he could have touched me just once to show he was glad to have fathered me, his first son."

What wasted years before we both understood, before we became true father-and-son. All those years growing up, I believed wrongly that his silence and restraint were measuring me against himself and the other men of our German clan, that the silence meant rejection or denial, that love is voiced only in words.

Unlike my mother, whose side of the family was garrulous, sentimental, and histrionic, my father came from that German stock which values formality, consideration, and reserve. Miss Manners would have loved him.

He was a little man; "Shorty" was his nickname. But he was strong, muscular, solid. His strength and perseverance were the legacy of his pioneer parents, people of sacrifice and long suffering, as well as the legacy of years of farming and, later, of construction work—dams mostly. He did not know how to complain: he endured. He was a gentle man, something I overlooked in my fear of his disapproval. A quiet man, a man of few words, he seemed to be mocking me when he laughed at my foibles and differences. How could I have known?

It was after my sixth birthday when he asked me if I'd accompany him to the pasture where he was going to "take care of" one of our cows that had broken her foot stepping into a gopher or prairie-dog hole. I sensed we were on an adventure, driving through the prairie grass, for normally we walked the pasture, usually to herd the cows home for milking. Not until Dad had pulled up beside the cow, still standing near the fatal gopher hole, and pulled a rifle from the trunk did I realize with a sudden terror what was about to happen.

"Aren't you coming out of the car?" Dad asked me in German.

I could only shake my head. When I saw him raise the gun, I quickly rolled up the windows, ducked below the steering wheel, and squeezed my eyes shut while plugging my ears with my fingers. And I was in pain, a new pain I'd never before felt.

I heard the gun go off, then heard the car door open. "What's wrong with you?" Dad asked me. "Afraid of a gun?" (Or had he said "Afraid of *the* gun?" The difference matters to a child's interpretation.) I thought he was mocking me, belittling my horror. Still I refused to look at the spot where the milk cow had stood. We drove back to the farmhouse in silence.

Those were the years, too, at ages six and seven, when I took to wearing aprons, pretending I was a girl as I played in the barnyard, the cornfield, the loft, the house. Sometimes I'd even tie my shirt around my head, letting it fall in back, making believe I had long hair. If ever Dad commented on my games, he never spoke a word to me. Silence can be the voice of approval or acceptance also, but what does a child know of that?

Over the next few years Dad took my brother Gary and me fishing several times. But I could rarely sit longer than ten minutes or so with my pole in the water before I'd be off to explore the riverside or the nearby woods. When I was ten, he took me fishing for the last time. I'd made a determined effort to sit longer than usual—probably no more than twenty minutes—when once again I rose restlessly, set my pole at an angle by shoving it into the side of the grassy bank, and romped off to explore. Returning thirty or forty minutes later, I found my fishing rod lying in the grass. I'd had a bite at nearly the same time my father had hooked a fish, and he had just managed to keep my pole from being dragged into the river. I knew I had disappointed him when he never asked me to go fishing again. On the other hand, he may simply have accommodated my lack of interest in fishing; that interpretation did not occur to me then.

At age eight I exchanged my aprons for my mother's discarded skirts, wearing them until I was eleven, even in the backyard after we'd moved to town. I didn't notice that Dad—not only Mom—allowed me this freedom until I outgrew it.

When I was eleven, we moved from North Dakota to northern California, where Dad began to work at construction sites long distances from home. Consequently, he would often be gone during the week, home only on weekends. More and more he seemed on the periphery of my life. Little teasings—taunts I thought they were—come back to me: when I refused to eat hot chili peppers, he would say, "Takes a man to eat these"; when I'd bend a nail while hammering, he'd say, "Hold the hammer like a man"; when I'd speak enthusiastically about my male friends, he'd ask, "Do you have a girlfriend yet?" Though he never barked, snapped, or scolded, I was convinced that he disapproved. I was not like my younger brothers or my many male cousins. Except for track and tennis, I participated in and cared about no sports. I read novels and poetry and listened to classical music. And I was an adolescent who secretly loved boys my own age. How could he approve?

Yet one memory of my teenage years stands out like an exclamation mark to contradict the censure I felt from my father. Though unable to afford it, my parents sent me to a Christian boarding school in Oakland, birthplace of Robert Duncan, childhood home of Gertrude Stein. I'd come home for a short holiday during my sophomore year but had seen little of Dad, who worked long shifts at the Oroville Dam. And he'd already gone to work long before the time I had to return to the city. Ticket in my hand, I was slowly moving in line toward the door of the Greyhound bus when a Pontiac squealed to a stop behind it. Dad jumped from the car. Had I forgotten something? No, he'd just come from work during his break. "Well, uh, you be good and don't do anything I wouldn't do," he said. Then he leaned toward me and kissed me good-bye.

All the way back to Oakland I kept thinking, "Maybe he loves me after all."

But the years shuffled on, each year seeming to put more distance between us. One brother joined the army, and two other brothers immersed themselves in sports and girlfriends. I continued my little affairs with peers and other men. It seemed Dad and I had little to talk about. Even when I began teaching school, education was not a shared topic. He had quit school at age fourteen, did not read much—certainly never a book—and knew next to nothing of art, music, other cultures, those topics of my own interests. And while my brothers spoke of their "love lives" to him, I hid from him my own devastation when at twenty and again at thirty I lost the love of two men to whom I'd been devoted.

However, smoke appeared on the horizon—promise of fire, promise of change. When I was thirty-three, I met Chris. This remarkable and atypical gay man had grown up on an almond farm in northern California, had milked cows, plucked chickens, had studied with Diebenkorn, Mel Ramos, Bob Bechtel, among others, become an artist, worked in New York publishing, met Muriel Spark, Elie Wiesel, and a host of other writers, then left the wordy world of name and fame behind and returned to the West Coast to remain true to himself. Whether it was Proust or Janet Frame, movies or ballet, Egyptian mythology or Chinese history, Balenciaga or Nero Wolf, he could discourse knowledgeably on the subject. In short, he was a Renaissance man, one who, unlike most people I knew and know, had clear convictions about nearly everything in his life. When we met, we were both living in San Francisco. We'd been visiting and dating each other constantly for about ten months when, for Thanksgiving, I drove home to southern California where my parents had moved a few years before.

The evening I arrived at their Santa Maria home, Dad and I were seated across from each other, he in his rocker and I on the sofa, a wide empty space between us. After one or two perfunctory remarks about the weather, we lapsed into our usual silence. I picked up a magazine, *Family Circle* or *Woman's Day* most likely, and flut-

tered through it. Suddenly the room thundered. Dad had burst out,
"Why in hell don't you talk to me like my other boys do!" and
stormed from the room. I was stunned. For a long time I sat listening to the echoes rumbling in my heart.

The next morning on our way to buy fresh eggs at a farm
outside town, I said, "Dad, before I return to San Francisco, I have
to tell you something."

"So whyn't you tell me now?" he asked quietly, glancing at
me from the steering wheel. His face seemed gentle.

"Because I'm scared. I need more time."

Accepting my reason, he began speaking of the farmer we were
about to visit, of how he himself still enjoyed eating farm-fresh
eggs, of how he sometimes missed farm life.

"But it's a good thing you keep such a large vegetable garden,"
I said. "You stay close to the earth that way. Besides, you're not as
healthy as you used to be. A farm would be too much for you now."

He agreed, and our conversation wove itself into a tapestry of
"the old days" on our North Dakota farm.

I too still loved the earth, its soil, its grass, its fruit. Like
father, like son. The next day I called him into the bedroom where
I slept when home. As I waited for him, a sudden memory washed
over me: The winter after my sixth birthday a blizzard had piled
snowdrifts seven and eight feet high. Dad had had to dig us out of
our little farmhouse. And once he had tunneled a pathway for us,
he called to me. Climbing up a snowbank, I found him waiting
with a little sled. In a flash I was seated on it, and he was pulling
and pushing me over hills of snow. I remembered a silent world of
snow crackled by the glee of my laughter. Where had it gone? My
palms were moist, my armpits trickled sweat, my heart raced like
that of a terrified fledgling fallen from a tree and now held in a
gardener's hand.

I was pacing when Dad walked into the room. "Whyn't you
sit down?" he asked me.

"I'm too nervous," I said, then stopped abruptly a few feet
from him. Looking at him, I went on with a rush. "Dad, I'm in
love with someone I'd like to spend the rest of my life with. It's a
man. I'm in love with another man."

The sky didn't fall, lightning didn't strike me, hell didn't open at my feet. But Dad, my father, opened his arms. Taking a couple of steps toward me, he put his hands on my shoulders and said, "You're my son. As long as you never turn on your mother and me, you'll always be my son." And then he held me against his chest.

Between the old life and the new life lies the seminal moment, the moment of bestowal. What had been underground had now surfaced. What had been our winter had now become our spring. I was a son born again and he a father renewed. I had feared his rejection, he had feared mine; now our lives with each other were given true life at last.

We are converted, changed through the body. Words would not have been enough. And so he held me. Hands, chest, shoulders, the nest of arms. In that embrace we spoke to each other as never before, profoundly, irrevocably.

The next time I drove home for a visit, Chris was with me. Dad welcomed him immediately. I knew he liked Chris because on the second day of our visit, when asked once again to drive out to the farm to buy fresh eggs for Mom, Dad suggested Chris and I go along. Chris sat between us on the front seat. At one point as he and Chris talked of farming and of raising chickens, Dad affectionately clamped a strong hand on Chris's left thigh. As sexual as the act seemed to me, I was thrilled.

Over the next decade, Chris and I invited my parents to San Francisco to spend weekends with us. And they came. Sometimes while my mother and I fixed meals, Dad joined Chris outside for a smoke. Seeing Chris as an extension of myself, he gave Chris as much attention and affection as he gave me.

In 1985, a couple of years after Dad retired early (his health having deteriorated), I agreed to drive my parents to North Dakota for a family reunion. It was a rich time. Though Mom and I had an occasional disagreement during those two weeks, Dad and I seemed to see eye-to-eye about everything: where to stay, where to eat, where to go, what to see, what to do. With each other we confirmed our love of the land, of the gently sweeping prairies, the pronghorn antelope that wandered it, the wide open skies, the bow-

ing wheat. Once, because Dad could no longer do so, in his stead
I helped my uncles shovel oats from a granary into the hopper of a
churning elevator that spiraled the grain into the bed of a huge
truck. Dad's arms too had once strained with the weight of a grain
shovel, Dad's back too had bent into the golden oats. Dad's skin
too had itched from the chaff dust. Like father, like son.

But back in California it was the hours we shared by ourselves
that I treasured most. Often those times were spent in the large
vegetable garden my parents maintained in town, a substitute for
the farm. Here, whenever I was home for a visit, Dad and I worked
side by side, picking beans, picking peas, pulling up radishes and
carrots, digging potatoes, watering the corn, the cabbage, the beets.
Sometimes he'd pick, say, a ripe tomato and hand it to me, beam-
ing. "See what the earth can do." Other times we pitched horseshoes
in the backyard or played pool. We spoke those times but we didn't
speak much. I had learned to understand his silences, their spare
eloquence. Like my father, I began to know the waste of words, to
understand that we talk most things to death. We say "I feel that"
when we mean "I think that," confusing thoughts or words with
feelings. We blunt and bury our deepest emotions in an avalanche
of words. I no longer needed to hear the words to know and feel
the intensity of my father's emotions.

For Christmas 1988, Chris and I invited my parents to spend
the holidays with us at the home of Chris's parents near Sacramento.
It was to be Dad's last Christmas.

Before we opened the gifts under a towering tree, Chris and I
and our families stood around a baby grand singing the old songs.
When Chris's mother asked the three of us Schramms to sing carols
in German, we blushed but rose to the occasion, our voices shaky
at first, then strong with the pride of our heritage and the love that
bound us. "Stille Nacht," "O Tannenbaum," "O Du Fröhliche." I
wonder if Dad recalled, as I did then, those long-ago cold North
Dakota winters of snowdrifts so deep no automobile could get into
town and him hitching a team to the sleigh to drive us, his young
family, into town as we sat, huddled and snug, under a buffalo
robe. I could still see him, stalwart and silent in his black astrakhan
coat and a cap with earflaps tied under his chin, as he held the reins

of the horses that pulled us through a white, undulating world without road, without river, without any human beings for miles.

We had come a long way, my father and I, and we had only a short way yet to go. That following spring, I resigned from my teaching position of eleven years in order to work on a book of poetry and to complete a long short story I'd been struggling with for years. I would go to Europe, traveling with Chris for a month, then stay on to write. Late that summer, shortly before Chris and I were to leave, Dad had a heart attack. Mom called me after he'd been hospitalized and seemed to be doing well. He'd told her from his hospital bed that I was not to cancel my trip nor change my plans on his account. Still skeptical, I called his nurse, who reassured me that so far all signs were in his favor, that there was no vascular damage. When I spoke to Dad, he insisted he was all right, that I was to take my trip, to follow through what I had begun. He sounded cheerful as he wished me a safe journey. Later, when I called home from Scotland, he was still doing well.

Once Chris had returned to the States, I traveled for two weeks in Italy, then went to Spain, where I settled in a white, hilltop town. When the Loma Prieta earthquake struck the San Francisco area, I was in Sevilla. For two days I tried to get through by telephone without any luck. On the third day I connected with Chris's sister, who immediately assured me that everyone I cared about in San Francisco was safe and fine.

"But there's still some bad news," she said. "Oh, Darrell, I'm so sorry. Your father died."

I hung up slowly, walked to the nearby Plaza Nueva, sat under a lamp, and wept.

This man, my father, had loved much, silently and deeply, had given of his love through work and sacrifice, without comment or complaint. Yet he'd watched the shortcuts of technology, chemicals, and credit replace the hands, hearts, and minds of people, watched his culture shift from neighborhood to selfhood, from self-sacrifice to accumulation, and he couldn't understand. He saw his world as one which brandished power more than knowledge, evidence that it considered human beings insignificant, and he couldn't understand. In his last decade, much of what he had struggled for was all but

swept away by insurance premiums and medical bills. Hard work
and devotion had garnered and guaranteed little. Sick and disillu-
sioned toward the end, he had wanted to die.

I thought those thoughts then, in that Spanish plaza. And I
remembered, too, our last words to each other, long-distance words.
"Dad," I'd said over the telephone, "I love you."

"I love you too, son," he said. "And give my love to Chris,
okay?"

"Dad, it's good to hear your voice."

There was a pause, and then Dad's voice broke as he said good-
bye. I believe he knew even then.

I, a man who loves men and the land, shall have no sons to
carry on the love of sons and the land. But sometimes, digging in
my garden, I remember him; and sometimes, seeing Chris smoke a
cigarette on the back porch, I remember him; but most of all I
remember him when, loving Chris and aware of my own body, I
know that I am his flesh and his love continuing.

james carroll pickett

kentucky 55 south
a visit with dad

You're forty. Not going to live forever. Sean's dead more than a year now. You've been diagnosed. Time to go back to Kentucky and have a talk with your dad.

Your best friend's widow picks you up at the airport in Louisville. It's been sixteen years since you hit the road. Kentucky is so green, so wet. You had forgotten. The Widow Bailey, not yet forty, is dazzling. You want to rush into her arms. Hold her. Be held. Weep. Rage at the loss. Her husband, Phillip. Your lover, Sean. Embrace lightly instead in the lobby of the American Airlines terminal. Drive to the working-class neighborhood of Crescent Hill where perched atop a hill is the house she and Phillip renovated, decked, painted, and nurtured into a showpiece worthy of San Francisco. Drink club soda and reminisce.

Dinner is at Dietrich's, a movie house converted into a bistro so hip the entire staff is perceptibly gay—except for the somber busboy, a nineteen-year-old redneck, face etched with acne, a basherin-waiting. This is the old Crescent Theatre. As a teenager, you drove girlfriends from the country forty miles into town hoping to get them hot watching uncensored European art films that showed tits and ass, and, if lucky, a flash of snatch. In '66, Larvida Perkins came to town with you to see *The Pawnbroker*, which had boxcars and barbed wire, but no snatch. It introduced you to the fact of Jews, a well-hidden subject in Kentucky, and that night on the drive back to Shelby County the yearned-for heavy petting was supplanted by discussions of the Holocaust. What, you wonder, ever happened to Larvida?

Drive the Widow Bailey's Toyota Camry out I-64 to 55 South, a narrow blacktop with grass creeping over the asphalt edges, through the sleeping burg of Finchville. It is six miles to the gravel lane on the left that winds up the hill to the 118-year-old farmhouse where you grew up. Your daddy grew up. Your granddaddy grew up. Headlights illuminate the towering brick house. The double front doors, used only for special occasions, are closed. On the back porch, greet your brother, Jack, and meet his wife, Marge. Thank her for the offer she made: "If there's anyone you'd like to bring with you," she had said, "anyone at all, know that he'd be welcome in our house." Regret there is no one left to bring home. It is late. Go up to your old room. Wish that Sean could have seen all this. Remember to take your medication. The crickets call all night long.

In the light of day, notice the paint is flaking and the brick and mortar are crumbling. There are two dogs, filthy and friendly, a pet tortoise, and innumerable cats. Outbuildings, weather-beaten and gray, lean at absurd angles. This farm has always been poor. Always will. Take a walk and observe your brother and his helper chopping tobacco in the shimmering midmorning humidity. Stand at the top of the hollow and admire the ancient oak tree that granddaddy loved so much. The trunk is ten, maybe twelve feet, in circumference now. Granddaddy's been gone since '61. Climb down the wooded bluff and hike along Brashear's Creek where the beaver have made a comeback.

Walk for two and a half hours and never leave your property.

Smell the woods, watch the deer and possums and squirrels. Go back to the house and imagine the ghosts of your ancestors rising up from the rich black loam.

Talk late into the night with Jack and Marge. Meet the children. Stare at photographs of relatives you have never seen. And never will.

Your grandmother is ninety-two and still living in her little white house in Finchville. She leaves the walker parked by the card table in the middle room, balancing herself on furniture as she navigates the front parlor and kitchen. Here is the refuge you sought as a boy. In the midst of family strife, she was sanctuary. Still is. She soothes you with corn pudding—not the canned stuff the Old Stone Inn serves these days, but the fresh kind she makes from scratch—and tells tales from the family lore, stories you've heard before, some dozens of times. Listen more carefully now because it is the last time you will hear them.

Great-Uncle Rector, it turns out, moved to Arkansas because he shot a man during a gambling dispute. It wasn't the law that made Rector a fugitive (Uncle Fitch was still sheriff then), but the risk of Old Testament justice delivered by the dead man's relatives.

Rector's brother, Rufus, was in the parlor the night *War of the Worlds* came on the radio. A devout atheist, Rufus nonetheless insisted the whole clan pack up and go to Elk Creek Baptist to await the Armageddon. Then Dad saved the day by telling everybody Edgar Bergen and Charlie McCarthy were still broadcasting on his crystal set in the bedroom. Surely martians, if they were really invading, would preempt Charlie McCarthy.

And there was the time Granddaddy got his hand caught in the hay baler. He carried the severed finger into the kitchen, wrapped in his dirty kerchief. "Lizbeth," he bellowed. "Chopped off my goddamned finger." Whereupon Grandmother, inspecting the grisly evidence, calmly stated, "Why you sure did." Disinfecting the wound in turpentine, she got out the sewing box and stitched the index finger back on the knuckle. It healed up nearly good as new.

Stay in the little white house until the afternoon shadows grow long, looking at family picture albums, yellow and brittle with age. Open Granddaddy's old pocket watch, hands frozen forever at nine-thirty-five. Hold the velvet-lined box that contains your father's Distinguished Flying Cross. Put out seed for the cardinals on the feeder attached to the kitchen window. Wonder if the birds will stay through the long cold winter. Wonder if your grandmother will make it through another season. Wonder if you will.

Promise you'll come back tomorrow for lunch.

Decide to call Billy Trimble, who has been bugging your sister-in-law to remind you. Try to remember exactly who Billy Trimble was. Look him up in the Mount Eden directory. His soft hillbilly drawl reminds you he was the fat boy who sat near the back of your high school classes. A little slower than the rest, but very nice. Billy's been married seventeen years, no kids, teaches school in Spencer County and barbers on Saturdays to make ends meet. He's kept up with your elaborate wanderings: New Orleans, New York City, San Francisco, Louisville again, Los Angeles. Billy's never left Kentucky. Talk for an hour and a half, startled at the tenderness with which he remembers your friendship. Suppress the desire to weep that ambushes you. State simply, without emotion, that he always was the sweetest boy in school. He tells you about his arrowhead collection and thanks you for helping him with remedial reading back in the summer of '66 when it looked like he might be held back a year. He appreciates your calling. Marvel at the goodness of this thoroughly straight man who has loved you all this time without condition, without so much as your knowledge.

Have supper with your dad and the Wicked Stepmother in their new retirement house. Notice the tremor that has invaded his right hand. Endure her catty comments about your ear stud. (How did this slight woman generate such uncontrollable rage in you as a kid?) Be polite about the deep-fried pork and heavy cream sauce. Eat salad. Claim that you are full. Make small talk about what happened to high school buddies. Pretend interest in the success of her two kids. Detach yourself from controversial topics and wonder when you'll have the courage for a heart-to-heart talk with your father. Go back to the farmhouse. Feel years of bitterness wash away. Try to sleep.

The next day, drive with your father in his pickup truck to check the sick cow in the back pasture. After lunch in Taylorsville, ride out to the lake and watch the boats. He talks about the war, something he refused to do in younger years. Ask questions about the B-24 Liberator he piloted for thirty-five missions over occupied Europe, and laugh when he tells you about landing his plane on the crater-pocked remains of a Nazi air base he'd helped destroy the week before. (Dad's high school flame, Jennie Sue Duvall, told you once how sensitive a boy Dad had been before he went off to war, about how the fighting had changed him.)

Try not to let him catch you staring at his palsied right hand. Tests have been run. It's not a brain tumor. It might be the heart medicine. He tells you about his will: Jack will get the farm and a third of the considerable trust fund; the Wicked Stepmother's kids will split a third. The remainder goes to you. Congratulate him on the success of his investments. Catch your breath. Tell him you have some news. Explain you have contracted the AIDS virus. You are optimistic, but there is a possibility (you resist saying "probability") that you will die before he does. You are on medication. Your own will has been prepared. Breathe slowly. Contain the emotion that threatens to erupt somewhere between your stomach and your throat. Continue. A small life-insurance policy will take care of your debts and interment. Tell him you wish to be cremated and scattered over the Pacific. You do not want to be returned to Kentucky if you get too sick or senseless to manage your affairs. You have made arrangements.

Wait through the long silence for his deliberate reply. "That's very disturbing," he says. "I think I'll file that information away. And try to forget it." Assure him you'll let him know about any changes in your health. It is never brought up again on your visit, but he stays close, wants to talk more than ever before. Your mortality has been revealed. It shows him his own. Late into the evening you are still together, and when he drops you off that night, he says, "If you need anything, just let me know." Tell him you will.

Mission completed.

Go back to Linda Bailey's house in Louisville for a reunion with eight friends from college days. Be awkward at first, a little too ingratiating. Notice Liz's boy, Tom Walker, a teenager, bright, handsome, mature beyond his years. (Later, Linda will tell you he has been through drug rehab and ask if you think he's gay. You do.) Loosen up. Recall the good times. Think your heart will break when Linda puts on the Crosby, Stills, Nash, and Young album *Déjà Vu*.

Remember love did come. Realize now he's gone.

On your last day in Louisville, meet Linda's friend, Tony Mavis, an artist and AIDS activist. Also meet Tony's assistant, Juan Ramirez, the only Puerto Rican in Louisville, who gives you a tour of the loft and its gardens. This is possibly the most beautiful man you have ever seen. He flirts, wiggles his ass, and smiles at inappropriate moments.

He calls you at Linda's later to see if you'd like a drink. A foolish idea—it's nearly midnight, with a 6:30 a.m. flight back to LA. Go with him anyway to Murphy's, a gay piano bar with six sad queens singing "My Way." He mentions his dog needs a walk. You say you'd love to meet his dog. Drive twenty miles up River Road. Not much time. Listen to jazz and undress each other on the white Berber carpet. Outside, the collie is barking. (Timmy's home, Lassie.) Spend two hours caressing, kissing, biting, making love. Let him take the rubber off. "Skin to skin," he insists. Exchange passion. You have not felt this since Sean got sick.

Sleep on the flight back. Be glad you made the journey. Enter the house in Silver Lake. Let the answering machine remind you of tomorrow's doctor's appointment. Take a nap. Dream of Linda and dead Phillip, of Sean, of the Wicked Stepmother who is a pale adversary now. Dream of Billy with his arrowheads, of Tina and Luckett and Steve and Tom Walker and Jim and Michelle and Kevin and Tony and Harris and Deborah and Mike and Cindy and all their babies. Dream of Juan Ramirez in your arms. Dream of your farmer brother, his wife and the five girls. Dream of your grandmother bathed in a special light of grace. Dream of your dad, the war hero, and wonder what you may yet need from him.

bernard cooper

my father picking plums

It has been nearly a year since my father fell while picking plums. The bruises on his leg have healed, and except for a vague absence of pigmentation where the calf had blistered, his recovery is complete. Back in the habit of evening constitutionals, he navigates the neighborhood with his usual stride—"Brisk," he says, "for a man of eighty-five"—dressed in a powder-blue jogging suit that bears the telltale stains of jelly doughnuts and Lipton's tea, foods that my father, despite doctors' orders, hasn't the will to forsake. It's difficult now to imagine him in the weeks following the accident, hobbling around the house, stopping to wince and catch his breath, the kitchen counter cluttered with salves, bandages, rubbing alcohol, Percodan, and anticoagulents.

He broke his glasses and his hearing aid in the fall, and when I first stepped into the hospital room for a visit, I was struck by the way my father—head cocked to hear, squinting to see—looked so much older and more remote, a prisoner of his failing senses.

"Boychik?" he asked, straining his face in my general direction. He fell back into a stack of pillows, sighed a deep sigh, and without my asking, described what had happened:

"There they are, all over the lawn. Purple plums, dozens of them. They look delicious. So what am I supposed to do? Let the birds eat them? Not on your life. It's my tree, right? First I fill a bucket with the ones from the ground. Then I get the ladder out of the garage. I've climbed the thing a hundred times before. I make it to the top, reach out my hand and . . . who knows what happens. Suddenly I'm an astronaut. Up is down and vice versa. It happened so fast I didn't have time to piss in my pants. I'm flat on my back, not a breath left in me. Couldn't have called for help if I tried. And the pain in my leg—you don't want to know."

"Who found you?"

"What?"

I move closer, speak louder.

"Nobody found me," he says, exasperated. "Had to wait till I could get up on my own. It seemed like hours. I'm telling you, I thought it was all over. But eventually I could breathe normal again and—don't ask me how, God only knows—I got in the car and drove here myself."

"You should have called me."

"You were probably busy."

"It was an emergency, Dad. What if you hadn't been able to drive?"

"You don't have to shout. I made it here, didn't I?" My father shifted his weight and grimaced. The sheet slid off his injured leg, the calf swollen, purple as a plum, what the doctor called "an insult to the tissue."

Like most children, I once thought of my father as invincible. Throughout my boyhood he possessed a surplus of energy, or it possessed him. On weekdays he worked hard at the office, and on weekends he gardened in our yard. He was also a man given to showy and unpredictable episodes of anger. These rages were never precipitated by a crisis—in the face of illness or accident my father remained steady, methodical, even optimistic; when the chips were down he was an incorrigible joker, an inveterate back slapper, a sentry at the bedside—but something as simple as a drinking glass left out on the table could send him into a frenzy of invective. Spittle shot from his lips. Blood ruddied his face. He'd hurl the glass against the wall.

His temper rarely intimidated my mother. She'd light a Tareyton, stand aside, and watch my father flail and shout until he was purged of the last sharp word. Winded and limp, he'd flee into the living room where he drew the shades, sat in his wing chair, and brooded for hours. Mother got out the broom and the dust pan and—presto—the damage disappeared. Shards of glass slid into the trash can, chimed against the metal sides. And when Mother lifted her foot from the pedal and the lid fell shut with a resolute thud, I knew the ordeal was over.

Even as a boy, I understood how my father's profession had sullied his view of the world, had made him a wary man, prone to explosions. He spent hours taking depositions from jilted wives and cuckolded husbands. He conferred with a miserable clientele, spouses who wept, who spat accusations, who pounded his desk in want of revenge. This was at a time when California law required that grounds for divorce be proved in court, and toward this end my father carried in his briefcase not only the usual legal tablets and manila files, but bills for motel rooms, matchbooks from bars, boxer shorts blooming with lipstick stains. It was his job to exploit every detail of an infidelity, to unearth the most tawdry and incontrovertible evidence of betrayal. Year in and year out, my father met with a steady parade of strangers and itemized insults, blows, deceits.

After one particularly long and vindictive divorce trial, he agreed to a weekend out of town. Mother suggested Palm Springs, rhapsodized about the balmy air, the cacti lit by colored lights, the street named after Bob Hope. When it finally came time to leave, however, my mother kept thinking of things she forgot to pack. No sooner would my father begin to back the car out of the driveway than my mother would shout for him to stop, dash into the house, and retrieve what she needed. A carton of Tareytons. An aerosol can of Solarcaine. A paperback novel to read by the pool. I sat in the backseat, motionless and mute; with each of her excursions back inside the house, I felt my father's frustration mount. When my mother insisted she get a package of saltine crackers in case we got hungry along the way, my father glared at her, bolted from the car, wrenched every piece of luggage from the trunk and slammed it shut with such a vengeance the car rocked on its springs. Through the rear window, my mother and I could see him fling two suitcases, a carryall, and a makeup case yards above his balding head. The sky was a huge and cloudless blue; gray chunks of luggage sailed through it, twisting and spinning and falling to earth like the burnt-out stages of a booster rocket. When a piece of luggage crashed back to the asphalt, he'd pick it up and hurl it again.

Mother and I got out of the car and sat together on a low wall by the side of the driveway, waiting for his tantrum to pass. "Some vacation," she said, lighting a cigarette. Her cheeks imploded from the vigorous draw. In order to watch him, we had to shield our eyes against the sun, a light so stark it made me want to sneeze. Sometimes my father managed to launch two or three pieces of luggage into the air at the same time. With every effort, an involuntary, animal grunt issued from the depths of his chest. Once or twice, a suitcase flew up and eclipsed the sun, and I remember thinking how small and aloof the sun really was, not like the fat and friendly star my classmates drew in school.

Finally, the largest suitcase came unlatched in midflight. Even my father was astonished when articles of his wife's wardrobe began their descent from the summer sky. A yellow scarf dazzled the air like a tangible strand of sunlight. Fuzzy slippers tumbled down. One diaphanous white slip drifted over the driveway and, as if guided by an invisible hand, draped itself across a hedge. With that, my father barreled by us, veins protruding on his temple and neck, and stomped into the house. "I'm getting tired of this," my mother grumbled. Before she stooped to pick up the mess—a vast and random geography of clothes—she flicked her cigarette onto the asphalt and ground the ember out.

One evening, long after I'd moved away from home, I received a phone call from my father telling me that my mother had died the night before. "But I didn't know it happened," he said.

He'd awakened as usual that morning, ruminating over a case while he showered and shaved. My mother appeared to be sound asleep, one arm draped across her face, eyes sheltered beneath the crook of her elbow. When he sat on the bed to pull up his socks he'd tried not to jar the mattress and wake her. At least he *thought* he'd tried not to wake her, but he couldn't remember, he couldn't be sure. Things looked normal, he kept protesting—the pillow, the blanket, the way she lay there. He decided to grab a doughnut downtown and left in a hurry. But that night my father returned to a house suspiciously unlived-in. The silence caused him to clench his fists, and he called for his wife—"Lillian, Lillian"—drifting through quiet, unlit rooms, walking slowly up the stairs.

I once saw a photograph of a woman who had jumped off the Empire State Building and landed on the roof of a parked car. What is amazing is that she appears merely to have leapt onto satin sheets. Deep in a languid and absolute sleep, her eyes are closed, lips slightly parted, hair fanned out on a metal pillow. Nowhere is there a trace of blood, her body caught softly in its own impression.

As my father spoke into the telephone, his voice about to break—"I should have realized. I should have known"—that's the state in which I pictured my mother: a long fall of sixty years, an uncanny landing, a miraculous repose.

My father and I had one thing in common after my mother's heart attack: we each maintained a secret life. Secret, at least, to each other.

I'd fallen for a man named Travis Mask. Travis had recently arrived in Los Angeles from Kentucky, and everything I was accustomed to—the billboards lining the Sunset Strip, the 7-Elevens open all night—stirred in him a strong allegiance; "I love this town," he'd say every day. Travis's job was to collect change from food vending machines throughout the city. During dinner he would tell me about the office lobbies and college cafeterias he had visited, the trick to opening different machines, the noisy cascade of nickels and dimes. Travis Mask was enthusiastic. Travis Mask was easy to please. In bed I called him by his full name because I found the sound of it exciting.

My father, on the other hand, had fallen for a woman whose identity he meant to keep secret. I knew of her existence only because of a dramatic change in his behavior: he would grow mysterious as quickly and inexplicably as he had once grown angry. Ordinary conversations would take confusing turns. One night I phoned him at home and tried to make a date for dinner.

"Sounds good," he said. "How about next . . ." A voice in the background interrupted. "As I was saying," he continued, "I'll have the papers for you by Friday."

"Okay," I said, stupidly. "What papers?"

"It's no problem at all."

"Dad, what's going on?"

"We'll have to have them countersigned, of course."

"Let me guess. You have company."

"No," he said. "Thank *you*."

After he hung up, I began to wonder why my father couldn't simply admit that he had a girlfriend. I'd told him on several occasions that I hoped he could find companionship, that I knew he must be lonely without my mother. What did he have to gain by keeping his relationship a secret? Or was it *my* existence he was trying to hide from her? I'd gone back to watching the evening news with Travis when an awful thought occurred to me. Suppose a robber had forced his way into my father's house, pointed a gun at his head, and ordered him to continue talking as if nothing had happened. What if our officious conversation had really been a signal for help? I tried to remember every word, every inflection. Hadn't there been an unnatural tension in his voice, a strain I'd never heard before? I dismissed this thought as preposterous, only to have it boomerang back. Nearly an hour passed before I decided to call him again. Six rings. Seven. His voice was dreamy, expansive when he answered, his "hello" as round and buoyant as a bubble. I hung up without speaking, and when I told Travis I was upset because my father refused to be frank, he said, "Honey, you're a hypocrite."

Travis was right, of course. I resented being barred from this central fact of my father's life, but had no intention of telling him I was gay. It had taken me thirty years to achieve even a modicum of intimacy with the man, and I didn't want to risk a setback. It wasn't as if I was keeping my sexual orientation a secret; I'd told relatives, coworkers, friends. But my father was a man who whistled at waitresses, flirted with bank tellers, his head swiveling like a radar dish toward the nearest pair of breasts and hips. Ever since I was a child my father had reminded me of the wolf in cartoons whose ears shoot steam, whose eyes pop out on springs, whose tongue unfurls like a party favor whenever he sees a curvaceous dame. As far as my father was concerned, desire for women fueled the world, compelled every man without exception—his occupation testified to that—was a force as essential as gravity. I didn't want to disappoint him.

Eventually, Travis Mask was transferred to Long Beach. In his absence, my nights grew long and ponderous, and I tried to spend more time with my father in the belief that sooner or later an opportunity for disclosure would present itself. We met for dinner once a month in a restaurant whose interior was as dim and crimson as the chambers of the human heart, our interaction friendly but formal, both of us cautiously skirting the topic of our private lives; we'd become expert at the ambiguous answer, the changed subject, the half-truth. Should my father ask if I was dating, I'd tell him yes, I had been seeing someone. I'd liked them very much, I said, but they were transferred to another city. Them. They. My attempt to neuter the pronouns made it sound as if I were courting people en masse. Just when I thought this subterfuge was becoming obvious, my father began to respond in kind. "Too bad I didn't get a chance to meet them. Where did you say they went?"

Avoidance also worked in reverse: "And how about you, Dad? Are you seeing anybody?"

"Seeing? I don't know if you'd call it *seeing*. What did you order, chicken or fish?"

It may seem as if this phase of our relationship was in some way an unhappy accommodation, but I enjoyed visiting with my father during that period and even found it challenging to find things to talk about. During one dinner we discovered that we shared a fondness for nature programs on television, and from that night on, when we'd exhausted our comments about the meal or the weather, we'd ask if the other had seen the show about the blind albino fish who live in underwater caves, or the one about the North American moose whose antlers, coated with green moss, provide camouflage in the underbrush. My father and I had adapted like those creatures to the strictures of our shared world.

And then I met her.

I looked up from a rack of stationery at the local Thrifty one afternoon and there stood my father with a willowy black woman in her early forties. As she waited for a prescription to be filled, he drew a finger through her hair, nuzzled the nape of her neck, the refracted light of his lenses causing his cheeks to glow. I felt like a child who was witness to something he shouldn't see: his father's helpless, unguarded ardor for an unfamiliar woman. I didn't know whether to run or stay. Had he always been attracted to young black women? Had I ever known him well? Somehow I managed to move myself toward them and mumble hello. They turned around in unison. My father's eyes widened. He reached out and cupped my shoulder, struggled to say my name. Before he could think to introduce us, I shook the woman's hand, startled by its softness. "So you're the son. Where've you been hiding?" She was kind and cordial, though too preoccupied to engage in much conversation, her handsome features furrowed by a hint of melancholy, a sadness that I sensed had little to do with my surprise appearance.

Hours after our encounter, I could still feel the softness of Anna's hand, the softness that stirred my father's yearning. He was seventy-five years old, myopic and hard of hearing, his skin loose and liver-spotted, but one glimpse of his impulsive public affection led me to the conclusion that my father possessed, despite his age, a restless sexual energy. The meeting left me elated, expectant. My father and I had something new in common: the pursuit of our unorthodox passions. We were, perhaps, more alike than I'd realized. After years of relative estrangement, I'd been given grounds for a fresh start, a chance to establish a stronger connection. The final hurdle, however, involved telling my father I was gay, and now there was Anna's reaction to consider.

But none of my expectations mattered. Later that week, they left the country.

•   •   •

The prescription, it turned out, was for a psychotropic drug. Anna had battled bouts of depression since childhood. Her propensity for unhappiness gave my father a vital mission: to make her laugh, to wrest her from despair. Anna worked as an elementary-school substitute teacher and managed a few rental properties in South Central Los Angeles, but after weeks of functioning normally she would take to my father's bed for days on end, blank and immobile beneath the quilt she had bought to brighten up the room, unaffected by his jokes, his kisses and cajoling. These spells of depression came without warning and ended just as unexpectedly. Though they both did their best to enjoy each other during the periods of relative calm, they lived, my father lamented later, like people in a thunderstorm, never knowing when lightning would strike. Thinking that a drastic change might help Esther shed a recent depression, they pooled their money and flew to Europe.

They returned with snapshots showing the two of them against innumerable backdrops. The Tower of London, the Vatican, Versailles. Monuments, obelisks, statuary. In every pose their faces were unchanged, the faces of people who want to be happy, who try to be happy, and somehow can't.

As if in defiance of all the photographic evidence against them, they were married the following month at the Church of the Holy Trinity ("The Holy who?" wailed my cousin Ruth. "Vey iss meer. No wonder he hasn't told a soul"). I was one of only two guests at the wedding. The other was an uncle of Anna's. Before the ceremony began, he shot me a glance that attested, I was certain, to an incredulity as great as mine. The vaulted chapel rang with prerecorded organ music, an eerie and pious overture. Light filtered through stained-glass windows, chunks of sweet color that reminded me of Jello. My old Jewish father and his Episcopalian lover appeared at opposite ends of the dais, walking step by measured step toward a union in the center. The priest swam in white vestments, somber and almost inaudible. Cryptic gestures, odd props; I watched with a powerful, wordless amazement. Afterward, as if the actual wedding hadn't been surreal enough, my father and Anna formed a kind of receiving line (if two people can constitute a line) in the church parking lot, where the four of us, bathed by hazy sunlight, exchanged pleasantries before the newlyweds returned home for a nap; their honeymoon in Europe, my father joked, had put the cart before the horse.

After the wedding, when I called my father, he answered as though the ringing of the phone had been an affront. When I asked him what was the matter he'd bark, "What makes you think there's something the matter?" I began to suspect that my father's frustration had given rise to those ancient rages. I could only imagine the tantrums Anna must have endured. But my father had grown too old and frail to sustain his anger for long. When we saw each other—Anna was always visiting relatives or too busy or tired to join us—he looked worn, embattled, and the pride I had in him for attempting an interracial marriage, for risking condemnation in the eyes of the world, was overwhelmed now by concern. He lost weight. His hands began to shake. I would sit across from him in the dim red restaurant and marvel that this bewildered man had once hurled glasses against a wall and launched Samsonite into the sky.

Between courses, I'd try to distract my father from his problems by pressing him to unearth tidbits of his past, as many as memory would allow. He'd often talk about Atlantic City where his parents had owned a small grocery. He'd worn short pants in those faraway days, played in his yard with a hoop and a stick, eaten saltwater taffy while he walked along the boardwalk. It was the unpleasant sensation of those short pants, in fact, that spurred my father to his first word; he'd cried they were "sour" over and over, though what he really meant to say was that the wool itched against his skin.

Sometimes my mother turned up in the midst of his sketchy regressions. Dad would smooth wrinkles from the tablecloth and tell me no one could take her place. He eulogized her loyalty and patience, and I wondered whether he could see her clearly—her auburn hair and freckled hands—wondered whether he wished she were here to sweep up after his current mess. "Remember," he once asked me, without a hint of irony or regret, "what fun we had in Palm Springs?" Then he snapped back into the present and asked what was taking so long with our steaks.

During those dinners, when remembering turned strenuous,

when my father struggled to find the right words, staring over mounds of salad and bowls of soup toward some vague and distant place, what I saw in his doleful eyes was a child crying *"sour, sour"* who knows he can't convey what he means with something as fallible as language.

The final rift between my father and Anna must have happened suddenly; she left behind several of her possessions, including the picture of Jesus that sat on the sideboard in the dining room next to my father's brass menorah. And along with Anna's possessions were stacks of leather-bound books, *Law of Torts*, *California Jurisprudence*, and *Forms of Pleading* embossed along their spines. Too weak and distracted to practice law, my father had retired, the house a repository for the contents of his former office. I worried about him being alone, wandering through rooms freighted with history, crowded with the evidence of two marriages, fatherhood, and a long and harrowing career; he had nothing to do but pace and sigh and stir up dust. I encouraged him to find a therapist, but as far as my father was concerned, psychiatrists were all conniving witch doctors who fed off the misery of people like Anna.

Brian, the psychotherapist I'd been living with for three years (and live with still), was not at all fazed by my father's aversion to his profession. They'd met only rarely—once we ran into my father at a local supermarket, and twice Brian accompanied us to the restaurant—but when they were together, Brian would draw my father out, compliment him on his plaid pants, ask questions regarding the fine points of law. And when my father spoke Brian listened intently, embraced him with his cool blue gaze. If the subject of Brian's occupation arose, my father seemed secretly delighted to learn that there were so many people in the world burdened with grim and persistent problems, people worse off than either he or Anna. My father relished my lover's attention; Brian's cheerful and steady disposition must have been refreshing in those troubled, lonely days. "How's that interesting friend of yours?" he sometimes asked. If he was suspicious that Brian and I shared the same house, he never pursued it. Over the years my father and I had come to the tacit understanding that I would never marry, and instead of expressing alarm or asking why, I'm afraid he simply assumed that the problematic examples of his own marriages had made me a skeptic when it came to romance, and therefore a confirmed bachelor. And if my father did understand, consciously or subconsciously, that Brian and I were in love, I liked to believe he was happy I ended up with someone sane and solvent—a witch doctor, yes, but a doctor nevertheless. My father, in short, never seemed compelled to inquire about the particulars of my life—it was enough to know I was healthy and happy—until he took his fall from the plum tree.

I drove my father home from the hospital, tried to keep his big unwieldy car, bobbing like a boat, within the lane. I bought my father a pair of seersucker shorts because long pants were too painful and constricting. "Do they fit?" I asked when he modeled them for me. "Not too tight? Not too sour?" I brought over groceries and my wok and while I cooked dinner, he sat at the dinette table, leg propped on a vinyl chair, and listened to the hissing oil, happy, abstracted. I helped him up the stairs, where we watched *Wheel of Fortune* and *Jeopardy* on the television in his bedroom, and where, for the first time since I was a boy, I sat at his feet and he rubbed my head. It felt so good I'd graze his good leg, contented as a cat. He welcomed my visits with an eagerness bordering on glee and didn't seem to mind being dependent on me for physical assistance; he leaned his bulk on my shoulder wholly, and I felt protective, necessary, inhaling the scents of salve and Old Spice, and the base, familiar odor that was all my father's own.

"You know those hostages?" asked my father. He was sitting at the dinette, dressed in the seersucker shorts, his leg propped on a chair. The bruises had faded to lavender, his calf back to its normal size.

I could barely hear him over the broccoli sizzling in the wok. "What about them?" I shouted.

"I heard on the news that some of them are seeing a psychiatrist now that they're back."

"So?"

"Why a psychiatrist?"

I stopped tossing the broccoli. "Dad," I said, "if you'd been held hostage in the Middle East for nine months, you might want to see a therapist, too."

The sky dimmed in the kitchen windows. My father's face was a silhouette, his lenses catching the last of the light. "They got their food taken care of, right? And a place to sleep. What's the big deal?"

"You're at gunpoint, for God's sake. A prisoner. I don't think it's like spending a weekend at the Hilton."

"Living alone," he said matter-of-factly, "is like being a prisoner."

I let it stand. I added the pea pods.

"Let me ask you something," said my father. "I get this feeling—I'm not sure how to say it—that something isn't right. That you're keeping something from me. We don't talk much, I grant you that. But maybe now's the time."

My heart was pounding. I'd been thoroughly disarmed by his interpretation of world events, his mine field of non sequiturs, and I wasn't prepared for a serious discussion. I switched off the gas. The red jet sputtered. When I turned around, my father was staring at his outstretched leg. "So?" he said.

"You mean Brian?"

"Whatever you want to tell me, tell me."

"You like him, don't you?"

"What's not to like."

"He's been my lover for a long time. He makes me happy. We have a home." Each declaration was a stone in my throat. "I hope you understand. I hope this doesn't come between us."

"Look," said my father without skipping a beat, "you're lucky to have someone. And he's lucky to have you, too. It's no one's business anyway. What the hell else am I going to say?"

But my father thought of something else before I could speak and express my relief. "You know," he said, "when I was a boy, maybe sixteen, my father asked me to hold a ladder while he trimmed the tree in our backyard. So I did, see, when I suddenly remember I have a date with this bee-yoo-tiful girl, and I'm late, and I run out of the yard. I don't know what got into me. I'm halfway down the street when I remember my father, and I think, 'Oh, boy. I'm in trouble now.' But when I get back I can hear him laughing way up in the tree. I'd never heard him laugh like that. 'You must like her a lot,' he says when I help him down. Funny thing was, I hadn't told him where I was going."

I felt a pang of regret for not having told my father about me and Brian sooner—what plain foolishness, what reserves of shame and fear had stopped me?—but I tried to postpone regret and listen. I pictured my father's father teetering above the earth, a man hugging the trunk of a tree and watching his son run down the street in pursuit of sweet, ineffable pleasure. While my father reminisced, night obscured the branches of the plum tree, the driveway where my mother's clothes once floated down like enormous leaves. When my father finished telling the story, he looked at me, then looked away. A moment of silence lodged between us, an old and obstinate silence. I wondered whether nothing or everything would change. I spooned our food onto separate plates. My father carefully pressed his leg to test the healing flesh.

martin palmer

my father

Although he died in 1944, I think about my father often and see him in scenes as vividly as if I were looking at slide projections in color, one vignette succeeding another, and with sound. I see his flexible thumbs, which I have inherited, as they rested against the steering wheel of his car when we drove in the country to see relatives or his patients, or holding my hand when I accompanied him to the curb market, or walked by him on the way to the M & N Café for toast and coffee. The filament of memory can become a stream, a river, sometimes a torrent when I evoke him, joining his own memories as he described them, this man, my father, born one hundred and twenty-five years ago, who in his sixty-first year fashioned me, his youngest child. When I was small, sometimes it was hardly possible to separate my memories from his own, giving me early a perspective of time and history that could form only with a parent his age. This sense stretches forward as well as back, a consciousness of endings as well as beginnings, a continuing flow in which I can discern now at this age my own ending yet see new beginnings in the skein of ever younger relatives who surround me when I visit them. It was through my father that I became aware of this biosphere and learned to examine it with intense curiosity.

I have pictures of my father when he was an infant, when he

was eighteen, when he was in his twenties and thirties, and on to the last year of his life. In my private office I have a portrait of him, and visitors who never knew him and barely know me remark on how much we resemble each other. I've chosen to wear a moustache, as he did, and as I move into my own old age I will look more like him as the years pass. And the same look around the eyes was visible in his mother, in his brother, in all four of my older half-brothers. I see him in my sister's face. In the daguerreotype I have of my great-grandfather, born in 1787, in the pictures of his sons, a resemblance takes me far back in time and makes me curious about their lives. I know, but without certainty, that some must have felt as I do. It would be against nature, a genetic impossibility, if all in this syncitium were wholly separate.

When I was twelve or thirteen years old my father looked up from a book he was evidently enjoying.

"This writer is just like you," he said to me, his eyes crinkling with amusement.

His book was *Lanterns on the Levee* by William Alexander Percy. At the time I was puzzled by this, but years later when I read it and when a relative of the author became a friend, I found out that Mr. Percy was gay—notably so, according to reports (though this was certainly not revealed in his book). My father knew. As a physician and as a person deeply interested in every kind of human being, he was not naive. I don't remember a single time that he condemned or rejected his sissy child. He didn't permit my hair to be cut until I was five years old. He was proud of its spun gold and let it reach a length that is usual for little boys today but which was uncommon then. I loved to climb on his lap and lie with my back against him in his rocking chair on the porch as he stroked my head and answered my endless questions about everything. Those summer nights we sat in the warm dark rocking gently, the katydids loud in the oaks and sycamores after the evening thunderstorms. My father was a demonstrative parent, affectionate and physically close to all of us, but especially to me. I felt loved and secure.

My father was the most important presence in the first seventeen years of my life and resonates in it still as I age. Having an elderly parent sharpened my perception of time. My father was a vigorous man, attending to all the details of his life from his medical practice to his children, his friends, his relatives, down to shopping, which he did himself, and the details of running a large household, which he supervised. He was one of the most hospitable men I have known. He expressed it by setting the best table, having the best food, and keeping the best cook, who was grumpily with us for many years. My mother's mother was his only rival in this. My grandmother's cook, Henry Thomas, was superb and Papa had to acknowledge this. When he courted my mother in 1911 he sent trays to her with his cook's best meals and his best linen, silver, and crystal. My grandmother's house was on the next block, so this was a convenient distance for the servant he sent with this display. I have never heard of this practice since then, but in his younger days it was a custom he had encountered. Born the year after the Civil War ended, he had passed his early years in a family impoverished by that conflict. This could have been why providing food was of such importance to him. This could have also been the origin of his need to provide well in every way he could. His father, a Civil War veteran and federal prisoner of war, returned embittered, useless, and mean. His brother Will's earliest memory of their father when he and his mother greeted him at the train returning from the war was of being immediately spanked for who knows what behavior in a three-year-old child.

My father was a resourceful kid. A baseball fanatic, he proved himself by catching bare-handed the fastest, hardest balls thrown by the older boys because mitts cost more than any money he could get. Once when he was asked to bring fifty cents for a project at Jefferson Academy where he was a schoolboy, his father humiliated him by his sneering command to ask his teacher for it if it was that important, sending him empty-handed to his class. He told me that when he was a child bananas cost five cents apiece, a high price in those days, and this was in Florida. He had a sunny attic filled with birds he caught and tamed to come at his call. He remembered the passenger pigeons, which were disappearing, and saw some of the last flocks of Carolina parakeets raiding his mother's fruit trees. The road from Monticello to Tallahassee thirty miles away led through swamps full of alligators and were loud with the roars of the bulls seeking mates in spring. He told me a panther could imitate a baby's cry exactly. Wild turkeys were plentiful. He clerked in Mr. Puleston's dry goods store where as a small boy he had put on his first pair of store-bought shoes, high-topped lace-ups with nickel-plated toes. Among the items he sold then were ladies' bustles. This fascinated me because I loved to look at the drawings of clothes of the period, and I made him describe these things in detail. A good student, he earned his way to college and then medical school at the University of Maryland with help from his Uncle Tommy. I have a photograph of him at eighteen, wide-eyed, handsome with his first moustache, and so young-looking. Later he sits at a dissecting table in medical school with two classmates, all in caps and rubber aprons, grinning at the remains of their cadaver. Chalked on the table in florid 1890s script is *"At Peace at Last."* From there he went to Hampton Roads, Virginia, where he was surgeon on a hospital ship in the US navy. Loving good clothes, good-looking, he was always a bit of a dandy to the end of his days. He attracted women all his life, and when he aged his old-fashioned gallantries charmed my sisters' young friends as much as they had his contemporaries. My aunts knew of an incident where he lost his wedding ring in a certain lady's bedclothes when he was a sought-after widower.

His photograph from 1892 shows him in a well-cut dark suit with wing collar and silk cravat, hazel eyes sparkling. He started his practice that year, and all the mothers with eligible daughters had their eyes on him. He chose a beautiful young woman from an old family, Maud Hamilton Myers, and held her hand, he told me, when he made a house call for some trifling indisposition which gave him that chance. She did not demur, and they were married in St. John's Episcopal Church, where he was a member the rest of his life. They had four sons before her death at the age of thirty in 1903 following the birth of their last child. In 1911 he married my mother, Sarah Lucile Saxon, a tiny, gentle woman and a fine musician twenty years his junior. They had four children, two girls and two boys, of which I was the youngest.

They were two guiding influences in my father's early life. The chief one was his mother, Mary Rebecca Gassaway Palmer. He adored her and she depended on him. A strong woman, she had

managed a plantation by herself during the increasingly hard years
of the Civil War while her husband was away fighting and then a
prisoner of war for two long years, holding her family together in
the bitter aftermath. She died in 1885 when my father was nineteen.
My grandmother named my father after an admired cousin, Henry
Edwards, who was blind. A landowner and cotton planter, it was
said that he could judge the exact state of his crops by walking
along the rows and feeling the plants with his sensitive fingers. As
convivial as my father was, he never drank and never learned to
dance out of deep respect for his mother, the devout daughter of a
Methodist minister. He had a cherished younger brother, John Reyn-
olds Palmer, whom he watched die in agony of what was then called
intestinal colic, but what was soon after treatable surgically as acute
appendicitis. My father often spoke of this episode and its part in
his becoming a surgeon. In the 1890s he performed the first appen-
dectomy done in Leon County, by lamplight and on a kitchen table.
It was successful; the patient, a woman, died fifty years later in a
car accident.

The other great influence in his life was his father's older
brother, Uncle Tommy, Thomas Martin Palmer. Uncle Tommy was
graduated from the University of Maryland medical school in the
1840s. He returned to Monticello where he practiced and inherited
the plantations and cotton manufactory of his father, Martin Palmer.
When the Civil War started he was made surgeon of the 2nd Florida
Regiment and sent to Richmond where he headed the Florida Hospital, and later Howard's Grove Hospital there. His dispatches to
Governor Milton during those years show him to be a sensible man,
excellent in his field and esteemed by everyone from the men in his
care to General Lee himself. In the last part of that war he was on
field duty at the scenes of battles with the army of Northern Virginia, where he could amputate mangled limbs swiftly when he had
to, and he had to very often under terrible conditions. Returning
to a destroyed world, he rebuilt his life as a physician ministering
to his district, where he was called "the Family Regulator." Everyone
took their problems to him: physical, personal, and political. In
1877 he was president of the Florida Medical Association. When he
was seventy-four, widowed, ill, and in pain, he shot himself with

his old army pistol in the house his father built in 1829 when they first came to Florida. He lies in the family cemetery hardly a quarter of a mile from the big house at the end of a sandy road beneath great oaks. My father had an obelisk of white marble placed over his grave.

These people, my great-grandfather, my grandfather and grandmother, my great-uncle and all their kin, were slaveowners. Their way of life was founded on agriculture and the slaves it required at that time. I have wills in which human beings are bequeathed the same way livestock or books or furniture or money was bequeathed. And they specified whether these possessions were "mulatto" or "Negro," giving one at least an inkling of the sexual exploitation that was a common part of life then. And I know from records that they bought and sold slaves. As their descendant, having heard of them often and even having known a couple of them in their extreme old age, and always in the flotsam and jetsam of their wake—letters, houses, wills, pictures, graves, values, opinions—I've had to face this aspect of their lives and to reach my own conclusions about it. I am too near them not to take this responsibility seriously and to ask why they could live with chattel slavery and still consider themselves upright, Christian, and moral, which most tried to be. I will never have a satisfactory answer to the question of why the United States of America chose to legalize slavery from their beginning until 1865, the year before my father was born; why alternatives were not taken; why we must live for centuries to come with the aftermath of this choice. I have lived with the effects of this all of my life, as any southerner my age must. In this narrative there will be attitudes that seem racist. I would be dishonest if I changed or omitted them. But from an early age, being conscious that I was different also made me aware that I was linked to others who were in any way different and who were labeled for it. Sooner or later I must acknowledge that all were my sisters and brothers, friends, nurturers, and lovers. And that I am responsible for myself, not for my forebears.

One of my earliest memories is of sitting in my high chair at the dining room table by my father's side, him cutting my steak in tiny pieces for me when I complained that the pieces I had were too big to chew. I must have been about four years old. Meals in our large dining room at the massive golden oak table were always a family affair, usually with guests my father brought up from his office on the ground floor of our house or friends and relatives he encountered on the street, in the market, at a meeting, or wherever, and brought along. Since he ordered all the food himself, he knew what we had. He always accommodated more if he wanted to. Around the room were glass cabinets filled with cut crystal and sideboards both large and delicate containing linen and silver. Each of us had our silver napkin ring, and he and I drank our water from chased silver goblets, mine with a small half-moon indentation in its bottom. I have these goblets with me still. He loved ice cream more than any other kind of dessert, his favorite being butter pecan. But he would try anything at least once and encouraged his children and guests to do the same. His patients brought him every kind of fruit, fowl, vegetable, and animal. Once we walked into dinner to find a roast possum in a thick layer of fat lying on a platter surrounded by sweet potatoes, looking like nothing so much as an oversized rat. Everyone but Papa, me, and old Mr. Hartsfield filed right out again. Mr. Hartsfield pronounced it one of the fattest, finest possums he'd ever seen. I managed.

On one side of the dining room was a tiled fireplace where fires in winter warmed bottoms while fronts shivered. The old house had a fireplace in every room that was supplied with fat wood to start the fires in season. During my first seven years my trundle bed stood at the foot of my father's great four-poster, and Mittie or Mary undressed me, slipped my nightshirt over my head, and tucked me in warmly while I waited drowsily for Papa to come hear me say my prayers.

"Po' little creeter," Mary often said softly. "Po' creeter. Your po' Mama so sick and all us tending to her when the Doctor looked at you and say, 'Who aint fed my child? Look! He's turnin blue.' And all us, sure enough, saw. . . ." She would hug me closely, but this hardly smoothed the cold dread that filled me with this account. My mother died when I was two weeks old. Because of this, her mother, my grandmother, kept an obsessive eye on all four children, my older brother and two older sisters. Papa always indulged her.

Every afternoon until I was five years old she swept into the house—
I remember her fur piece with its tiny sharp black eyes and its
braided clasp jaw clamped on its tail—to see that I had my bottle,
which I took lying on the sofa in the living room beneath the heavy
gilt mirror. My aunts blamed my buck teeth on this practice when
I started with the orthodontist at age seven.

Bryan, my oldest half-brother, thirty-one when I was born, had
eyes as cold as stones in an icy brook behind his steel-rimmed
glasses. Bald, he had been a handsome West Point cadet during
World War I and later managed his and his older wife's property.
Resentful of the spoiling his sissy youngest brother received, which
he had never had, he enjoyed flinging me in Orchard Pond with the
command, "Swim, then!" at my terror, or hiding behind a coatrack
in the cavernous dark hall and growling at me, abjectly frightened,
at night when I had to descend the stairs. After this horseplay our
relationship advanced to more subtle means of mental sadism in the
unspoken threat to take my sister and me over and "straighten us
out" when he had the chance. I loved my oldest sister deeply. Next
to my father she was probably the main influence on my young life,
and remained so. I loved my other sister, too, but we argued and
jockeyed for position as young ones will. She was five years older
than I. I saw little of my own brother, who was off at the university
and then medical school before entering the service in World War
II. Tom, another half-brother, was a man admired and loved. He
had children my age who were my playmates. I saw little of my
other half-brothers and there was no bonding to speak of.

In those days there were still in medical practices some patients
who, having become firmly addicted to opiates in the days when
laudanum was used to quiet teething babies many years before, were
authorized to receive their dole of morphine from a physician. Old
Mrs. Warner and a family of dilapidated gypsies named Adams were
among these. They showed up usually once or twice a month, creeping up on the front porch and sending for Papa. The servants treated
them with disdain, and my father was harsh to them, berating them
for their weakness, giving them their dole only after a castigating
lecture that they accepted with glittering-eyed humility, waiting for
relief. He could be that way. Since then I have always been fright-

ened of gypsies. Mary, my nurse, told me that they stole children like me "and Lord only knows what becomes of them." They would avenge themselves. Once, outside his consulting-room window, I heard him telling a male patient scornfully, "You were greedy, boy, just too greedy! Now you've got both, clap and the syph. I'm going to have to run this up you. . . ." I could see the long curved urethral sound in its cabinet and I shuddered in sympathy. Before antibiotics, gonorrhea caused urethral ulcerations leaving scar tissue that was broken through with such instruments—and without local anesthetics. Most often the sufferer was a young black man.

In our house we had a large library accumulated over the years that included books on every possible subject that could appeal to the bookworm I was. Dickens, Grimm, Dante (with the magnificent nude illustrations by Gustave Doré), Shakespeare, the Civil War in photographs, travel, all kinds of novels, histories, tales. In my father's medical library were Kraft-Ebine *Psychopathia Sexualis* with its grim case histories from nineteenth-century Vienna, Havelock Ellis, other medical and surgical volumes, all of which I had looked through by the time I was eleven. I knew what homosexuality was, but my understanding of it was strange. Having a literal mind, I puzzled over the weak-or-absent-father/smothering-mother models I found in these books. But I felt that it was better to be reticent in these matters. I never asked my father about them. When I was about five years old I was with my father one day in Wilson's Department Store where he was waited on by a Mr. Maxwell. While he was busy, I told Papa, finger in my mouth, that I thought Mr. Maxwell was "very handsome." My father burst out laughing and to my intense embarrassment told this to Mr. Maxwell. The sensibility of this episode, vivid in my memory, was distinctly sexual.

Susan Matilda Archer, "Mama Sudie," was an ancient cousin of Maude Myers, my father's first wife. After Maude's death, Mama Sudie remained with us because she had no other place to go as a gentlewoman without means. Her father had been a distinguished lawyer who died just before the Civil War, and her mother was the daughter of an early governor of Florida. When I was born Mama Sudie was in her late seventies, and I remember her fussing over me with my nurse, Mary. Mama Sudie often stayed at the dinner table eating tomatoes, which she loved. She told me that when she was young tomatoes had been thought poisonous. Years later I discovered that tomatoes were thought to encourage "unseemly passions" in the Victorians, and for that reason were avoided. They were called "love apples." When Susan Matilda Archer was a young girl, her mother's friend was Princess Achille Murat, an American lady, the widow of Prince Murat who had fled to Tallahassee to escape one of the European upheavals of the time. When I was about five years old the current Prince and Princess Murat visited Tallahassee, and Mama Sudie, as one of the last survivors of those days, was invited to a reception at the governor's mansion in their honor along with my father. She insisted that I go with her, and Papa obliged. I remember my white linen suit with short pants and a Buster Brown collar. Mama Sudie, a small, cadaverously thin old lady, put on her best black dress with her high jet beaded collar. She was placed in an armchair and the prince and princess were brought to her in one of the big rooms full of mirrors at the mansion, and then I was presented. I remember the princess in a dark flowing flowered chiffon dress. She had pretty blond hair and a kind manner. My nurse urged me to remember the occasion, which I apparently did—it flashes before me the way childhood memories do. Not long after this, at the end of a hot summer with the little green electric fan droning and rattling in the room, attended by my father along with Mittie and Mary and bottles of medicine, Mama Sudie died. She was eighty-four. The house was hushed as relatives waited, and I recall the different atmosphere with my father in charge. That afternoon when everyone was busy and before Mr. Culley, the undertaker, came, I crept into Mama Sudie's room where she lay under the sheet and slipped beneath it to hold her tiny hand, stiff as a dead bird's claw, and tried to comprehend this change from life to death. I was six. Early the next morning I slipped into the parlor, reeking with flowers, where Mama Sudie lay in her satin-lined casket. I remember that her mouth had fallen open to reveal a cotton ball resting on a dry tongue, and a file of tiny red ants were moving from her lace collar to the corner of her open mouth. I was fascinated and puzzled. After the funeral and the cemetery, that evening with my father on the front steps looking up into the darkness of the oaks and listening to the summer insects, I tried to tell him that in some way I could never explain and indeed had no words for, time itself had changed, had been fractured in some way, making me feel as if I were in another dimension, unreal. My father gathered me in his arms, saying, "You were a big help to me, son," and we went in to the large supper all the guests and relatives attended. I hadn't the words to explain to him what I had learned then about age, and death.

When I was seven years old my father married a rich lady a little older than he was, from Boston. In my memory she looks rather like Queen Victoria: small nose, gray hair, dignified, flowing clothes, a diamond watch deeply embedded in her wrist, and given to attacks of asthma for which she smoked Sweet Caporal cigarettes. Years later my older half-brother told me that she loved sex and importuned my father steadily. She did not take easily to precocious small boys and adolescent girls. She had a Boston bull terrier named Zab who snorted and farted and didn't like kids. Papa swore me to secrecy about this marriage, but as soon as I went to my grandmother's for Sunday dinner I couldn't resist telling an eager audience of aunts. This resulted in the first of two spankings my father ever gave me, the second being for pulling the tail feathers out of his flock of Muscovy ducks. This lady had a large "cottage" in York Harbor, Maine, where we went for the summer. At that time my passion was cliffs; I had read about them but there were none in Florida. Maine had almost nothing else. My father stayed in Florida because of his practice, but joined us for the last month. He liked Maine and enjoyed the people he met there. Across the point of land from Colonial Cottage lived a New York family named Stone with a girl and boy several years older, my sister's age. One day while I was riding in their chauffeured limosine—the kind that had a separate open front for the driver—Frances Stone slapped me sharply across the face and then brayed with donkey laughter. I was stunned by such behavior. I can't remember at all why she did this; I remember, vividly, just the incident.

Mrs. Ruge (she was always this in my mind; I called her Mother Palmer, but it never sounded right) could be stern. Our house had a large front hall from which the wide stairs ascended to the second floor. She knew I was terrified of the dark, filled with ghosts, monsters, crouching things, but thought this nonsense. So she had the hall and upstairs lights turned off, closed the living room and parlor doors, and sent me upstairs to fetch her sewing scissors. She was adamant; I must go, and I must turn on the lights when I got there. I went. Crying with every step, I made my way upstairs fully expecting to meet my doom either on the landing or at the top. But I survived. And I turned on all the lights. And returned with the scissors. And I don't recall ever being afraid of the dark afterward. I don't recommend this, but it worked. Another incident I recall is a birthday party that never took place. It was to be a surprise party, but somehow I got wind of it. In my excitement and pleasure, I tracked down a cache of party favors and triumphantly brought some to her. I was a rogue, she said, and canceled the party to teach me a New England lesson in propriety. I am sure I needed it, but I was not a Yankee, not by a long shot, and hated the word. After three years she and my father parted with, I think, relief all around and were divorced. I didn't like Maine even if it had cliffs. In York Harbor I had to get my hair cut in the beauty shop (where the movies were shown also); it was cold, too. It wasn't the Gulf of Mexico where I was with friends and relatives.

During Mrs. Ruge's time I was sent to expensive summer camps, trips I resisted as much as possible. Once there, I hated sports and chiefly wanted to hang out with the counselors, young men in their twenties at most, but who seemed to me very glamorous and physically attractive. The last summer of this I got sick and just wouldn't function. Finally my father came to get me and take me home. I think this was the purpose of my illness. We had a great train ride through Virginia and South Carolina, seeing all the historical places, and I was in buoyant health and spirits as soon as I was out of the camp compound.

When I was eleven my father started courting another lady, this time a winter visitor from Rochester, New York. I was having my own struggle, having discovered masturbation and sex in the form of two boys, one my age and one older; one white, one black. I was growing, my schooling was coming to an end at Caroline Brevard, the grammar school. I was deeply anxious. Finally my father married Mrs. Burgess in Rochester, and I was not present. When she moved into the house, I remember being very anxious to please her. I called her Leah. She was a cold woman who did not tolerate competition. Shortly after she became my stepmother she had Mary Larkin dismissed. Mary was my nanny and had been with us ever since I was born. I was desolated. Every night for months when she came to hear me pray (my father thought this would bring us closer) I wept without being able to say why I did. If I had been in her place, I would have become exasperated after a very little bit of this, but it is to her credit that if she was it never showed. By now my father was aging, but Leah fit in better than Mrs. Ruge had, and we took long Sunday afternoon drives to see just about everything and everyone in north central Florida. By 1941 my father was serving on the draft board, which meant that he and my stepmother had to go to a number of Florida towns. We spent summers on the Gulf, which I loved. I had entered junior high school and did well because I was eager to be liked. I had no liaisons there and I remember struggling with my sexuality because the only models I could discover in books called it a sickness and a perversion. I was a sissy kid, and I think the only reason I was not physically hurt was that other kids were afraid to harm me. I also had my good friends, and more and more I looked, with a bookworm's intensity, to older people as companions and models. Leah didn't like sharing my gregarious father with his friends, and our dinners had fewer guests and laughter. Leah was very conscious of her position as my father's wife. She looked on my remaining sister and me (my older sister by now had married) as spoiled and indulged, and she set out to correct this. She did this in two main ways: first, we were not to "bother" our father about "trifles," and second, she went to my oldest half-brother, Bryan, to help "straighten us out." Even more contemptuous of my sissiness, and jealous of our father's indulgence, he had no love at all for me although Bryan liked my sister well enough, a mere woman posing no threat. He could be menacing, and he took on the task with a mean relish behind Papa's back. War came. My father was busier than he had been, he said, since World War I because so many of the local doctors were off in the service.

At this time Tallahassee had an air base to train fliers and a large infantry training camp on the Gulf about fifty miles away. The town was bursting with this influx. Because of this growth the mayor and the city council began to have some grandiose ideas about the capital city. A couple of the main streets, one of them Adams Street where we lived, were lined by large old oak trees that had been there undisturbed for at least seventy-five years. In their wisdom, the mayor and councillors decided that these must come down. Only hick towns had large trees growing on main streets obstructing progress, not to mention views of the fair city. My father was outraged and vowed that the trees would stay. The council vowed that they would go. All of his life my father rose at five a.m., bathed and dressed, and was ready for the day by six. Every morning before his breakfast he patrolled Adams and Monroe streets after he found a tree-cutting crew ready to start and peremptorily ordered them off. His schedule never varied and because of this and because he was not a man to be crossed, he won the first round in the battle for the trees. But one morning the mayor had the work crew out before four and managed to cut down several trees before my furious father arrived on the scene with an injunction. With this, and because of his steady, tough opposition, most of the trees were saved, finally. Most of his friends stood behind him, and when the tree cutters approached the fine old oak pushing up a part of the sidewalk in front of St. John's Episcopal Church far down Monroe Street, the folly of the city fathers became clear. Now the trees are an ornament of the city, thanks to Papa.

In October 1942, my father celebrated his fiftieth year in the practice of medicine. On this occasion he gave the last of his big parties, held at our house where dinner was served for one hundred, with double that number from all over the state at the reception afterward. He had served as president of the Florida Medical Association, had been on numerous boards and commissions, served as president of the state Historical Society, Senior Warden of his church, and had many other honors he had earned. In 1942 he was seventy-six years old and still working full-time because of the war, and also because he wanted to. But I could see that he was tiring. Soon afterward my brother was commissioned captain in the Medical

Corps and sent to Pennsylvania for training. I could see the worry
in my father's eyes. The household drew in. Papa began to have a
series of small but painful illnesses: a stubborn eye infection, diver-
ticulitis, angina (which he concealed). But he kept on at his work.
Christmas of 1943 was gaunt. For the first time I could remember
no one had thought of going out and getting a tree as we always
had. Only my sister and I were at home now, and Leah increasingly
used the excuse that we were not to worry Papa about "trifles" (the
Christmas tree was a trifle) to isolate us. Finally I went out to
property we owned, found a tree, cut it, and brought it back. It
looked forlorn in the chilly, empty hall, at the foot of the stairs
because I couldn't find all the trimmings, and Leah, miffed, would
not help us. That Christmas was a bleak one. Papa was not well.
War news was dismal. The season was unusually cold. Fuel was
rationed. In February my brother was ordered overseas to the European theater with his medical unit. Papa's anxiety was plain as he
set out with Leah for Jacksonville, where my brother was stationed,
to say good-bye. While he was in Jacksonville staying with my older
half-brother, Tom, my father collapsed with a heart attack and was
rushed to Riverside Hospital. My brother George proceeded overseas.
I was in my last year of high school. My sister was in college. Our
house was empty except for me, and I was ordered to stay in Tallahassee until I was sent for or Papa was brought home. I would only
be in the way, Leah said.

Alone, I dealt with my feelings as best I could. Sick with
dread, I continued school. One spring day, feeling intolerably lonely,
I went down to Papa's office and sat for a while at his rolltop desk
with its papers and notes in his particular hand (though I could, if
I needed to, imitate his signature well enough for school purposes).
Then I went upstairs, laid out on the dining room table all his best
linen, crystal, and silver as if for one of our lively dinners in the
past. I picked flowers from the yard and filled two vases that I set
in the middle. Then I sat in my father's place for what seemed like
a long time, drawing strength from my memories of better times.
Toward evening I cleared the table, put everything away, folded the
linens, straightened everything up, and left only the flowers. Then
I went upstairs to do my assigned homework. A week or two after

this Papa came home from Jacksonville in an ambulance. The living room had been converted into a bedroom for him and his four-poster had been disassembled and brought downstairs. He was weak but glad to see me and glad to be home. I hoped for the best, but I could see that he was very ill. He was in congestive heart failure.

It was my father's wish that he be brought back to his house to die where he had lived, and his doctors obeyed him. One day I was sitting with him when Dr. Wilkinson came for his daily visit. I didn't leave, but sat behind one of the curtains in the tall window. After a while I realized from my father's choked voice that he was weeping. I had never in my life seen this strong man in any condition other than comforting others, everybody's mainstay in all situations, always aware and in charge. I was thunderstruck. Then I heard him talking to his doctor. He wasn't, God knows, afraid of death, he said. He had seen death all his life and his faith was strong. No. He paused. What worried him constantly now (he began once more) was what would happen to Martin and Mary Lucile, his children, after he died.

One evening a few days later Parson Alfriend came. Papa by now was drifting in and out of consciousness, lucid only in short periods. A small prie-dieu had been fixed by his bed and Reverend Alfriend—whom my father as Senior Warden had welcomed to St. John's twenty years before—gave him communion. That night when his mind was briefly clear I was able to tell my father that I loved him more than anyone else in the world and to say good-bye. Then I went up to my room to get out of the way of the nurses and the tubes and the ineffectual oxygen mask, and the others in his room. Sometime in the early morning my brother Tom opened my door gently and called my name. He saw that I was awake as he came over and put his hand on my shoulder.

"Martin, Papa's dead." I had no reply.

The funeral was held from the house where my father's open coffin stood against the bay windows in the parlor, then proceeded to St. John's for the service. From the church he was taken to our family plot in the Old City Cemetery where he was buried beside my mother, sharing the headstone. Before the coffin was closed, the last view I had of him was of his hand, lying against his gray suit in a position familiar to me in his life, his limber thumb exactly like my own.

bob summer

jim my father

There have been three Jims in my life—Jim my brother, an All-American youth who became an air force officer; Jim, the FFV (First Families of Virginia) golden boy and marine captain with whom I spent an intense summer the year President Kennedy was assassinated; and Jim my father. Each of these remarkable men left his imprints on me in various ways. To a large degree, my life has been a reaction to the example of a maleness society deems orthodox, which my older brother set for me to follow. Jim the sensitive FFV scion ennobled me with a vision of what two men can find together if fate smiles upon them. But although my father and I were not close for much of his life, he is my life's greatest loss.

Oh don't worry, this is not going to be another of those "I Never Sang for My Father" types of reminiscences. An outwardly unaffectionate man, at least until he was well into middle age, my father would be embarrassed by that. So even if such maudlinness was my style it would be inappropriate to his memory. Instead I want to sort through our perplexing responses to each other to see if I can find the answer to why it is that I have missed him so much since he died in early 1977.

Is it guilt? Yes I am sure there is some of that, but I am just as certain that that is not the entire reason. Indeed our tentative

approach to each other, and for a span of time almost total alienation, was rife with complexities. He had many qualities I admire
in a person, mixed with some, like most of us, of a baser nature.
And when I was very young, probably up to the time I was in the
third or fourth grade, I kept him on a pedestal. I favored him in
looks, people told me, and even then I was aware from family stories
that he had triumphed over an early life of hard knocks. In the
South, storytelling—our vaunted, but not wholly positive, oral tradition—does more than just entertain; it passes down myths. And
the stories told by uncles, aunts, and my grandparents that focused
on Daddy left me with a virtual reverence for him.

Both sides of my family have deep roots in the rural Dutch
Fork community in mid–South Carolina just above Columbia, the
state's capital. When my father, the sixth of his mother's children,
was born in 1902, that hard-scrabble area was locked into a long-
term depression due to the failure of its cotton-based economy to
recover from the Civil War's destructiveness forty years or so earlier.
(Sherman and his foraging troops had skirted the eastern side of the
Dutch Fork on their route to North Carolina after the burning of
Columbia.) But the situation of Daddy's family was made even worse
when his father, a railroad conductor, was killed in a train wreck
the week before his last son was delivered.

Somehow, probably through pluck more than anything, my
grandmother kept the family otherwise intact on their farm, almost
the only thing of fiscal worth her husband left her. And my father,
whose formal schooling was scant, went to work when quite young
to help support the family from pickup jobs at cotton gins, saw
mills, and construction sites. After electricity came to the area he
developed a skill for electrical wiring, and eventually enrolled in a
course to better learn that trade. But the course was offered in
Chicago, not in South Carolina, and from the money he had saved
he bought a train ticket to head northward. In a way that was the
real beginning of his life, since it set the stage for what would
follow.

Within a few years, back in South Carolina, he met the young
woman who would become my mother and they were married before
he returned to Illinois for a job he had there as an electrician with

a large construction company based in the East. After he died many years later, I asked Mama why she had married him. Even during the worst years of the Great Depression when they were wed he kept a "good" job, she told me, and always had "lots" of money. And her father, a dominating Southern paterfamilias type called "Pa Joe" by his grandchildren and "Cap'n Joe" by others, thought highly of him. "Jim had a good reputation," she added, and everyone in the Dutch Fork regarded him as "a real go-getter." Curiously she didn't mention love, although I'm certain that was involved too. At the time of his death, they had been together for close to fifty years.

But I'm getting ahead of my story. During the first years of their marriage, they lived in Illinois, Pennsylvania, and Baltimore as his company moved him from one construction job to another. But they were always surrounded by other South Carolinians. When possible, he would find jobs for friends back home and send word for them to join him.

When time came for their first child to be born, however, the process was reversed and my mother returned to South Carolina. Jim my brother was born at her family home, as was traditional in the South. But a few years later when I came along that tradition had fallen to "progress" and I was born in the Columbia Hospital. Except for her young brother and his wife Mama was alone, though, since my father had been delayed in getting away from his job up North. When he finally arrived and saw his second son for the first time, according to a family story still told at reunions, his reaction was to ask, "Is he going to always look like that?" I was tinged red from my tiny toes to the wisps of curly hair on my head.

Fortunately my skin soon cleared, although the red curls remained. And in a tinted photograph made in a Columbia studio when I was about a year old, my long fiery curls make me look more like a girl than a little boy. That was Mama's doing, I'm sure; no similar picture of my brother exists, nor undoubtedly was ever made. Mama called him her "little man," and that must have been his role from the beginning. Since my father was usually away fulfilling his role of family provider, my mother, with *her* role as homemaker, must have seen my brother as a substitute for the man in the house Southern women of her era were raised to rely on.

But Daddy returned home to be with us every chance he could get, and at other times he would send small gifts in addition to his regular money for food and clothes. Once he sent my brother and me matching sailor suits, and I still have a snapshot of us smilingly posed arm-in-arm while showing them off. I don't have any Christmas pictures from those years, though, but I know he was always with us for the holidays, making certain that Santa Claus remembered my brother and me with a toy we had set our hearts on and the traditional Southern stockings filled with pecans, apples, oranges, and tangerines. It never occurred to me that Christmas might be an emotionally down time for him until I heard Grandmother Summer in her deathbed ramblings say that Christmas was always a sad time for her though she tried to conceal it. Her husband had met his sudden death shortly before December 25.

Still, Daddy, who inherited the late Victorian code of "manly" restraint, did not easily show his tender side in those years; he did not even cry at his mother's funeral. But he had provided much of her livelihood, since his brother with whom she lived on the family homeplace was a poor manager and another brother was left an invalid from the gassing inflicted upon him as a foot soldier in the trenches of France during World War I.

Daddy, in short, was the only son she had to depend on. Indeed, compared to other relatives still living in the Dutch Fork, he had done quite well for himself. And by that time he had advanced to become a section foreman in the large plant he worked at in Oak Ridge, the East Tennessee site the federal government chose for the Manhattan Project, which developed the atomic bombs that were dropped on Hiroshima and Nagasaki to force the Japanese to surrender, ending World War II.

A job in Oak Ridge was enviously sought after by workers across the South, and the fact that Daddy had landed one added further to his reputation back home. Now certainly his job as an electrician was a much lesser one than those of the scientists at the Oak Ridge National Laboratory, who oversaw the diffusion of uranium, Oak Ridge's purpose. But nonetheless he was proud of the small part he had in the national effort, and he had an abiding loyalty to both the place and his union. After all, Oak Ridge pro-

vided him with the best job security and highest income he ever
had or probably dreamed of having.

To be sure, Oak Ridge did not make him a wealthy man. But
he was able to buy there the only house he ever owned and settle
with his family into a community, albeit one much different from
that in which he was raised. The stark new town the army had built
almost overnight in the aged Tennessee hills gave him—and us—a
hard-earned security.

The piano he bought, ostensibly for me, symbolized the attain-
ment of all this, although Mama again was the impetus for it. Her
sister, whose husband found an Oak Ridge job about the time Daddy
did, had purchased one in nearby Knoxville for her daughter. Mama
and Aunt Fannie always played their own private keeping-up-with-
the-Joneses game, and when I saw the spinet model in my aunt's
house I knew it wouldn't be long before we had one sitting in our
small living room too. Not that I didn't want it. I had my aspirations too and, happily, when I began my weekly lessons my teacher
said I showed promise.

Maybe Daddy got some satisfaction from my developing talent.
I hope so, but he never said and didn't attend my recitals. What
did spark his excitement, though, was my brother's growing involvement with sports, especially football. Fall Friday nights saw Daddy,
with Mama and me in tow, in the bleachers at Blankenship Field,
along with other workers from the Oak Ridge plants, lustily cheer-
ing on the town's favored sons as they clashed with opposing teams
from area high schools.

Of course, there wasn't much else to do in town on Friday
nights, since everyone was at the football game. Besides, it gave the
town the topic for the following week's conversation. And soon that
conversation centered on the feats of my brother. Beginning in junior
high, Jimmy (as everyone called him) had steadily risen to stardom,
and in his senior year of high school he was team captain and won
a football scholarship to Georgia Tech.

I guess I realized I was overshadowed, although I tried to
pretend it didn't matter that Jimmy's exploits made anything I did
pale by comparison. My inclinations were more artistic, I rational-
ized. Anyway, the pedestal atop which I set Daddy in my childhood

had long been toppled. No longer did I laugh at his stories. And although he may have single-handedly raised his status, I noticed we were still considerably below the economic and social level enjoyed by the scientists and plant managers who lived in the larger, better furnished homes I envied. I was uncomfortable to be alone with him, since I always seemed to unleash his anger. At night, on the other side of the thin wall separating my and Jimmy's bedroom from theirs, I could overhear him questioning Mama about why I did this, why I wasn't better at that. When he tried to teach me to drive it was, predictably, a disaster, and I failed the first test I took for my driver's license.

Once a high school friend of mine was given an assignment in his journalism class to interview someone who had been in Oak Ridge since its beginning years. He told me he wanted to interview Daddy, to which I responded, "Why? He hasn't done anything worth talking about." And when, at Mama's urging, I tagged along with him and Jimmy down to Georgia Tech to move the family star into the athletic dormitory there, I was embarrassed by my father's childlike glee. Amid all the beefy football players and coaches we met (including the legendary Bobby Dodd, then Tech's head coach), Daddy was like the proverbial kid in a candy shop. But the car was icily quiet on the long drive back to Oak Ridge.

That tenseness between us continued on into college. I went to the University of Tennessee in Knoxville, since my father would only cover my educational expenses if I enrolled at an in-state school. And to his credit he fully kept his promise, although I must have sorely tested his patience when I changed my major from business administration to liberal arts. But I made by far my best grades in history, and since I was at UT rather than the out-of-state college I wanted to attend I decided to concentrate on what I, not he, thought best for me. After his initial outrage, he never said anything, although Mama mentioned he told some visiting relatives they ought to read some of the history papers I brought home marked with As. I was unaware he had read them.

Later, after a trip to New York (my first, made at my expense) with some friends during spring break my senior year, Daddy reported to other relatives on what I had seen—the Empire State

Building, United Nations, Metropolitan Museum of Art, Macy's, Brooklyn Bridge, and so forth. An aunt relayed to me that he also had pointed out to them that New York was a long way from the Dutch Fork. Now Daddy wasn't a braggart, and what he said, I think, had to do with the fact that New York then was still the ultimate city in the minds of Southerners. That a son of his had finally gotten to a place neither Daddy nor any Summer had seen with their own eyes was a source of pride.

But again I wondered why he wouldn't talk directly to me, why he had to get everything I said secondhand through Mama. Perhaps I had wounded him by not following Jimmy's football (and other athletic) accomplishments. (Someone in high school my freshman year told me Daddy had promised the football coach a new hat if he could get me to try out for the team.) Mama said the reason we couldn't get along was that both Daddy and I were "stubborn as mules." As he got older, friends would occasionally tell me he was charming, and with his teasing sense of humor he could be— but to others, since he never showed that side directly to me.

I can't claim, however, that he ever failed to meet his material responsibilities for me, although he was a tight man with his money. When I made long-distance calls home, he and I would barely say hello before he put Mama on the line. That was because, she explained to me, he did not like long-distance charges. He also abhorred interest charges and would permit her to have charge accounts only if they could be paid in full every month. Nor did he approve of allowances to children; both Jimmy and I, and later my sister, had to earn our own spending money when we were growing up.

On the other hand—and that was to me the baffling thing about Daddy; there was always an "on the other hand"—he lent me the down payment for my first house (after Mama's intercession on my behalf). And he was generous with hospitality; no one ever left our house hungry or thirsty. He bought canned food for our church, Grace Lutheran, to give to needy families, in addition to the tithe he annually made for what he called the church's good work. And after he retired, he became active with Grace Lutheran's project for the resettlement in Oak Ridge of Asians whose lives had been made chaotic by the regionwide catastrophe brought on by the Vietnam

War. It was the first such project in Oak Ridge, and many people there—including Mama—initially did not approve of bringing non-Caucasians into a mostly white, middle-class town where the political allegiance had shifted from Democratic to Republican. But despite that Daddy argued the resettlement was commanded by the church's mission.

Thus he enthusiastically helped gather furniture, clothes, and other household items for the Mouas, the family from Laos the church pledged to sponsor. A home was found in a housing project, a menial job for the father (a former Laotian army officer) was located in one of Oak Ridge's scientific facilities, and individuals were assigned to help them become acculturated. So when the family of ten arrived in Oak Ridge the year the United States celebrated its bicentennial, all was ready for them to begin their lives anew far from the refugee camps they had left behind.

Even if neither Daddy nor I had forgotten the past perceived wrongs our life together had wrought, both of us had mellowed and by then were learning (or perhaps relearning) how to talk with each other. He never questioned why I was not married, since he had not done so himself until age twenty-nine. To him that (as well as sex in general) was a private matter. Instead, he always wanted to know about my jobs and the places where I lived or visited. Geography and demographic facts fascinated him, and each year he bought an almanac to supplement his world atlas.

That year I was back in Oak Ridge for Christmas when Daddy over Saturday breakfast broached the matter of a holiday gift for the Mouas. Mama dismissed the idea outright; he had done enough for them already, she declared, and besides she had more than enough to do to finish getting ready for Jimmy and my sister who would be coming in shortly with their families.

Undaunted, Daddy mused that a basket of pecans, apples, oranges, and tangerines would be a gift all the Mouas could enjoy, and he turned to me and asked if I had time early the next week to drive him over to the farmers' market in Knoxville. I leapt at the invitation, and early on Tuesday we headed out on our little expedition. On the way over, he reminisced about what would have been happening in the Dutch Fork at Christmastime when he was growing up.

The older he got, the more vividly he elaborated on his memory of those early years. "Papaw, tell us about ole times," was his grandchildren's key to getting his stories started. And since he was reared on a farm he was right at home in a farmers' market. I knew that while filling the bushel basket we brought with us he would exchange stories with each of the farmers there. Indeed he enjoyed that swapping so much that it was late afternoon before we were headed back to Oak Ridge. And the temperature was dropping so that it was much colder. The TV weather forecast on the evening local news raised the specter of snow, the season's first, but when we finished supper and were leaving with the brimming basket for the Mouas I thought the air lacked enough moisture for that.

Someone from the church had called Mr. Moua to tell them we were coming, and their outside porch light was on for us. And when we knocked on the door, I could hear him telling his children, I guessed, how to act. Then when he opened the door, he smilingly welcomed us with gestures and faltering, staccatolike English. Meanwhile, I glimpsed his wife shepherding the children out of the small kitchen into the living room.

Daddy, talking loudly and deliberately, explained why we had come and signaled for me to follow him in. I looked for a Christmas tree under which I could set the basket, but there was none. So I set it in a corner of the small room, exchanged smiles with Mrs. Moua, and watched the children align themselves in descending order according to height (and perhaps age) beside their parents.

Daddy continued talking as if sheer volume was enough to make himself understood, and Mr. Moua responded by bobbing his head up and down with small punctuating laughs. But the smallest of the children, a young boy and his younger sister, didn't know whether to direct their attention to us or the gift basket in the corner. What their mother wanted, though, became clear when the little girl reached to touch an apple and was reprimanded with a pat on the head and a stern look. But once again attentively assembled, each child followed their father's lead by arranging their hands together, palms pointed upward. Daddy looked befuddled, and for

a second I thought he was going to follow their example before he
dropped his hands down to his side.

Mr. Moua began talking. He and his family, he said to Daddy,
were honored by our visit and grateful for the gift. He then bowed
to Daddy, and his wife and children followed suit. I looked at
Daddy, whose perplexed smile revealed his uncertainty about how
to respond. But, his voice calmer, he answered by saying we were
happy they had come to America and wanted to wish them a Merry
Christmas. Then he extended his hand to the much smaller Laotian.
"You thanked me your way," Daddy remarked, "but I'll answer
with mine." And he went down the line, bending and grasping in
his hand that of each member of the family, wishing everyone a
Merry Christmas.

That little ceremony seemed all that was called for. Noting we
had interrupted the family's supper, we took our leave so they could
return to their kitchen table. Mr. Moua saw us out, while his wife
tried to muster the children back to their evening meal. But the
basket was a magnet drawing their curiosity, and as I left I saw
they were hovering over it, perhaps, I later realized, because in their
temperate homeland they were unfamiliar with apples.

We had not stayed long enough to remove our coats, and
Daddy, after exchanging goodnights with Mr. Moua, hurried back
to the car. I added my own "Merry Christmas" and followed. But
on the way out, I noticed that a light from a source other than the
one on the porch was widening in front of the house. Looking back
toward a large front window, I saw that little girl, probably standing
on a chair, holding up a curtain with one hand while, in the other,
she held an apple.

When I got back to the car and climbed in on the driver's
side, Daddy too was watching the scene. What was he thinking? I
wondered. When I first saw the little girl in the window, my first
Christmas memory—a large decorated cedar in Pa Joe's house,
brightly lit with colored lights and shimmering with tinsel—suddenly came rushing back to me. Was Christmas imagery from the
Dutch Fork in Daddy's mind also? Was he hearing ol' Mims and
Holly blazing Christmas greetings across the Piney Woods with

shotgun blasts rather than the customary firecrackers? Was he remembering his mother's once-a-year pineapple upside-down cake.

I didn't ask. Nor did I hear his usual, "Let's get going." He seemed to be silently relishing what was happening. The faraway gleam in his eyes told me that, and I was certain Christmases in other times and places were resonating with us as we sat there on the fourth night before Christmas 1976. How strange that this exiled family from halfway around the world could be the agent for bridging the gap between Daddy and me.

I switched on the engine to get some heat into the car. Then when I pulled on the headlights, the beam of light picked up flakes of a beginning snow. And across the way, Daddy and I saw the little girl being joined by an older brother who held an apple in his hand also. Both were wonderingly looking out at the snow and us, and time for a precious moment was seamless. Christmas present and Christmas past were joined, and Jim my father and I were together.

Silent night. Holy night.

albert clarke

my entire life, and my father

When I was a boy, the phrase "Honor thy father" used to drive me into a rage, and I think that my profound distrust of the Bible probably originated with those three simple words.

There was very little to honor about the man. He was defensive and narcissistic, with an obdurate, cynical sense of his place in the universe—the kind of man who envisions life as a card game in which all the players, except for himself, have been dealt beautiful hands and who comes, as a result, to despise both the players and the game. He was harsh and unaffectionate, with a fierce, volatile temper, and being told to honor him was like being told to honor a killer tornado or the man across the street who'd been arrested for trying to poison the neighbors' dogs. I didn't want to honor him; I wanted to escape him.

And yet, perhaps perversely, I loved him—despite the emotional rampages, the times when he threatened (and once even actually tried) to kill me, or the hundred smaller abuses, both physical and emotional. When I was twelve years old, some part of me still desperately wanted to recapture the warmth of those few fragile moments when he had once scooped me up in his arms and hugged me. Demonstrations of affection mysteriously stopped when I was about five years old. To this day, I don't know why.

Several years ago, when my mother was cleaning out her house, she sent me a box of memorabilia from my childhood: old copies of my high-school newspaper, letters and postcards from various trips I had taken, some family photos. Near the bottom of the box was a postcard my father had sent me when I was four years old. It showed a deer at the Grand Canyon, and my father (who was then traveling cross-country on business) wrote: "Daddy saw a deer just like this today. It was all brown and fuzzy. Daddy loves and misses you a lot." I looked at it with incredulity and checked twice to make certain it hadn't been addressed to my brother. In the same box, there was a Polaroid snapshot of me at five years old in a cowboy outfit and my father—stern, pockmarked, his lips rammed together in what seemed like perennial anger—kneeling next to me. My only thought, with an ache of abandonment that went right through me, was, How could that man have wound up doing what he did to that happy and innocent boy? I was just a child. . . .

A more perspicacious youngster might have seen where all his unhappiness came from. If I had been alert to his business worries, his regrets, his general feeling that time was passing him by, I might—*might*—have had an easier time of it, or at least might have had some rationalization for his behavior. The one thing I knew for certain early on, even without understanding the full implications of it, was that his own parents were crazy.

His mother was a voracious mountain of flesh. She weighed over three hundred pounds and whenever she came to visit, our dogs would sniff in a frenzy at her monstrous calves as she slowly made her way, with an odd waddle, across the living room floor. She ate incessantly, uncontrollably, and I remember when I was a child she was not above reaching out for a cookie I was about to put in my mouth and saying, "You don't really want that, do you?" A second later, the cookie disappeared between her lips.

She was a mean-spirited and carping woman who needled my father mercilessly about everything from his income to his acne scars. "Poor Eddie's face is a mess," she used to say disgustedly, addressing everyone in the room but him. "When is he going to do something about it?" She was addicted to enemas and took a variety of pills; the only cars she could ever travel in were convertibles, because the only way she could ever be squeezed into an automobile was to first remove the top. As she got older (and even more obese), my sister, mother, and I used to joke we would soon need a construction crane to take her anywhere. In fact, there came a time when she couldn't travel at all anymore, and instead sat all day in her big armchair, watching the daytime soap operas, reading *The Saturday Evening Post*, and ridiculing the neighbors and the world.

I remember that, more than anything else in life, she feared and detested "sissies." She was obsessed with them. When John Kennedy was elected president, she agonized over the Free World being led by a "sissy" (and a Catholic one at that). "Now Joseph McCarthy," she used to say, "there was a *real* man." Anyone with money or a college education was a "sissy." Anyone from the East Coast or in show business or with a taste for classical music was a "sissy." And, closer to home, I, too, was a "sissy."

When I was nine or ten, I overheard a conversation in which she complained to my father that I was growing up to be a "sissy." My father didn't defend me or object; in fact, he didn't say much of anything—I knew he agreed with her. I was a skinny, bookish, painfully shy boy, not effeminate, really, but rather anxious and unassertive. I suppose I hated my father for not defending me, but more than anything else I was stricken with panic by his silence. I suddenly knew I had no allies in that family and felt some of the creeping terror people experience when they run into trouble in a foreign country where the language and expectations of the natives are incomprehensible to them. The pathetic part of it was, I suspected (from later clues) that my father had once been a boy much like myself—overly sensitive, emotional, bookish—whose virtues and kindness were swept away in the path of his mother's obsession with manhood and weakness.

His father was little better. He ridiculed everyone, but particularly the Jews and the Democrats and the Communists (without making any distinction among them). He prided himself on being something of a learned man but looked down on universities and intellectuals; he pronounced the word "intellectuals" with such contempt there was no need to add the "goddamn" that otherwise pervaded his conversation with numbing regularity.

One of his only obvious pleasures in life was farting jokes, and at holiday dinners he would suddenly ask, with a wry and wicked smile, "What's the definition of a narcissist?" The answer: "A man who smells his own farts." Then he'd lean forward, as if sniffing a really juicy one, and throw back his head in helpless laughter, nearly falling off his chair in the process. He was also an avid, amateur genealogist and spent most of his final years tracing our family tree back to medieval Ireland. That family tree, once completed, covered several square yards, and as a family we would sometimes gaze at it in awe as it lay sprawled, like some beguiling pool of time itself, across the living room floor.

I'm told that the two of them—my father's parents—often had bitter fights and would sometimes go at each other with kitchen knives, letter openers, and whatever else was handy. My father and his siblings were, as children, forced to hide in closets to avoid injury. Early on in the marriage, my grandmother and grandfather decided they hated each other and seriously discussed the possibility of divorce; the irony was that they finally decided to stay together "for the sake of the children."

I grew up in a house full of holes—literally. There were doors my father had kicked in and walls he had punched holes through. It sometimes made a titillating story to tell friends that the three craters in my bedroom door had come from my father and that the door frame itself was loose because he had, just a few nights earlier, kicked in the entire thing while trying to attack me. The upstairs hallway was full of pictures that hung in odd places, too low or too high, to hide the various holes my father had put in the walls.

As poignant to me somehow as the damage to the house was the fact that our entire backyard—a huge backyard, full of roses and wisteria—was untended and overgrown like the garden of someone who had died. Meanwhile, the house's upstairs rooms—which were only partly finished when my parents bought the place—remained unfinished for thirteen years, the naked wall studs a symbol of my father's exhaustion, a sign that nothing was really worth doing.

More than anything though, his sad craziness was typified to me by a locked file cabinet that stood rather ominously next to the breakfast table in our kitchen. In it, he hoarded cookies, Scotch, cashew nuts, and other food. He was terrified of deprivation, and was so distrustful that one of us would eat these things that he locked them away. But the cookies always went stale and grew moldy and had to be cleaned out by my mother every few months; the Scotch remained unopened, the nuts went unconsumed. On the couple of occasions when I tried to pick the lock, out of curiosity and mischievousness, I was walloped brutally; his anger was wild and murderous, as if I were attempting to steal the last provisions of his survival. He also on one occasion padlocked the refrigerator to protect "his" eggs from being eaten and "his" milk from being consumed. I soon learned to survive on "Instant Breakfast" mixed with water (my sister and I sometimes fought if there was only one left), and once I passed out in grade school because, as usual, I had nothing to eat in the morning. Both my parents were shocked and humiliated when they were called in by the school nurse, who explained to them the need for sound nutrition in growing children. For several days afterward my parents regarded me with vicious anger, as if I had deliberately betrayed some family secret.

I suffered daily abuse at my father's hands. I was slapped, kicked, and pulled by the hair; once he kicked me up an entire flight of stairs (one hard kick to the buttocks every two or three steps). On another occasion, he locked me in my bedroom on a diet of bread and water because he thought he had recently detected criminal tendencies in my personality (a ludicrous suspicion, considering I drained myself trying to be the perfect little boy). Among his many idiosyncrasies, he hated the sound of crunching—celery, potato chips, raw carrots, and ice were all banned from our dinner table; and if you were unlucky enough to get a crisp piece of lettuce in your salad, you paid the consequences, usually an agonizing kick under the table or a hard whack across the face. He also cringed at the sound of sneezing, and it wasn't until I was nineteen that I first learned how to blow my nose, as my father had always forbidden us from blowing our noses in his house.

Oh, how I hated the man! He dealt with his own bizarre behavior by boisterously dismissing it as fiery and eccentric, as if he were some colorful character from history—which is, I think, exactly how he viewed himself and his family: the colorful Rutledges, unique, misunderstood, full of passionate, raw emotions. He glorified all of his inner turmoil, and subsisted on that glory until recently, when, as he approached his seventieth birthday, he suddenly collapsed in a heap of depression and immobility and was put on Prozac by his physician.

I first started looking for a man to replace him when I was nine or ten.

In the fifth grade, I became infatuated with the most popular boy in the class, a blond, athletic boy who was always elected to student council and who, it seemed to me, had a perfectly wonderful father: the kind of father who mowed the grass every Saturday and who could be seen in the front yard on Sunday afternoons throwing a baseball back and forth with his son. It was obvious to me then, just looking at them, that they weren't the kind of people who hoarded cashews and Scotch in a safe by the breakfast table, and I doubted there was a single hole in any of their hallways or bedroom doors. I loved them both—father and son—and often rode my bicycle in silence, back and forth in front of their house, on evenings and weekends.

In seventh grade, I became infatuated with our P.E. coach, Mr. Carlson, who—not incidentally—often wore extremely tight, white jeans. As a freshman in high school, I loved a varsity wrestler. By the time I was seventeen or so, I had had dozens of fantasy fathers, some of them culled from real life, others—such as Robert Conrad or William Shatner—taken from movies and TV. And yet—*yet*—if one of them had presented himself at my door, I would have sent him away, because actually taking a surrogate father meant acknowledging once and for all that mine was a monster, and few children are prepared to embrace that kind of hopelessness, even if it means escape. I lived with my longings and my fantasies.

Meanwhile, my real father still hit me across the face for clacking my fork against my teeth at the dinner table; occasionally ordered me to take down my pants for a whipping, usually with his belt.

The other adults in my life remained pointedly oblivious to my situation. My mother—an intensely beautiful but vain and rigid woman—couldn't bring herself to fully acknowledge what was going on in her house. While she knew how my father treated me, she put it out of her mind, the same way she avoided thinking about the starving masses in Bangladesh or the threat of nuclear war.

And then there was Mrs. McCauley, an English teacher I tried to talk to once in seventh grade. *She* told me just to be thankful that I wasn't like that poor little girl who had recently been in the newspapers—the girl's father had tried to exorcise her of the devil with hammer blows to the head, and she was now in a coma. "Just remember," she told me anxiously (and I can still see her nervous expression as she maneuvered me toward and out the classroom door), "it's still a pretty good idea to honor your mother and your father." She seemed afraid of being sucked into some awful, sticky torrent that might threaten her career or well-being.

The major effect all this had on me was to make me, for many years, almost pathologically shy. I had few friends, in part because I could never trust anyone enough to get close to them. I spent Friday and Saturday nights lying in the dark on my bed imagining what other kids were doing at that exact moment. Other effects were almost crippling. It wasn't until I was nineteen or twenty that I could get up in the middle of a movie and go to the restroom without a sense of running some dark, silent gauntlet of ridicule and derision; the long walk up the aisle was hell. If a teacher ever called on me in class, I immediately darkened and started shaking, and my tongue turned so dry I couldn't get a word out. Meeting new people was a horror, crowded elevators threw me into a panic, and talking to people on the telephone . . . well, I usually let a ringing phone go unanswered or had other people answer it and say I was out.

Other effects that lasted well into early adulthood included a nervous habit of quickly eating my food, wolfing it down without chewing it, and then fleeing from wherever I was eating. I also suffered for years from a feeling of impending doom, a bitter depression that would descend on me every afternoon at five o'clock sharp; this clockwork melancholy vanished in my midtwenties, when I finally realized that five o'clock was the time every day when my father had gotten home from work.

Through all of this it never occurred to me that I might be sexually attracted to my father. Indeed, the only two episodes in which I saw any part of his genitalia were disgusting to me. In the first instance, he had a badly infected boil on the small of his back, just above the cleft of his buttocks, and I was in my parents' bedroom when I saw it: he was lying face down on the bed, his pants down to his thighs, and my mother was applying some kind of ointment to the infection. His buttocks seemed to me broad and flabby and flat. I looked at them for several seconds feeling repulsed. I was about twelve or thirteen.

In the other instance, he was lying on his bed at night reading a book. He was wearing boxer shorts, very loose around the thighs, and he had one leg cocked up with his book propped against his knee. I came into the room to ask him a question (I don't remember what), and I could see straight down one leg to his testicles. They seemed very dark and molten, loose-sacked not firm, and there was nothing appealing about them. In fact, I winced at the sight of them, and he may have caught my glance because in the next moment he suddenly dropped his knee and rearranged his shorts.

By my late twenties, though, I got some kind of fleeting glimpse that he had indirectly entered my libido. I suddenly noticed I was extremely attracted to men who wore glasses—and the only person I'd ever known well in my life who wore glasses was my father. I pushed the thought from my head (the thought I might be attracted to him cut too close to the psychological bone), but further glimpses only confirmed my fears. I realized I was sexually drawn to big men—my father was tall, very broad-shouldered, and while not fat at all, he had a certain imposing bulk, a stature that made him doubly frightening when he was angry. There was also the issue of men with bad complexions and the same pursed lips he had.

The realization of all this threatened me so much at first that I couldn't masturbate without a sudden image of him intruding into my fantasies and wrecking the moment. It exasperated and frustrated me, and I would sometimes pointedly search through porn magazines looking for men who were *not* like him at all. They became, for a time, the only ones who were safe to fantasize about.

I've since reconciled myself to the issue. It can be frightening to learn that our libidos and fantasies are shaped by all sorts of individuals, including people we've despised. Shaped as we are by our experiences with these people, a detailed examination of what turns us on would probably yield a sometimes troublesome gallery of faces and influences we might not want to face too directly.

Once, when I was home from college, I was sitting alone with my father in the family room, and I suddenly asked him, out of curiosity, what I'd been like as a little boy. He told me then that I'd been an awful brat, a constant trial to his nerves, "too god-damned smart for your own good, and I swear to God I thought you'd eat us out of house and home." (At the time of this conversation, I was 5'10" and weighed 120 pounds.) "But you know," he added abruptly, in an anxious voice, "I never mistreated you. I never laid a hand on you, not once. Not once . . ." And with that, he suddenly gave a hard kick, for no reason at all, to one of the dogs sitting near him. The dog yelped and ran into the bathroom.

I stared at my father in astonishment. I thought at first he might be joking. But, he wasn't. It seemed that the final damning craziness of his life was that he erased everything that was inconvenient to remember. He had started some crazy inner voyage, deeper and deeper into some pacifying dream in which he was the perfect father and had only done what was necessary to keep our perfect family together.

In later years he also began whitewashing his own childhood. At a family reunion recently he got into a fight with his brothers and sisters: they were all recounting the terrible fights their parents used to have and joking about having to hide in the closets. "That never happened!" my father exclaimed furiously. "That never happened at all! Why do you make up such things?"

I used to have this dream: My father was dead and lying in an open coffin at the funeral home. Walking up to his body, I felt nothing but rage and resentment. I wanted to spit in his face. But I couldn't. Not because it was dishonorable or unseemly, but because I was afraid to. Afraid that his anger—that dark, relentless anger that was at the core of his being—would transcend death, and he'd get up from the coffin and tear me to pieces. In the dream I just stood there, shaking and helpless.

I don't have that dream anymore. Sometimes, now, when I dream of him (which is rarely), he's often a crazy old woman in a shabby, oversized dress with a ragged scarf tied to his head. Sometimes he's just sitting there mumbling to himself, lost and confused; in one dream, he was sitting on the toilet and pulling houseflies apart with his fingers. Other times he's just shuffling around our old house talking to himself. But always, he's this crazy old woman. In the dream, as in life, he can't hurt me anymore. All I have to do is walk away.

my brother on the shoulder of the road

My brother Ken, who died of AIDS at thirty-seven, almost died in a car accident when he was three. My mother almost ran him over.

This was in Illinois, before I was born. So for me the accident takes place in a mythical prehistory that shapes everything to come. For me it's almost as if it takes place in the womb.

It was on a family trip. My father and Uncle Pete were driving in one car, with Ken and my oldest brother, Paul, in the wide backseat. Following in the next car was my mother, who was driving, and Aunt Helen and my two sisters. My father and uncle got involved in conversation and weren't watching the boys. Nor did the men notice that the doors were unlocked. Apparently Ken grew restless and decided to experiment with the door handle.

So, driving along a two-lane highway at sixty miles an hour, my mother sees my two brothers fly out of the car ahead of her. She swerved, only narrowly avoiding the boys as they rolled onto the pavement.

My brothers and the two cars all came to rest on the shoulder of the road. I imagine the cars were black or dark green, with tiny rounded windows, and there were light green wheat fields off to the right.

Miraculously, neither of my brothers was badly hurt: a chipped elbow for Paul, a broken leg for Ken. But this became one of the cautionary stories that ruled the family. After that, my father wouldn't pull an inch out of the driveway without making certain the car was secure. I remember we'd be all ready for a pleasant drive, and suddenly the air would be filled with tension. Urgently, sometimes angrily, my father would ask: "Did you lock your doors, boys?" To me, who came years after the near-tragedy, his caution seemed ridiculous. And to this day, when any of us comes for a visit, my father continues the drill, even though obviously we're all adults, and no one is going to decide to just open the door when the car is hurtling down the highway.

Ken was in a sense my only sibling. The others are much older and were all out of the house by the time I was seven. My sisters, born fourteen and sixteen years before me, are more like beloved aunts. And when I say "my brother," without using a name, I don't mean my oldest brother, Paul. I could only mean Ken.

My family moved a lot, so Ken and I spent a lot of time together despite an age difference of six years. By the time we got to California, the two of us played and fought on surprisingly equal terms. Paul had been left in college in the last state, and my mother started working, so now just Ken and I were at home. And we moved across town only six months later, when my parents bought a house, so Ken and I had to change schools just as we were making friends; the two of us were thrown together again. I was nine and he was fifteen. We started playing a lot with a dozen or so hand puppets given to me by our Uncle John. First we told stories about them, then we started making props and clothing, and eventually, over the next few years, we created a whole world with them.

They were made of molded plastic and were painted either blue or yellow. We called them muppets. The blue ones frowned and had bulbous green noses, and the yellow ones smiled with big red mouths. They came in pairs, stuffed in small corrugated boxes, and each of them had distinctive features depending on how he had been packed with his partner. To adults they all looked the same, but Ken and I had no trouble telling them apart. For instance, one of the yellow ones had been smashed so flat in his box that his smile was completely gone, and Ken called him Dead Codfish. He was a gangster.

We made the frowning blue ones female, which may have reflected my mother's temper, and perhaps an underlying sadness or fragility that we sensed in her. The yellow smiling ones were always male, and they had high voices. One of them could play either Ken or me, or sometimes my father, in his amiable, accommodating mode. But my father could also be represented by a blue muppet. In our cartoons, if you were a yellow muppet and you got really angry, you'd turn into a blue muppet. But if you were a blue muppet you were always a blue muppet, and if you were angry you simply grew ten feet tall.

In fact, we made up a special word for the blue muppets to express their anger: "Dih." It could be either a swear word or like "blah-blah" for rage. Usually the blue muppets resorted to strings of "Dih" when reason failed them, pummeling the yellow ones into submission. I think my mother's moods made about as much sense to me when I was growing up: "Dih, dih"—Die, die.

The muppets were my opportunity for revenge and conspiracy. Whenever Ken and I were in trouble, we could go into my room, shut the door, and reenact the scolding scene with my parents completely in the wrong. We drew cartoons or set up scenes in the muppets' houses, and the parent muppets would rant and rave ridiculously. (Perhaps the muppets prefigured a later conspiracy, when Ken and I were out only to each other, or still later when, at least until he was gravely ill, I was the only one in the family who knew Ken was HIV positive.)

Even my best friends at school never quite entered fully into the muppets' world: it was Ken's and mine. We used to say "Dih" to each other even as adults, which expressed both a particular kind of exasperation—that is, that we knew it was futile to be so mad— and the intimacy between us.

Ken made up countries for them, and each pair was a king and queen. They lived in suburban houses, open-topped corrugated boxes, and their furniture and clothes were mostly construction paper. I sat on the floor in my room for hours with the glue and scissors and Scotch tape. I wanted them to have everything on *Let's Make a Deal*: kitchen ranges, refrigerators, cars, boats, minks. My mother sewed them royal robes that tied around the neck, with terrycloth fur trim. Ken and I cut up bits of paper and made money.

All the muppets were mine except one pair, which was Ken's. Harold and Victoria were rulers of the smallest but most powerful country, Heere. Harold owned the casino where all the others lost their money. Victoria owned the Beauty Baths, which we set up every once in a while in the bathroom—some lounging in the sink and others sitting to dry up on the plastic decorative shelves above the toilet, next to the fake fish bowl. This was the analog of the wig and beauty shop where my mother was bookkeeper and about which she complained nightly at dinner. We soon discovered that the tap water actually helped chip their paint, which for the muppets was a sign of aging. "So really they're ugly baths!" Ken cried.

(It was Harold and Victoria that I would search for most desperately in Ken's house in San Diego after he died. I couldn't find them, and so I took other childhood objects: Matchbox cars, a worn stuffed dog, and two early handpuppets, Tiger and Ruff, a furry tiger and puppy whom I remembered but had never really played with. As it turned out, Harold and Victoria were still at my parents' house up in San Jose; I found them the following Christmas, staring up out of a box in the garage.)

For a time we took delight in making the muppets the most outlandish clothing and furniture because Ken said they had a mental disease called "opposit-itis." It meant they liked ugly things. I'd make a green-checked bedspread and then put black-and-pink snow-flake wrapping paper up on the walls. "How lovely!" Ken would exclaim, speaking in the high voice of the yellow muppet. "How elegant!" They had "bad taste," Ken said. Later they all got over it and had to redecorate.

Besides the obvious, is there something inherently gay about these games? Could two straight brothers have constructed the same world? Or one straight and one queer? Somehow the answer is no, and lately I like to think of my time spent playing with the muppets as the height of a gay childhood.

As if to prove this, at school that world soon became suspect. It was said that Cliff *played with dolls*. For I made them clothes and furniture. "They're not dolls, they're *puppets*," I would reply. The muppets hardly resembled people, I reasoned, and their clothing and houses weren't at all realistic. Besides, I thought, everything was made out of construction paper, and I didn't buy anything, the way a girl would buy Barbie clothes; I made everything myself.

Early in sixth grade I made the mistake of bringing a pair of muppets to math class one day, setting them up in the corner of my desk so I could look at their faces. Mr. Lang said I had to put them away, and then began asking pointed questions. *Do you play with them all the time? Do you sew them clothes? Do you make them doll houses?* Like a doctor he nodded a short "uh-huh" to each answer, and then he turned in his gray suit back to the blackboard.

The year before, it had been Mr. Lang who wouldn't let me give a puppet show to his regular class. Perhaps my own teacher said something to me about his not approving. In any case, somehow I knew Mr. Lang's refusal wasn't because he thought my show would disrupt his curriculum, but because of me.

It was also about then that the other kids began calling me names: girl, fem, fag. My friend Chipper had moved away the year before, and my new friend, David Vickers, called me a fem all the time.

But at home in my room I still had my own, safe world if I wanted. Here there was nothing wrong with me. "The other kids play with GI Joe, don't they?" Ken would point out. "GI Joe is a doll."

Even as the year went by and I began to move on from the muppets, it was always a world to return to—as Ken and I knelt on the floor beside the cardboard houses and each took a puppet in hand. It might be a fight with my parents, or just plain boredom, that brought him into my room. But then we could draw a cartoon or take the muppets and move them about in their open-roofed houses, which were growing dusty now, and act out a story.

So it was a refuge, but a betrayal was coming.

It was the summer before Ken went away to college. My mother, who worked full-time, was paying him to clean house for her, and babysit for me. I had a cruel streak, and I teased Ken mercilessly when he was vacuuming or dusting. Like my parents, he had a terrible temper. It was easy even for me, six years younger, to get his goat. I would stand in the path of the vacuum cleaner and make faces, or I'd follow him around while he was dusting and make farting noises. Sometimes I'd just lean in the doorway of the bathroom and stare at him until he turned from his cleaning and said, "Do you mind?"

I also defied him as much as possible that summer. Perhaps I was angry that he was going away to college in the fall. Perhaps I had simply reached the age to rebel, and Ken was more available than either of my parents.

David Vickers and I had set up the train table in the living room for the summer. In self-defense I had put the muppets aside and now played with trains every day, a more boyish activity. David and I had built bridges from the train table to the two steps into the sunken living room—and this was the cause of perhaps the worst fight I ever had with Ken.

It was hot, and the sunlight pressed against all the windows of the house. I had no doubt been teasing Ken all day, and now he wanted to vacuum the steps. I remember he came into my room and asked me to move the bridges.

"No," I said, fingering the curtains. "I don't feel like it."

He grabbed my arm, I began to scream, and things went on from there. He managed to drag me out into the entryway above the living room, and he hit me a few times on the shoulder. Still I refused to help him. "Cleaning is your job," I said. By now he had pinned me to the cold tile floor and was kneeling over me, his face and arms red with fury. I struggled, and then came his worst blow:

"Stupid little faggot!"

He had never called me that before. Or if he had, somehow it had never hit me in quite the same way. We stared at each other a moment, and I think my face must have changed its shape. Perhaps

I screamed. What I felt, and could not find words for, was this: *Not you, too.*

I tore myself from his grasp and ran down the hall, an incredible and shameful grief pushing up behind my eyes. It was one of the last times until adulthood that I would really cry. Once in my room with the door closed behind me, that privacy did not seem enough either, and, as if to confirm the power of a future metaphor, I ran and shut myself in the closet.

Ken came into my room after me. Somehow I had known he would see the seriousness of the situation and not open the closet as well. He stood outside the sliding door, and I sat fingering the opaque plastic door handle, a cap over a hole in the door and the only light that came in. "Come on," he said. "I hardly touched you."

But I kept still. My head hurt with trying not to cry, and it was hot in there. Ken waited a moment longer. "What's the matter?" he asked.

As much as we fought, and as often as Ken hit me, he was sensitive and he knew when he had really hurt me. I think he was sorry now, but still I didn't speak. I couldn't have explained it anyway, and at that moment I just wanted to be left alone to cry.

"Okay, be that way," he said, and I heard him go out.

The following spring, it was a chance remark by Ken that made me understand that I was gay.

He came home one weekend from college with his girlfriend, Kathleen. This was Ken's first girlfriend, and I don't remember my oldest brother, Paul, ever bringing anyone home, so this was new to me too. The air seemed charged with sexuality. My mother approached Kathleen gingerly, as if on tiptoe; my father teased her. On Saturday afternoon Kathleen and Ken sunbathed on lawn chairs in the backyard. I followed my mother out with the tray of iced tea, and as Kathleen walked barefoot to the patio in her yellow bikini, her browned hips and breasts flowing out, my mother exclaimed, as she always did during sexy scenes in movies on TV, imitating a huffy matron: "Well!"

I had been lonely since Ken went away to college, and I wanted to sunbathe myself now in his and Kathleen's brief presence. I wanted to know them, their private jokes, their world together. They called each other "Rabbit." They surfed. They smoked pot. They had a communal way of talking, Southern Californian and ironic, with certain phrases that seemed unusual and hip to me: "How odd," they'd say. Or, "Mr. Meat says, 'Make a mess!' " I didn't know where the phrases came from or even what some of them meant.

Saturday night I went to the movies with them. Or maybe we went miniature golfing, I don't remember. By the end of the evening it was like I was drunk on their company. As we drove home, in the darkness of the backseat I grew more and more vivacious, trying to imitate them and their phrases as much as possible. Maybe I was really imitating Kathleen. Anyway, after seven months of junior high constraint, I let go completely.

I like to think of that utterly fluid moment in seventh grade, before I quite knew the names of things, the proper boundaries between masculine and feminine, gay and straight—where my personality was so unformed and changeable that I could, with a little encouragement and excitement, let my guard down and emerge as a flaming queen of a child.

"Oh, how odd!" I cried, giggling. "Make a mess!"

I was scarcely aware of whether Ken and Kathleen were listening or not, so happy was I to be with my brother and his girlfriend, this wonderful alternative to my hate-filled life at school.

"Why are you acting so strangely?" Ken asked as we turned onto our block. All the houses were dark.

I stopped and thought. I was so happy, I wasn't even offended by his question. "I don't know," I said. "I usually don't act this way. How am I acting?"

"Really femmy," was his reply. Maybe he was embarrassed in front of Kathleen. And yet I like to think there was a strangely nonjudgmental quality in his voice, as if he were simply describing a fact.

"Really?" I said.

"Yeah, femmy," agreed Kathleen genially. She didn't seem to care.

"Hmm," I said. I looked for a reason. "I am acting differently. Maybe it's because of being with you two."

Then Ken said something very strange. I'll never forget it, though I don't remember his exact words, and it was only a joke. He said something like, "Maybe you're a *contact homosexual*."

"What's that?" I asked.

And he explained that it was someone who was homosexual only in contact with certain people, or in certain situations. It was a phrase he and Kathleen had learned in psychology class.

Shame began to ring in my head like a bell. We had pulled up in the drive a few minutes ago, and now we got out of the car. As I followed them up the dark walk to the house, in the California night air, I was beginning to put it together—what homosexual was, what fag was, what I was. Inside, I said goodnight to my parents, who were getting ready for bed. Ken and Kathleen went to their rooms—they had to sleep separately—and I went to my own room quickly, as if holding my discovery close to my breast. I closed the door and looked up the "H" word in the Encyclopaedia Brittanica and confirmed that I really was what the other boys at school said I was.

Ken came out to me when I was twenty-one. He had been living with Kathleen nearly six years when he started seeing men. He had moved with her to the East Coast, where she was getting her PhD, but he couldn't find work in Vermont and had to move to Boston. Now, a year and a half later, they had broken up and he had just moved back to California. He was staying with my parents while he looked for a job, and so now it was I who came home from college to visit one weekend.

Saturday night we went to a ferny, brightly lit bar in the next town where you could play backgammon. We sat down and had beers.

I didn't know Ken had something to tell me. His initial strategy was to remark on how other men in the bar were cute. I was so far from letting myself look at men that I had no idea what he was talking about. I remember at one point a stocky blond guy came in the door, at the far end of the room. Ken pointed discreetly. "Oh, there's a cute one," he said.

I turned. "Uh-huh," I said vaguely, guardedly.

I must have been frowning.

"Do you think it's strange for me to say that?" Ken asked.

"I don't know. I guess you're scoping out the competition, huh?" I meant his competition for the women in the bar. I genuinely thought this was some sort of "swinging singles" technique.

Ken did one of his joking double takes, a fidgety gesture he had. He was always very nervous, his hands shaky and his eyes darting, in the manner of everyone in the family, to your face and shyly away again. He had ruddy skin and a high forehead that furrowed easily. "Not exactly," he said. Then he just blurted it out: "I'm trying to tell you that I'm gay."

I almost think I had the same feeling of fear as that night when I was thirteen, when Ken made that chance remark—only now the feeling was more like elation. "Really?" I said. I saw him fidgeting with his beer, waiting for my reaction. It was as much to put him at ease as to satisfy any desire to talk about these things that I told him about myself too. "I've had those feelings," I said, faltering. Then I was a little more honest: "Actually I've had them a lot."

Ken did another one of his false double takes. But he was happy now.

We talked first about our mutual surprise. "I guess I always thought you were basically straight," Ken said.

"No . . . I thought that about you, too." And I have a particular image in my mind of Ken as a straight man, which was perhaps my model for any straight man: Ken washing his red Ford Falcon in the drive. His teenager's manly persona was, in fact, part of my own ideal self-image, nurtured throughout high school—that of the kind of guy who fixes things, who swears, who smartly ruffles the newspaper before he starts to read. I wonder at how we had fooled each other all that time with these personas, or rather with the idea that such a persona could not be gay. We each believed in this "basically straight" guy, and we each fooled ourselves with him.

So it was that we began to compare notes. I had had no experience and was still too scared to be planning any, so I had little to tell. I did manage to say I had felt this way since I was five. Ken countered that he had had no sexuality at all until after high school. In the back of my mind, I attributed this to the family's moving constantly, which meant that Ken went to three elementary schools, two junior highs, and three high schools. It seemed logical that he might protect himself by feeling nothing sexually. But I wonder now just how much to believe him, or just what he really meant. Anyway, he explained that it was in graduate school in San Diego (the city where he would later settle, and where he would die) that he started looking at men: "On the beach, when I used to go surfing," he said. "The other guys."

I think this probably seemed a little too real to me at that moment: sitting on the beach; surfers in wet bathing suits; looking at them. . . . But the story continued.

Back East, he and Kathleen had had to live apart and they began to fight. In Boston Ken started seeing a guy from work on the side. Within a few months Kathleen figured out something was up. Ken had never hinted to her anything about being attracted to men, so she assumed he was seeing another woman. There was the expected confrontation. "I told her, no, I'm seeing a man," Ken explained, smiling angrily now, seeming to take a certain pleasure in that exchange—the kind of scene where you're holding all the cards, and you lay them all on the table at once.

"So what happened?" I asked.

There were more fights, he said, and he and Kathleen stopped speaking altogether for a while. Then Kathleen started seeing someone else, in Burlington, and she and Ken decided finally to break up.

There was a pause. Ken was upset, and I imagine him frowning and staring down at the table, the same frown he'd had since childhood.

Then began the most curious part of the conversation.

"Why do you think you're gay?" I asked.

Ken waited a minute and said, "I think it was because of the accident." He meant when he was three.

I knit my brow. "How is that related?"

Then he said: "I could have died, you know. . . . I think after that, Mom clung to me too much."

Now, how did those fifties' shrinks propagate that dominating-mother story so effectively? I think it was even in the Encyclopaedia Brittanica. Anyway, even then I didn't put much stock in what Ken was saying, or maybe I was just jealous of the idea of his being so close to my mother—so I tried to make a joke of it all. "Well," I said. "I wasn't in any accident. So how does that explain me?"

But now I too want to make connections to that accident as a means of creating some kind of order from my brother's life. I want for a moment to see a random event, Ken's illness, as part of some pattern.

For instance: It was always said that when Ken was three, after he returned from the hospital, he never complained about the cast on his leg. Similarly, my mother says, he never complained as she and my father cared for him in the last months of his life.

But more important: Two and a half years ago, it was a car accident that marked the onset of my brother's final illness. Suffering from dementia, he ran his car off the road one day and was found wandering like a three-year-old along the banks of the freeway. Paramedics took him to the hospital, but this time there was no miracle. His moments of lucidity were less and less frequent, he was in great pain, and he died, more quickly than expected, just two months later. So I lost him by the side of the road. I wasn't present at his first accident, which was before I was born, nor at this last one, which took place three thousand miles away, and I was on my way to visit him when he died.

john
champagne

---

to my brother
with love

In my favorite photograph of my brother and myself, our faces are mirror opposites of each other—this, despite the fact that we are dressed in identical striped shirts. Ted's round brown eyes stare directly into the camera. My almond-shaped, hazel eyes look off to the left, outside of the frame. His plump, three-year-old face is surrounded by soft brown curls of hair. My face is angular, my hair, straight. Even though I am one year older than my brother, he already seems bigger than me. Ted is smiling, the rosiness of his cheeks visible even in this black-and-white photograph. My face is pulled into what is already by now its familiar frown, a look my father refers to as a "funcha." It's a Sicilian word my father learned from his in-laws. It is a certain kind of frown, an expression of sadness and displeasure, a mixture of fear and fatigue. This expression is much too serious for the face of a four-year-old. It will follow me into adulthood, insinuate itself into my features so that, unless I am smiling, this "funcha" almost always takes over my face. It leads people to ask me what the matter is when nothing is wrong. One of my friends refers to it as "that puss."

There was never any kind of explicit sexual activity between my brother and me. And yet I would still argue that I learned some of my earliest lessons about loving men from my brother. These lessons were usually of the negative variety—lessons in how love can go wrong. I have only recently begun to see how the sometimes difficult relationship I had and still have with my brother was inflected by my mother's illness. Using that illness as a kind of backdrop, I want to begin to explain to myself why my relationship to Ted has been marked by so much pain and misunderstanding.

My mother had her first nervous breakdown when I was four, shortly following the birth of her fourth child. Although she has been hospitalized briefly only once since then, her illness has been a constant presence in the life of my family. From a very early age, we were informed, both through direct observation and my parents' explanations, of the features of the illness—a "nervousness" that led her to walk at times with a kind of hitch, a pulling at the top of her buttoned blouse, and most noticeably, a tremor that caused her to shake almost uncontrollably whenever she went to kiss or hug one of her six children. (This last "symptom" I had forgotten until well into my adult life, when Ted reminded me of it once again.)

But even when these symptoms weren't directly present, we were always reminded of our mother's illness. There would be bouts of crying behind the closed door of her bedroom or in church and appointments with her psychiatrist every other Saturday afternoon, when my father would take us to feed the ducks along the shore of Lake Michigan or to the meat-packing company owned by my mother's aunt. And even when my mother's symptoms disappeared temporarily, we never forgot this family secret. In an effort to keep us from being frightened, my parents had explained to all of us just what my mother had gone through—the hospitalization with its accompanying shock treatments, the gradual regaining of her memory as the effects of the electricity wore off. And through it all, my father remained by her side, taking care of his young children.

■   ■   ■

Not only was Ted always heavier and taller than me, he was also considerably more outgoing. If I were to characterize the most common emotion of my childhood, it would undoubtedly be fear. I was afraid of everything—school, small animals, doing the wrong thing, going anywhere by myself, leaving my house, being laughed at by my peers. While the specific causes of the fear shifted over the years, the emotion stayed fairly consistent. Ted's most common emotion was defiance. He always appeared to me to be afraid of nothing—not the world outside our parents' house, not the teasing or laughter of other children, not the disapproval of our mother and father. In fact, in all the places I was frightened, Ted was brave.

I think it isn't coincidental that Ted's bravery matched my fear. It strikes me now that we were both reacting to my mother's illness, but in very different ways. I saw my mother's illness as proof of how threatening and dangerous life could be, and I fought to hold on to what little security I had by avoiding much of the world outside my home. My fear assisted me in that avoidance. Ted realized that the world we called home, marred as it was by the constant threat of mental illness, was at least as precarious as the one outside the family. His defiance allowed him to deny the pain of a family perpetually on the verge of a nervous breakdown, a family with a mother who might at any moment disappear into madness. Our complementary modi operandi—my fear, his defiance—created between us a relationship of dependence, the kind of relationship many people call love. My fear in fact fed Ted's defiance, convincing him that he—unlike me—could in fact escape the instability of our family. His defiance kept me all the more locked into my fear, locked into my belief that, as tenuous and painful as life inside my family was, life outside was somehow even worse.

Before the age of fifteen or so, I was fairly terrified of the outside world, so much so that I rarely did anything on my own. From the time I was six to the time I was fifteen, my brother Ted accompanied me almost everywhere. We took piano lessons together, joined the Cub Scouts together, took tumbling class together, had our hair cut together, went on errands together. If I ever had to venture into a public restroom, Ted inevitably accompanied me there, so terrified was I of walking across a crowded room of strangers alone. If I wanted to go to a movie or shopping, he was always at my side. He took up the role of my protector almost automatically, ordering food at McDonalds for me, helping me to learn to ride my bike. He was my closest friend and confidant, the person I depended on most in the world; the only place in which I ever expressed any real autonomy was in school, where he obviously could not always accompany me.

What strikes me today is how closely our relationship resembled a certain (admittedly dated) heterosexual model of romantic relationships. Ted was the man, taking care of me, protecting me from the world outside the relationship. I was the woman, passive, protected, unable to do things of her own accord. What this most obviously resembled was not coincidentally that of our mother and father. My mother was deeply affected by other people's opinions of her, so much so that she rarely ventured into any arena where she might possibly be subject to criticism. My father could care less about other people's opinions of him. My mother was shy and withdrawn in public. My father was gregarious and outgoing. My mother was the victim, the one who needed to be saved from her illness; my father, her savior. This was the model of romantic relationships with which I grew up—a model explored in the course of my first novel *The Blue Lady's Hands*.

The feelings I had for Ted were similar to those I would eventually feel for other men, feelings which I would ultimately have to call into question in order to arrive at some kind of "healthy" relationship with another man. I needed my brother desperately. I couldn't imagine living without him. He saved my life so many times, just as my father had saved my mother's. And Ted got from me some of what my father got from my mother. For where he was emotionally distant, I was emotionally alive. The price of his defiance toward the world was a certain inability to be comfortable with his emotions, and a difficulty in being accessible to others. One of the only benefits of my fear was that it allowed me to feel—often too much, and in ways that might accurately be described as "self-indulgent." But those were the two choices you got in my family. Either you were so in touch with your feelings—like my mother—that you were perpetually on the verge of an emotional breakdown;

or in such a state of denial—like my father—that almost nothing could disrupt your life. Ted and I provided each other with what the other was missing.

My "romance" with my brother went smoothly for several years. Then, at some point, I really can't say when, things began to turn sour. Ted changed. He seemed resentful of my dependence on him. Or perhaps his own sense of defiance needed some kind of reinforcement. In any case, he began to play a very cruel game with me. I would ask him to accompany me somewhere, anywhere, and he would agree to join me. But then, just prior to our leaving, he would change his mind. Terrified of the thought of having to go out on my own, I would beg and plead with him to keep his promise. This begging would continue until, finally, he relented; but he often attempted to keep me in this state of panic and fear for as long as possible, insisting over and over again that he had changed his mind, that he had never actually promised to accompany me, that he just didn't feel like going to the store or the mall or wherever.

Eventually, I got tired of all the begging and disappointment and learned to do things on my own. But Ted's actions—actions I now recognize as put into play by both my ever-increasing dependence on him and his increasing need to assert his independence—transformed our relationship. Our "romance" became a "love-hate" relationship. While I still felt a great deal of affection for him, I also resented the control he exercised over me—control that I had obviously handed over to him.

My brother similarly both desired and resented my dependence on him. My dependence gave him feelings of independence. This was at least partially due to the fact that a couple in my family was always defined as two people who were the opposite of each other. My father was strong, my mother weak; my father secure, my mother afraid; my father healthy, my mother sick; my father stoic, my mother emotional. If Ted and I were a couple, then only one of us could be independent—the one who was like my father.

I was not like my father. I was told this over and over again. Whenever I would complain to my father of how much it hurt me when other kids at school called me names like "fag" or "teacher's pet," he would say, "You're just like your mother. What should you care what other people think of you?" When I would tell him how afraid I was of being laughed at in gym class for being so small and awkward, he would say, "Why do you listen to that crap? You know, you're just like your mother."

Ted must have realized that to be like me was to be like my mother—something he would have to fight desperately if he wanted to survive in the world outside of our family. Though kids at school often called him names too, Ted never let them see how it affected him. And if anyone ever laughed at him, he just laughed right back in their face. I became for my brother a kind of yardstick against which to measure his own independence, an independence synonymous with his difference from my mother. As long as I still depended on him, he knew he was not like me, or her.

At about fifteen or so, Ted began taking singing lessons. We had both studied piano when we were young, though Ted eventually stopped taking lessons by the time he was a teenager, while I continued my studies into adulthood. Shortly after he began singing, we discovered that Ted was in fact a very gifted classical singer. He pursued his talents throughout his later years of high school, entering contests, performing in recitals, and studying with important teachers. Throughout the early years of his career, I acted as Ted's accompanist. Whenever Ted performed anywhere, I was his pianist.

Neither of us had small egos, and the pressures and pleasures of our new relationship as performers only exacerbated the tensions of our "love-hate" relationship as brothers. At sixteen, Ted sang for Lucianno Pavarotti at the Chicago Lyric Opera House, where the great tenor was giving a master class open to the public. Pavarotti's accompanist, John Wustman, had heard my brother sing at one of his own master classes and had arranged for what we thought would be a private audience with Pavarotti. But Pavarotti decided that, before he heard my brother privately, he would like to give Ted the opportunity to sing publicly for the audience assembled for the master class.

Ted and I walked from the audience to the stage, both of us a bit unnerved by the fact that what we thought was going to be a private voice lesson had been transformed on the spur of the moment by Pavarotti into a public performance. As I straightened my music and readjusted the piano bench, Ted turned his back to the audience and whispered to me, "Make sure it's slow enough." I was perhaps feeling a bit insecure that day, worried that I might not play well enough and irritated by what I felt was my brother's increasing tendency to take my work as his accompanist for granted. "If you don't like the way I play, get somebody else," I whispered back to him. "You always have to ruin things for me," he retorted, and then spun around to face the audience and begin his piece, a popular Italian art song called "Caro Mio Ben." All this took place in a matter of seconds, under our breath and before the unsuspecting eyes of a few hundred people.

While I loved playing for Ted, and got immense pleasure from hearing him sing, there was no way to separate our relationship as embattled "lovers" from our relationship as musicians. However well we may have been getting along on any particular day, neither one of us had any way of knowing when the doubt and fear we both harbored about the other's affections might surface and disrupt our actions. Yet, if ever one of us were faced with some kind of threat from the outside world, we would immediately close ranks, and find in each other the mutual strength and protection on which we so often relied.

For example, following our performance for Pavarotti, which went extremely well for both of us, we were asked to remain on stage for a private lesson. As the crowd filed out, one of the other students from the master class, a tenor several years older than Ted, approached my brother, ostensibly to congratulate him on his performance. "I've never heard anyone sing 'Caro Mio Ben' publicly," the tenor said. Both Ted and I recognized this as a barely veiled insult. The tenor was implying that the song wasn't suitable for a public performance; it was "light fare" compared to the "serious" arias sung by the other, older students in the master class. "Well, you have now," Ted smiled through his teeth, amused by so obvious a display of jealousy. For we had both done our homework: Pavarotti himself often performed "Caro Mio Ben" in recital.

Whatever animosity may have arisen that day between my

brother and me immediately dissipated in the face of this inter-
change, deflected as it was onto the other man's bitchiness. I adored
Ted's ability to say "fuck you" to this tenor without ever losing his
smile, and felt that sense of admiration I often felt when I saw my
brother defend himself in ways I never imagined I could.

These swift changes in mood between the two of us were characteristic of our relationship. When the threat of losing love hangs so
perpetually and precariously over one's head, it is impossible to treat
those you do care about with kindness and respect. Our mother's
mental illness represented to both of us that threat of the loss of
love. Our way of making sense of that threat was to develop a
relationship which allowed us to both affirm and deny our need for
the other.

I have always said that my brother left me for his first lover.
This is obviously an overstatement, and yet I have sometimes felt
that some of what Ted once needed from me he eventually found in
his lovers. Ted and I came out within a year of each other—though
I can't recall, despite our apparent closeness, a single conversation
in which we discussed, prior to coming out, our feelings for men.
There was, however, at least one instance where we both were forced
to confront, if not each other, then at least ourselves, with our
growing sexual desires.

My father had a habit of packing all eight of us up in our
station wagon, renting a camper, and traveling across country for a
family vacation. This particular summer, we were heading from
Milwaukee to North Carolina, where my father's sister lived. I was
fourteen, Ted thirteen. At some roadside stop along the way, Ted
bought, completely by accident, a paperback novel called *Fire Island
Pines*. Neither one of us had ever heard of the Pines; we had no idea
what the book was about. It turned out to be a kind of gay soft-
core porn romance set in the New York rag business.

Ted pretended to be completely scandalized by the book,
though of course he read every last word of it. I for my part found
the novel fascinating and scary. I distinctly remember my own surprise and discomfort at the fact that a particular scene in the book,
in which two men swimming together begin making love, gave me

an erection which I had to conceal beneath the blankets in the back of the car. (We didn't dare let our mother know that we were reading such a book, so we took turns reading it in the furthest reaches of the station wagon.) As soon as we had both finished the book, Ted destroyed it (much to my disappointment), claiming perhaps a bit too self-righteously that it was pure trash. Though we never talked in any detail about our reactions to the book, I'm sure that my brother must have been as drawn to, and disturbed by, it as I was. (I recently came across a copy of this book in the library of a friend. It was really wonderful to reread it and try to imagine how I must have felt, huddled in the back of that station wagon, waiting for my erection to disappear.)

When, at sixteen, I first told my brother that I had had sex with men, he started to cry. He insisted that he wasn't crying because I was gay. Instead, he was crying because of the men with whom I had been—men whom he believed treated me badly. I only half believed him at the time, assuming that his tears were also ones of fear—fear that he was gay, too.

For, despite the difficulties of our relationship, there were always also feelings of great intimacy between us, feelings often expressed in the most furtive of ways. We were not a family that encouraged physical intimacy, and yet there were moments when my brother's touch—say, his hand straightening my collar as I tried on a new sweater—conveyed a great deal of his love to me. And we had, after all, been taught those many years to imagine ourselves as a kind of couple. Perhaps he heard my telling him that I was gay as telling him that he was gay, too.

But when he eventually did come out, the reaction in my family was generally one of disbelief. Unlike me, whom my family "accepted" as gay shortly (a few months at the most) after my coming out, Ted was always suspected of being straight, or perhaps bisexual. He had, after all, had a steady girlfriend all through high school. Even when my parents learned of Ted's steady relationship with a man, they still wondered if in fact this weren't some kind of stage which he might outgrow.

The suspicion that Ted might in fact be straight extended from my parents to my third cousins. (I come from a family where there is no such thing as a secret.) I deeply resented this charade, because I felt it was evidence of my family's homophobia. I resented the fact that certain cousins of mine who would laugh at me behind my back would simultaneously express their shock and doubt that Ted might also be queer. Of course, Ted encouraged this speculation. To this day he is uncomfortable at large family gatherings. He is relatively comfortable with our immediate family—which in our case encompasses our parents, siblings, aunts, uncles, and cousins. But for some reason, he can't tolerate our second and third cousins knowing that he is gay. I can't say I really blame him, considering the way I feel when they whisper about me.

My first relationships were with men who treated me like my brother, men who contributed to and perpetuated my reliance on them, and then resented me for being too "needy." I tried to present this kind of relationship briefly in a passage from *When the Parrot Boy Sings*, my second novel, in which the main character, Will, describes his past relationship to his ex-lover, Tony:

> I hated him. I hated the way he made me feel help-
> less, the way
>   he was always saying
>   "Stop putting yourself down," or
>   "Why are you so frightened?" or
>   "I can't do it for you,"
>   when what he really meant was
>   "I've got you right where I want you, right
> under my thumb."

I have two particularly vivid memories which seem relevant here: I was standing in line at a sandwich shop with my first lover, a man who was six years older than me. The dynamic of our relationship was such that he was always trying to "help" me to become more assertive, less frightened of the world outside our relationship. Meanwhile I always felt as if he wanted me to look to him for guidance and advice. He was always telling me what to do with my life—how to dress, what to study in school, how to act in front of other people. And while he seemed to deeply resent my dependence on him, at least part of his attraction to me was rooted in his playing "daddy" to my "little boy"—so much so that he would encourage me to dress in such a way as to play up my youth: he liked me to keep my hair cut short, sport no facial hair, and to wear white jockey shorts.

As we approached the cashier, and it became our turn to order, he asked me what I wanted to eat. "A turkey sub," I said. "Don't tell me, tell him," he shouted at me, motioning to the cashier. The cashier overheard him and laughed at me. I was deeply humiliated. I felt as if I were being tricked by my lover into depending on him, and then publicly shamed once I let myself actually rely on him.

Several years later, Ted and I were waiting in line at a bakery. He asked me what I wanted. "A jelly donut," I told him. He proceeded to tell the cashier for me. I was shocked that Ted had assumed that I wanted him to request the donut for me. At that point in my life, I was no longer afraid of doing things on my own. I realized in that moment how deeply ingrained the pattern of our relationship was.

Ted's discomfort with his being gay is sometimes a point of conflict between the two of us today. I sometimes feel as if I ought to be ashamed of who I am when I am around him. I know that he disapproves of the autobiographical quality of some of my fiction. He believes that certain things ought not to be spoken about in public. And he is sometimes smug about the fact that he can still "pass" as straight if he so desires—something I apparently can no longer do. Yet I know that he is deeply torn about his sexuality and would like to be able to express it in whatever ways he desires.

Our relationship since coming out has in fact improved. It has allowed us to become close in ways we perhaps never were as children. There are things we can share with each other that we would be reluctant to share with the other members of our family. Because I am "out" in a way that he is not, I am a person he can go to when he needs to express something that might meet with disapproval elsewhere. In fact, I am probably the only person in my family he would ever consider talking to about sex or boyfriend problems.

The most persistent point of conflict in our relationship today concerns our respective choices in terms of partners. One of my lovers once insisted that my brother and I together treated him worse than anyone else had ever treated him in his life, and though the statement seems to be an exaggeration considering the limited contact Ted had with this man, it is true that my brother has sometimes treated my boyfriends with contempt and arrogance. I for my part have not always been as gracious as I might be to his lovers. Perhaps on some level neither one of us can control, we perceive other men as a threat to our intimacy.

Ted and I now live hundreds of miles apart. He is currently pursuing his career as an opera singer in Europe. I see him a few times a year and speak to him by telephone at least once a month. I would like my brother and I to love each other in an as yet undefined way. When we speak or are together, he sometimes seems emotionally distant, unless he is in some kind of crisis. Then, he relies on his older brother for advice. I once resented the fact that he only seemed to "need" me when he was in trouble emotionally. But I have come to recognize his behavior as part of a larger family pattern. In my family, we don't know how to love each other unless one of us is unhappy. We never learned how love and happiness might occur together, how it is possible to love someone without being dependent on him.

But as my relationships with men have improved, so has my relationship with Ted. We are for the first time able to talk about some of the difficulties of our own interactions. But this is all very new stuff for both of us. We have both only recently come to re-imagine how we want it to be with men. He is trying to fight the pattern of being with men who depend on him for their happiness and feelings of safety in the world. He has sometimes been trapped in the kind of "you and me against the world" relationship we had as children, a relationship in which we fought desperately to maintain, against our fear of our mother's illness, some semblance of stability in our lives. I am learning to be with men who allow me to have a life separate from their own, men who really want me to be independent and comfortable with the choices I have made.

I can't say specifically when or how Ted and I have managed to come to this tentative truce in our relationship. A number of things seem to have come together recently. On my side, I would point to my own recent willingness, in therapy, to discuss my childhood. Having been forced to do such banal things as draw pictures of my family members and show my therapist photographs of them, my own resistance to discussing some of these things has finally worn down. I have also recently begun work on a third novel, which has helped me to confront some of my unresolved feelings toward my parents in particular. There is also the trauma of turning thirty and the accompanying re-evaluation of one's life to date, as well as a relatively new relationship with a man who has no interest in controlling my life. We have completely different careers (I am an "academic," he is an employment manager for a hospital), separate as well as mutual friends, varying interests (he likes *Pretty Woman*, I like *Jungle Fever*; he tolerates my singing, I drag myself through his aerobics class), and a healthy sense of ourselves as capable and independent adults—we have separate residences, separate bank accounts, and sometimes even separate vacations. While these differences may seem trivial to some, they have allowed me to begin to see that I can exist in relationships that do not mirror the unhealthy patterns I learned as a child.

On Ted's side, I can't really say what has allowed him to change. Perhaps it is the physical distance from my family and the fact that his career has allowed him to define himself in something other than a relationship of opposition to my mother or me. Perhaps we are both just growing up, giving up the childhood antagonisms that seem so petty and trivial today. Perhaps our mutual career successes and our attempts to forge new kinds of relationships with men have made it possible for us to overcome our fears of becoming our parents.

I can't provide a resolution here. I can't tell you that my brother and I have reached some kind of peace in our relationship. For now, there is this "story," a story which helps me to understand why my relationship with Ted has been marked by so much love and pain. The last time I spoke to my brother, he told me that he loved me very much. As soon as he said this, he started to cry. I recognize this behavior. I, too, used to cry whenever I told anyone I loved them. Perhaps we are afraid that love is so ephemeral, so fragile, it will disappear if it is ever spoken. Perhaps we are just overwhelmed with emotion because we have finally spoken what is in our hearts. Perhaps it is both these things at once.

Ted knows that I am writing this piece. It has in certain ways been very difficult for me, and I don't want to show it to him until I feel it is truly finished—if anything is ever finished. Hopefully, this story will provide the conditions of possibility for the telling of a new story, a story where my brother and I come together to imagine a different kind of love than the one we have known. A love less tyrannized by the fear of loss.

michael bronski

the brother, the glasses, the crackers, the turtle

I. Now

It is Saturday morning. I get up at 7:00 a.m., make a quiet cup of tea, and begin to make notes for an essay on what it is like to have a gay brother. Walta, my lover of sixteen years, continues to sleep as I sit at my desk scribbling down ideas and abstracts for my article. At 8:30 I am startled out of my writing by a ringing phone, a call from my brother who wants to know if I am ready to go with him to the local supermarket to do the week's grocery shopping. I throw on my jeans, sweatshirt, and boots, walk the half block and we spend the next forty-five minutes comparing prices on meat, complaining about our parents, and discussing our boyfriends.

This is what I tell people when they ask me what it is like to have a gay brother. It is not enough for an essay.

I am forty-two, my brother Jeffrey is seven years younger. This means that when I was a senior in high school Jeffrey was in fifth grade. When I was going to college, while living at home, Jeffrey was not yet in high school. In 1969, when I was becoming involved with gay liberation, my brother was not yet in high school. Throughout all of those years when I was first beginning to act out on my sexuality—even though I had been aware of my homosexual desires from the relatively early age of eleven—I had little relationship with my brother. Later, after I had left New Jersey to move to Boston and go to graduate school, and my brother began to act out on his sexuality, he had little relationship with me.

We became friends later on in life through his visits to Boston and my seeing him when I visited my parents. I lived in Cambridge with my lover, he lived with his lover, two towns away from my parents. Our family—parents, another brother, Stephen, and a sister, Suzanne—acknowledged our relationships; lovers were invited to dinners and family functions—but no one really spoke about our gay lives.

It was much the same way between my brother and myself. There were no emotional explosions or revelations but also little discussion between us about our gayness or even the earlier life we had spent together in the same house when we really didn't know each other. (My family's emotional life is founded on methodically working through problems without really discussing them and, surprisingly, most issues are eventually dealt with.) I don't know if he had crushes on boys in grammar school or lustful dreams about his high school gym class. We went to the same parochial grammar school and high school, but that seven years' difference was crucial. Gay male porn was nearly unobtainable when I was in high school; seven years later the corner newsstand sold *Mandate* and *Blueboy*. I grew up with *Life* magazine exposing the "gay scene" in San Francisco; he grew up with *Time* chronicling "Gay Power." Although we grew up in the same home, the same family, the same town, our early years were not similar.

Even today our lives are, in many ways, quite different. I am a freelance writer working in the gay and progressive press whose life revolves around queer activism and speaking gigs. Jeffrey is a computer systems programmer who works for Harvard University. We each have our own friendship circles, although there is some overlap. And we have continued to have very separate relationships with our parents.

Thinking about my relationship with my brother I recalled, after some thought, three incidents from our early life together. Each seems, in varying degrees of obscurity, to say something about our own relationship as well as our relationships to the rest of the family.

II. The Glasses

It is 1969, my junior year at college, and I am living at home. I had become something of a hippie, with the requisite long hair and beard, and had become involved in leftist politics and the antiwar movement. None of these things thrilled my parents but their objections were garden-variety generation gap—an inability to accept my growing autonomy rather than to any specific social ideology. Although Stonewall was several months away I was actively homosexual and this was not discussed.

My social circle included politicos, artists, and writers—a concept and level of sophistication for which I had been yearning for years. My friend Marianne had taken an eight-by-ten full-face photoportrait of me of which I was very proud. There was nothing special about it but I felt it made me look, with my horn-rimmed glasses, beard, and cable-knit sweater, like an intellectual. It was the first time that I had ever seen myself represented as an adult, or as a sexual person. I had left the picture prominently displayed in the family living room as a way of establishing myself, and my new identity, amid my family.

One morning at breakfast I glanced at the picture and discovered that someone had defaced the photo by painting over the eyeglasses, and my eyes, with black poster paint. I became furious, rageful. My anger frightened and startled my family; they had no idea what the photo meant to me. I quickly discovered that twelve-year-old Jeffrey had been responsible for the damage and turned my wrath upon him. I was nearly inarticulate with rage and while everyone dismissed the incident as a joke—the paint did wash away easily—I was determined on revenge. That night after everyone had gone to bed I found Jeffrey's glasses on the kitchen table and painted both sides of the lenses with the same black paint. The next morning, when he found them, he was furious and threatened to wake up the next night and cut my long hair while I was asleep. (We shared a bedroom with our other brother and a younger, orphaned cousin who was staying with us.) I scornfully told him that he got what he deserved and the rest of the family declared a truce between us.

Thinking back on this it is clear that Jeffrey was striking out (partially fueled by unspoken signals from my parents) against my newly found personal, political, and sexual independence. Did he, on some level, understand that I was gay and feel threatened by that? Did he realize that *he* was gay and feel obliged to protect himself from guilt by association? It is interesting that we both chose symbolic castration—the removal of the eyes—to attack each other, and that he countered my attack by threatening tonsorial demasculinization. Or was this just a standard sibling squabble centered on petty mischief followed by petty revenge?

III. The Crackers

My second memory of growing up with Jeffrey takes place five years before the incident of the glasses. Jeffrey was seven and I was fourteen. It was early evening and Jeffrey and my sister, who is a year older than he, had just been put to bed. My parents were in the living room reading the papers, my other brother and I were with them, doing homework. In the midst of a quiet moment Jeffrey called from the bedroom: "I'm hungry. Can I have some crackers?"

"No," my mother responded, "it's time for you to go to sleep and you know that you aren't supposed to eat in bed."

There were a few moments of silence and suddenly Jeffrey spoke again.

"Daddy."

"What is it?" my father responded wearily.

"I'm hungry. Can I have some crackers?"

"Your mother said no."

"Daddy?"

"What?"

"Can you sneak them up?"

There was a moment of silence and everyone began laughing. Everyone except my mother.

"This always happens," she stormed. "They think they can get around what I say by turning to you."

I don't remember what was said next. Certainly Jeffrey did not get his crackers. My brother and I stifled our laughter and my mother's not unreasonable pique subsided and the episode was dismissed.

Although the memory of this always makes me smile I wonder now what it meant to Jeffrey. Did he feel a rejection by both my parents? Was my father's refusal to bring him the desired crackers a sharper pain? Why didn't he think to ask one of his two older brothers to sneak him the crackers? Did his turning to my father, which by its public nature negated my mother's presence, indicate some preference or desire to turn to men?

And how did I perceive all this? My father would have let us eat crackers in bed (since he did not have to worry about the resulting laundry) but did not interfere with my mother's decision. Did this teach me that I should not trust men? Did I learn from the difficult position in which my mother found herself that women are often scapegoated for making logical, necessary choices in their lives? How did I view my brother who, through his humorous naïveté, exposed an already existing tension between my parents? Why do I remember this evening so well and not the thousands of others that we spent together?

IV. The Turtle

The earliest memory of my brother is from four years earlier. It is our first house—a too-small Cape Cod bungalow in a working-class development—and it is summer. We have a small yard that is defined by tacky split-rail fences on either side and a high cyclone wire fence that separates us from the Western Union factory on the other side. After several years of living in a cramped apartment in Astoria, Queens, or with my grandparents, this house and its small, green yard seems like paradise. I am ten years old, my brother Stephen is nine, my sister Suzanne is four, and Jeffrey is three.

It is a hot summer day and Jeffrey comes in from the backyard in uncontrollable tears. We gather around him as he tells us, through sobs, that, several hours ago, he took our pet turtle—a small, five-and-dime store creature who lived in a shallow basin on the kitchen counter—out for a walk in the backyard "because he looked lonely." Now he was missing. We all rushed out to the yard and looked for the errant reptile but he was nowhere to be found. Jeffrey's tears continued and although no one else was terribly upset about the loss—he was a circumstantial pet, won at a church bazaar and unremarkable except for the fact that my mother claimed he sometimes made small noises when she fed him—it clearly was emotionally devastating for him.

Jeffrey cried most of that afternoon. His tears stopped for a glass of Kool-Aid and later a Good Humor popsicle—treats that were usually only brought out for emotional emergencies—and we other children eventually became tired of attempting to comfort him and continued our own games and pastimes. The tears continued sporadically through dinner and Jeffrey went to bed looking as though the world was soon coming to an end. Although the turtle was not mentioned the next day (no one would dare mention him for fear of setting off another deluge of tears), Jeffrey's grief was apparent for several more days. Eventually he overcame his loss and life, of course, went on as usual.

Thinking about this now—thirty-two years after the fact—I am amazed at the amount of grief Jeffrey's three-year-old existence could contain. What could that turtle have meant to him that its disappearance could be so cataclysmic, so emotionally wrought? Was this a reflection of some undercurrent, some extraordinary tension in our family, that made Jeffrey himself feel on the verge of abandonment? He claims today not to have any memory of the afternoon. He was, after all, three years old but can such a feeling ever be really forgotten? From what I generally remember as a happy collec-

tive childhood this afternoon stands out as a mystery. Did we see
his reactions as babyish and dismiss them as immature? Could we,
should we, have done more to comfort him? How? I think of Jeffrey's
profound grief and see it around me today as friends die and as more
and more become ill. I understand grief today better than three-plus
decades ago, but I still don't know what to do, how to overcome it
in myself or in others.

V. Home and Not Home

As I write this piece I am deeply curious about why these three
moments in time are my main memories of my early life with my
brother. I am too much of a Freudian to think that they are only
random bits of brain cells that have escaped being burned out by
acid or pushed out of place by movie trivia. Yet I am somewhat
unwilling to ascribe them too much importance, too much regard.
Do they have a deeper significance or are they only loosely, randomly
connected to my relationship with Jeffrey?

When I first mentioned to friends, a decade ago, that my
brother was gay, almost everyone had the same response: "That's
wonderful. It must have made it so easy for him, with an older gay
brother, to come out." But I don't think that that was the case.

In a very profound way I think that my public exploration of
my newfound identities in college—political activist, hippie, gay
liberationist—and my parents' reaction to them set up a danger zone
for my younger siblings. If Stephen and I were the "bad" children,
my sister Suzanne and brother Jeffrey had to be the "good" children.
Having an older gay brother gave Jeffrey not so much a role model
but an example of how not to please his parents.

On some level this, I suspect, is what caused the tensions that
resulted in his painting over my photograph and even informed my
revenge for the act. My declaration of my homosexuality—which
took various forms, some covert, some less so—in Jeffrey's young
years was probably not a guiding light for him but a symbol of
family disruption. If he was discovering his own homosexual feelings
at this time (it is more than possible—he was twelve years old; I

consciously knew my own sexual orientation at an even younger age)
he may have felt that my blatant behaviors would eventually lead
to the discovery of his own secrets.

From the age of ten or so I had a desire to leave my parents'
house and strike out on my own. In my fantasies this meant moving
to New York City—which was only forty-five minutes away from
us—and living in Greenwich Village. I wanted to do this even before
I knew that there was very good reason for me to move to Greenwich
Village. Once I discovered, at the age of fourteen, that the Village
was both the metaphoric and actual center of a gay male community
I was even more determined to find my own community, my own
home, and move there. The emergence of gay liberation in 1969
allowed me to broaden my vision and see in other cities—such as
Boston, where I did end up living—the potential for security and
pleasure that I once saw only in the Village. After I moved away I
made it very clear that there was a separation between myself and
my family. I hardly ever went home for the major family holidays,
preferring to find and build my own gay family.

This desire for flight from my roots seems to be in direct
contradiction to Jeffrey's life. Even after he came out and was living
with his lover he remained closely connected to our parents. Not
only did they live a few miles away but he and his lover had weekly
dinners with our parents and helped out with lawn work and other
household chores. This would have been a nightmare for me; I
sometimes feel suffocated (mostly by memories, not my parents) even
on short visits to the home where I grew up. But as I was writing
this piece I began to wonder how much of my brother's actions were
a direct reaction to my emphatic flight from my family. Did he, on
some level, feel that I had also left him when I moved? Did he need
a sense of biological family more than I did—I can't help but think
of the missing turtle and the terrible grief that Jeffrey felt at the
time—or were we just two separate people with differing needs,
differing expectations?

Clearly both Jeffrey and I had different relationships with our
family. It is difficult to say why. Was it the difference in our
position in the family? The fact that I came to adulthood during
the height of the 1960s and felt more of a social demand, and

permission, to rebel? The fact that my parents were, perhaps, more comfortable *as* parents by the time that Jeffrey was born? I think of Jeffrey calling out for my father to bring him crackers in bed and wonder how much more complicated life must have been in a family of six than in a family of three, four, or five. How much more difficult to maneuver the emotional pitfalls and hidden agendas in the scary process of growing up.

I don't know why we have had such different lives, such different reactions in dealing with our family. In the long run it doesn't matter very much. In the short run it is all speculation.

VI. Men in Love

Lesbian writer-theorist Jill Johnston tells a wonderful story that appeared in one of her *Village Voice* columns almost twenty years ago. She is having one of her usual fights with her mother about her open lesbianism when suddenly her mother says: "Well, if you love women, why don't you love me?" Johnston admits, probably for the first time in her life, that she has no answer.

I have often thought of Johnston's predicament and felt that it applies also to gay men. If we do love men, why so often do we have such hard times loving our fathers and our brothers? Regardless of the object choice, all people learn how to love by first loving members of their own family. If we, as gay men, love men, we have also learned this—as infants, toddlers, children—from loving our fathers and our brothers.

To a large degree I have not given a great deal of thought to having a gay brother. Since he moved to Boston several years ago we have become much closer, but it is a closeness based on our everyday lives, not on political or emotional analysis. We share errands and a car, we go to the movies and theater; frequently we have dinner together. In many ways it is the way that a traditional family spends time together—perhaps we are now going through the daily rituals, the weekly routines that we never had in our parents' home because the difference between age twelve and age nineteen is much greater than the distance between age thirty-five and age forty-two.

As I get older and my relationships with my family change—and as I get more distance from the maelstrom of growing up in the nuclear family—I can see more and more how my interactions with my father and my brother Stephen have influenced my adult relationships with other men. I can see similar patterns in my emotional responses and my emotional needs. But this seems to have very little to do with my brother Jeffrey. Although I am grateful we have an adult relationship and friendship now, our early life together feels distant, vague. I understand that siblings have all manner of complicated relationships—love, envy, support, jealousy—and I am sure that our separate awareness of our gayness played a part in our perceptions and feelings of each other. But on some level it feels almost irrelevant to our relationship now.

And yet I am faced with the question of those three recollections—the glasses, the crackers, the turtle. Perhaps there are real, concrete, if psychological, reasons why those are my primary memories of my brother. Or maybe my writer's mind is just attuned to the striking, if useless, detail. But they remain as much of a mystery as how families function or why two adults—who happen to be brothers, and gay—are friends.

a r n i e
k a n t r o w i t z

---

uncle sam

As far as anyone knows, I am the only gay person in my entire family, which includes, aside from my parents and grandparents, ten aunts and uncles and their spouses, and seventeen first cousins. But although no one could ever ask him about it directly, I may have one predecessor: my Uncle Sam, a dear and gentle man who probably locked his sexual orientation away in some Pandora's box many decades ago.

That was one reason why, in June of 1989, my lover Larry Mass and I made a pilgrimage from our Manhattan apartment to northern New Jersey, where Uncle Sam's eightieth birthday was going to be celebrated in a restaurant near the nursing home that is his current address. The closer we got to the restaurant, the edgier I felt. My coming out of the closet had dropped a bombshell at a family gathering nearly twenty years earlier, and the only time we had all reunited without visible strain since then was at my father's funeral in 1986, a time when no one felt like discussing sexual identities—except for Larry's mother, who had cheerfully asked another uncle if he thought Sam was gay like me and had received only widened eyes and a dropped jaw as a reply. I wasn't concerned about seeing Uncle Sam for the first time in several years. We had long since made our peace with each other. But in order to pay my respects to him, I would have to deal with relatives with whom I had not been on good terms for a very long time.

As we rode through the suburban towns that dot the mountains of New Jersey, I tried to remember how things used to be long before the family schism, when I was an innocent little boy, frightened because I knew I was somehow different, and Uncle Sam was in his prime, part of the world of adults whose approval I yearned for. He lived with my father's parents in a two-and-a-half-family house my grandfather had built on Leo Place in the Clinton Hill section of Newark. My parents had lived in the cramped top-floor apartment when I was born, but they had soon moved to a similarly cramped apartment a ten-minute drive away because my mother had needed to break free from the cloying ties that bound my father's family together. In spite of my mother's feelings, I was as bound to that house as any of the others. My mother's relatives lived far away in southern New Jersey, so my father's family were my kin. They were the people I looked like, and theirs was the home where I belonged.

A visit to Leo Place was always an event for me. I loved to watch my grandmother prepare her cholesterol-laden offerings of salami and eggs fried in chicken fat, which she offered each member of our overweight family as a greeting at the door: "You want something to eat? A pfahnkuchen maybe?" I loved to listen to the stories of my grandfather, who ruled as a benevolent patriarch, wisely judging and tolerantly accepting his children's foibles. I loved the dreams spun in a rich baritone at the kitchen table by my father's brother Albert, who had a genuine talent for show business, which he had set aside to raise his children in the suburbs—but not too far away to prevent several visits a week. And I loved my father's sister Dorothy, a timid and sentimental, yet staunch, woman who lived several blocks away from her parents with her husband and their daughter, Adrienne, who was my favorite playmate.

Uncle Sam, however, held a special place in my heart. He was a soft-spoken, sweet man with a cherubic face, and behind his eyeglasses there was a compassionate look in his warm eyes. Although his features were similar to the rest of the family's, his interests were different from those of the others. He was the only bachelor among them, a scholar, whose bedroom, located right next to his parents' room, was filled with books, piled pell-mell into their bookcases and overflowing into piles stacked on the floor—much the way my own study looks today. Otherwise, I am very tidy, but his room always looked like a tornado had just paid a visit, with bedding and clothing chaotically shrouding all the furniture and doorknobs, and every available surface filled with sheaves of musical scores and resin for his violin bow, fountain pens and pencil stubs, loose change and crumpled bills, tubes and bottles of minor medications and toiletries, collar stays and cufflinks, neckties and bowties, elastic suspenders and lots of white handkerchiefs, both crumpled and neatly pressed, and, of course, more books. Amid hurriedly abandoned shoes, his violin, carefully placed in its open case, usually lay on the floor, next to a folding metal music stand on which stood the sheet music for whatever he had practiced last.

In spite of all the havoc in his room, Uncle Sam was the neatest-looking, most carefully groomed man I had ever seen. He always wore starched white shirts and never left the house without a jacket and tie. He spent hours in the steamy, white-tiled bathroom that always smelled of soap. Its floor was usually covered with newspapers because it had just been washed. Sam stood at the sink, endlessly trimming his moustache to perfection, shaving and reshaving and scrubbing his skin until it was pink. My grandmother, who did the family's wash at a scrub board in the basement sink, confided in me with a hint of exasperation that he changed his white boxer undershorts and athletic undershirts several times a day.

Sam's fastidiousness extended beyond the bathroom to the kitchen, which was the heart of the household. His scrupulous cleanliness was legendary, the butt of many a family joke. He was the only person we knew who washed bananas before peeling them, and he had once been found scrubbing a lemon with Brillo and soap before inserting a slice of it into his glass of tea. When Albert carelessly dipped his used spoon into the mayonnaise jar, Sam, just as casually, capped the jar and threw it in the garbage, a gesture that could not go unnoticed since the garbage bag sat prominently on an unused kitchen chair against the white-tiled wall. Germs and illness were anathema to him, and the entire family was often sent on a search for the slightly open window that he thought might be the source of a dreaded draft he imagined he had felt.

If one were looking for Uncle Sam, the first place would be at his post in front of the open refrigerator door, where he spent enough time to gladden the electric company's heart, pondering the possibility of a new "taste thrill." Whatever he produced to share with anyone else had to be preceded by a long lecture on the special qualities of the item: its rarity or uniqueness and its exquisite deliciousness, a ritual intended to engender premature salivation and undying appreciation, even if he were discussing a simple tomato. "Do you know where this comes from?" he would ask, and without waiting for an answer he would continue, "I had to go to a greengrocer in New York that only a few people know about because it's on a very small street. He has them imported especially for his shop from Italy." (Or it might be from Mexico, or, if we were particularly honored, Israel). "Just look at how red it is. Touch it, but don't bruise it. Smell that aroma. Now that's a tomato! You can't find tomatoes like that around here." (New Jersey, "the Garden State," produces the best beefsteak tomatoes I have ever eaten, but New Jersey was not exotic enough for Uncle Sam.) "Do you know who used to eat tomatoes like this? The medieval popes." (Or Emperor Maximilian, or, if it was particularly luscious-looking, King Solomon.) Then he would slice it ceremoniously, with the precision of a *moyel* circumcising a Jewish infant, sprinkle it with a large helping of coarse kosher salt (that would be considered lethal today) from the bowl kept on the table, and present it with a flourish. Finally, he would wait for the verdict.

No one would have dreamed of disappointing him. Everyone hurried to agree that his introductory comments had not been exaggerated, that indeed this was a rare treat, the tomato of tomatoes, a gift from Mother Earth that equaled the ambrosia enjoyed by the Olympian gods. How had he been lucky and clever enough to find it? Wouldn't he draw a map to the store? Were there any others like it? He would sit by, smiling benignly at the pleasure he had wrought, until the tomato—or bread, or chicken, or soda—was entirely consumed.

As the years went on, his spiritual values were applied to his diet, and he abandoned meat because he did not want to ingest the cow's karma to add to his own future reincarnations; then he left vegetarianism for fruitarianism because he felt it was sinful to kill an entire plant for his nourishment, and a diet of fruit could be obtained without killing any vegetation. Unfortunately, it also wreaked havoc with the digestive system, so he eventually returned to a more balanced diet, but always with a sad appreciation of the fact that he gained his nutrition at the expense of other life forms. As you can see, a tomato was never merely a tomato for him: it was a child of God. In short, for Uncle Sam eating was a religious experience. Religion was Uncle Sam's greatest involvement. Most of the books that cluttered his room were about various forms of spirituality, both traditional and esoteric. As he read about each one, he absorbed its principles and points of view so thoroughly that he, in effect, converted, but never with formal ceremonies, only with his enthusiasm. He would read about Zoroastrianism and explain to everyone the glorious light of Ahura Mazda. Or he would study Quakerism and be found sitting quietly, listening to his "Inner Voice." He was persuaded by Baha'is and Buddhists, by Hindus and Holy Rollers, by saints and Sufis. When he studied Islam, he told me, "My heart is in the desert," and when he returned to Judaism, he whispered that he had the key to the Kabbalah. Mysticism of any form was his meat, and he had some difficulty keeping his feet on the ground. He expounded on his discoveries at great length to the other members of the family, but their concerns were in the concrete world, and they rarely bothered to mask their impatience with his endless discourses.

When I was a teenager, Uncle Sam confided in me that he had had a mystical experience. "I was lying on the living room couch," he explained, "not quite awake, but definitely not asleep, when suddenly I felt my consciousness detach from my body and float upward to the ceiling. I looked down to see my body still lying on the couch, while my awareness was encased in a shimmeringly translucent blue replica of my form, attached to the body of the couch by a silver umbilical cord that stretched from navel to navel." I was completely mystified by what he told me, but he went on to say that after his experience he had read about the phenomenon called "astral projection" (out-of-body experience) in Madame Helena Blavatsky's *Isis Unveiled* and that the school of mysticism she had founded, called Theosophy, was the true spiritual path.

The true path of the month, I thought to myself, but I was nonetheless fascinated and went to the library to find out about astral projection. I looked into works by Madame Blavatsky and her follower Annie Besant, and, inspired to continue the quest for the secrets of existence, I also read *The Ocean of Theosophy* by William Q. Judge and Gurdjieff's *Meetings with Remarkable Men* and Ouspensky's *Tertium Organum* and Bucke's *Cosmic Consciousness* and others, so that eventually, when I was in graduate school, I was able to apply my learning to a paper about the relationship of images of astral projection to sexuality in Walt Whitman's poetry, which my contemptuous professor awarded a grudging "B + ." But I was undaunted. In later years, I went on to have my own mystical experiences. Some of them were natural, like the glowing vision of cosmic unity called satori, and some of them, like hearing a reassuring heavenly voice at a lakeside in England, occurred with a slight assist from LSD, but thanks to Uncle Sam I was not unfamiliar with the territory I had entered. I even tried being a vegetarian for a year and a half, until my enthusiasm for ratatouille began to wane.

I tried to explain my excitement to Sam, but his interests were already elsewhere, and he seemed unimpressed. I tried to tell him that I thought I was my generation's version of him, but he was suspicious of my admiration of Walt Whitman, whose mystical homoerotic poetry had been denounced as coarse when he was in school, and he didn't seem to understand the link between us. Perhaps it was because he was so used to being barely tolerated by his bemused siblings that he had long since stopped expecting anyone to really understand or believe in his adventures of the soul. He knew I was bright. He always repeated the story of my six-year-old's response to his inquiry about my sore thumb: "The pain has abated somewhat, thank you." But he couldn't get past the notion that he was ultimately alone—one of a kind—because he was different.

Before I grew up and visited seven or eight countries, Sam was the only member of the family to have traveled abroad (excluding my grandparents' long immigration voyage from Eastern Europe). A wood-framed oval tray made of blue and yellow butterflies' wings, arranged under glass into pictures of Rio de Janeiro, hung on the wall among the massive Victorian furnishings of the dining room, a testament to the journey he had made as a member of the band on a cruise ship. He played his violin in a musical group at bar mitzvahs and weddings, but the work was only part-time and didn't provide much of a living. He had begun medical school, but had decided not to finish. Later on, he attempted to sell Bibles for a while, but that didn't work either. (Perhaps that was the reason he was the only person I ever heard of who actually invited the door-to-door Jehovah's Witnesses missionaries in for a chat—or maybe it was simply his yearning for spiritual conversation.) There was also a half-hearted attempt to sell real estate, but that, too, proved fruitless. Basically, he was not much of a wage earner, and for most of his life he depended on his parents for sustenance, as they depended on him for care in their later years.

In the mid-1960s, I returned to Leo Place to live. I had been teaching at a college in Upstate New York and had started to come apart at the seams. Deeply closeted, I had confined my sexual adventures to combing my hair in the men's room near the gym (whose mirror reflected the open door of the men's locker room and the unclad hunks who occasionally hurried past it) and a great deal of compulsive masturbation to the accompaniment of daringly bought physique magazines that I hid at the back of my living room closet, in a box covered with loose bricks. My attempted affair with a woman in the English department had brought things to a head. I had finally confessed to her that I was gay, and then slashed my wrists. Eventually, my father agreed to take me in. My parents had been divorced, and he had returned to live with his sister Dorothy on the top floor of the house on Leo Place, where he had lived when I was born. On the first floor, my grandfather, now a widower, was dying of bone cancer, and Uncle Sam was looking after him. He was a devoted and loving nurse, long-suffering and compassionate, as good an attendant as anyone could hope for.

He would occasionally disappear for the day on one of his mysterious trips to New York, and he would return triumphantly with grease-stained brown paper bags, from the glatt kosher Hassidic shops of Williamsburg in Brooklyn, containing exotic pastries and Eastern European culinary concoctions that would have been beyond even my grandmother's expert range. I wondered in later years if he had conducted a sex life during any of those excursions, but of course no word was ever said about the subject. As far as anyone knew, when he was quite young, his heart had been broken by a mysterious woman he had been in love with, who had chosen to marry another man. And that was all that was ever said about Sam's sexuality, except for one conversation I remember in which several family members speculated about what he did for sex—whether he was totally asexual or whether he might be secretly homosexual—but the subject was put away immediately because no one had a single clue to go on, and on one ever dared ask him directly about what was clearly a forbidden topic.

After my grandfather died, Sam got a clerk's job in Newark's city hall. The house on Leo Place was sold, and he, my Aunt Dorothy, and my father all moved to separate apartments. I moved to New York, where I led an active but furtive sex life, cruising the tearooms and the postmidnight streets of Greenwich Village. During the day, my own sexual identity was as suppressed as Uncle Sam's, and not even my closest heterosexual friends knew about my other life. With the exception of my parents, who knew why I had attempted suicide, the rest of the family knew me only as a cousin, a nephew, a teacher, and a Jew.

I remember one lovely afternoon when Uncle Sam and Aunt Dottie came to New York, and we all went to the Lower East Side, where we stuffed ourselves with the kind of heavy food my grandmother used to make and went to a matinee at a Yiddish theater on Second Avenue. The movie was an old-fashioned tearjerker about an old couple separated by their unfeeling children, and the stage show, replete with acrobats, songs, skits, and comedians, was entirely in Yiddish, but it was the audience we enjoyed the most. We laughed for years afterward about their graceless old-world manners, their loud demands made in the cranky style permitted only to older people, their conversations yelled across the aisles, oblivious of the show they had paid to see. Accustomed as we were to soft-pedaling our Jewishness in public, it was an image that seemed embarrassing to our assimilated eyes, and we were as foolishly uncomfortable as many gay preppies are when confronted with a loud drag queen on the streets.

When I was twenty-nine years old, after years of anguish and a second suicide attempt, I suddenly came out of my closet. I decided to join the Gay Activists Alliance early in 1970. Within months, I was its vice president, angry at the long years of silence and lies that had been forced on me, and eager to tell everyone I was gay: my employer, my students, newspaper reporters, politicians, police, the salesman who sold me a piano, strangers I met on a bus, and finally my family. It was at the Passover seder in 1971 that I decided to take the plunge. My grandparents had already died, and I had already told my parents and my brother. Now it was everyone else's turn.

Passover was the one time of year the whole family still gathered. While my grandfather was alive, everyone had sat in respectful silence at the table, the men all wearing traditional skullcaps, while he read through the entire Passover Haggadah in Hebrew, not allowing anyone to begin eating until he had finished. Once he was gone, the solemnity had given way to playfulness. We read only portions of the book—in English—and the traditional yarmulkes were exchanged for an assortment of chapeaux, ranging from Davy Crockett coonskin caps to bright red firemen's hats, so I felt free to express my secularism by going bareheaded. The laughter was as bountiful as the food, and gales of hilarity pursued each other up and down the long table, as the joy of being a family clearly took precedence over religious ritual. When the meal was done, Uncle Al and Aunt Dottie would take turns at the piano, accompanying Uncle Sam at his violin, as we all sang our favorite Yiddish folk songs. Sam's fingers were especially nimble on those nights as he raced with agility through the complex strains of "Hora Staccata" or "Romania" and made his violin wail with the age-old Jewish sorrows expressed in "My Yiddishe Mama" or "Mein Shtettele Beltz" ("My Hometown Beltz") or brought a nostalgic tear to our eyes with my grandmother's favorite song, "Shayn Vie Die Lavunnah" ("As Pretty as the Moon").

Not wanting to interrupt the festivities, I quietly took each member of the family aside and explained that I was gay, that I had always been gay, but that now I was glad about it and had become a political activist, so I might have to speak out publicly and I didn't want them to learn about me in some impersonal way. I told them that I loved them as I always had, and I was sure that they still loved me, since I was still the same person I had always been. Everyone seemed to take it quite well. At least no one said anything negative, and it wasn't until the next year that the cracks began to show, when one of my aunts called up to insist that I show respect by wearing a yarmulke at the table. "Everyone else wears silly hats. What you really mean is that I should keep quiet about being gay, don't you?" I responded, and we launched into an hourlong yelling match that left us both exhausted.

The following year, the whole thing exploded in my face. Shortly before Passover, along with two other gay activists, I was on *The Jack Paar Show*, the predecessor to *The Johnny Carson Show*, explaining to the late-night audience why we found Paar's antihomosexual jokes offensive. He had been saying things like, "If your child's tooth comes out, tell him to put it under the pillow, and a member of the Gay Activists Alliance will come and leave a quarter there."

I had my head shaved in those days, but in deference to public relations, I removed my earring and my rose-colored glasses for the evening. Nonetheless, Paar seemed intimidated by us. "Shouldn't I be offended when a writer like Jean Genet talks about having sex with a goat?" he asked defensively.

"If anyone should be offended, it's the goat!" I answered, and the audience seemed to be on my side. In despair, Paar offered us the microphone to say whatever we wanted. I took my opportunity and said to America, "Some of you are sitting next to your own children or brothers or sisters who are gay and afraid to tell you, because they're afraid you won't love them anymore. You may be loving their lies. Why not give them a chance to be themselves?"

I was pleased with my performance, but I soon learned that my family was not as thrilled as I was.

My cousin called to tell me that the family had met after seeing me on television and had decided that it would be a good idea for me not to come to the seder.

"But why?" I asked, naive enough to be genuinely amazed.

"They said you were shaming our good name. Uncle Sam said that as far as the family was concerned, you were dead."

"Tell them that it's my name too," I said. "Good-bye."

The next day, I was walking on Christopher Street when a gay stranger came up to me and said, "How could you go on national television to represent us all looking so weird with your shaved head? You've probably set us back five years!"

"Fine," I said. "Next time, you can represent us on TV, and you can pay the price!"

A few days later, Uncle Sam called the gay commune in the SoHo section of Manhattan, where I then lived with my current boyfriend, and asked if he could come to visit me!

The morning of his visit, remembering his penchant for cleanliness, I scrubbed the kitchen floor. He rang the bell exactly on time. I opened the door to find him much smaller and frailer than I had remembered. He was getting old. Although he had initiated a Russian-style kiss on the cheek between the male members of the family years earlier, I was self-conscious because it was my custom to kiss my gay male friends in public as a political statement, so we ended up shaking hands and embracing awkwardly.

I showed him around the house, trying to make its gay identity manifest: "This is where my lover and I sleep," but I could have had sex right in front of him and he wouldn't have noticed. He kept changing the subject to food, reminiscing about my grandmother's chicken soup and chopped liver.

"Do you want to go to lunch?" he finally asked. We went to a nearby restaurant, which I had always thought of as a straight place since there were so many gay hangouts in nearby Greenwich Village, but to Uncle Sam it was a gentile establishment: "I notice they serve ham here. Maybe I'll just have the eggs." When they arrived, he said, "These eggs are delicious. I bet the chef got them someplace special. Do you know who used to eat eggs cooked this perfectly? Only the royal families . . ."

Eventually, with nervousness, he raised the subject he had come to discuss. "Ah . . . about your, er, difficulty."

"What difficulty, Uncle Sam?" I was in no mood to make things any easier for him.

"Well, I read of a young man who had an operation, and now they say he's very happy, or rather she's very happy as a woman."

"You mean you think I should have a sex change? What for?"

"Er . . . ah . . . this, uh, deformity of yours." He saw my brow knitting angrily. "Uh . . . maybe you don't call it that. You have to understand: I was raised to see things a different way."

"So was I," I said. "But I've changed. I like being just what I am: a gay man."

"Well maybe some hormone shots?" he suggested limply. I knew he was trying to be helpful.

"Uncle Sam, what needs changing is your lack of information. I'm not a thalidomide baby, you know, only a homosexual."

"You have to understand," he replied, "I'm just not used to talking about this." Then he leaned toward me and whispered, "Tell me, what can two women do with each other in bed?"

"I've never seen two women in bed, Uncle Sam. You'll have to ask them."

He changed the subject. "How come you wear those red glasses? Isn't it bad for your eyes? And what did you do to your hair?"

I changed it right back. "About the seder . . ."

"It wasn't the way it used to be. They invited some business friends. . . ."

"And if I talked about being gay, it would have made a bad impression?"

"They wanted me to entertain them on the fiddle, but I couldn't."

"But if that's all it was, why did you declare me dead?"

"Everybody got me all excited. I didn't even see the show!"

"I never wanted to split the family apart," I said, looking down at the table. "I only wanted to do some good for a lot of unhappy

people." Then, hearing a strange sound, I looked up. Uncle Sam
was crying! I handed him a tissue.

"The family has to stay together, no matter what," he said.
"Next year I'll make the seder. . . ."

I'm sure he meant it when he said it, but it never happened.
It wasn't until afterward that I realized I had been so intent on
discussing my position in the family that I had missed the only
opportunity I was ever likely to have to ask him about his own
sexuality. But his ignorance itself had told me a great deal about
how limited it must have been, whatever direction it took.

The next time I remember talking to Uncle Sam privately was
when Aunt Dottie died. I called him up, and we wept together
on the phone. At her funeral, I had only the most perfunctory
communication with the others, except for her daughter Adrienne,
who was always my friend.

Half a decade later, when my father became an invalid, Sam
retired and moved to an apartment building for older people at the
Jersey shore, so he could be near enough to help his brother. There
he was very popular with the aging widows of blue-collar workers,
who loved to listen to his lengthy discourses on food and music and
religion, awed by his learning and his ingratiatingly gentle manners.
Glad to have someone to cook for, they brought him plates of their
homemade food, and of course he knew just how to impress them
with his appreciation of their culinary skills. I visited him there and
found things changed. His apartment seemed spartan compared to
all the clutter I remembered. But while there was little furniture,
the center of the living room floor was dominated by a huge pile of
books, pamphlets, and magazines, all with their open pages facing
down, as if abandoned in midreading during a frantic search for the
ultimate truth. It looked like someone was about to put a match to
it. Sam had lost his jovial potbelly, and although he still wore a
shirt and tie, he no longer looked quite as neat in his ill-fitting polyes-
ter clothes. He looked like a pilgrim nearing the end of his quest.

Around that time, I was invited to a cousin's wedding, but I
declined, feeling that if I wasn't good enough for a seder, then I
wasn't good enough for a wedding. I began to go to seders at my
gay friends' homes, and I even attended the gay synagogue, Beth

Simchat Torah, for a while, but although I kept my ethnic identity, except for Adrienne, who kept me abreast of the news, my family roots seemed severed.

It was my brother who had arranged Uncle Sam's eightieth birthday party, and when he asked if I wanted to come, out of respect, I said yes. Sam hadn't been well for some time. Vascular disease had made it impossible for him to walk more than a few steps. His arthritic fingers could no longer play the violin. He was usually depressed, with little appetite and less desire to talk, a totally different person from his younger self. He probably didn't have long to go, and I wanted to see him before it was too late.

When we finally arrived at the restaurant, I learned that my trepidation had been in vain. I mingled with my relatives as if the intervening years hadn't happened, and knowing how our family was shrinking, we were genuinely glad to see one another. Our faces were all aglow when Sam was helped in, and when we all yelled, "Surprise!" and presented him with an engraved watch, he wept to see us all together in his honor.

At eighty-two, Uncle Sam is still going back and forth between the nursing home and the hospital. I have visited him in both places, and the prognosis isn't very good, but the family has survived. Following his birthday party, I was invited for the first time to the homes of my cousins, and finally, this year, I was invited back to the Passover seder for the first time in ages. I sat proudly with Larry, and tears sprang to my eyes when Uncle Al raised a glass to the people who could not be there: my father and Aunt Dottie and Uncle Sam. With Uncle Sam's absence, Uncle Al and I have discovered a new closeness, when he sits at the piano and plays the Yiddish tunes of the past—a trio of one—and I sit nearby, enthralled by a nostalgia that we share in a special way.

But there is something else that haunts me, something that I can't easily share with the others. What was Uncle Sam's internal life really like? Was he a heterosexual with experiences no one in the family knew about? Or did he actually abstain from sex following an early disappointment in love? Was he a covertly gay man who was raised when all sex was a secret and the last thing one could discuss was a variation on the theme, perhaps something so repressed that he himself never even knew it because he was one of those uncountable loners who never made that lucky contact with the secret gay world? Or was he a totally spiritual person who simply had no interest in physical matters?

My studies of Walt Whitman have showed me that America's great homosexual poet was a combination of homoeroticism and mysticism, as I know I myself am, and yet Whitman was called an asexual ascetic or forced to wear a heterosexual mask for decades before gay scholars revealed the truth about him. Perhaps Uncle Sam's life is the same. Perhaps he channeled his unacceptable sexual feelings into spirituality and scholarship, and the aesthetics of music and food. He would not be the only gay man to have done so. As many similarities as there are between us, there is one essential difference. I know who I am, and I'm glad enough of it to proclaim it. Maybe he secretly knows who he is, too, but I'll probably never find out. Part of me will always wonder: Who is my Uncle Sam?

andrew holleran

my uncle, sitting beneath the tree

It's a warm May afternoon in north Florida: the still, sullen morning heat has given way to a slight breeze off the lake, and the sun is dimmed by the recent arrival of the big clouds that will, in three or four hours, give us our daily thunderstorm. But it's still a warm day.

My uncle is traveling south and has stopped for the weekend before continuing on. The one thing I dislike doing in the yard is mowing the lawn—there is no way to make it interesting—and my uncle has done me a favor by doing it for me. He always does something when he stops by: rakes leaves, fixes a smoke alarm (whose constant beeping I thought was a frog caught indoors), mows the lawn. He has worked all his life, and though he is now retired he still seeks out projects and tasks. After mowing the lawn this morning, he checked the oil in the car, got rid of a wasp nest, came in, took a shower, and went back out to sit under the water oak by the lake and read. I went to look out the window and saw him there, in his khakis, white T-shirt, and sandals, silhouetted against the smooth blue water. Though he's now in his sixties, and the hair at his temples is silver, he seems to me still—seated by the lake—the young man who served as an officer in the army in World War II and Korea, reading a paper on the grounds of some military base. He has that air of cleanliness, order, regularity, and discipline we associate with the military.

My uncle never married. After the war, he went to work for the phone company in Washington and worked for it till he retired just a few years ago. He has led, however, a life in the world, working with men who are mostly married, obtaining everything men are supposed to obtain in this society, save a family of his own. The family that produced him he has always remained close to; he lived with a sister and her husband for years after their children had grown and gone off on their own. Now, retired, he is living alone on the Gulf of Mexico. But he still makes a point to telephone every month, takes a trip with a brother each summer to visit the widow of another brother, and visits us. He watches his blood pressure, he does his own taxes. He has opinions, but is never strident or argumentative, he is amiable, intelligent, a man of good manners, yet not officious or insincere. Careful to keep his independence intact, he never stays long. He is also fastidious about his appearance and health—and, I have always assumed, since I began to lead a homosexual life, he is homosexual, too, though of a generation that did not act on it so frequently as my own.

On this, however, I may be wrong; just as heterosexuals are often incredulous to learn so-and-so is gay, homosexuals sometimes cannot believe that an unmarried man or woman may have remained single (especially men) for reasons other than an interest in the same sex. I assume that all heterosexual men would rather marry, perhaps because I see marriage as nothing but advantages (tenderness, rootedness, a place in society) rather than the tumultuous, painful accommodation its detractors claim it is. In this sense, my uncle remains a mystery. I, who brood over the fact of being single, who am embarrassed to state the fact on applications, who feel sad when I exit an airplane and see the throngs of wives, and children waiting for their daddies, am proud that my uncle has led a full, productive, interesting, sane, enjoyable life while remaining that thing which all statistics predict will lead to auto accidents, bad health, drinking, and unhappiness: A Single Man. The novel by that name by Christopher Isherwood is superb because it depicts perfectly the loneliness, the need, the drab reality of such a person. But looking at my uncle I cannot associate any of these qualities with him; he sits now under a tree by the lake, freshly showered after having mowed the lawn, reading a newspaper, still somehow an army officer taking a break on the lawn of some base in the Far East: orderly, handsome, neat, and contented, which I surely am not, which makes me wonder—is it the difference between our generations, or our selves?

So much has happened since my uncle grew up—to America itself—that homosexuals of my generation are asking themselves: Was it me, or the times, that led to the behavior that did not cause, but that enabled, a virus to broadcast itself so rapidly among us? Am I, in short, the casualty of an historical mistake: fast-food sex? My uncle traveled, on business, in war, much more than I, but I have no way of knowing whether he traveled in the sexual sense. Most people, Proust wrote, are like houseboats moored in a stream; they never move up or down it. My generation did. I accomplished, in a way, all the traveling I wanted to do—in the sexual and social sense—by staying in the same place: Manhattan. Now we learn there was something in the bloodstreams of our partners that was infinitely more lethal than any unboiled glass of water drunk in a Mexican or Filipino village. And so I look at my uncle seated in his middle sixties under the water oak by the lake—the lawn around him freshly mown, the mimosa tree drooping in the humid air, a heron settling down into the marsh weeds to his left—and think: Did I give up the world for just a portion of it? Was his way better?

Almost everyone feels he threw his life away on something, I suspect, but my uncle seems never to have considered the thing that occupied my youth; and now he sits there cool and clean under the water oak, while I stand here at the window fearful of the consequences of acts that at the time had no consequences. Or so we thought. Even now the itchy sore of lust endures beneath the worry. How did he scratch it? (If he ever did.) My uncle, in a country addicted to so many things, does not seem addicted to anything.

He does not smoke; never has. He seldom eats sweets, and in the evening he laughs at the invitation to have some ice cream, because he watches his weight. Or, most amazingly, if he accepts he has one small cup and not another. He is the man who always brings us a box of Fannie May candy, but seldom has any of it himself, or when he does, is able to stop with one.

The despair therefore, I would assume, of advertising agencies, he nevertheless enjoys commercials on television. He watches the nightly business report on television, too, and the occasional baseball game, which leads me back to my confusion.

His interest in baseball and basketball—both of which he enjoys watching—makes me think he is not, cannot be, homosexual; but then why has he never married? When my age, he was the only one of seven children still living at home, and took care of my grandmother in her final illness. My mother once said my uncle loved my grandmother too much ever to transfer the emotion to another person. Perhaps he didn't want to love someone else who would die; or perhaps he didn't want the mess, the chaos, the screams and emotion of family life, since he has always seemed to prize peace and calm, and is above all a man of moderation.

He swims once a day in a public pool, even now plays golf, goes to bed before midnight, and rises before I do. Often he is gone when I awaken the next day: the perfect guest. A ghost. No one understands why he doesn't stay longer. In spring he always puts a bug screen on the grille of his car. The day he got here he asks me if I have checked the oil in mine, and watches me do so. He washes the windows, hoses down the screens, advises me to call the roofer again and remind him of his promise to scrape the dripped tar off the gutters and remove the TV antenna lying in the yard. The branch of my family he belongs to has two strains—Irish and Norwegian—and if one can use the Irish to denote high spirits, unpredictability, nerves, a slight lunacy, and the Norwegians to denote fastidiousness, reserve, calm, this uncle, I think, seems to me more Norwegian than Irish. Yet—and here is the perplexing part—there is nothing melancholy, brooding, or repressed about him; he seems not to have exacted any price for his discipline.

Once I asked my sister if she supposed he ever suffered in love, was unhappy, disappointed, or hurt (things I find hard to imagine his being), and she said, "Of course," on the assumption that everyone who lives has to have experienced these emotions at some point or another. I doubt that we will ever know, however. When he lived with my aunt in the sixties, she said: "I never ask him where he's going, or when he's coming back. It's none of my business." (This fact startled me at the time—but now it seems to me the essence of that courtesy members of a family extend one another: the right, within this most intimate context, to have a completely private existence.) When he lived with my aunt, my uncle was very friendly with a married couple, both artists, with whom he owned a small motel on the outskirts of the city and took vacations. To this day I have no idea what that relationship involved. He is, needless to say, a man of whom I've never asked a personal question. So I really have no idea what lies behind the man I see beneath the tree at this moment—the man who once was young, who must have asked himself why he did not marry, who has surely suffered along with everyone else. Yet I've always wondered if he did not, when he came out of the YMCA after taking his swim all those years, feel desire for another swimmer or loneliness or some sense of a truncated life.

It would be too simple to say he solved all the problems of life by going to work for the telephone company, and yet I am tempted to. Working for the telephone company may have done just that, I think. The civilian version of the army, a vast organization that provided him an identity in the same way the church might have in the twelfth century, a society that met all one's needs. He traveled, he worked, he rose in the hierarchy, he had a secretary. The portion of his life not covered by the telephone company—the "love" portion of the "love and work" duo—the evenings he must have left the office or the YMCA after taking his swim never presented the question: "Can I go home to an empty house? Should I stop by a bar first? Why must I sleep alone tonight?" because he slept in a house owned by his sister and her husband, in a town not far from the one they grew up in. The family continued to hold him. He came and went as he pleased ("I wouldn't dare ask," my aunt said), but he did so from the solidarity a family provides. He has always been rooted. My generation seems less so—families scattered across the country. If his generation included the first Americans to move abroad and set up companies in foreign lands, my generation is accustomed to using airplanes as cars or buses. Airplanes are no longer things one puts on a coat and tie for, and long-distance telephone calls are no longer considered permissible only for important news. It was a symbol, perhaps, of an earlier generation's rectitude that my uncle seldom used the privileges we assumed he had while working for the telephone company (free calls). It was only after retiring, and leaving his sister's house for a rented condominium in Florida, that he began calling every few months to keep up on the family. He is the one who passes on the news among the few brothers and sisters still living. He is the one who comes to us now for Thanksgiving and Christmas and brings candy he does not eat.

Did he ever do something he regrets? It seems impossible to have lived more than forty years without answering "yes," yet looking at him beneath the water oak, beside the still lake, in his pressed khakis, his white T-shirt and sandals, I think: perhaps my uncle is that desideratum of philosophy, that rarest of birds—a moderate, reasonable, and happy man.

I say nothing to him of my own life, which seems now to have consisted primarily of that stab of desire when I emerged from my own swim at some YMCA in a city up north; of the principle of never working for the telephone company; of fleeing the family he has remained part of all his life. Who cannot decide—now that it is time to draw up a will—whom to leave his things to? I am sure my uncle has faced this question already, but I cannot guess the answer as I look out at him, seated beneath the water oak. A person, a group of persons? A university? I can no more imagine the recipient of my uncle's wealth than I can imagine his being compelled by desire to do furtive things. I can only consider his talc, his aftershave lotion, his bug screen, his sandals, and conclude he is happy. Which makes me glad. Since—given the fact that most gay people are going to have to deal with the difficulties, social and personal, of not founding a family of their own—there is no relative more important to, or closely watched by, the gay child than the uncle or aunt who never married.

philip
gambone

---

second cousin

In my family, even if you don't much like them, you're expected to associate with your first cousins. It's the first cousins, plus the aunts and uncles who spawned them, who properly constitute the clan, the *famiglia*. They're the ones who are, you're told, "important."

As a kid, I had twelve first cousins: eight on my mother's side, four on my father's. But for me, not even one of them came close to being important in my life. On Mom's side they were all much older than I, some by as many as twenty years. When they came to call, it was to socialize with my mother and father, or to pay respects to our grandmother, who lived with us. On Dad's side, though my first cousins were my age, we hardly ever saw them. (Something about the sisters-in-law not getting along.)

Even more important—and an eight-, nine-, ten-year-old knows this, long before he knows he's gay—they were all straight, the whole dozen of them.

I used to listen with envy to friends who told me stories about their relationships to special cousins: about overnights at cousins' houses, about spending whole summers with their cousins on some

farm in Indiana, about learning to golf or fish or jerk off with a
cousin. So lonely for such a cousin was I—so hungry for that kind
of buddy and family member all in one—that I used to refer to my
uncle-through-marriage's sister's daughter's son, a boy almost exactly
my age, as my "cousin" Raymond, even though he was no blood
relation at all. But Raymond lived in New Rochelle, which, in the
days I was growing up, was a half day's trip from Wakefield, the
town north of Boston where my family and I lived. Raymond and
I saw each other, at most, once a year.

Fifteen years ago, when my brother got married, he and my
mother argued for days about inviting all of our first cousins to the
wedding. My mother was adamant.

"They're your first cousins!" she tried explaining.

"But who ever sees them?" my brother countered.

"That doesn't matter. You can't not invite them."

My brother eventually relented. The first cousins came (the ones
on Mom's side), bearing gifts and congratulations. And then they
went and my brother was right: most of them we didn't see again
until the next wedding or funeral.

Or "homecoming."

Such was the case when, late in the summer of 1973, the
summer I turned twenty-five, I returned to Boston from a six-week
trip to Europe. My parents met me at the airport, where they announced that they'd planned a little "Welcome Home" party for
that evening. The party turned out to be a rather elaborate affair,
an end-of-the-summer family gathering, full of aunts and uncles and
most of the first cousins (again the ones on Mom's side).

I was in no mood to celebrate. I'd been away with my first
lover, a man my family knew only as my "roommate," even though
we'd been together for five years. It was to have been our *Wandersom-
mer*: the cathedrals of England, the chateaux of the Loire, the great
museums of Italy. But halfway through the trip, Dan and I broke
up. Our love affair had been stagnating for over a year. The trip
was supposed to perk things up, but within days of our arrival in
Europe, we had started bickering and fighting, lobbing accusations
at each other, nursing jealousies. The tensions might ease for a day
or two, only to erupt again, more hostile than ever. At the end of

the six weeks, each of us was left exhausted by the ordeal, stinging from the wounds.

Back home, at my parents' party, I somehow managed to put on a happy face, to find the requisite happy stories to tell about "our" trip. (First-person plural pronouns must be the saddest words anyone going through a divorce, even a closet divorce, can use.) But eventually, after watching my former lover merrily chatting it up with this relative and that, I retreated to my old bedroom for a few minutes of solitude.

I wasn't there long before there was a knock on the door. It was my cousin—my second cousin—Fred.

"What's the matter?" he asked.

There's a look that Fred gives me to this day—a mixture of love, concern, and no nonsense—that says, "Come clean." That's the way he was looking at me that night in my bedroom. I told him everything.

Fred listened. He must have said things, too. Things like, "There'll be other guys." Or, "I never liked Dan anyway!" Or, "Too bad you didn't break up before the trip so that you could have enjoyed all those gorgeous men in Italy." Maybe he said all those things—they have a vague ring of familiarity, that mixture of wisdom and humor that I love in Fred—but in situations like this, what someone says to you isn't nearly as important as the fact that he is listening. And Fred did. He listened to everything I had to say. And I spared him none of the details.

At the time, Fred was married. He had four kids. He was best pals with my mother. On paper, as they say, he didn't exactly fit the description of the kind of person a young gay man comes out to. And yet, it felt utterly natural to tell him all about myself. In fact, I'd been waiting a long time to come clean with Fred.

Fred's grandmother, Jenny Marasca, and my maternal grandfather, Louis DeVita, were brother and sister. His mother and my mother were first cousins. Which makes him my mother's first cousin once removed and my second cousin. This story properly starts back in the nineteen-forties when Fred was a kid and my mother, unmarried but well into her thirties, "adopted" Fred and his brother Alfred. (The absurd similarity in names is only an accident of English: Fred was baptized Ferdinando.)

"I'd take them to the beach," my mother used to tell me, "or to the museums. I called them my teddy bears."

The beach was probably Revere Beach, which they could easily have reached, via the "trains" (now part of the Blue Line on the Boston transit system) from Fred's home in East Boston. I imagine wicker picnic hampers, sunsuits, sketch pads, and boxes of colored crayons. Lots of crayons. My mother was an amateur artist, and Fred and Alfred were already showing promise in that direction.

In 1947, when Fred was ten, my mother married—"late" by the standards of the day—at age thirty-five. Over the next few years, Fred and Alfred, her teddy bears, became teenagers with teenagers' interests and activities, and my mother started raising a family of her own. The crayons and trips to the museum passed on to me and my brothers.

Then, one Sunday afternoon—one of those interminable Sunday afternoons when my family paid a visit to yet another relative I'd never heard of—I found myself packed into the Ford with my parents, my brothers, and my grandmother, headed for East Boston. We were going to Aunt Jenny's.

"Who's *she*?" my brothers and I demanded, itchy and irritable in our Sunday best.

"Nanna's sister-in-law."

"So why do we have to go?"

"Don't fuss. Your cousin Fred will be there."

"Who's *he*?"

Aunt Jenny turned out to be an ancient woman, slightly stooped, with a copious mound of white hair on top of her head and a wily gleam in her eye. She smiled benignly at my brothers and me, said something in Italian, then retreated with my grandmother to talk. The other adults were my mother's cousin (Aunt Adeline), Adeline's husband Pat, and their son Fred.

Fred was twenty-one, a senior at the Massachusetts College of Art. He sported a crew cut and the hooked Marasca nose. He seemed delighted to meet his little second cousins, and he expressed that delight by talking to us exuberantly about our interests and hobbies,

all the while managing to keep up with the adults' conversation as
well. Back and forth, between us and them, he'd talk and joke. I
was immediately struck by his laugh, a hiccuping kind of belly
laugh that made us giggle with delight. (A few years later, when
my voice changed, I started copying that laugh, making it my own.)
I began to think that Fred was the most playful adult I'd ever met.

Fred dragged out a box of marionettes that he and Alfred had
played with as kids. The strings were tangled and broken, but by
the end of the afternoon he had managed to repair them, bringing
the dolls back to life. There was a princess, a king, a Spanish
señorita, a dashing young man in a flowing cape—close to a dozen.
I was enthralled.

Fred showed us how to manipulate the strings and rods, how
to make the marionettes walk and bow, brandish swords, genuflect,
slip and fall on their fannies, then bounce up and begin gesticulating
all over again. Some could even be made to open and close their
mouths and eyes. We played all afternoon. Most wonderful of all,
at the end of our visit, Fred piled the marionettes into a couple of
large cardboard boxes and gave them to us. Not one or two, but
the entire troupe.

I didn't see Fred again until two or three years later when, on
a similar visit to Aunt Jenny's, he was there once more, this time
just out of Columbia with a master's in teaching and a fiancée.
Perhaps the occasion for this visit to East Boston was to meet the
fiancée, Jeanne, a cute, perky woman with the exotic virtue (for me)
of being non-Italian. The afternoon was centered on the two of them,
on conversation about the wedding and how they'd met and what
their plans were for the future.

I liked the way they included me in the conversation, too, in
that radiantly generous way that soon-to-be-weds extend to even the
remotest members of the families. At twelve, I'd already been to a
number of my first cousins' weddings. But this one seemed more
special, more radiant, more full of youthful romance. Fred and
Jeanne. I felt something effervescent bubbling up whenever I spoke
their names. Maybe the first sugars of romantic feelings were fer-
menting in me. Or maybe I was displacing onto Fred and his fiancée
my unconscious infatuation for him alone.

Perhaps that is why, on this visit, I paid more attention to Fred: to what kind of person he was, to the details of his life, the way he put things, his jokes, his mannerisms, that laugh, so full of energy and delight. Even though he was eleven years older than I, I felt as if I'd found a cousin who, more than just being fun and playful and generous, actually liked me. A cousin who, at last, I could be my total self with, unguarded and unafraid.

From here on, Fred's life and mine began to weave together in a complex network of associations and relationships: older cousin-younger cousin, teacher-student, parent-babysitter, adviser-advisee, artist-apprentice, bohemian-acolyte, friend-friend.

In the fall of 1960, the fall after he and Jeanne were married, Fred took his first permanent teaching job, at Wakefield Junior High School, the junior high school I was just then entering. I was thrilled with the prospect of having Fred as my teacher. But, whether through scheduling difficulties or deliberate finagling on the part of the school authorities, I wasn't assigned to him. There seemed a kind of rightness in this, as if "Life" could not be expected to hand you anything nearly so perfect as your favorite cousin for a teacher. It was enough, almost, just to know that Fred was at the junior high; enough to hear from the kids who did have him how much they liked him, how funny and original and encouraging he was; enough to hear them affectionately call him Freddie behind his back.

That Christmas, Fred decided he would decorate his art room in something other than the traditional red-and-green color scheme. He chose purple and orange. He hung large purple and orange shapes—squares, circles, and triangles (no silhouettes of Santa and his sleigh for Fred)—all over the bulletin boards in the art room. It was something of a scandal, but he got away with it. Students and teachers from other parts of the building came into his room just to look, and I loved him for it.

There was a lot that was slightly scandalous about Fred. His age alone—he was twenty-three when he started at Wakefield Junior High School—in a faculty of middle-aged teachers was slightly suspect. He mocked the safe, traditional art projects of some of the other teachers; selected prints for the bulletin boards that were not necessarily "pretty" (I remember he told me he hated the word "pretty"); told jokes and laughed a lot.

Fred drove a Volkswagen. This, too, was something of a non-conformist practice in those final days of Eisenhower's complacent presidency. On afternoons when my friends and I stayed late at school and missed the bus, Fred would pile us into his VW (sometimes as many as six or seven of us) and off we'd go. I suspected we were breaking the law, crowding into one car like that, but breaking the law with Fred seemed okay, seemed like the gateway into a world where conventions and rules didn't count. It was the year I learned the word "beatnik."

That year, I got to know Fred in another context, too. He and my mother opened up a Saturday morning art school in the basement of our house. The first students were, as one might expect, mostly girls. But a few boys, including me, took lessons as well.

I remember these Saturdays as happy and frustrating occasions. Happy because there was always music playing (Fred brought a record player and lots of recordings of Broadway musicals) and plenty of teenage chatter, mostly "girl talk" about hair and clothes and boys, to which I paid rapt but silent attention. The frustrating part was that I had little talent in the visual arts, or at least for the kind of meticulous draftsmanship and brushwork my mother espoused.

Fred, I was happy to discover, was looser about such standards. I'd already been to his apartment a few times and there I'd seen examples of his work: bright, bold abstracts done with thick impastos of paint. It surprised me that my mother liked his work, so different was it from her own tightly controlled technique. (As a young woman, she'd studied with an old Italian "professor," who had taught her in the classical tradition.) When it became apparent to Fred that I hated the fussy little still lifes that I was expected to paint, he suggested I try some imaginary nature scenes in German expressionist or Fauvist style. I could paint purple tree trunks, blue grass, yellow skies. What mattered, he explained, was not accuracy of color, but accuracy of emotion.

Fred also seemed looser in his classroom manner. Whereas my mother kept herself constantly busy, making her way from one easel to the next, Fred took time to join the students in their chitchat, oftentimes to initiate it, passing along tips on hair care and fashion. Before too many Saturdays had passed, he'd even brought combs, brushes, and hairspray and was giving demonstrations to the girls on how to tease their hair.

The next year, my eighth-grade year, I finally got to have Fred as my junior high art teacher. My memories of that time are telling: a collection of seemingly irrelevant details that only now, through my awareness of myself as a gay man, make sense. I remember the small museum-reproduction head of a Greek god that Fred kept on his desk; the admiring way he referred to a fellow male teacher's skin tones as "olive"; and how once, on a field trip to the Museum of Fine Arts in Boston, we met a handsome French college student at lunch and how jealous I was that this man gave all his attention to Fred and none to me.

The homoeroticism of these moments was not apparent to me at the time. In fact, at the time, I was in love with a girl named Earlene Weller, and called upon Fred to listen to my moony, thrilled descriptions of my feelings for her. But I was also beginning to feel other stirrings, an interest in male bodies. Frequently I would baby-sit for Fred and Jeanne, and on those nights, after their infant son had gone to sleep, I would pour through Fred's art books, closely studying the photographs of Greek nude sculpture. I had no interest in the female figures (whose bodies seemed abstract and "aesthetic," frozen in the realm of art), but the male bodies—athletes, gods, soldiers, *kouroi*—these bodies attracted me with their exquisite, incarnate beauty. I studied them for hours, the faces, the musculature, the turn of the legs, the genitals.

In the spring of 1963, under the auspices of their art class, Fred and my mother organized a three-day cultural field trip to New York. The idea was to take in some of the great museums, the architecture, the artistic atmosphere of the place.

We did all the important museums—the Guggenheim, the Met, MoMA—but what I remember most vividly is our final evening, when, as part of the "cultural" variety Fred and my mother had planned, we attended a performance of the off-Broadway revival of the 1938 Rodgers and Hart musical *The Boys from Syracuse*.

At age fourteen, going to the musical theater was not a new experience for me. For several summers, my parents had taken me and my brothers to various summer-stock musicals at the Cape Cod Melody Tent in Hyannis and, in Falmouth, to productions of Gilbert and Sullivan by a troupe from Oberlin College. But *The Boys from Syracuse* was of an entirely different order. It bristled with sex appeal. So much so that I have always assumed it was Fred's, and not my mother's, idea to take us.

Sex was everywhere in this show: in the scantily clad, leggy choreography, in the full-fleshed orchestrations, in the lyrics with their racy double entendres. "I shook the tree of life one day/And got a cold potato," warbled Karen Morrow, playing Luce, the sexually frustrated kitchen maid, about her husband, Dromio of Ephesus. (Could this mean what I think it means? I asked myself. I had never heard such overt, exuberant references to sex before, and, in the darkened theater, I kept stealing glances at my mother to see how she was reacting to all this.) The show was full of sex talk. And while romance, love, marriage, and fidelity formed the dominant direction of the plot, there was a healthy dose of skepticism about such virtues. *The Boys from Syracuse* takes a lighthearted attitude toward adultery, promiscuity, prostitution, "fooling around." For the women as well as for the men. You don't find stuff like this in Gilbert and Sullivan. It was all very new, and very exciting.

The dreamboat of the cast was Stuart Damon, who played Antipholus of Syracuse. In some presexual way (certainly prehomosexual way), I knew that I was paying an inordinate amount of attention to him and that whenever he came on stage I felt warm and happy and ready to cast off everything about my suburban life for whatever life it was that he represented up there in his trim beard and thigh-revealing tunic.

I still have the New York cast album of *The Boys from Syracuse* that Capitol records put out that year. Damon's voice is smooth and silky and slightly boyish, a little like the voice of an accomplished college glee-club soloist. There's an unthreateningly virile quality to that voice that for me still represents everything bright and lovely about falling in love with a man. Did I fall in love with him that evening at Theatre Four? All I know is that for the next year or so I played that album a lot. And that Fred's taking us to that show has never seemed an accident.

Not much later, Fred got a new job, teaching in a high school a few towns away. Though he and my mother continued to run the Studio Art Classes together, I saw less and less of him over the next several years. Then I went away to college, fell in love with Dan during an idyllic summer when we were both employed at Tanglewood, and eventually moved with him to the Midwest where we got teaching jobs together. Then came the summer we went to Europe, the breakup, and the coming out to Fred.

Fast forward now a decade, to the early eighties. Fred and Jeanne have gotten a divorce, Fred remarries, divorces again. He's on the faculty of one of the state colleges, teaching color and design courses. In his spare time, he's also doing some freelance interior design work. He moves out of the suburbs, takes an apartment in Boston's South End, just then emerging as Boston's new gay ghetto. His friends are artists, dancers, fashion designers.

It seems incredible that I still had no idea he might be gay. But Fred's live-and-let-live attitude, that spirit of bohemian laissez-faire ("Whatever floats your boat," he's fond of saying), left me assuming that his comfort with my gay life, his *exuberance* for my gay life, was just another manifestation of his unconventional spirit.

With Fred I shared each milestone in my developing life as a gay man: the first article I wrote for a gay paper, my first visit to Provincetown, my first bout with VD. Tales of bar life and beaches and boys—all the stuff that constituted so much of what life was about for young gay men in the seventies and early eighties.

Even so, I didn't make a great effort to see Fred very often during these years. Maybe that's because I was too preoccupied with assembling a family of gay friends. But, if I'm brutally honest with myself, I know it's also because I was embarrassed by my life. Not that I'd done anything particularly sleazy or objectionable: after all, I'd completed a master's degree, worked in a library, gotten a teaching job. Eventually I'd settled down with another lover. We'd bought a house together. But, in comparison to Fred's life—or the life I supposed Fred had—mine seemed utterly conventional, impoverished of that exuberant spirit he had in abundance. Here was this straight man, eleven years my senior, whose life was so much more like the one I wanted. To my mind, I wasn't gay enough in any sense of the word. Fred's "gayness," his unafraid gladness of heart, stood as an indictment of my safe, restrained achievements.

I don't recall how Fred actually came out to me. I know it wasn't through any grand, dramatic announcement. Probably, in the middle of one of our conversations, he just shrugged his shoulders, threw up his hands, tossed his hair off his forehead—gestures I've seen him use on many occasions, gestures I still wish came naturally to me—and declared through that hiccuping laugh of his, "Okay, what the fuck, I'm gay, too!"

I do remember the story he subsequently told me about hitchhiking to Ogunquit (Maine's version of Provincetown) to test out his newfound identity, picking someone up on the beach, and the ensuing weekend of lovemaking.

"I wanted to experience it *all*," he told me. When Fred delivers a line like this, it's with the kind of reckless gusto that an Auntie Mame or a Gypsy Rose Lee might use.

We talked. This time I listened. And nodded my head at all the familiar stories and feelings, the euphoria, the self-consciousness, the doubts, the humor of it all. In the years since, we've talked a lot more, but never once has Fred expressed any regret about coming out so late. There's never been much room for regret in Fred's life. "Regret? Who's got time for regret?" he'll say.

He came out to my parents, too. Long before I did. How could he not? He still calls my mother his "best girlfriend." They've confided a lot to each other, conversations I'll probably never know about, though many of them have, I'm certain, focused on me. How could they not? The more I kept from my parents who I was, the more my mother must have sought out her former teddy bear to help her understand this son who seemed so uncomfortable with her yet so comfortable with him. (Fred is the only male relative whom I have always kissed in greeting, a custom that just evolved spontaneously, and which we somehow have always gotten away with. Italians, you know.)

"Fred told us he's gay," my mother said to me one day about eight years ago when she and my father had taken me out to lunch. We were in a restaurant in Harvard Square. The conversation had been characteristically perfunctory up to that point, and I was determined to keep it perfunctory. I sensed that Mom was opening up *the* topic.

"Oh, yeah?" I said, matter-of-factly.

"Did you know?"

"Yeah, I think I did."

"So what do you think?"

"Whatever floats your boat."

And that was it. We went back to pleasantries about the food.

I can now see how hostile this kind of behavior was, and I'm amazed that Fred never called me on it, never pushed me to tell my parents what they already knew anyway. But this is also typical of him, the way he's always let me, let anyone, find his own pace, his own style, his own story. He must have known how much easier it would have made things if I'd just come out to my parents, but he also knew—I now see—that it was my life and that he could not lead it for me.

I suspect that this is one of the biggest lessons he's taught my mother, too: that she could not lead my life for me; that, as well-meaning as she was, she could not direct the choices I was making. To a pretty remarkable degree, my mother has refrained from direct meddling in my life (Dad was always more of a natural at this), which is not to say that my mother hasn't sent subtle "messages" over the years. I'm sure that it has been Fred's example and advice to her—to stand back and trust that I'll make my own way—that have significantly influenced her relationship with me.

In the last few years, Fred's life, at least the outer trappings of it, has mellowed. He's moved from the South End to a comfortable suburb just outside Boston. Having retired from teaching, he has a successful interior design business that he shares with his lover, a beautiful younger man named Billy. (*"Younger?"* Fred will exclaim with that stage-voice extravagance. "He could be one of my *sons*, he's so young!")

In turn, some of my old embarrassment about not matching up to Fred's level of gayness has dissipated. This is particularly the result of my doing more of what I've always wanted to do, putting together, like Fred, a life in the arts. I'm also not hiding from my family anymore. But that took a crisis, a crisis Fred helped me through.

In the spring of 1989, my lover of twelve years and I broke up. Unlike that summer of 1973, when Dan ("just my roommate," after all) could disappear from my life without so much as a comment from my parents, here the situation could not be avoided. Glenn and I owned a house together, he'd become part of the family, even though my parents did not acknowledge that we were lovers. (For twelve years, they sent us separate Christmas cards.) When I began showing up at family parties without him, my parents began to pick up that something was wrong.

"How's Glenn?" Mom would ask, and I, ever evasive, would give her a succinct, clipped, "Fine."

This went on for several months, until Christmas, in fact, when my attempts to direct the activities of my life around my parents' scrutiny finally proved impossible. It was time to come clean once again.

"They've been asking about Glenn," Fred told me one day.

"So they know?"

"What they know is that you two aren't living together anymore."

"Then why haven't they said anything?"

"They don't know what to say."

"But, damn it, they know we've been lovers."

"They feel awkward. They don't understand why you've kept it a secret all these years."

"I haven't kept it a secret; they just never asked."

In the end, with my relieved, cowardly permission, Fred told them. And shortly afterward—again in a restaurant, again in Harvard Square—my parents and I talked it all over. Well, not *all* of it over, but enough to finally, after twenty years, get the gay thing on the table. They said all the right things (those horribly corny, horribly necessary phrases you read in coming out novels: "We still love you. All we want is for you to be happy"), and I assured them I was happy. The next week, just before New Year's Eve, Fred and Billy even arranged a small supper party so that my parents could meet my new boyfriend.

There is a terrible stubbornness in me, a stubbornness that might have kept me from ever letting my parents into one of the most significant aspects of my life. Fred must have sensed that and, despite his philosophy of letting people find their own pace, did something to bring me out of the closet. I wish I could say I did it all on my own, but during that cold, gray December I needed a push, and he was there to give it.

Where are we now, Fred and I? Closer than ever, but also at a crossroads. We continue to spend time with each other, sharing news and gossip, griefs and joys. I've attended the openings of some of his shows; he's helped me select wallpaper for my apartment. We've gone dancing and clubbing together in Provincetown. In the spring of 1991, when my father was dying, Fred was often at the hospital, and when Dad passed away Fred was there through all the events of the next several days. Two months later, when my first book was published and I threw a book party, Fred contributed hours of time, meticulously arranging three spectacular bouquets of flowers, and hours more during the weeks prior reassuring my mother that a book of gay short stories and a party to which I'd invited everyone (gay and lesbian friends, straight colleagues, even some of those first cousins) were going to be just fine.

By the time this piece is published, Fred will have become a grandfather. Ever since his son and daughter-in-law told him the news, he's been riding high. (So has Billy, who, when Fred told him, managed to exclaim through tears of happiness, "I'm going to be a grandmother!") Ever the designer, Fred has already been helping with plans for the baby's room.

"I can't believe how into it I am," he told me. "It's like the completion of a cycle that began when I became a father."

I listened to this with a mixture of excitement, confusion, and anger. There was something about Fred's feelings that seemed like a betrayal, like a turning away from what gay life is all about. Getting worked up about grandchildren? Suddenly, he seemed so middle class. How could this man who, for over thirty years, had been my countercultural hero now espouse such Hallmark-card kinds of sentiments? I didn't want him to feel the way he was feeling. This grandchild had nothing to do with what he was all about, I wanted to tell him.

But of course this grandchild has a lot to do with what Fred is all about. For Fred has always been about having his feelings— all of them—even the ones that are supposed to be inappropriate or embarrassing or politically incorrect. No conventions of propriety or party lines have ever stopped him from feeling, and expressing, whatever it was he was feeling at the time.

And this, I now realize, is really the reason why, in comparison to Fred's life, I've often felt embarrassed by my own. There was a dishonesty in my life that went beyond the dishonesty of the closet. I was filtering all my feelings through the screen of what others might think. What would the girls say if I joined in their conversation about teasing hair? What does Mom think of this *Boys from Syracuse* show? What will all those first cousins say if they know I'm gay? Somehow, Fred never learned those self-doubting questions, or if he did, he never took them to heart. In idealizing his "bohemian" lifestyle, I'd lost sight of what I truly admired in Fred, his integrity of feeling and expression.

Years before, in those art classes, Fred had told me that it's not accuracy of color but accuracy of emotion that counts. I'm finally catching on to what that means.

charles
henry fuller

when my sister laughs

Home is as much a state of mind as a place fixed in time and space. After renting these five rooms for over ten years, I consider this apartment home. When I am fed up with the rude world outside my door or when I crave a hot meal and the safety of my partner's embrace, I take great comfort in the phrase, "Let's go home." However, if it is confusion and loneliness that plague us at the beginning and end of our lives, it is dislocation that haunts the years in between. When my sense of world-weariness is most intense, I inevitably listen for the familiar voices and sounds that dominated those distant rooms I will always know as home. My sister's laughter is the surest key to unlock this estate of memory that is my adolescence. Her laughter alone says that perhaps not everything that happened there was sad, and that perhaps today's miseries may also become tinged with humor tomorrow. At the center of her laughter is the confidence that hard times can be weathered with dignity. I find this possibility tremendously reassuring.

My sister and I have always used dark humor to distance ourselves from the horrors of our biological family. Recently, after a series of colossal blunders illustrating the poor judgment that has defined the decade since his retirement, my father was forced to sell our childhood home for a pittance. I listened over the telephone as my sister filled in each grim detail, lingering over the fact that our emotionally disturbed older brother, who has always lived at home, is now staying with my father in a rooming house. It was impossible not to hear the lack of expression in her voice that underscored the seriousness of the situation. Then, her recital ended, she breathed the extravagant sigh that is the signature of many black families in trouble and asked, "If he truly intended to tear down everything he's built up all these years, what took so long?" I let the 130 miles of fiber optic cable between us pulse for a moment before observing, "Well, he was *always* a perfectionist."

Then we rocked with laughter, letting each irreverent howl cleanse our palates like sherbet between courses. Neither of us, for all our romantic notions of ruined childhoods and dreams deferred, has a gift for tragedy. Pragmatism is the table we have set for ourselves, with survival as our main course. And as we whooped and hollered our way through years of examples of our father's determination to do it his way, a thought occurred to me that I have not been able to forget. If there is truly a balm in Gilead to heal the sin-sick soul, its power is no less strong than the purifying fire of my sister's will to survive. At last, I asked what we ought to do about Dad *this* time. Her response cut with a knife's precision.

"We haven't come all this way to be dragged down into a fiery pit with *his* name on it. He'll do what we tell him, or he'll land in the gutter. We've fed his ego long enough."

My sister is a social worker by trade, well practiced in the art of excavating fragments of hope that were plowed under years ago. But on that particular afternoon she was in no mood to reframe the situation. She was right, of course. Some dreams do come to dust on the road. Better to admit it and move on than to sit contemplating what might have been while life barrels past you. Though easily one of the nicest people I know, I have few illusions about my sister. She will put up with a lot, a very lot in life, but once her back is to the wall, look out. Either you talk sense, or you're soon talking to yourself.

My sister was the only girl in a house of three boys. To keep peace in the family, she was named after each grandmother. My brothers and I readily agreed that she had gotten stuck with a terrible "old timey, colored name"—Beulah Estelle—that clanged like a cowbell in a yard that rang with David Daniel, George William, and Charles Henry. Beulah went through adolescence claiming that at age twenty-one she would legally change her name to something with less cotton dust on it—Alexandra led the pack for quite a while—but she never did. The blend of feistiness and humility that a downhome name required made her secure enough in her identity not to mind the occasional smirk or rude comment. Also, after our mother's death in our teens, my sister felt closer to Mom, who, after all, had been saddled with Ada-Nellie for fifty-three years. Still, Beulah was careful to give her own children beautiful names, names I find myself repeating just because of the music they leave in the air.

But time has a way of compensating. After a rather unpromising girlhood, my sister developed a lovely figure, a cute face with large, expressive eyes, and a winning disposition. Everyone liked her. Even during puberty when girls changed best friends almost as often as headbands, she had a faithful following. There just wasn't any sport in running down the quintessential good girl. She made friends easily and, unlike many of her classmates, kept them for life. You move in and out of my sister's field of vision, not out of her thoughts, and certainly not out of her heart. Kindness is rewarded with lifelong devotion, betrayal with bottomless enmity.

Though she would deny it if asked, Beulah has a dread of being overlooked or marginalized in life. Most of us pay a price for our ticket through life—my sister does not want the extraordinary cost of her passage dismissed. Success was never a given in her life, so remembering the struggle has real value for both of us. Having been there, having seen what was demanded and how each fee was met, our bond is close. The road was not—is not—easy. We won't let anyone say otherwise.

My sister and I were marked as special from an early age, as much by the times in which we lived as by our parents. Dissatisfied with the inadequate and partial education they received in the colored public schools of Depression-era Virginia, our parents pooled their combined intelligence and industry to quit the Jim Crow South of the forties and join the great migration to the industrialized North. In New Jersey, New York, and finally Connecticut, Charles and Nellie Fuller scuffled and shuffled as laborers, did whatever they could to ensure that their children's way in the world would be easier than their own. Their resolve to help "uplift the race" was strengthened by the articles they read in the black press about *Brown v. The Board of Education*, the Emmett Till murder trial, and the growing "respectability" of White Citizen Councils throughout the country. They were especially impressed by the Southern Christian Leadership Conference's young spokesman, Martin Luther King, Jr., who had a talent for getting the mainstream press, that is, white America, to admit that the race problem was not confined to Birmingham, Alabama. For all the harshness of their experience, Mom and Dad were dreamers and the sixties was a time for dreamers. The election of John Kennedy, the passage of the Civil Rights Act of 1964, and Lyndon Johnson's plans for The Great Society *seemed* like the better days they had imagined for so long.

Still, necessity made my parents realists. From the first set of tears they wiped from our eyes because someone had called us "niggers," my parents made it a habit not to shield us from the irrational, blinding prejudice that would confront us, they insisted, for the rest of our lives in this country. The message was received loud and clear: You'll always have to be twice as good to get half as far. Paternalism—what they derided as white people's funny-acting ways—was the fabric of American life. So we were taught not only to set our sights high but to give equal thought to *how* we would get over. "Meaning to" and "getting to" were not synonymous.

As I sat listening to my sister explain the few remaining housing and health care options my father had not systematically destroyed for himself, I again marveled at her resourcefulness. Though we are similar—each committed to our parents' teachings of survival and upward mobility—I felt their energy, their passionate sense of outrage burning more brightly in her during this latest family crisis. Listening and sighing as she answered my questions about how a ten-room house and one's life savings could be lost in a matter of months, I felt every millisecond of my thirty-six years.

The fact that this exchange of energy is cyclical, a finite reserve we have been passing back and forth for years, eluded me that afternoon. Fully ready to hate her strength of purpose and clearheadedness, I was rescued from fratricide by the familiarity of her laughter. For all the finely drawn lines in her words, what moved me was the subtle way her desire for a positive outcome overwhelmed her fear. If her nervous laughter asked, "Am I doing the right thing?," mine answered reassuringly, "Of course. I'll tell anybody I supported everything. You were not—are not—alone."

My sister's laughter, its rhythmic click-clacking before it is allowed to soar out of her, always puts me in mind of our childhood home. Specifically, the sudden shift from ladylike chuckle to earthy, side-splitting belly laugh reminds me of my mother and the safe world she created for us. Though she appreciated the humor of our adopted middle class—word plays, double entendre and social commentary—it was always the pratfall, the rude bodily functions, and life's other unexpected ironies that made Mom laugh until she cried. My sister becomes more like her every day. Beulah's laughter, seasoned as it is by what was hoped for and what ultimately came, feeds the hungry child in me. And the similarity does not stop there.

As she speeds through her thirties, my sister looks more like my mother than ever. No amount of rouge can make her cheeks appear less "squirrel-like" than our mother's, her middle and bottom are already thicker than she would like, her breasts insist on their matronly weight, and the color under that henna rinse is not as dark as it once was. But it is not all a heartless tale of the approaching middle years in which everything will be diminished. I noticed recently that my sister's shoulders, arms, and hands are shaped exactly like my mother's: strong, graceful, searching. Beulah's gestures, even her movements when bending and stretching, have such familiarity to them. But it is only when my sister laughs, when her eyes sparkle as those eyes once did, that I firmly believe in magic. For all their differences, biology has finally taken pity and given me a composite glimpse of my mother at just the moment I feel most in danger of losing all physical memory of her.

The resemblance stops there, of course. As close as they are in biology, mother and daughter are dissimilar in temperament. Having survived life with three brothers, a domineering father, and an equally narcissistic husband, my sister is quite a bit more assertive than our mother. For all her polite surfaces, Beulah does not suffer fools gladly. Neither do I. And we appreciate that in each other's company we can tell it like it is.

Today, I hear this laughter that I need so much and wonder how it is possible. When we were growing up, poor black children were told a lot of foolishness about themselves. We mid-fifties babies stumbled into the black power and civil rights movements after a decade or so of taunts that included, "You liver-lipped, Brillo-headed animal, keep your nasty black hands off me." As difficult as it was for me to find self-esteem in such a world, I realized early on that it was worse for black girls. Race and class issues are tough enough; girls also had to put up with sexism. I watched as most of the men and women that my sister came in contact with treated her differently. When I got good grades or landed a role in a school production, these were quantitative successes that moved me one step closer to that gold ring that was a scholarship to college. However, when Beulah did well, the criteria for evaluation shifted to the qualitative. Was she pleased with her accomplishment? How did she feel others were dealing with her success? Did her boyfriend mind that her grades were creeping up?

Don't get me wrong. We were both expected to succeed, but what constituted success for each was different. My stage was to be the world, hers the universe of home and hearth. Through her eyes I, too, came to resent the double standard, the sexist mumbo jumbo women were expected to live by. But unlike her, I had the choice to speak out or remain silent on sexism. She *had* to master the "feminine game" to reach her goals. So twice as good was not going to be good enough on the job; Beulah had to inspire confidence to be seen as promotable and yet appear soft enough not to be viewed as a threat to the male ego. And male egos had to be soothed at home, too. That she can smile at all is amazing, living proof of heavenly grace.

Sexuality, or rather the way our society deals with sexuality, is the only wedge that has ever separated my sister and me. Beulah is twenty months older than my twin brother and me. Since our older brother is seven years older than I am, we younger three were thick as thieves until puberty hit. I was amazed at how quickly things changed. Beards sprouted, breasts budded, shoulders broadened, and legs became alternately curvy and hirsute. My twin became a crude womanizer and suddenly my best buddy—Beulah—couldn't wait to huddle in her bedroom with girlfriends and discuss this week's heartthrob. Since the only homosexual role models I was aware of at that point were whispered about over back fences, I suppressed what was natural in me and retreated into my writing, music, and books. All of this boy-girl foolishness was too . . . too . . .

One afternoon, my sister walked into the room where I was writing and told me once again how much she liked my performance in our high school's production of the musical *Carnival*. Her opinion meant a lot to me, especially since I had taken a risk artistically with this role. To give the B-grade script some juice, the director and I decided to play the vindictive owner of this broken-down carnival—Schlegal—in a very flamboyant manner. No one ever said homosexual—"peacock" was as close as we came—but, given the player, that's where my interpretation settled.

I thanked Beulah and turned back to my work. But she wanted to share her reactions to the entire production so I let her talk. Now it was completely out of character for my sister to evaluate any of my performances in any great depth. Usually, like my mother, she was glad I showed an interest in something other than the shape of some "fox's booty" and was pleased that others took note of my efforts. That's why I was surprised when her general comments suddenly became quite specific: How could I, as a young black man, choose to play a homosexual?

Though I saw myself as the sensitive one in the family, my father and society were grooming all three of his sons to be "real men," that is, hard-drinking, skirt-chasing good ol' boys. (It was still seen as somewhat uppity for black boys from my neighborhood to show too much interest in building careers. Steady employment should be enough to content us.) By contrast, my sister was measured against the yardstick of genteel Southern Baptist womanhood as personified by my mother. Given these standards, Beulah and I were bound to fail because we were originals, not copies. Until that moment, this recognition had been a valued strength in our relationship. Still, life is change. Like everyone else in our hometown, she had her suspicions about me, but no proof. Proof would not be provided until my mid-twenties when my fear of being alone forever would overtake my fear of ostracism from the black community. Until then, she, who had always built her defense of a *funny* brother on the bedrock of the sensitive artist, would be shut out.

So that afternoon as I saw her cozying up to the sort of small-minded bigots that catcalled me and others in the street, I could not allow myself to trust her fully. At seventeen, I already knew that in desiring a special male friend I did not want to replace women in any straight man's life. I wanted a man who wanted a man—nothing less. Even so, clear as that concept was to me in 1972, I had no experience, personal or otherwise, on which to build my defense. I waffled, I bullshitted, I tried to change the subject. When Beulah asked where the character's walk had come from, we both realized she was scratching at something deeper, unspoken and dangerous. I hadn't changed my walk for the character and she knew it. Still, curious as she was, my sister was always sensitive to the pain of others. She decided on mercy and let me squirm away. Soon that glorious laughter of hers put everything in perspective. Plays come and go, but family is forever. And besides, the character was funny. She had laughed as loud as anyone.

To me, that humorless exchange made it clear that a line existed between us, one that I was not to step over. As strong an advocate as Beulah was, even then, for personal difference, she was not about to spend her life explaining or defending a mincing queen. The world would not understand—or forgive.

Exhausted by our discussion of what to do about Dad, Beulah and I turned our thoughts to careers and loved ones. My sister was now in the middle of a separation from her husband. The particulars of their discord are at once colorful and simply put: they have become too skilled at hurting one another. Even if she has fully come to terms with the limits of their love, Beulah says their children deserve better, and she wants them to have it. I felt for her. Like her joy, her pain is infectious.

Talking on the phone, I felt guilty realizing that my relation-ship with my life partner has evolved and grown over the last decade to become one of my proudest accomplishments in life. After watching the tremendous energy my sister has poured into saving her marriage these last six years, I have learned that not all bad marriages are loveless. You can remember so intently who someone was that you cannot accept what they are becoming. But all the love in the world cannot leap a wall of denial erected before it. I actually considered telling her this before I came to my senses. This was no time to score easy points. Instead, I told her that things are fine between my partner and me, then turned the focus back to the safer day-to-day issues—school, children, and summer vacations.

Like most of our telephone conversations over the last fifteen years, my nieces and nephew vie for Beulah's attention. Sentences on the most intimate topics are decorated with nonsense commands: "Stop pinching him!" "Can't you see I'm on the phone?" "No means no, damn it!" Usually, I ignore these interruptions, but that after-noon I responded to them until my sister laughed and said, "I'm glad *somebody* listens to what I say."

Listen. That's what I want to shout at my father, brothers, and brother-in-law. *Don't you realize this woman loves you and only wants what's best for you?* Of course, they don't. What makes her counsel inaudible to these important men in her life is that, first, it comes from a woman and, second, this woman doesn't lie. Beulah will do many things for you—but give you the chance to catch her "telling stories"? Forget about it. Having been lied to her entire life about the contributions minority women have made to the world, my sister places special value on the truth. Beulah has an extraordinary ability to deal with what life gives her. She will lend you her full support as long as you agree to face facts. Only by acknowledging what hasn't worked is my sister able to see what choices remain, how the goal might yet be achieved. The fact that so many men in her life have been unable to "own" their failures has brought her to some-thing of a personal crisis. The unspoken question laced through her laughter is, "Will every man I love lie to me?" The answer weaving through mine is, "Yes, but not habitually."

Is it true that some men are more afraid of the power of women than self-deception? I know that I don't feel diminished by the reservoirs of strength I find in my sister. And as I let her power breathe wind back into my sails that afternoon of horrible truths, I felt lightheaded at the wonderful, adult relationship that is finally taking root between us. After so many years of sorting out personal pronouns, where she begins and I end, who's right and who's wrong, we seem comfortably at home with each other.

Time has worn us down. Today, I look more like my father than my father does. And for those split seconds in the half-light as we walk beside each other, I become the father who finally listens, praises, and validates her accomplishments, while she becomes the mother who loved me without qualification. We are a family of two who carry our home wherever we go. And when my sister laughs and my own laughter rushes to join hers in the air above our heads, I savor the joy of being a witness who has lived to tell the tale, who has found his voice, like hers, heavy with the passage of time but full of hope and promise. If it turns out we are truly on a blue highway—some forgotten back road that dips and sways as it makes its way to the city—then let our laughter shorten the journey and warm us, sister, just in case better days are farther off than we think.

david rakoff

my sister of
perpetual mercy

At a Christmas party in Tokyo, I told a young Japanese man that I had a small pea-sized lump in my neck. He placed his fingertips at the side of my throat below my left ear and gently pressed and kneaded, his eyes never leaving mine. "What a fabulous accessory," I thought. It was a week later, when it had become the size of a largish grape, that I had to admit that what was growing inside of me was possibly an entrapment of a different sort. I quit my job in a Japanese publishing company, abandoned any hope of continuing a burgeoning courtship, and moved back to Canada. I was living in my parents' home again and diagnosed with Hodgkins lymphoma, a highly curable form of lymphatic cancer that strikes many young males. Scarcely four months after lighting out for the territories at age twenty-one, I put my life on hold: the Young Turk cut off at the knees. At the same time my sister Ruth, older by two years, was flying home from Tel Aviv, where she was living, to take care of me.

My parents had called Ruth in Israel almost immediately after I called them from Tokyo to tell them I was coming home. She decided of her own accord to return to Canada. Her job as a cook in a restaurant in Tel Aviv was grueling and unrewarding, and she could take care of me and take a break as well. I accepted her return as a matter of course. I expected nothing less of my sister; we had always been close. As children, we had a club—the "pals" club. If one member frowned, the other one patted his or her head, immediately eradicating the frown and replacing it with a smile that magnified into a transfiguring grimace of sheer joy and ecstasy, until the now-cured pal would expire into saintlike rapture, faith in the cosmos restored, unhappiness banished. The world suddenly seemed huge to me and Ruth. We wanted to be on the same continent.

Surprisingly, my liberal-Jewish-medical-psychiatric family never discussed sex all that much; until I came out formally, my sexuality was clandestine and never inquired about, a state of affairs facilitated by my being away at college in New York. We were rather intelligent children so we could certainly understand sex, but we were much smaller than average and grew so late that for years sex was something theoretical, something that happened to other people. I felt allied with Ruth in our refusal to stoop to something so unseemly or pedestrian as puberty. In my intellectual family, athletics, sex, the life of the Body in general were deemed less important than the life of the Mind. Ruth, I was horrified to find out, did not feel this same alliance of celibate virtue. I remember the first time I was aware that my sister was a sexual being. I was eleven and we were at summer camp. She was thirteen and standing next to a boy; spontaneously, she leaned over to whisper in his ear. Her arms crept up around his shoulders, one hand playing with his other ear as she spoke to him conspiratorially. I thought, "What on *earth* is she doing with that awful boy?" and, simultaneously, "Who does she think she is? She's too young for that gesture." I felt utterly betrayed and exacted punishment by glaring at the boy for the rest of the summer. What was she to do, after all? Ruth had started to grow breasts and was well on her way to becoming a bit of the raven-haired sultry Jewess, while I remained tiny and prepubescent for many years after that.

When I was fifteen, I had a brief and thwarted flirtation with a boy at the same camp—the younger brother of the corrupter of my sister's virtue, in fact. Ruth came up and told me she heard I was "experimenting." There was no judgment in her voice nor, for that matter, surprise. Throughout my childhood I had never made any great effort to appear straight. The slightest examination of my character would have revealed what I already suspected to be the case. Beyond that tacit acknowledgment from her, however, we never talked about my being gay until years later when I was away at college.

Ruth arrived at her unequivocal acceptance of my sexuality by sheer osmosis. My gradual emergence as a gay man was simultaneous with my general maturing. For so many years she had assumed and known that I was gay. Just as I, after my initial shock at age eleven, accepted her as a sexual being, a straight one, she accepted me. The shock she may have experienced at the disclosure of my desires and actions was rooted in the fact that her baby brother was growing up and having sex, not that he wanted that sex to be with boys.

I had for years been asking Ruth to casually mention to my parents that I was gay, something she absolutely refused to do in favor of my telling them myself. The night I finally came out to my parents, I had warned her minutes before that I would do it. She waited in her room with her boyfriend. Afterward, I walked down the hall to her room where, immediately upon closing the door, I began to cry from relief. She and Tom and I sat on her futon. I think she cried too. What about? I didn't even conjecture at the time. Relief? The hardships she thought I'd face? I worried the next day that perhaps my parents had missed the point. I hadn't actually said, "I'm gay." I had said, "I haven't had any girlfriends and I think you can guess why." "Maybe they just think you have a fear of intimacy," she joked. I moved to Tokyo a few weeks after that and she to Tel Aviv with her boyfriend. When we reconvened in Canada it seemed my being gay was immaterial and not germane to the matter at hand. It seemed merely a newly acquired and slightly irritating trait—like a bogus English accent acquired after a summer term at Oxford—that, at best, was something to be disregarded in the climate of illness that demanded cooler heads unclouded by issues of character. At worst, before I was diagnosed with cancer, I feared my sexual orientation could be the cause of my illness. I treated my sexuality upon my return like a too-loud shirt bought on holiday in the Caribbean that gets stowed in the bottom drawer. There was nothing so desexualizing to me as the total betrayal of my body.

When I found out that it was not AIDS but a highly curable form of cancer, my relief was alloyed with a sense of being a sham and a charlatan—doubly so, since I could not justify for myself a place within the hierarchy of suffering that belonged to either the gay community or those who had had to live through, or die of, truly serious cancer. I was embarrassed by having gotten off scot-free, and so I shut most everybody out. Without a career or, to my mind, a legitimate reason not to have one, I clung to my sister for support and shelter. Each day she drove me to the hospital where I received three minutes of plutonium radiation, and then home where I, depleted, slept for hours. I did not have many friends left in Toronto, and certainly no gay ones. Time accordioned and I was as sexless upon my return as when I had originally left Canada to go to college. If I was going to show someone my ass, it was to have a bone marrow test.

Ruth became my ally. Her boyfriend was thousands of miles away in Israel so she, too, was profoundly single. We resembled nothing so much as two aged celibate siblings, a fantasy bolstered by my geriatric infirmity as we walked down the street, me leaning on her arm. We had never lived together as adults in our parents' home with time on our hands and our needs provided for. In solidarity with me, she became as useless a member of society as I. We tooled around in my mother's car looking for fun food, cheap pajamas, kitchenware. Occasionally, even we were overcome by our lack of achievement and found ourselves in a bakery where Ruth, a cook by trade, would expound to the staff on sorbitol sweetener while I declared in a loud voice that I had never had anything so tasty when I was *living* in Tokyo—octogenarian football stars desperately waiting to be asked to recount the final minutes of the big game of 1927. We went to the movies in the middle of the day. "My God," Ruth exclaimed in a crowded theater at midday, "does everyone in town have Hodgkins?"

We fought only once during that time, to my recollection. It involved an errand she had wanted to run on the way to treatment that I did not. I snarled something about letting me out of the car, that I'd make my own way to the hospital. We both knew this was impossible since I was very weak and, having no real need of money, carried none. I sat in my seat seething and impotent, unable to make good my threat to get out and walk. Silence in the car. This was the first fissure in the veneer of total politesse that had existed between us during my illness. I felt closer to Ruth at that time than anyone else, but I had not discussed my feelings with her. I had no feelings to discuss and she had not pushed or pried. I was shocked by my sudden impulse to make a claim I clearly didn't have the goods to deliver. I hated my sister at that moment for being witness to that kind of impotence. She hated me back, I'm sure, for that very weakness that forced her to quell whatever tide of fierce childhood invective had been called up in her. She hated me, however briefly, for being ill and therefore requiring her to rise above the altercation and take the Moral High Ground. But take it she did. As we drove by Maple Leaf Gardens, the hockey arena, she said, "I bet people who buy their skates in that sports shop think they're really much better quality because they bought them at the Gardens." We both laughed, sports and sports enthusiasts being an endless source of derisive amusement in our decidedly unathletic family. She put her arm across the back of my seat and rubbed my neck.

When she went back to Israel after a month to reclaim her job, Ruth started to cry at the airport. "You really have to get out more," she pleaded. I, for one, had no intention whatsoever of getting out more. With Ruth I didn't have to be charming or a professional invalid. I did not have to answer the inevitable party question—"What do you do?"—with, "Vomit and sleep, and yourself?" My recent time in Tokyo felt distant and abortive. To talk about it was, to my mind, grandiose and pathetic. The drugs puffed up my face and I was unattractive. Such was my level of emotional strangulation that I was truly baffled by Ruth's tears. She, in turn, was baffled by my lack of self-esteem. She found my capacity for steely reserve alarming. How wonderful to have someone like her around who still found me funny and smart. My sister was the ultimate no-pressure date, the husband who looks across the room at his wife of twenty-five years and still sees the girl he married.

Ruth and Tom, her boyfriend, came home that summer to be married. I was declared in remission but not getting better. I developed a wracking cough and lost thirty-five pounds. I had avidly watched Oliver North's testimony on television, but by the time John Poindexter took the stand I was in too much pain to concentrate. Some undetected cancer outside the field of radiation had been growing steadily, and it was determined that I was in fact much sicker than when I had first presented with the disease and that I would have to have chemotherapy. Ruth became my caretaker again. Because of my extreme weightloss and the constant pain I was in, I was swinging wide and free emotionally. On good days, I was the aesthetic arbiter of her impending wedding, tyrannically deeming things either timeless or vulgar. On bad days, I would cry uncontrollably, once while watching *Sleeping Beauty* in the middle of a sticky-floored theater full of children, Ruth with her arms around me, comforting a child of her own.

I resumed my role as cancer patient rather than unmarried gay sibling. I joked to my family that if anyone was stupid enough to ask me when I was tying the knot, I would turn to them with tears welling up in my eyes and say, voice cracking, "Well . . . if I live that long." It occurs to me now that these assembled friends and strangers found me far more sympathetic as a man with cancer than as a queer. Perhaps some of them thought that Hodgkins was merely a coverup for what was really wrong with me. I had, in fact, been denied an invitation to a friend's engagement because her father-in-law, a physician no less, thought I had AIDS. At that point, however, being gay and being sick were ineluctably joined. I burst into tears a few weeks before the wedding, saying, "I'm in too much pain to be nice to anybody. No one's going to like me." My sense of self at my sister's wedding depended on both things being manifest. Ruth spoke of her wedding as something that might be a nice break for all of us from the utter joylessness of my illness, the true concern of the family. I had known my brother-in-law since I was twelve, and the three of us, Ruth, Tom and I, had been a contained unit for some time. I was made to feel that it was a party as much about their union as about my eventual recovery. I have a photograph of the three of us from the wedding: Ruth, Tom and I. We all have linked arms and it's tricky at first to pick out the bride and groom since we all look like we could be related—until one sees that they are the ones whose faces have broken out from nerves like adolescents. I can't even remember, though, if I'm standing in the middle or on one side.

At my nadir, about two days before the wedding, Ruth and Tom had tried to take me swimming to relieve some of the intense pain in my back. It was too cold for me and I started to weep. They sandwiched me between them so tightly I could no longer feel the water.

I have now been in remission for well over three years and it is likely that I will make it to five and be deemed cured. I have since moved to New York, where AIDS is now the illness that pervades every aspect of my and my friends' lives. Ruth and Tom are now endlessly solicitous and supportive about the illness of my friends, forever asking after their health. When newly returned from Israel, they came to visit me. Ruth had asked me a great many times, when we had seen my gay friends, "Is he positive?" (having just learned the difference from me between positivity and full-blown AIDS). She was slowly beginning to understand both the invisibility of HIV and its seeming ubiquity. When I decided to be tested, Tom was the only one in my family I told. When I found out I was negative, I gave him permission to tell Ruth. The illnesses and deaths of my friends have separated me from Ruth in a way. I have my worries about the people who are my fictive family here, and she has her worries about me and my health, fears she does not speak of with me.

Tom, Ruth and I are still very much a unit of three within my family. I now wait anxiously for them to have children who I, perhaps unrealistically, will consider to be partly mine, which they have not denied. To this day I still look at my sister and see a female version of myself with long hair and breasts. Ruth does not see the same strong resemblance, and never has. I see something in my sister's dark Semitic face as vital as a kidney, as untraceable, yet present, as the phantom pain from a limb long since gone.

b r a n d o n
j u d e l l

---

my sister hated
little richard

"Little Richard . . . yeuchhhh! He's such a faggot! He makes my stomach crawl."

—Linda Diana Judell, circa early seventies

Last week I was in a Stroudsberg, Pennsylvania, movie theater for more than an hour watching Julia Roberts comfort her love interest as he vomited from chemotherapy, solace him over his baldness, and coax macrobiotic foods down his unwilling throat. Finally, the moment comes when Julia's about to utter her Norma Shearer three-hankie speech, questioning why she should love someone who's going to croak soon. I station my popcorn box on the floor and get ready to turn on the waterworks. However, at that very moment, outside the theater's doors, the ushers drop what must be either a two-ton garbage can or a Brobdingnagian cymbal. KAWANG! Tears don't come, and since I'll probably never see *Dying Young* again, a moment of catharsis is lost forever.

Today my luck's better. I'm receiving free Showtime, and I get to view *Steel Magnolias* twice. This time it's Julia with one foot in the grave. My tears slide down my cheek onto my soiled sofa cushions. I search the floor for a tissue box I had seen a week or two ago. There's William Burroughs on the cover of *The Advocate*, a *Lear's* sporting the "Fable-bodied Raquel Welch," a press release announcing Zina Bethune as the new prima ballerina in *Grand Hotel*, an empty Pepsi can—and, by the window, partially buried by who knows what, is the local registrar's Certification of Death, Cert. No. 0652760. Date of Death: January 11, 1991. When you have death certificates sprawled on the floor, you know it's time to clean.

It's strange to bury someone young and straight nowadays. Di was forty-seven.

Before I was tested (result: HIV negative), I was sure I was going to go first. Having had hepatitis B plus non-A–non-B, amebiasis ten or more times, anal gonorrhea, frontal gonorrhea, lactose intolerance, sex in the Mine Shaft and in Macy's bathrooms, I should have, if there really is a God of morality, been pushing up pansies by now.

But Di left first, leaving her unused potty in my living room. It's white plastic in an aluminum stand. You supposedly fill it with cold water before using. I'm thinking of utilizing it as a tree planter.

Di, by the way, was a divorced mother of four tattooed boys (John Battista, Jr., Dominic Patrick, Christopher Joseph, and Joseph Anthony) and a pierced-ear girl (Adele Theresa). She got disunited from her Catholic-Italian hubby after he turned over the Christmas dinner table and tried strangling her. John Jr. and I yanked him off her. The hubby then got a rifle and chased her down Iris Road and I pursued. A heavy snow was falling—massive thick flakes like Upstate New York used to have before the Green House syndrome overtook us. I finally phoned the state police. They came and handcuffed the father while the five kids stood there whimpering. No wonder four of them wound up in AA, an organization Richard Chamberlain's father helped start. (Please note that I had brought as a present the Harveys Bristol Cream that was the direct, unintentional instigator of this Christmas fiasco. No one remembers this fact except me.)

Well, Di moved in with an awful alcoholic man and remained

with him for the next ten years. (She had Polaroids of her house after he tore it apart.) She also joined AA. I never knew why. I never saw her drunk or even dewey-eyed. But then we had grown apart for a while after she had given up custody of the kids to their father. I never totally forgave her.

Oh, I guess I did. At least on some days, I did.

As a gay boy who never would fertilize any eggs of his own, I thought it would be romantic to help raise her brood of five. In fact, it wasn't until my thirty-eighth birthday, two years ago, that I outgrew my I-Want-to-Be-a-Daddy syndrome. I have since developed attacks of I-Don't-Think-I-Even-Want-to-Own-a-Cat and Just-Because-I'm-a-Homosexual-Do-I-Really-Have-to-Go-Out-with-Men-When-They're-Such-Shits.

It's funny that I don't remember telling Di I was gay. I remember when I told my stepsister.

(Time out for family structure: I have a brother Jay and had a sister Diana. Our mother died when I was four from a brain aneurysm. My father [dead in '85] remarried a year later to Gerda, who had a daughter Evelyn from a previous marriage. We can continue now.)

Well, I was on the phone when I told Evelyn I was gay. She tried to outdo me by telling me how a dildo had changed her life.

Maybe I didn't tell Di, however, because she always seemed shy about sex, even though she was pregnant when she was married. One time she came to my house and sat on the sofa next to a copy of *Playgirl*. While I chatted on the phone, she kept turning it over to peruse the cover and then she'd quickly flip it over again. Di didn't have the chutzpah to check out penises in front of me.

At this very moment in time, as I'm writing this, Pumpkin has started bleeding. She'll be nineteen in October, which everyone tells me is ancient for a feline. It makes her almost as old as Hermione Gingold in human years. The blood is dripping from the left side of the litter box. There's a puddle right to the left of this chair, and I just discovered one in the living room. I lift her up and the blood is coming from her vagina. Now she's on my bed, and she just got blood on a copy of *Bound & Gagged* (Issue No. 23). It's the paragraph that starts "Getting back into the truck we started off toward the back roads and came across a [sic] old dirt road and he pull [sic] over and stop. He had to take a piss and so did I."

That's really amazing because Pumpkin cannot piss now. She's on the litter pan again and only a drop of reddish water comes out. Also bloodied is an unopened money request from the Sierra Club and a MoMA press release: "Cannes: Le Festival, 45 Years of Cinema."

My sister had trouble going to the bathroom, too, while she stayed with me. She had a fifty-foot oxygen tube that let her walk down my long hall to the bathroom. Did I say she was staying in the living room on the sofa bed? Did I even tell you what she died from?

Sorry, Diana died from lung cancer. She smoked a lot.

Anyway, eventually my living room became a hospital room. Homemedco finally delivered one of those electric beds you see on TV, where the mattress can be twisted into all shapes. We also got a large oxygen tank, a small portable one, the plastic toilet, and from some other organization we got cans of a fattening nutrition drink.

So I'm in the cab now heading for the Animal Medical Center on East Sixty-second Street. I'm shaking. I'm sure Pumpkin is going to die, and this will be the death that sends me over the brink. I have suicidal thoughts a lot. In fact, I always have. From the age of eleven on, I used to cover my head with those plastic dry-cleaning bags or I'd try to smother myself with my pillow. For a few nights when I was twelve or so, I even tried to saw my left wrist (I'm right-handed) with my Boy Scout pocket knife. I never got further than a few red creaselike marks.

One day, I took the window screen down. This was when I was eleven, and we lived in the Bronx on the fifth floor (Dad, Stepmom, and me). I opened the window and was going to jump. I stood on the ledge and imagined myself falling through the tree below. It was a big tree, about three stories high maybe. I wondered if its branches would catch me or poke out my eyes if I fell. I stood there, trying to grasp for a few reasons not to jump. The one I came up with was that Di was married and pregnant and that she'd be sad if I jumped. I'd also never see her baby then. I fell for that excuse.

I'm running out of excuses.

When Di got cancer, I was furious. I knew I only had her and my stepmother to live for. Mom's now eighty-three. Who's going to keep me alive? Almost everyone I have had a history with is gone . . . even the minor characters. (I'm getting bored with this train of thought. Too maudlin.)

Di as a teen had "bad" friends by Jewish Bronx standards. They were Italians or Gentiles. *Goys*. In those days, she wore something that was called a Garrison belt. It was thick, black, and wide. She also used to sit in the bathtub and let her jeans dry on her, so they'd be like a second skin.

Being eight years older than me, she had to babysit a lot.

One time we went to visit her gang, and this older, muscular type, sixteen or so, picked me up and rode me on his bike. My foot kept getting stuck in the spokes of his front wheel, so he lost his patience with me. I was scared and titillated and who knows what else.

Another time Di was babysitting for me at home and she had two guys and a girlfriend visiting. I kept bothering them and refusing to go to sleep. So one of the guys brought me back to my room and tied me with rope to my desk chair. A few minutes later, I was back in the living room, pulling the chair behind me.

This was a rather famous chair, by the way, in the Judell family, having been sat on for decades. In its near final moment, when I was nineteen or so, Dad picked it up and threw it at me. The seat came off the legs, but that didn't stop him. He picked up two of the legs, which were still attached to the other two by a rod, and chased me around the apartment. I grabbed the other two, and we played a game of push-and-pull. I pushed too much, and Dad fell. Shocked because of my Germanic upbringing and forced memorization of the Ten Commandments (respect one's elders), I ran out the door barefoot, zooming down five flights of stairs, moved to Manhattan, and became a *practicing* homosexual.

(Sadly, I'm still *practicing*, having not perfected the craft yet: I can't disco . . . and having my knees forced against my shoulder blades usually makes me feel more like a gymnast-in-training than a orgasmic bunny.)

Childhood memories . . . There must be more.

Di promised to take me to see *The Ten Commandments* and *Snow White and the Seven Dwarfs*, but she saw the movies with her friends instead.

I was just decontaminating the bedroom floor when I found the guidelines to writing this piece for this anthology under the bed, where I lost it about two months ago. It was under some Chad Allen photos (he played the boyfriend in *My Two Dads*). It was certainly time to clean up.

Well, I decided to go whole hog and use my Quik-Broom II, which Evelyn, the dildo-sister, gave me when she visited Di and me last year. She felt Di, in her condition, shouldn't be exposed to as much dust as she found here. I argued it wasn't dust but mobile carpeting. Anyway, we all went down the street to take Di out to eat. Di ordered her first steak in months and cleaned the whole platter up. Then she went to the bathroom. Evy followed and said Di was throwing up. Then we went home and Di went to the bathroom. When she came out, she said she had thrown up in the sink but cleaned it up. I replied, "Good." I detest vomit. I've actually read sex ads, maybe one, where vomit was included. I hope this perversity doesn't catch on.

Anyway, I was just vacuuming now and the cord pushed a coffee cup that Di had bought me off the speaker, and it broke. She had given me four black mugs manufactured in West Germany. She knew I loved Deutschland and wanted to move there. I now also have her very nice set of white microwave dishware, her VCR, her double cassette player, her jewelry that I mete out to relatives, our mother's mah-jong set, which she wanted to give her daughter but which I absconded with, her thousands of medical bills, and five of her remaining death certificates.

Di's the biggest part of my Museum of the Dead, although I wouldn't exactly call her the biggest draw or the one of highest societal importance. Nevertheless, she could be labeled the sentimental favorite.

Was just reading Vidal: "Pages from an Abandoned Journal." In it there's a character who's also written about in Capote's *Answered Prayers*. Well, whoever this homo was, he's dead now and the line goes: "Hard to believe someone you once knew is actually dead, not like the war where sudden absences in the roster were taken for granted."

I really can't write today. The cat's on antibiotics, and when I was on the subway platform station, heading for the New Music Seminar at that awful Hotel Marriott, I imagined my body lying on the tracks, in crucifixion position. . . . No, I was spread-eagle . . . and the train was speeding over me and slicing me to pieces neatly.

I used to fantasize about being hit by cars a lot in my early twenties.

I remember back in the early seventies, I was living upstate with Diana, her hubby, and I think there were only three kids then. I was working in Camera Craft in Parkchester in the Bronx. It must have been close to a three-hour train-and-subway ride each way, and I read Nijinsky's diary and Plath's *Bell Jar* one after another. I was living life as an impotent heterosexual when this adorable older man (thirty or something) made a pass at me on the train going to Brewster. I had so much sexual energy pent up in me that when I talked to him, I must have sounded crazy. I think my arms did weird things, too. Anyway, I scared the chap off into another car.

I'm not even sure how this section started off anymore. I wanted to talk about how there was no time for mourning anymore. But I also wanted to tell you about being in the Marriott today and attending the New Music Seminar. Well, I was going up or down an ugly escalator when I realized how I can't really touch people. Hugging or petting or holding a hand is like a big deal for me. I have become robotic.

Anyway, I remembered the only time I hugged Diana. It was in the living room, and she had just been told by the doctor over the telephone that she would no longer have a regular nurse visiting her. She would have a hospice nurse. Di asked, "That means there's no hope, right?"

I was standing in the hall listening because the doctor had spoken to me first.

Di put the phone down, and we went to each other and hugged and cried. It wasn't the light tears. It was like the heavy, heaving tears.

I think I might have hugged Diana one other time. Just after her doctor told me she had six months to live (she never knew), and I had her move in with me, I had a fit in my bedroom. I started pulling books off the shelves, and I broke my GE phone against the wall, and I was screaming and crying, and I ran into the street and called Evelyn, the dildo-sister, at work.

"I can't take it. I can't take it."

When I got home, Di said, "I don't want to make you unhappy. I don't want to cause you pain." I think we might have hugged then, but that's a little foggy.

Oh, during that fit, I almost destroyed my computer and fax machine, but I wasn't that crazed. Whenever I have a fit, a little controlling voice says, "Destroy only what you can afford to replace."

I've finally got a full-time job. During the year I took care of Di, I brought in $5,000 as a freelancer. We sort of lived off my fourteen credit cards. Anyway, my old bosses from '85 called me back. It appears one of their editors was murdered by a trick; another had a spinal operation. After two years of being rejected by every gay organization, God stepped in and knocked off a few people *for* me.

So I'm editing a story today—and for half an hour I am weighing whether it's okay to say that Christ had a "hard-on" while getting crucified. I finally "red" it out. Arousing the Lord is almost as bad as sticking him in a glass of urine. Why rile the censors more than you have to?

Di, by the way, converted to Christianity without telling me. I always felt it was an AA thing. Going to Alcoholics Anonymous in certain areas upstate is like having your foreskin sewn back on. When I found out, I didn't talk to her for more than a year. Now

I don't feel Judaism is the end all, but most of our relatives were killed for being Jewish and our father was a mess because he was Jewish during the Nazi period, so I actually feel we the survivors owe our ancestors something. I feel that if you have to convert, you don't turn to another organized religion, especially one that really messed up the world and used gays as faggots. You turn instead to Buddhism, Taoistic sexual massage, biorhythm, astrology, meditation, reflexology, water tanks, psychoanalysis, Weight Watchers.

It was sort of strange: here the homo was throwing the Christian out of the house—or in reality just refusing to communicate with her. (For Diana's last Christmas, though, I almost broke down and bought her a rosary. I wound up not buying her anything. I have this weird something-or-other that says I can't buy expensive gifts for people who I know are going to die in a month or so. I want to. I go into store after store, but I just can't do it, and then I hate myself for not buying a gift for the rest of my life. A Jewish self-flagellation tendency, maybe.)

I finally made up with Di and let her go her own way on religion, but I knew she knew it riled me. When we were signing her into Sloan-Kettering, the sign-in secretary asked, "What religion?" Di waited a few beats before she could answer "Catholic" in front of me.

Then when she moved in here, there were the magazines (e.g., *Unity*) and the tomes (*Book of Miracles*). They all gave her hope. Part of me didn't want her to have hope. Be realistic. Say you're going to be dead and buried in a few months and get ready for it.

I remember when I had to push Di around in her wheelchair. She wanted a new pair of eyeglasses. So we went into this expensive shop on Columbus Avenue because it was the closest. The bejeweled-with-attitude saleslady hawked three-hundred-dollar frames at us. Her big sell was how strong they were. "They are guaranteed for seven years."

What have you in the seven-month range? I almost asked, but you couldn't do that in front of Di.

It's the same with certain AIDS folks. Craig used to joke that he was one of the Living Dead. Tolin, on the other hand, even when he lost his ass and most of his other body fat, was worried whether

he'd have enough money to live on for the next ten years. Get real,
kid. Ten minutes is more like it.

I should have let Di buy the glasses. I talked her out of them
though.

I am moving upstairs this weekend to an apartment with a
terrace. For more than fourteen years I have lived on the ground
floor, forced to keep my venetian blinds drawn. No sunlight. In
New York City if people on the street see what you have inside
your house, it's soon inside theirs. It would have been nice for Diana
to be able to wheel herself to the balcony and get sunlight.

I hate writing this piece. I hate feeling the loss. I still haven't
finished paying off the Coble-Reber Funeral Home, possibly because
this way I'm keeping her from being totally buried. Also I didn't
like how they sort of brown-coated her green-blue face. Anyway, for
the last six weeks of her life, Diana stayed with her daughter Adele
in Pennsylvania. Diana need to be bathed and helped to the bathroom, and her morphine drip had to be monitored. It was best that
there be a woman to take care of her, and it was best that Adele
and Diana recement their relationship.

I visited on weekends and for Christmas. Then Adele called to
say that Diana was having nonstop hallucinations. I caught the earliest train to Harrisburg possible.

Sister was in her wheelchair, going on about cups of coffee,
that there weren't enough for everyone. There were three of us and
three cups, but Diana felt someone else was coming, and that there
wouldn't be enough. She started getting really distraught.

Adele and I finally got her to bed. The bed was always in a
sit-up position. Diana even slept that way. Then I got Adele to
rest. She'd been up for over twenty hours trying to calm her mother
down. Now it was my turn.

Out of nowhere, on her hospital-type bed, with the oxygen
tubes attached to her nose, Diana would scream, *"It hurts! It hurts!
Why are you doing this to me? Why? It burns."*

I'd open the window and tell her the breeze was blowing the
pain away. Diana would calm down. Then I'd tell her she was going
to heaven. She'd smile. I told her our mother, our Uncle Herman,

our Aunt Lena, and our father would be there. Diana started screaming, *"Not him! I'm not going to see him! No! No! No!"*

It's strange how even through the strongest morphine hallucinations, reality fights its way through.

(Did I tell you Di once had belt marks under her eye from our sweet Germanic father? I can't even remember now if I have written about him. It's strange how months have gone by since I've started this piece. Maybe that's why I have avoided shrinks lately . . . in fact, for the last decade or so.)

I have a wall of dead now in my new bathroom. Friends deceased from AIDS, or soon to be, smile at me as I try to get rid of the gas that's symptomatic of my lactose intolerance. It's sort of like them nodding in amusement and saying, "You just try kvetching about being bloated."

After soothing Diana's worry, telling her that Dad wouldn't be up there in the clouds (I can't remember how I got out of that one. I'm sure I didn't say he was now a security guard in hell or something like that), her new worry was that she had forgotten one of her children. I helped her count them on her cold, emaciated, stiff fingers. "John's in Panama with his new wife, Trini. Adele is resting in the next room. Dominic is in Upstate New York, learning to be an airplane engineer. Chris is selling kitchens and venetian blinds. Joey is in school in California." A momentary smile would light across her face. Then anguish.

"No! No! Someone is missing." For the next half hour or so, we would repeat this process. Then Adele came in. We both stood at the foot of the bed and looked at my sister gasping like a fish out of water. I wanted to take her pillows and smother her. I would have done it, too, if Adele hadn't been there. I really felt I had the strength. Instead, I left the room to call her hospice care workers.

"Can't you give her anything to sleep? To put her out? She's in pain. She's in agony."

"Your sister's on a very high dose of morphine. Nothing will probably work."

Remembering Shirley MacLaine's big scene at the end of *Terms of Endearment* (and I really did), I screamed, "Don't you think we should try? *She's in pain.*"

The woman said a prescription would be waiting at the local pharmacy, which was great since there was no one to pick it up for us.

I went back into the makeshift hospital room. Diana was screaming that she needed to go to the bathroom, to the potty next to the bed. Adele and I lifted her into my arms. She fell upon me, and I grasped her as best I could. It was like I was hugging a skeleton. As I maneuvered this body, it started screaming, *"No! No! No!"*

I put Diana back in bed, straight on her back. The oxygen tube kept falling out of her nose; I kept replacing it. There was mucous hanging out of her mouth. Either Adele or I wiped it away. Then Adele told me this was the end. She had been instructed by the hospice care workers to recognize oncoming death—something to do with veins in the neck or forehead or coloring. I don't remember. So we stood there, maybe holding Diana's hand, waiting.

Soon she was dead. I was so glad. The hospice care workers showed up ten minutes later. Adele and I kept going back into the room to look at what was left. During the final minutes, I had almost expected to see a spirit pulling itself out of that body. The moment of death is, however, sadly anticlimactic.

I possibly hugged Adele, then started making the death calls to the funeral home, to relatives, to friends. And somewhere during this time—or maybe the next day—or maybe it never happened, Adele told me how she had wanted to smother her mother at the very same moment I did, when we were both at the foot of the bed. She didn't because I was there. Then she said she was glad I had placed Diana on her back.

"What?"

"You knew she couldn't breathe on her back."

"No."

"That's why she always slept sitting up."

The New York Times ran the following paid obituary:

JUDELL—Linda Diana. The much beloved mother of John, Adele, Dominic, Christopher, and Joseph Scalera. The nurturing sister of Brandon, Evelyn, and Julian. As Annie

Dillard wrote: "I am a frayed and nibbled survivor in a fallen world and I am getting along. I am aging and eaten and have done my share of eating too." Sadly, Diana hadn't eaten or aged enough, dying at 47 of lung cancer. But she had survived child abuse, adult abuse, and alcoholism, never complaining and always being there, physically, financially, and emotionally for those who came to her door. Funeral service Tuesday, 11AM, at Coble-Reber Funeral Home, 208 N. Union Street, Middletown, PA.

Having a terrace in New York makes you feel like a rich person. Hopefully, I'll be able to buy some lounge chairs soon. In the meantime, I'll sit on Di's unused commode, read the Sunday *Times*, and feel very grand.

ronald l. donaghe

---

my sister and i

My sister, Libby, burst out laughing as she turned over an album cover in the light. "Someone kissed his picture!" she said, then went on laughing.

I cringed, feeling my face turn hot. Just a turn of the picture in the light revealed the impression of my lips on the cellophane. The album was my copy of Herman's Hermits, with a close-up of the group's lead male singer. I was afraid she'd turn and ask if it was me who did it. Just a bit more reasoning by her about whose album it was, who had access to it, and she would have flung open my closet door, with me cowering inside.

But such a thought would not have entered her mind back then. It was 1965. She was thirteen; I was seventeen. We lived on a farm near Deming, New Mexico, with our parents and a younger brother and sister. We were so naive and sheltered that neither of us had a word for the way I felt about boys.

In a visceral way I knew, but I didn't know to say, "I'm gay," or "I'm homosexual." I never told Libby that it was me who kissed the singer's picture. When she laughed about it, without realizing my secret, I was relieved but also ashamed. It was laughter of surprise, not of meanness, but it made me realize that laughter was one way people might react if they knew about me.

I didn't think in terms of closets and being something other than what I felt, which had no name. I just happened to like boys— a lot. Libby and I were normal, active teenagers as far as I could tell. She had many girlfriends, best friends she had gone to school with all her life. We were both "good" students; the teachers liked us.

We both dated, both mooned over boys, but she didn't know that. She could talk to me about her crushes, especially when they were on some of my male friends; but I couldn't talk about mine. So I retreated to safety, pointing out girls, saying that they were pretty. That was the only way I could talk about such feelings.

To get close to boys I found attractive, I begged my parents to allow me to throw parties. My whole purpose in giving them was to invite the boys I was in love with. But because that might be too obvious, I invited as many people as I could think of.

Although Libby didn't know my motives, she was my ally in convincing our parents to let me throw the parties. She was also a familiar, helpful face among the crowd. With her reddish hair and a spray of freckles across her nose, her otherwise creamy complexion and good Irish looks attracted many of my male friends. And even though she wasn't yet in high school, she mixed well and was kept busy dancing with them. So for both of us, the parties were enjoyable. For me, however, the enjoyment was bittersweet. I would have been in heaven if one of those boys whom I secretly longed for had snuck away with me and confessed his same longing for me. But I didn't share my secret with anyone—not even Libby.

Although I had frequent contact with most members of our large family, there was an internal struggle within me about being homosexual. We were a gregarious bunch. Family vacations were always spent among relatives. We could travel across the states of Arizona, New Mexico, and Texas—some fourteen hundred miles— and spend every night at some relative's house along the way. And in all the contact I had with my male cousins, there was only the most cursory sexual experimentation—pissing in the toilet together, comparing penis size, or "jacking off" out in the field while moaning about girls. In all my extended family, I heard no hint of the proverbial uncle, of whom no one spoke, nor the suspect male cousin who spoke with a lisp or had been caught in a dress. I was the one, the only one, I thought.

Libby and I were close enough in age that we played with the same cousins and, before one of our trips, we made plans as to what we'd like to do once we got to Waco or Lubbock, Texas, or Apache Junction, Arizona—depending on which set of cousins were there, which ones had a car that we could ride in. As we grew older, she began to wonder, "I hope they (meaning any number of our cousins) know some cute boys I can meet." I hoped the same thing, but I couldn't say it. With a pal like my sister on those vacations, I enjoyed myself, and I felt welcome in the family; but I was still alienated as a result of a self-imposed fear of how Libby or others might react to my burgeoning homosexual feelings.

When I started college in Las Cruces in 1966, only sixty miles east of Deming, I still dated women but longed to date guys. By then I liked calling myself a homosexual. I sometimes looked at myself in the mirror and repeated a litany. "I am a homosexual. A homo-sexual." For three more years, I may as well have told myself that I was the *only* homosexual in New Mexico. I still had not met another gay person.

Yet those years propelled me into many directions at once. I blossomed as a student "leader," which meant being a student senator, the state president of a nationwide organization of education students. In that capacity, I once spoke before five thousand teachers and, for three years in a row, attended national conventions in Houston, Texas, Washington, DC, and San Francisco, California. At the same time that I outwardly appeared to have goals and plans, my inward life was still one of doubt and confusion.

I was unable to ignore the increasing realization that dating women was a sham and that I had to do something about my inner feelings. I searched in those dark days for other gay people, but could still find no real evidence that there were others, except for reading about them at the university library.

When I became familiar with Las Cruces and El Paso, Texas,

farther south, I drove to Deming to get Libby and, with pleasure, did what a big brother is supposed to do. I took her to the "big city" of El Paso for a Coke and to drag its main streets. Both being true hicks, we gawked at the lights, the bustle, the El Paso teenagers at their Sonic drive-in, which seemed bigger, brighter, and better than anything Deming had to offer. I took Libby to a couple of the college football games in Las Cruces, a dance or two, hoping she'd decide to follow me on to college.

But she didn't. Like our two sisters before us, she married right out of high school. By the time she graduated in 1970, I was dropping out of college, due to massive changes in my life.

They began in 1969 when I was a junior in college and attending a Student Education Association convention in Washington, DC; there, I finally entered one of the gay bars I'd read about in *Life* or *Look* magazines, lost my virginity during a one-night stand, and felt lucky for it. When I returned to Las Cruces I knew for sure that I was homosexual. I guess it showed, oozed from the pores of my skin, attracted other gay people to me, or I to them. It turned out that my roommate was homosexual, that he had secretly longed to tell me, but it wasn't until after I returned from Washington that he confessed his secret.

He took me to a gay bar in El Paso where I soon became a regular on weekends and sometimes in the middle of the week. Shortly after that, I had my first male lover. My friendships in college began to change. My new friends were guys in other dormatories I'd met in El Paso and older men who weren't associated with the university.

I didn't regret the turn in my life toward the gay world, but as my focus shifted more and more toward it, my relationship with and thoughts about my family became fuzzy. As I got more involved in the gay scene, I stopped making those frequent trips home. I stopped taking Libby to the places where I hung out. By that time, she was busy with her own friends and dating. I recall one weekend night when I was at home, in Deming. She was on a date with the man she would eventually marry. When she got home I happened to be just inside the living room door, where her boyfriend kissed her goodnight. It seemed odd to see her kissing this man, and I realized with regret that her life was changing, too, and that she was no longer my kid sister, but a young woman.

I still visited Deming occasionally but cut the time short so that I could get back to the nightlife in El Paso. For about six months, I was happy having finally made contact with others like myself, having a place to go where I could be with them. My grades soared. Years of anxiety fell away. But this new gay life I had discovered was in the backwash of the gay world. Eventually, I began to feel sad at the condition of the gay life in El Paso and Las Cruces. And when Libby asked me about things, I pretended I was dating women from El Paso.

Because I felt the need to lie, I felt even more alienated and, as soon as the newness of finally being a sexual person wore off, I got weary of the "gay" life. It began to go in circles. The bars were the only places where gay people in this part of the world congregated. The emphasis was on having sex, falling in love forever for an evening, breaking up tragically, and doing the same thing again one weekend later. The normal life Libby had, of dating, of bringing her fiancé home to meet the family—all seemed so much better. I listened to her with mixed feelings—at once happy for her and yet envious that I could not bring home Bob or Tom or Dick, or whoever my current fling was at the time.

In the middle of my plunge into the gay world, I turned abruptly and married the first woman I found attractive, nice, and willing to accept this terrible secret of mine, someone who would help me to change myself. Rather than thinking in terms of trying to change the gay world, I became disgusted with it. In getting married, I was trying to go from being homo- to heterosexual, to repackage myself, to padlock and chain my closet door shut. It became dark and dank in that part of my mind, again a secret— even from myself.

I got married perilously close to April first. Libby married a man from Las Cruces a few months later. I think my parents sighed with relief when I got married at age twenty-one, which was getting a little late in my family for the men to settle down and have children. Libby's marriage was approximately right on schedule for the women in our family. While she and I lived in Las Cruces and saw each other occasionally, my marriage began to unravel right away.

My wife and I and her two girls from a previous marriage moved into married-student housing on the campus. With this marriage and the psychological pressure cooker my mind had become, my grades in college sank to their lowest ebb. The next semester was my last. I began to feel alienated on almost every level of my life.

My wife seemed to have an innate ability to add to that feeling by taking up the banner of changing me from a homosexual, but she chose degrading ways to go about it. She began instructing me in my overt behavior. "Hold your wrist stiff," she urged when I took her hand during a romantic moment. I wanted to withdraw my hand from hers at such a remark, but I dutifully tried to stiffen my wrist, ignoring the shame that coursed through me. "Come up on the balls of your feet," she'd say as she watched me walk away from her. These comments came from the blue and were hellishly effective in making me feel like a freak, even in her supposedly loving eyes. I often thought I saw mockery in them. In comparison to Libby's marriage, where she and her husband were buying a house, mine was continuing a downward spiral. It was the loneliest time of my life.

At what point it became unbearable, I don't remember. But I followed the mistake of my marriage with another one. Suddenly, out of college with only a year left before I could graduate, married and feeling lonely, I left my wife, my family, and Las Cruces, stepped off the planet Earth, and entered Hell.

Vietnam was going strong in 1971 when I dropped out of school. No longer a student, I was threatened with the draft, so I abruptly joined the air force. It was also a convenient way to temporarily step out of my marriage.

After basic training, however, my wife and her children joined me, and I felt doubly trapped. We picked up fighting where we had left off a few months before. To "save" our marriage, we conceived a child. We lived together for four more months in a shabby house outside Wichita Falls, Texas. Our lives continued to deteriorate.

Getting letters from Libby about her apparently happy, but childless, marriage only made my pain more acute. When I was sent to Brooks Air Force Base in San Antonio, Texas, my pregnant wife and her two daughters moved to Colorado. A few months later, she wrote to me declaring our separation.

I was delighted. Although I had not cheated on her, nor even considered it, her letter suddenly made me feel free. I went immediately to my closet door and flung it open to have another look. My absence from the gay world had made me grow fonder of my previous experiences, now recalled with rose-colored clarity and, once more, I entered the gay world.

This time, with the new gay activism that was spawned at Stonewall Inn in New York City, I decided to work on my pride. My military life became irrelevant and I would soon use my homosexuality and the military's stance against it to get out. Before I did, however, I met the man with whom I would spend the next decade and a half of my life. I became happy again, this time with a vengeance.

But when I called home and spoke with Libby, our roles had reversed. While my life was on an upward spiral, hers was beginning to decline. I listened to her small voice on the telephone as she told me of the draconian way her husband's family lived. Her husband, like the rest of the men in his family, considered himself above reproach. Libby was his slave, his chattel, like his mother was to his father. At every meal, the men ate first while the women stayed in the kitchen; then, if there was anything left to eat, the women were permitted to sit at the table and eat the leftovers. Libby told me that when her husband took her to a restaurant, she had to keep her eyes on him or on her plate. She told me of the bills that were piling up; while she was expected to work steadily, he permitted himself the luxury of quitting a job whenever he wanted.

The best I could tell her was to treat the debts like a game and not to let them overwhelm her. About her marriage, I could only listen with sympathy and ache for her, recalling my own failed marriage.

When my lover and I finally got out of the air force with honorable discharges and were living in our first apartment in a gay ghetto of San Antonio, I wrote to various members of my family to tell them that I was gay. I still didn't have the courage to tell them over the telephone. Oddly, I didn't begin with Libby. I wrote my first confessional letter to one of my older sisters. She maddeningly referred back to my failed marriage by saying that my exwife was probably not the right woman to turn me into a heterosexual and that two sick people couldn't make a marriage. When I told Libby, she seemed to accept my homosexuality rather than trying to argue me out of it. She was the only one who invited my lover and me to visit if we ever made it to Las Cruces.

By my own experience I had found that being gay was not a choice to be made. She seemed to understand that, too, when I told her that *acting* on my gay feelings *was* a choice—but being attracted to members of my own sex was not. In my letters to her, I tried to explain it in terms that anyone could understand, whether they were heterosexual or gay, by saying that I had no choice in finding sunsets beautiful. I just do. But if someone told me that it was wrong to love sunsets and I believed them, my only choice in the matter would be to refuse to watch them.

My parents were silent on the matter, but when, a few years later, I brought my lover to Deming to meet them on one of our first vacations together, they seemed to know that we were more than friends, though no one, including Libby, could quite treat us as if he and I were married. My mother had always made a point of setting up her daughters with domestic items when they got married. That usually entailed a complete set of dishes, everyday silverware, bedding, and such as that. There was none of that for us.

Even as the years passed and my lover and I stayed together, there was still none of the legitimacy of a marriage, even as far as where we spent our vacations; neither his family nor mine thought it important that we switch back and forth for the holidays, so we frequently spent them apart. There was just that silent ascent that they knew what was involved, and they preferred not to talk about it.

When my lover and I moved to Las Cruces in 1977 and opened a bookstore, we began having a lot of contact with my family.

During that time, Libby was working at a department store and her seven-year marriage to her first husband was coming to a close. When it ended, she moved in with my lover and me. This was the first time in years that she and I had lived in the same house. Here, it was as roommates. She paid her portion of the rent, her portion of the groceries and utilities, and pitched in with the housework.

That arrangement only lasted a few months, until she was able to get on her feet after the divorce. But as I remember, it was pleasant, and this time there was none of the alienation I had felt when we lived in the same house as teenagers. In that sense, I felt free. If there was any talk among the rest of the family about my lover and me, Libby could report back to them with some authority that we shared a fairly ordinary existence, doing such mundane and everyday things as taking out the garbage, cleaning house, and working to make ends meet.

That was the seventies, the decade when gay liberation began, after Stonewall, and after the APA or some such changed its official position of what homosexuality is—whether it is a disease that needs to be (or can be) cured or a developmental problem that the afflicted can live with. Members of my family, mainly my siblings, went along with the shift, having my lover and me as examples to show that homosexuals come from the same environment that they do.

Time has simply worn down the barriers between me (as a gay person) and my family. In 1987 when my lover and I parted ways after fourteen years because he said he was heterosexual, my family knew that I was going through a bad time. My mother asked me one day if I thought that Jim and I would ever get back together. My father asked about him occasionally, wondering if I ever heard from him. My two older sisters offered a little sympathy for the breakup, one going so far as to say that it was like a real divorce, adding, "Isn't it?" Libby, however, was the only one of my family I could talk to, the only one to whom I could give the gory details of our breakup. But beyond the initial sympathy, even from her I kept my real pain, the years-long hurt that came over me.

With the publication of my first novel came another step for us as a family, far beyond those feelings of alienation I had as a teenager.

In 1989, Libby and my brother came to a party given for me at a lesbian friend's house, upon the publication of my novel. Close to a hundred people attended. Former professors of mine, a lawyer friend, their spouses, people from my job at the local university, and droves of gays and lesbians attended. Libby brought her second husband. My brother brought his girlfriend and a male friend of his from Deming. My brother and sister were curious, kind, glad for the turnout. That's as close to celebrating my homosexuality as they have ever come.

My family doesn't approve or disapprove; they know that I'm happier as a gay person. I doubt that any of them, including Libby, will ever be *glad* or celebrate the fact that I'm gay. But now that I have met another man, after almost five years of being single, I am confident that Libby is glad for me. Whether this pairing will last is the same crapshoot that it is for her.

On the subject of our marriages to men, Libby has often complained (with some justification) that men are selfish creatures. Of the six children in our family, and of the four of us who have been married, we've collectively had five divorces.

Libby has just gone through her second divorce. Her first one she often said was a happy occasion, as mine was. But her second one was just as bad for her as mine was for me. Unlike me, however, she went to a counselor for help and was able to charge back into life. She once asked how I got over my divorce to my lover without counseling. I told her that I handled it by wallowing in abject self-pity for a year or so.

At times I can look at Libby and recall the little girl I was once the big brother to; at others, all I can see is the woman she has become. In ways, her experiences have made her more mature than I am. She says she is glad to be single, again, now that the shock of her divorce is over. I still wrestle with the fear of living alone.

There are still vestiges of anger in Libby at the shabby way her second husband went about getting his life in order before asking for the divorce. But I understand her anger, her need for counseling, and I admire her strength to pick herself up at thirty-eight to yet again go through the dating scene (I was more weary of that than she is).

Recently, she and I rummaged through the male photos of a gay magazine sharing our delight in the pictures; it could just as well have been *Playgirl*. I told her which men attracted me. She told me which men she liked. As our discussion widened to include singers, we agreed on country-western singer George Strait, disagreed on Randy Travis. I gave her a pinup poster of Clint Black. I wonder if, when she turns that picture of him into the light, she will burst out laughing, or smile, seeing the impression of my lips on his picture? My bet is she'll laugh warmly and hang it in her bedroom as she said she was going to do.

christopher wittke

sisterly advice

July 1979

"Whatever you do, you can never, ever tell Mom," my older sister Connie said through quivering lips. Tears welled up in her eyes as she explained, "After Dad dies, Mom will finally be free. If you tell her this she'll worry about you for the rest of her life."

It was a typically hot summer day and we were standing in the backyard of my family's home in Manchester, Connecticut. The occasion was my first attempt at coming out to someone I trusted, that is, anyone other than myself and the men I had had sex with in the few preceding years. I had graduated from high school the month before and it slowly occurred to me that the way I had been living my life—being attracted to men sexually and acting on that attraction—was, in fact, destined to be The Way I Would Be Living My Life.

I also realized that I wasn't going to be able to keep secret for long my dabbling in nearby Hartford's gay community. I had been dating a writer for a sleazy bar rag called *Nightshift* (b. 1979, d. 1979), and for a couple of weeks I had been making up unlikely

excuses for overnight excursions with my new friend. Without telling me beforehand, the writer included my full name in an article
he had written about gay people working on electoral campaigns.
Even though I was nervous about having my name printed in association with a gay issue, I told myself that it was a good thing that
it happened, because there was probably little chance that anyone I
knew would actually read the article. It also gave me a feeling of
being open and honest about my sexuality, which was sort of a
theme for a lot of people in the late seventies. Of course, this
reminded me that I had some catching up to do, family-wise, in
the openness-and-honesty-about-my-sexuality department.

Connie seemed like the obvious choice for first family member
to get the news. Although eight years my senior, she was closer in
age to me than my two other siblings. In the summer of '79, I was
seventeen and Connie was twenty-five, a nurse in the emergency
room in our town's hospital. We were the last of the four kids to
still be living at our parents' home. We were also similar physically
and psychologically (squishy and borderline misanthropic) in the
same way that our older brother and sister were of a type (ectomor-
phic and generally upbeat).

My oldest sister, Jane, was thirty-two in 1979, and my brother
Rudi was twenty-nine. They both had long escaped our emotionally
tense household for lives, such as they were, of their own. Connie
and I, on the other hand, were still stuck in the mire of our cramped
two-family home with our father, who was getting progressively
sicker and debilitated with the emphysema he had suffered for as
long as I could remember, and mother, who probably would have
divorced the tyrant she had married in order to escape her own
emotionally tense family's household, if, a) she hadn't been a devout
Roman Catholic, and b) my father hadn't been chronically ill for a
very long time.

But that was the situation I had to come out in—I couldn't
exactly divorce my family and go find another one—and although I
knew I would soon be telling all of them that the baby of the family
was queer, I chose Connie for the season opener. I could then continue in ascending chronological order, telling my brother, my oldest

sister, and Mom. At some point after that, I imagined, we could all get together and figure out what to do about Dad, if anything.

Connie was the first stop on the road from the closet and (I convinced myself) she was destined to be the most supportive. Besides the fact that she always seemed to genuinely like me, we both had endured my father's emotionally abusive verbal outbursts (he was too weak to be physically abusive, but still had the lung power to bellow and belittle). Connie and I developed a kind of war-weary relationship, like soldiers bonded together in hard times.

Although Connie was just like most other members of my extended family in that she was distrustful of "difference"—in people or places or activities that didn't conform to the well-beaten paths upon which most of them had chosen to live their lives; Connie had often said, "I'm not a feminist, I like it when men open doors for me"—I was me and she was Connie. My telling her that I was gay certainly was not going to fundamentally change anything. I believed, as truly as any seventeen-year-old queen who survived twelve years of Catholic school right-and-wrong black-and-white indoctrination and an emotionally stunted home life could possibly believe, that my announcing my homosexuality was "No Big Deal." And that was how I decided to frame my announcement.

I picked that specific July day to tell Connie for no other reason than the fact that when I glanced out my bedroom window I saw her in the backyard. That was the only place we ever really had conversations away from parental ears. My father was sitting in his living room chair, which is where he sat like a sentinel for all of his waking hours. I stepped over the long green tube that delivered oxygen to his nostrils twenty-four hours a day and that snaked throughout most of the rooms in the house like some flexible futuristic wiring system. My mother was reading the newspaper at the kitchen table, whistling along (off-key) with the radio.

I strolled quickly yet casually through the house, out the back door and down the porch steps. Connie was scooping up dog crap in the pen out back by the garage.

I can't remember the small talk I used to get us into the conversation, but I do know that I started to cry. The fact is, I hadn't read any of those helpful coming out books that suggest that you never cry in front of the person you want to come out to ("because you want to give the impression that you believe you are sharing good news"). At seventeen, I didn't even know such books existed. Connie asked me what was wrong and seemed genuinely concerned, if uncomfortable with handling such naked emotion.

"It's no big deal," I sniffled, and then I told her that I had recently done some "work for a gay community newspaper in Hartford," which was true if you counted the amount of time I spent sneaking around with the bar-rag writer "work." Connie nodded the nod of a person who had only ever said homophobic things about gay people if she ever said anything at all. And she kept nodding, not wanting to make the obvious connection in her head. So I added, rather cleverly I realize now, "And that's a community I think I may be a part of," as if to convey that there was an organized entity for me to fall back on for support should she reject me. I then realized that using the word "may" was giving Connie some sort of qualifier to seize upon, so I amended my statement by hastily blurting, "*am* a part of."

"It's no big deal," rumbled repeatedly through my head like a mantra that was also a blatant attempt to convince myself that it was truly not a big deal. But Connie's silence led me to believe otherwise. Her lips began to tremble as she told me, not that it was no big deal, but rather who I shouldn't share this information with. I remember feeling unprepared for this response and thinking "I can't tell Mom?"

While Connie may have had a point about Mom's finally being liberated from the shackles of a bad thirty-year marriage on the occasion of my father's death (which would come about eighteen months later), I remember thinking it was ghoulishly presumptuous of her to speak of his death as if it were some approaching holiday. "After Dad dies" indeed. Honestly, there was no love lost between my father and me, but I had this vision of my sister twisting a knot in his oxygen tube and gleefully rubbing her hands together as his face turned blue.

I shook that image out of my head when I realized that it would probably be best if I focused on the moment at hand, concentrating on what I had just told Connie and her reactions. This was my moment, my issue to deal with, my no-big-deal announcement. But it was playing out as Connie's big moment and as she hugged me—neither of us an experienced hugger—I remember thinking how utterly free of emotional support the gesture felt. As I walked back to the house wishing I had never opened my mouth, I saw my mother watching us out the back window.

"Is something the matter?" my mother asked as I shuffled through the kitchen.

"No, everything's fine," I said, hoping against hope.

Back in my bedroom I wrote in my journal that everything was going to be okay, that in a day or two Connie would come around to seeing how unimportant my being gay was in the ultimate scheme of things and that eventually she would probably consider it a novelty. I wrote, "I can even imagine her saying things like 'This is Chris, my gay brother,' like I was just the latest and coolest thing." But I wasn't convincing myself. I still couldn't shake the feeling that telling Connie was the biggest mistake I could have made. She made it clear to me that I had just delivered the worst possible news a sister could get from her brother.

Three days later I was propped up on my bed writing adolescent poetry in my journal. I had actually not seen Connie since my announcement, our conflicting work schedules and finely honed avoidance techniques had seen to that. But eventually there came a knock on my bedroom door and Connie poked her head in.

"Hi," I said. It didn't feel the same as it would have a few days before, I knew that for sure.

Connie walked into the room and sat on the far corner of the bed. She immediately started to cry. Feeling sort of like the adolescent heroine of some disease-of-the-week TV movie, I said, "Don't cry for me anymore."

"I'm crying for me now," she sobbed, but it was impossible to visually tell the difference between these and the earlier tears. Connie had given me no indication that the tears on the day of my announcement had been for anyone but herself. "Those tears must have been for Mom, who can never know," I thought.

We didn't talk at all about my sister's advice, a fact I realize now probably indicated to Connie that I felt her warnings about telling my mother were correct and that of course I agreed to never tell Mom. Watching my sister sob, I thought, "God, I'm never gonna tell anybody again; this is really terrible."

So I tried to make light of the subject. I said, "Listen to what I wrote in my journal." I turned back a few pages and read the entry about how one day Connie would think my homosexuality was a novelty, that it was cool. Connie's face turned ashen and she said, "No, no. I won't." I tried telling her that my experiences in the gay community had largely been positive, that I had been "seriously" seeing somebody (even though I was only in the fifth of a fourteen-week "relationship," which was eons to me at seventeen) and that was why I wanted to share my happiness with my family. Connie smiled wanly and after a few halfhearted pleasantries, she left the room. I vowed at that moment to steer any future conversations away from homosexuality as quickly as possible in the unlikely event that Connie ever brought it up again.

December 1979

A few months before my father's death, Connie announced her engagement to a local police officer. That came at about the same time as my brother Rudi's announcement of his engagement to a woman he had dated for a long time. The family was awash in anticipation of celebrations of heterosexual happiness. It was easy to let the topic of homosexuality slip between the cracks.

Certainly, Connie and I never talked about it. The dynamic was such that we were both aware of the conversation we had had—how could anyone forget such devastating news?—but we never mentioned it.

I found myself doing conversational dances with Connie. I hoped she wouldn't bring up my announcement and did my best to finish off any dialogue between the two of us as quickly as possible. At this same time, I found myself feeling queasy about my decision to come out—even to "be gay," I must have felt somewhere in my consciousness—and started to avoid gay-community activities. At the time in Hartford, that pretty much meant going to bars. Though I had made a few acquaintances in the scene, they couldn't call me at home so there were no real lasting friendship connections. After quickly breaking up with the wag from the rag, I felt uncomfortable being in the bars at all, since they were his occupational habitat. I considered seriously the possibility that maybe I had jumped the gun: maybe I hadn't really been gay at all.

After all, I had just turned eighteen and was unaware of any gay and lesbian group or network to help teenagers come out. And Connie's display of support had amounted to telling me not to tell people. It seemed a logical leap from not telling to not being.

One day in the hallway outside our bathroom, apropos to absolutely nothing, Connie said, "Are you still seeing that guy?"

"No," I replied, feeling my pulse rush. "It didn't work out."

That was the last we spoke of the issue for well over a year. And my avoidance of both the topic and the truth of my homosexuality went forward full-steam ahead.

August 1981

After a year of trying to be celibate and happy and only being celibate ("asexuality" was a hot topic on talk shows that season and I had aspirations to a guest spot on David Susskind), I found myself in the backyard of my mother's house with Connie again. My father had been dead since the spring of 1980, and it was indeed true that my mother—and our entire family—was more relaxed now that the decades-long ordeal with his miserable health and even more miserable personality was over.

Connie and I were playing with her dogs when, again apropos to absolutely nothing, she put on a rather forced smile and a high-pitched voice that belied the seriousness of her intentions. Something we had casually spoken of must have cued her on the topic of homosexuality and it was as if she had been waiting forever for entrée.

"Oh, yeah," Connie said in a sort of singsong voice, "I keep saying to myself, 'I have to remember to ask Chris if he's still gay.' "

It was a study in indirect questioning. With split-second timing I replied, "Not really."

Connie heaved a theatrical sigh of relief.

"I'm not really doing anything with men anymore," I said, which was true, "and I could give you a list of women I've been with," which wasn't. I think I was motivated to tell Connie what she wanted to hear so that we could forever be rid of the uncomfortable topic.

"So it was just a phase," she said, which—in spite of my own sexual denial—pissed me off. Leave it to her to use such a cliché.

"Well, I dunno," I hedged, not willing to see her leave the conversation as smug as I thought she appeared in that instant. "Maybe I'm bisexual."

With her hand on her chest as if she was having a case of the vapors, Connie said, "Even that would make me feel better."

Even that. Half a straight person is better than none. But the fact is, I was caught in limbo. A month earlier, *The Hartford Courant* reported that *The New York Times* had just reported the first cases of "gay-related immune deficiency syndrome," and ever the hypochondriachal germ-phobe, I decided right then and there to never have sex again. I was convinced that I had done whatever it was that those people who had what later came to be known as AIDS had done, which was true. So if I made it official that I wasn't gay, I could avoid their fate. It seemed the surest way to survive, be happy, and never have to burden a family member with devastating news of homosexuality—or gay illness—again.

January 1984

"You've been here six weeks, and you've talked a lot about feeling depressed and conflicts with the memory of your father and issues with your family. But it occurs to me you've never mentioned anything about your sexuality," the social worker assigned to my case in the "mental health unit" of the hospital where Connie worked told me.

"What are you saying?" I asked.

"Just that. You've been in intense private therapy for well over a year and something your psychiatrist wrote in your admission notes reminded me that I've never heard you talk about your sexuality."

"What did he write?" I asked, focusing as usual on personality clashes with my shrink rather than the issues at hand. This is basically how I kept my psychiatrist focused on "Chris is depressed" as opposed to "Why is Chris depressed?" twice a week for over a year (not including group).

"He wrote that you avoid talking about sexuality," she said simply. I felt relieved that she didn't say, "He wrote that you won't deal with the fact that you are most likely gay."

"That's not really an issue right now," I said. I had actually convinced myself of this at the time.

"What is the issue?" she asked.

"That I'm depressed," I said.

"I see that," she said. "The whole staff sees that and everyone writes in your notes that you're working very hard in therapy. But you're not feeling any progress?"

"Well, a little progress," I replied.

The social worker, whom I liked a lot and who had always seemed to be "on my side" during my voluntary hospitalization for clinical depression, leaned back in her chair and thought for a moment. After tapping her pen on her desk for a few seconds, she looked me in the eye.

"What would you say if I told you I believed that our ability to masturbate reflected our own propensity for homosexuality . . . for our ability to give and receive pleasure to and from members of the same sex?"

"I'd say that's an interesting theory, but what has it got to do with me?"

"Maybe I'd just like to see you have an emotionally fulfilling relationship with another adult," she said, "of either gender."

"But I'm not looking for that," I countered.

"What do you fantasize about when you masturbate?" she asked.

"Nothing," I lied. "Absolutely nothing. I just jerk off to clear out the pipes and it's over and done with. I don't even enjoy it."

Which was, of course, a lie. I fantasized about hairy chests and erect cocks and getting fucked and blowing strangers in peep-show booths, and all the things that seemed to be causing gay men to die of AIDS in big cities in Reagan's America, as judgmental a place as any Catholic school or any backyard with a reactionary sister. In reality, I fantasized about all the things I did in my teenage years, right up to the time I told Connie the bad news.

"I really don't have much interest in sex," I lied again; I was simply terrified of sex. If I could make it true that I was uninterested, I could protect myself from the grief I had been through with Connie, and from the potential grief and terror of AIDS.

At a later family meeting with the social worker at the hospital, Mom, Connie, and Rudi offered their emotional support in my "time of crisis." They all seemed to come away with the feeling that I was officially depressed, as defined by the experts, since I was, in fact, in a loony bin. They seemed as confused about why I was depressed as the social worker had been. But none of them asked me about it directly.

January 1985

The lure of the gay bars could be ignored no longer. I found myself cruising a popular auto loop in downtown Hartford one night, excited and scared at the thought of physical contact with another man. It had literally been years.

After going home with a man I had slept with in the summer of 1979 (who didn't seem to recognize me these few years later), I found myself in his bed. I fondled his naked body. We explored our propensity for homosexuality by masturbating and giving and receiving pleasure with members of the same sex. It was my first real moment of sensual pleasure since the summer of '79. We did it all safely and it was heaven.

At my next shrink appointment I said, "It's been AIDS all along. That's why I'm here. But it's going to be okay now. I've been really scared, but I'm not quite so scared now."

The shrink was a bit disbelieving that it was all that simple, which of course it wasn't, exactly. But when I asked, "Have you known for sure that I was gay all along?" he nodded. I could never tell if he was just saying that and wanted to look as if he was smarter than me.

Spring 1985

After weeks of hemming and hawing with my shrink, I decided to get the then-new hepatitis vaccine (considering myself ever-prone to every infection, I figured I should protect myself in whatever ways possible), and to come out to my family. I worried that my mother would reject me or that it would, in fact, worry her for the rest of her life.

First, I came out to my family physician, a man I adored. I told him I wanted the vaccine because I was "a member of the gay community." There was that phrase again.

He was wonderful about it. I told him I was glad that he was taking it so well (establishing a pattern I adhere to today: if I come out to someone and they're not horrible about it, I think they're really nice!) and told him that Connie had been rather upset on receiving the news years before. He knew Connie on both professional and medical levels. He just shook his head.

"I went to med school at NYU," the doctor, who had become a sort of father figure to me over the years, explained. "We were exposed to a lot down there."

As time went on, I came up with a plan to come out to my family. I decided to do it in much the same order I had intended in 1979, starting with my brother and ending with my mother. I knew all along that I was going to leave Connie completely out of the loop. I was still worried about rejection or inflicting undue pain on any member of my family, but so much of my depression lifted on the night I jerked off with my old friend that I figured admitting to being gay could make my life resemble a Busby Berkeley musical.

I called my brother Rudi one Sunday afternoon. "Can I come over?" I asked. "I need to talk to you about something important."

"Sure," he said in his no-nonsense Gary Cooper tone, behind

which lies a sensitivity I don't normally associate with people who are skillful amatuer athletes.

We plopped down on his couch to talk. His wife was at work and his daughter Jennifer (this was the 1980s) was playing in her room. I told Rudi that I was a member of the gay community and that I would appreciate his being available for consultations when I told our mother in the coming weeks.

"I think everyone deserves to be happy," he said. "Um, you remember when you were in the hospital?" he asked.

"Why, yes I do," I replied blithely.

"Remember how upset I was because it was hard to figure out just why you had been depressed for so long?"

"I guess so," I said.

"And you know what a big mouth Connie has . . ." he said with a half-smile.

"Are you telling me she told you I was gay?"

My brother nodded affirmatively and added, "She was as upset as the rest of us and I think we were all looking for answers."

I steamed with the information that The Keeper of the News had come out for me a year and a half before this. I began to see Connie's original response as a meddlesome attempt to be in control. "How very straight," I thought in my new queer-positive way of thinking.

Weeks later, I was out for a drive with my older sister Jane while visiting her in southern Connecticut. "Did Connie ever mention anything when I was in the hospital?" I asked her. I hate telling jokes that people have already heard, and I had recently learned that I hated coming out to people who have been clued in on that punchline, too.

"No," Jane said. She had avoided the family meeting at the hospital, so perhaps she had been spared Connie's efforts.

"Well, I need to talk to you about something important. Um, I'm gay and I'm gonna be telling Mom soon."

Jane winced. "Do you have to tell Mom?"

Not her too, I thought. "Yes, I do," I said. "But don't you think she already knows; didn't you know?"

"When your little brother's in his twenties and he's never had a girlfriend and he never mentions being interested in women, you get an inkling."

Jane handled the situation pretty well considering that at fourteen years my senior, she's practically from a different generation, if not planet. I wondered if, in the inevitable "Is it something I did?" portion of our discussion, Jane would blame my homosexuality on the hot curler she rolled into the front of my hair when I was four years old. But that seminal event—which probably didn't seem incongruous with my being such a sissy four-year-old—was never mentioned. After discussing some of her other concerns (Jane would have been immensely pleased if I'd signed a document swearing I would never engage in public displays of homosexual affection), I told her the tale of Connie from 1979.

Exasperated, Jane said, "The woman is a nurse for chrissakes."

Summer 1985

Chris:
> *Have a great vacation and know that you are loved. No conditions.*
>
> > *Mom*

I brilliantly chose to come out to my mother the day before a weeklong vacation I had planned to spend in Boston. Although it seemed sort of cowardly, I thought, "Hell, if she explodes or something I'll have already high-tailed it out of Dodge."

I came out in the same sort of blunt matter-of-fact community-based way I had come out to most of the others. And, even though I had read a couple of coming out books by this time, I still cried all the way through it.

I gave my mother a copy of the book *My Son Eric*, which detailed one practicing Catholic woman's coming to terms with her young son's gayness. I asked her if Connie had told her long before this and she told me that she hadn't. I asked her if she didn't have some idea anyway?

"No," Mom replied, "you always said you weren't interested

in relationships, so that's what I always thought." The one person who believed the line!

I told Mom about how I had tried coming out to Connie all those years before and how she told me I could never, ever share this news with her. My mother said that maybe Connie had a point, I was only seventeen then and my father was still alive (and would never have accepted my homosexuality, my mother informed me). And my mother felt she had acquired a certain wisdom with age that she might not have had even six years earlier. I wondered if this wasn't just my mother's particular inclination to think the best of her kids or to cushion Connie from my lingering hostility. I kind of wanted her to say, "The woman's a nurse for chrissakes, hadn't she been exposed to the world?"

But she didn't. Instead, she told me about a neighbor she knew when she was first married and how she had a husband who was "different." We talked about difference and people being unable to handle it. We talked about how Connie seemed to be one of those people. We retired for the evening, and I was relieved that my mother didn't look like she was about to worry "for the rest of her life." (This could be partly due to the fact that, in a rather uncharacteristic move, my mother read the entirety of *My Son Eric* in one sitting. Usually it's six pages and she's out like a light. She later told me that the book had addressed most of her questions and concerns.)

When I woke up the next morning with my bags packed for my vacation, Mom had already left for work. But I found her note on the kitchen table. I left it there, hoping that it would still be on the table when Connie stopped by later that afternoon.

"Hi, how was your vacation?" Connie asked as soon as I picked up the phone.

"Really good," I replied. "There's so much more to do in Boston, I think I might move there."

Our voices still had the same tension that reflected the fact that neither of us ever talked about what we wanted to talk about. For once in my life, I tried to go against that tendency. "I came out to Mom before I left," I blurted.

"I thought so!" she said with a cross between amusement and high-school-cheerleader-like enthusiasm in her voice. "I saw that note Mom left you on the table and the thing about 'no conditions' and I thought, 'I wonder if Chris came out to Mom.' "

I wanted to say, "I was surprised you hadn't already done it for me." But I didn't.

September 1985

Some time before my twenty-fourth birthday I decided that I was going to move to Boston. I could finish school (delayed a bit by my trip into depression and psychotherapy) at Emerson College (where Fonzie went) and find a niche in what appeared to be a much bigger gay and lesbian community than I had been used to in Hartford. Jane seemed relieved that I had plans to be more politically active in Boston rather than Hartford, where I might manage to get a picture of myself kissing a man in the daily paper or something.

In a phone conversation with Connie, I mentioned how well everything had gone since I came out to the family, although to this day we haven't ever talked about her "outing" me to my brother. I made a quick allusion to the fact that the family had been very supportive since I told them and that I attributed part of that to the fact that I had left her out of the process. I said I figured this made sense, given the traumas of the summer of '79.

Again, as if Connie had been waiting for entrée to this conversation for centuries, she leapt on the topic wholeheartedly. It had obviously been on her mind.

"I was talking to Mom about that," she said cheerily. "I told her I felt bad about what I had said and Mom said 'What's past is past.' And you know she's right."

I was a bit dumbfounded that Mom had forgiven Connie for me and that it appeared that I was just meant to go along with it. Connie continued, "It's true, it's water over the bridge and we can't go back. But, really," and I swear she said this, "it's no big deal."

And we've never talked about it again.

william
haywood
henderson

sister

My sister was a tough little girl with a short, square haircut. She was fast, out of reach, darting through the shrubs, climbing fences. There were times when I could have rescued her, comforted her—I have no excuse. At age four she split her forehead in a fall from a runaway bicycle, and I was left to watch her as my mother called the doctor. Instead of watching her I crouched at the foot of the bed, watched my own feet, listened to her uneven breathing until my mother returned and took her away. A year later, as we walked home from an afterschool showing of *Alice in Wonderland*, she ran from a German shepherd that had burst through a screen door—I watched her flee, watched the dog bring her down and nip her on the back.

She grew into a slender girl with long brown hair. She played Peter Pan at the Little Theater, gave up the saxophone for the violin, ballet for gymnastics. My parents moved from Colorado to South Carolina, and my sister had a frizzy-haired, blue-eyed gentleman for her first boyfriend. His parents disliked my sister, this Western girl too fast for their boy, but it was he who, toward midnight, arrived at my sister's window and urged her to climb down. She followed him beneath the dogwoods, beyond the hammock. And on a night when my parents were out of town, he pounded at the kitchen door, came in bloody from a fight, and my sister soothed him, removed his shirt, dabbed at his scrapes with a warm cloth. Someone like him, I thought, would be good for me, but my sister was still a young girl. She placed her hands on his shoulders, shifted them to his hips.

I bussed tables at a steakhouse that summer, off through the South Carolina woods, and the waitresses, sharp and sweet college women, huddled with me, teased me, and mixed me drinks after hours. I would give them rides to and from, promise to send post-cards from Colorado, where I would return to finish high school, eventually to start college. My boss, a skinny Greek as pale as a harmless cloud, watched me with the women and asked which one I loved, which one I was taking home. I was as thin as him, afraid to touch anyone, much less these women in their tight black nylon short-skirted uniforms and white aprons, but I never denied, just smiled and shook my head slowly. And then one night when I was on my way out, as he waited to lock the door and return to his office, he caught me against a stainless-steel counter, pressed me with the full length of his body, and whispered. I pulled away and drove home with the windows open, the din of the tree frogs. He'd said something foolish, cryptic, something I wouldn't interpret until years later. I saw again the knots of his dark hair, the tired sheen of his skin. Perhaps he was twenty-five or thirty. I'd rarely seen him outside the steakhouse, the windowless block of brick and dark carpet. Once I'd found, in the storeroom, a book about a photographer and a string of young men, a book I slipped into my jacket and took home. The cover was stamped with the name of a local, mysterious adult library. The book belonged to the cook, I told myself, or to the man who scrubbed the potatoes. But, of course, my boss wanted to hold me, to unfasten my shirt, pull me back through the kitchen to the littered square of his office. All forgotten the next day. If he'd pushed it a step further—

I was home when my sister's boyfriend picked her up for a

formal dance. She wore a long, pale blue evening gown. Her hair was set with a light curl at the tips, her eyelids and lips were colored, her cheeks sparkled faintly as she laughed. She was beautiful, clearly, and her boyfriend seemed surprised at just how beautiful. He held her tightly against his side as my father took their picture.

Was I close to my sister? We practiced dance steps together for her first cotillion, made home movies of frenetic piano playing, challenged our older brother to a group wrestle (we always lost—he proved his strength and we proved our success at taunting him into action). She took a curling iron and gave my hair a clownish wave. Left alone on the bunny slope, we taught ourselves to ski. We drove the foothills, stopped in at Windy Cave, ate egg salad sandwiches at Johnson's Corners. But then, as I finished high school and headed to college, we were always apart, saw each other only during holidays and a few weeks each summer. I knew little of her life. I suppose she was curious about my various girlfriends, at least as curious as my girlfriends were about my intentions. None of these women had her grace or intelligence. I'd tell a friend, a guy in the dorm or a classmate, that my sister was beautiful, produce as evidence a picture taken at the Jersey shore when we were tan and smiling together, tell him that he would want to meet her, that when she came to visit perhaps she would like him and want to go out for the evening. What must these young men have thought of me pushing her like that? They did seem intrigued by her picture, and they might have thought only of her, dreaming about when she would arrive.

During my second year of college, my parents bought a ranch a few miles outside a tiny town in the Wyoming mountains. Along the miles of dirt road out to their place, in the sagebrush flats beside the creek, the local teenagers threw regular bonfires and beer busts. I'd seen the flames, the sweep of headlights, the circling forms blank against the arches of the cottonwoods. With an old friend from high school, a boy who had known my sister for seven or eight years, I drove up from Colorado for a visit. I had thought that my sister would entertain us. Instead, she had met a local boy at a bonfire, and they spent their days fishing together, hiking, spent their evenings at parties, playing pool, lost somewhere among the cabins and mobile homes in town. So my pal and I goofed around like kids, drove to Jackson Hole to ride the aerial tram, wandered across the fields to climb the badlands or find a spot to eat our picnic lunch—if we had a pack of cigarettes, we might have snuck a puff or two. My sister would return home toward dawn and sleep in the old sheepherder's wagon behind the house, cut off from our voices and rumblings. Her new boyfriend was tall, my height, with a heavy, cleft chin and uneasy shyness. He was my age, three years older than my sister, had left college after a semester to build houses. A few days into our visit, with my sister almost constantly absent, I went out to the wagon early and sat on the narrow side bench beside the mattress. My sister was so still and heavy on the pillow that she might have been drugged. She was being selfish, I told her. Couldn't she forego her new boyfriend for a day and take us around, be with us? She didn't move. I became more strident. Not a twitch or flutter. Whatever my protest, however shrill, my sister paid no attention, and in a year she too had left college after a semester (to return later) and moved to New Mexico with this man. I remember a phone call, after a promise to my mother that I'd use my influence, intervene, sure my voice could save my sister; all I could muster were echoes of my parents' dire warnings of ruin spewed into silence. I would erase that lecture, now, if I could. She married him. She loves him. He's my good friend.

Getting on with my own business, I transferred from Colorado to Berkeley and came out. I called my mother, and she cried, got over it. I called my older brother, and he said it was cool, he knew lots of gays in the men's clothing business—if he'd had any homosexual leanings himself, he said, they would have surfaced by now, what with spending his days crouched at men's crotches with a measuring tape.

I came out to my sister, and she laughed. "I knew it," she said. "I guessed." She demanded details. I defined lists of terms, named names and places, described, as if realizing for the first time, my boyfriend's physical beauty—his blue eyes and high forehead, the softness of his straight blond hair over the wavy darkness of its undergrowth, the heft of his thighs and chest. "Yes," she said, "I know all that. But how do you *do* it—what do you do?" I explained.

And later she told me that her husband would attempt to persuade her with my line, "Just think of it as a lollipop," and, if she acquiesced, he'd lie back and whisper toward the ceiling, "Thank you, Bill."

I took to sending her greeting cards of frightening leather men with coiffed poodles, swimmers wet from the pool, a smiling woman embracing an immense bratwurst. Inside the cards I'd concoct lavish tales of demeaning liaisons. She would read one of the cards, amused, perhaps, by the details, the twists of my imagination, and then slip the card back into its white envelope and file it with the others in a drawer of the bathroom vanity. And she went back to her chores around the house, studied for a class or went off to work, carrying with her this world that I'd created, far worse than I'd lived, far less than what was available. I have never tried to imagine, have never asked her what she thought my life was like, day to day. I have always assumed, I suppose, that she was secure in the knowledge of my fundamental innocence. But I'm also sure that I've told her, on more than one occasion, of my moments of poor judgment and the thrill that followed.

What could we know of each other? There were the points of surface fact . . .

I lived in San Francisco. On a Saturday night I might flinch as the men dancing around me flung sweat my way, snapped open fans, and cut more room for themselves on the dance floor. I might lie in the spring grass in the Berkeley hills, hand my boyfriend an orange, watch in fear and hiding as a large lesbian carried her tiny lover along the fire trail below.

My sister lived in Laramie. She worked at a copy center, worked as a waitress, kept at her studies as the money allowed. She fought with her boyfriend, ran from him and returned, drove a Porsche as fast as Capote, kicked bad habits before the cops could zero in.

But there were all the vague underpinnings that we couldn't know. If she'd ever asked me, point-blank, what I felt on day X, at moment Y, while watching individual Z pause to tie his shoe, I wouldn't have, couldn't have, formulated an answer—too much to explain, too much I couldn't explain to myself. Not surprising. My mind emptied when I tried to focus on *her* private fits and starts and moments of unclaimed desire.

There was a day, though, on which we wandered Laramie with her boyfriend, gazed up at the sandstone façades, paused out of the wind in a dusty entryway. And then the afternoon warmed, the spruces on the university campus seemed plump and fresh, the students had a healthy, hungry look about them, the green-and-yellow light beneath the cottonwoods seemed to hold us close to the ground, seemed to protect us from the cut of wind across the plain, from the distant sharp bulk of the Medicine Bow Mountains. In a Mexican restaurant, we were hungry but too flushed and ruffled to eat much of what we ordered, so my sister and I leaned back into the darkness of the recess, watched the busboy, whispered our unison urge. We would have chased him, pinned him, held him between us.

In Germany, at the edge of the Alps, my sister and I met up with a young Australian man on the last curves of the road before entering through a castle's gate. He joined the group that gathered for our tour. I'd watched him at breakfast in the hostel. We wandered the castle's halls, wound its stairs, passed through the grotto into the bedchamber.

As we descended the road, the young man joked with us. I kept pace with him, stayed at his elbow, and as he mapped out the rest of his day I shifted our plans and registered surprise that, yes, we too were headed in the same direction. My sister made little protests as I continued. What about lunch? she asked, and the edge to her voice stopped us all. The young man caught my disappointment, my moment of fumbling, and he laughed, rubbed me on the shoulder, and said that he would be fine alone, he'd been traveling alone for weeks, that we should go on about our plans and not worry about him. We continued along the road together, tried to restart our conversation, but soon he had taken another fork, heading higher into the mountains, and my sister and I found the trail toward town.

Above the wall of the woods, the white castle shadowed us. Where to have lunch? I was the guardian of our money, and I urged restraint. Maybe we could find a grocery and buy some bread and cheese? She wouldn't have it—she wanted hot food in a restaurant. We argued. She stopped on the path, and I continued alone.

The German woods were lovely and dense. The well-kept path traced along the uphill edge of the steep meadows, near the darkness of the eaves. Soon I glanced back and saw nothing but the path and the woods and the castle above, with my sister lost to the trees and the folds of the hills. Silence but for the scuff of my strides. I might come across a stranger, exchange a few trial greetings until we settled on a shared language, and he and I would wander together toward town, to a room somewhere. The sun was blaring, the air still.

I came to a bench in the shade of two pines, sat and waited, looking back up along the path. What would we be doing at that moment, if she hadn't caught me out and sent us down toward town for lunch? The young Australian would be leading us past waterfalls into the cool of higher canyons, and I'd be watching the back of his neck or the swing of his hands, my blood sugar dropping, feet dragging, trying to remain witty. And then, toward dusk, we'd descend, my sister and the young man and I. We'd part after a lazy, rich dinner, or at our bedroom doors in the hostel, or perhaps we'd share a conversation in a dim corridor. Hazy with cheap beer, he'd continue his generous laughter although I'd be tangling empty syllables. And, eventually, far too early in the morning, with fatigue crowding out memory and desire, we'd leave him behind at the train station, going another direction, fast.

My sister knew only that it was time for lunch. She also, I suppose, knew that she disliked my awkwardness as I matched my pace to the young man's. She wanted to pull me away from him, cut my disappointment before it solidified, and get us something to eat. What was it? Soup and hot bread and heavy steins of beer.

I watched the path, and minute after minute she didn't appear. No movement at the windows of the castle above, no voices in the dead air. Beneath the trees, there was weight to the blackness. These were the woods of wolves and trolls, evil stepmothers who snatched away their children's goodies. Perhaps I was alone. Perhaps someone had already carried my sister away, too quickly for her cries to reach me. Hard to believe, surrounded by such manicured meadows, that anything wrenching could happen, but I leaned forward and listened more intently. What was the tone of her voice? Would she want me to answer, to rescue her, to pull her along with me?

She came wandering into view, looking at the pines or into the air until she was close. Then she smiled and said, "I'm hungry. Aren't you?"

"A restaurant," I said. "I've thought of one. A pub across from the old stone building where they locked the children in *Chitty Chitty Bang Bang.*"

Harmony again. An easy drifting. Three more countries, and my sister and I watched the sun set into the Aegean. We came in from the balcony of our room, headed down the hill, across the dip of the road, toward the lights in the mass of white plaster buildings, in through the dark gaps where the stone pavement carved. In a basement jazz club, my sister and I sat at a table in the back corner and sipped our Orgasms and Ouzo, watching the tourists. She had her eye on a tall, bearded American—her Wyoming boyfriend waited for her in Laramie, but she wasn't blind. I had selected a German who had arrived on the same latenight ferry with us, a stocky little elf in purple T-shirt and lederhosen, who danced alone, bouncing, kicking, flailing his hands above his head. For days no one approached us, until finally we danced out into the crowd and my sister caught her tall American in conversation. They'd thought we were European, perhaps married, out of bounds. She was immediately taken up in their group—two brothers, a boy from Buffalo, a woman from Vancouver, and a drunken, curly-headed youth who chanted endlessly that she was the most beautiful woman he'd seen in months of travel. I edged into their conversations, edged out, drank more, and danced alone. I circled my German, my elf, and took on his jumping moves. He faced me and kept dancing. He closed his eyes.

Hours later, with the music still echoing too loudly from wall to wall and out across the island, my sister took her sleeping bag and headed down the hill to the beach with her American and others. Alone in our room, I pulled out my postcard of Michelangelo's *David* and attempted the pose. I turned off the lights, stood on the balcony, and looked west toward the next island. Too far to swim, adrift in warmth. Close, hidden below the edge of town, along the fringe of the sea, a group scattered, following the hiss of voices, circled and stumbled across one another. Such an easily gathered mob.

Another island, another week, and we were heading south from Santoríni to Crete, to windmills, canyons, the pigment of ancient temples. Our ship, a scow rocking so wildly the motion seemed induced by some crazy internal pendulum, emerged from behind the black island cinder cone and docked. We cursed and boarded, found seats in the open air on the highest deck, and watched the cliffs shift perspective as we cruised through a gap and out into the frothing swells.

Six hours of aching nausea. I left my sister at her grip on the rail, found the stench of a clogged restroom, tried sitting in the food lounge but caught a whiff of cheese Danish, and finally laid myself out flat on the lowest deck toward the prow. My eyes slit open to momentary visions of lurching clouds. I fought the sensation of fluid sloshing between my ears, through the hollow of my gut.

On the first ferry ride of our trip, two months earlier, my sister and I had traveled from England on our way to Amsterdam—I'd had in mind the bars filled with pale Nordics. Among the passengers I spotted some fellow travelers from the States—a group of four or five men with harshly cropped hair, dark shirts, jeans. When my sister and I entered separate restrooms, and when I emerged first and found myself alone, I took the opportunity to wander the boat and hunt a little. Down obscure halls, up a narrow flight, I found a deck perched at the prow, cut off from the rest of the ship, and among the people in the full wind on the rows of benches, I found my fellows. On a parallel bench, I sat and twisted myself slightly toward them, watched their loose movements, their fingers touch at shoulder or thigh, their laughter and the momentary hard focus of their eyes as they glanced. Perhaps they saw me, I don't know, I kept glancing away. Chiding myself for foolish shyness, worried about sunburn after twenty minutes, a half hour, I yawned, rose, and headed back into the boat to find my sister. Not in the lounge. Not along the railing. I cut through the center of the ship, past the restrooms, and there she was, beside the door where I'd left her.

She leapt toward me, a spark to her movement—"Bill, you're here!"—and then, as she took hold of my arm, she lost momentum and tears started. "Where the hell have you been? I thought you were gone. I waited and waited. I sent someone into the bathroom to see if you were sick. I asked one of the crew to look, to do something—I thought you'd fallen overboard, you were dead." No, no, no, I soothed, sitting her down on a sofa, and she sobbed, caught her breath, relieved and furious. "I was on the deck," I said. "I just thought I'd wander a little. I'm sorry. I was just out in the sun for a few minutes. Too long. Don't worry." And then I was afraid of her anger, afraid of her tears, and I stuck close to her, took her with me to a tiny gay pub in Amsterdam, sat in the back corner, watched the few regular patrons hug and kiss dramatically as they checked for our reaction. She would need me with her, need to know where to find me, and so I'd watch the men but never risk contact, never reach for anything that would take me away.

But on the ferry from Santoríni to Crete, I lay perfectly still for the better part of six hours, and I thought nothing of her, thought only of the passage of time, the solidity of earth, the cycle of calm breathing. When we docked, I found my sister on deck and we staggered into town, looking for a place to sit and something to weigh down our empty stomachs. We talked of the ferocious rocking, the dream of a cheap flight back to Athens, a package of Dramamine. Intrepid travelers.

Two weeks later, we had slept on a beach beneath olives, ridden a tiny fishing boat from the mouth of a remote canyon back toward civilization, come to blows with the fisherman over the agreed fee, hidden in the dunes through a windy night afraid the fisherman would round up a posse to extract his missing drachmas, and finally we were on a school bus at dawn heading north across the mountains of Crete toward a port, another ferry, Athens, and on into the Peloponnisos. Women shrouded in black genuflected frantically as we passed each of the hundreds of tiny shrines along the cliffs and slopes—a cross and a white box, a photo of a lost love. The bus lurched to a sudden stop, and the driver's assistant jumped out, threw a rock at something in the underbrush on the steep slope, the people cheered, and the man came back onto the bus with a dazed bird clutched in his hand. The tiny head swiveled, the beak rested against the yellow thumbnail. As he returned to his seat behind us, the man held his fist toward my sister, mocked her fear, brushed his free hand across his crotch and asked her to share his seat. I scowled, tried to sit up straighter, but I wasn't much, wasn't there, and he was already on to other jokes.

That night in our hotel in the port city, set above the bright noise of the narrow streets, my sister told me of the rest of that rocking trip from Santoríni to Crete. After I had already found my low-lying deck and closed my eyes, she found the same fouled restrooms I had found, tried the same couch in the lounge, but to her the food-bar attendant offered assistance. Out along the open walkway on a middle deck, in through a locked door, he showed her the narrow bed in his room. He left her stretched out there. She tried to sleep, listened to the rumble of the ship, braced herself against the swells. The attendant returned. The room was dim, airless, the walls peeling paint, rust on the ceiling. He lay down along the outside edge of the bed. I remembered him—the worn whiteness of his shirt, the shadow of his dark skin, dark hair, the blackness through the cloth, light of his eyes, moustache. My sister made to get up, felt her stomach surge, and he calmed her, "No, no, we lie here, we sleep, like brother and sister." She wouldn't move, wouldn't fight to climb across him, settled back in the heat and for a few minutes thought they really would sleep and she would be fine. But his arm locked across her, hand pressed to the back wall, he rolled against her, and he said, "I love, I love." And she was away from him, he let her go, she was out onto the deck and looking for a place to sit, up higher, where the wind was full.

"Why didn't you let me help you? Why didn't you tell me?"

"We were both sick. How could I have found you? It was over. Why worry you?"

At my brother's wedding reception, my father danced with a woman from our old neighborhood. I remembered her as tall, exotic, smart, and frightening. And there she was, fifteen years later, elegant in her dark red dress, smooth in my father's shuffling, sliding guidance. Smiling and serene, she was unlike the other women, and

I didn't talk to her much, only marveled when I shook her hand as she came through the receiving line. As she watched me move through the ballroom in my tux, as I tried to keep upright and avoid conversation, she turned to my mother and said I still walked as I'd walked back then, in junior high and high school—sort of sideways, angling toward my destination.

And at the same reception, in an equally silky red dress, my sister danced with uncles, neighbors, new relations, my brother's old pals. I snapped her around in a quick jitterbug, our cotillions paying off. She was lighter, faster than the others. She would intimidate even the bravest young neighbor.

My sister lives in Denver with her husband. He is the foreman for a busy contracting company, and he has taken to buying racks of sports shirts in bright colors, piles of work boots (looking for a fit that will coddle his tender feet), and playing golf on weekends and straight through vacations. My sister, now that she has two children, has quit her job as a property manager and plans to stay home with the kids for a few years. They've finished perfecting their home inside and out. Now they occasionally drive into the foothills looking for property on which to build, to get up out of the city and place the children in those clean mountain schools. As her husband pulls up to the curb in his new Chevy truck, my niece slaps her palms against the screen door, jumps and squeals, "My daddy's home, my daddy's home. . . ."

And I've been around, gone off to graduate school, returned to San Francisco to rekindle friendships, watch others fade away. My boyfriend and I stopped in Denver on our way to our new home in Mississippi. My niece, two years old, took to him, and he took to her. He sat cross-legged on the floor, and she stood behind him with her lime-green plastic brush, smoothing and smoothing his hair, carefully patting at the waves with her delicate hands. She calls him "Uncle."

I returned to spend a month with my sister and her family. The scent of the children—the girl as she soured toward bathtime, the boy as he faded toward sleep on my shoulder—became palpable, nourishing.

Now my sister sits at her dining room table and holds her new son to her breast. My niece runs through the room and into the backyard. Turning to me, my sister asks if I will take her children if she and her husband died. I laugh and say, "Sure. How much do you think they'll bring on the open market?" But she persists, wandering through the more logical choices and arriving back at me. She would want them in my care.

"You don't think people would protest?"

"That's why I'm asking, so we can write a will."

"The likelihood of you both being killed is very low."

"Of course. But what would you do if it happened?"

"I'd raise your children."

"Good."

There is the implicit loss that I won't dwell on, not at the moment, hopefully never. But perhaps my sister, as she hands me her new son and I stand him up on my lap, knows that, if the time came, her children would help me as much as I would help them.

My sister and her husband were married in a tiny, log church in Dubois, Wyoming. After the ceremony, we all drove out the dirt road, wildly rutted from the spring rains, to my parents' ranch. The Buffalo Chips played mountain tunes on the deck behind the house—banjo, base, squeezebox. The locals, the ranchers and loggers, had dressed themselves up as far as clean jeans and a bolo, the out-of-town relatives had gone a notch past casual, and among them all circulated the wedding party in their tuxes and yellow satin dresses. My older brother laid down a challenge, someone brought a rifle from a back room, and the fancy-dress group headed out past the cottonwoods and into the sagebrush. We all milled around, glowing and elegant in the afternoon sun, sipping champagne, as someone lined up tin cans on a distant hunk of wood. "Cheers," we all said. My brother took his shots, knocking off most of his targets. Someone replaced the cans, and my sister stepped up. Her gown was lace at the shoulders, tiny buttons up the spine, a long, full skirt smudged slightly by its trek across dirt, short grass, out among the sage. Hefting the rifle carefully, settling it against her shoulder, tipping her eye to the sight, she lined up the cans and shot. She was the victor, easily. We all laughed and toasted again. We all said it was clear how she'd landed her husband. And she laughed as hard as anyone as she switched on the safety and laid the rifle gently aside. She is in control.

I call her when I need family, and I chat with her husband briefly and try to coax a few sentences from my niece. We analyze the lives of our parents and siblings, telling ourselves, to bursts of laughter, how happy we are that we've turned out so well.

contributors

MICHAEL BRONSKI is the author of *Culture Clash: The Making of Gay Sensibility*. He is a columnist for *Z Magazine*, *First Hand*, and *The Guide*. His articles on books, film, culture, politics, and sexuality have appeared in *Gay Community News*, *The Boston Globe*, *Fag Rag*, *Radical America*, *American Book Review*, and *The Advocate*, as well as numerous anthologies including *Hometowns: Gay Men Write About Where They Belong*, *Personal Dispatches: Writers Confront AIDS*, *Leatherfolk*, and *Gay Spirit*. He has been involved in gay liberation for more than twenty years.

JOHN CHAMPAGNE attended three other undergraduate schools before completing his BA at Hunter College in New York. He also planned seminars for dentists, taught day care, worked in wholesale, and played piano for ballet classes and cabaret acts. He completed his MA in Cinema Studies at New York University in 1988. He is currently a PhD candidate at the University of Pittsburgh, where he also teaches. Champagne's first novel, *The Blue Lady's Hands*, was called "pornographic and sacrilegious" by *Inches*. His second novel,

When the Parrot Boy Sings, was published in 1990. Champagne's work on film has appeared in *CineAction!*

CLIFFORD CHASE's short fiction has appeared in *Yale Review* and *Threepenny Review*, and *Boulevard* has been selected by the PEN Syndicated Fiction Project. He studied creative writing at The City College of New York and has been a resident at the MacDowell Colony and Yaddo. He lives in Brooklyn and is currently working on a book about his brother and his family.

ALBERT CLARKE is the pseudonym of a well-known gay author.

BERNARD COOPER's *Maps to Anywhere* received the 1991 Pen USA/ Ernest Hemingway Award. His essay "Beacons Burning Down" was selected by Annie Dillard for *The Best American Essays of 1988*. His work has appeared in *Harper's*, *Grand Street*, and *Yale Review*, as well as in the anthologies *Men on Men 3* and *Indivisible: Short Fiction by West Coast Lesbian and Gay Writers*. He is currently working on a novel.

RONALD L. DONAGHE, after working as a technical writer for many years, is now working as an openly gay writer in Deming, New Mexico. He has published a novel, *Common Sons*, and is working on a sequel. He lives in Las Cruces, New Mexico, with his mate, Cliff.

LARRY DUPLECHAN is the author of three critically acclaimed novels: *Eight Days a Week*, *Blackbird*, and *Tangled Up in Blue*. Duplechan's work has appeared in *LA Style*, *The New York Native*, and *Black American Literature Forum* and in the anthologies *Black Men/White Men*, *Revelations: A Collection of Gay Male Coming Out*, and *Hometowns: Gay Men Write About Where They Belong*. He holds a BA in English Literature from the University of California, Los Angeles, where he teaches writing as part of the Continuing Education Program. A native of Los Angeles, Duplechan lives there with his spouse of fifteen years. He has recently begun working on his fourth novel, which has the working title *Jazzin' for Blue Jean*.

CHARLES HENRY FULLER is a freelance writer and human resources consultant based in Cambridge, Massachusetts. Though trained as a classical singer at the New England Conservatory of Music and Hartt School of Music, he now channels his creative energies into his essays and literary criticism that has appeared in *Gay Community News*, *Windy City Times*, and *Seattle Gay News*. His work has also been anthologized in *Brother to Brother: New Writings by Black Gay Men* and *Gay Life: Leisure, Love, and Living for the Contemporary Gay Male*. He is currently completing a book on job-hunting strategies for black Americans and is finishing research for a novel.

PHILIP GAMBONE has published short stories in over a dozen magazines including *Gettysburg Review*, *Tribe*, and *NER/BLO* as well as in *Men on Men 3*. A former fellow of the MacDowell Colony, he has also been listed in *Best American Short Stories, 1989*. A collection of his short stories has been published as *The Language We Use Up Here*. He has taught writing at the University of Massachusetts and Boston College; currently he works at the Park School in Brookline, Massachusetts, and teaches at Harvard. He makes his home in Boston and Provincetown.

HARLAN GREENE is the author of the novels *Why We Never Danced the Charleston* and *What the Dead Remember*, and of the nonfiction *Charleston, City of Memory* (with photographs by N. Jane Iseley). He lives in Chapel Hill, North Carolina, with Olin Jolley, M.D., his lover of many years.

WILLIAM HAYWOOD HENDERSON was born in 1958 and raised in Denver. He is a graduate of the University of California at Berkeley and Brown University, and was awarded a 1989–91 Wallace Stegner Fellowship in Creative Writing at Stanford University. He has served as an adjunct lecturer in creative writing at Brown University. His fiction has appeared in *Crescent Review* and the anthologies *Men on Men 3* and *The Faber Book of Gay Short Fiction*. He is the author of the novel *Native*.

BRANDON JUDELL lives in Manhattan and has written for *The Village*

Voice, *New York Daily News*, the *Bay Area Reporter*, *Detour*, *The Advocate*, *Philadelphia Gay News*, *Au Courant*, *Art and Antiques*, *VLS*, *Diversion,* and *Bulletin* (Funders Concerned About AIDS). He's served as a researcher for three of Rosa von Praunheim's films (*Army of Lovers, or Revolt of the Perverts*; *Tally Brown, New York*; and *Silence = Death*). He has appeared in Charles Ludlam's *Hot Ice* as a streaker and a bingo-card salesman, has written for and appeared with the Sheila Kaminsky Dance Company, for which he was singled out by *The New York Times*, was a minor media celebrity on the Gay Cable Network for six years, and is currently producer-host of the five-year-old, monthly *The Write Stuff* on WBAI-FM, a literary program. He has also served as vice president of the Gay and Lesbian Press Association and as president of the gay caucus of the National Writers Union.

ANDREW HOLLERAN is the author of the novels *Dancer from the Dance* and *Nights in Aruba*, and of a book of essays, *Ground Zero*.

ARNIE KANTROWITZ is an associate professor of English at the College of Staten Island, City University of New York. His essays have appeared in *The Advocate*, *The Village Voice*, London's *Gay News*, *The New York Times*, and other publications. His poetry has appeared in *Trace*, *Descant*, *The Mouth of the Dragon*, and other literary magazines. He is the author of an autobiography, *Under the Rainbow*: *Growing up Gay*, and he has recently completed a novel about a modern disciple of Walt Whitman.

BRIAN KIRKPATRICK, a fiction writer, grew up in Connecticut, lived in Boston and San Diego, and has recently moved to Amsterdam with his lover. A chapter from his memoir-in-progress, *Ambassador to the Garage: The Journey of an Adopted Son*, appeared in *The James White Review*.

ERIC LATZKY has lived in Paris and Los Angeles, and currently lives in New York City, where he was born. His articles and essays on contemporary art, literature, and culture have appeared in *BOMB*, *Interview*, *High Performance*, *L A Weekly*, the *Los Angeles Times*, *The*

Advocate, and other publications. His first novel, *Three Views from Vertical Cliffs*, was published in 1991.

R. NIKOLAUS MERRELL was born in Spokane, Washington, and raised in Montana and Idaho on Indian reservations and in logging towns. He attended graduate school in Mexico City and holds an MDiv from the Church Divinity School of the Pacific in Berkeley, California, and an MA in counseling psychology from Santa Clara University. He now lives with his lover and their adopted seven-year-old Honduran-born son near San Jose, California. He is a contributor to *Hometowns: Gay Men Write About Where They Belong*, and is currently finishing his first novel, *Bitterroot*, a German-American heroic adventure set in the Pacific Northwest.

MICHAEL NAVA was born in 1954 and raised in Sacramento, California. At seventeen, he left home for Colorado College where he wrote poetry and eventually obtained a degree in history. He spent the following year in Buenos Aires where he studied and translated the poetry of Ruben Dario. In 1978, he entered law school at Stanford, graduating in 1981. While working as a prosecutor for the City of Los Angeles, he wrote his first book, *The Little Death*, a mystery featuring Chicano attorney Henry Rios. There have been three other Rios books, *Goldenboy*, *How Town* and *The Hidden Law*. He lives in West Hollywood with his lover, Andy Ferrero, and still practices law.

MARTIN PALMER was born and educated in Florida. He is a graduate of Johns Hopkins Medical School and trained afterward at Tulane University Medical School in New Orleans, where he lived until he moved to Alaska in 1968. He teaches English and Speech at the University of Alaska–Anchorage, where he received his MFA. He lives in Anchorage where he practices internal medicine. He is a poet and finds the land, the people, the progression of the seasons, and above all the quality of light in the Far North an inexhaustible source of renewal. His fiction has appeared in *Men on Men 3*.

JAMES CARROLL PICKETT is a playwright and cofounder of Artists

Confronting AIDS. He curated the Gay Writers Series at A Different Light bookstore in Los Angeles for three years, and is Writer-in-Residence for the Beverly Hills Playhouse. As a producer of the theater docudrama *AIDS/US*, he received the LA Weekly Humanitarian Theater Award, and an Alliance for Gay and Lesbian Artists Media Award. His plays, *Bathhouse Benediction* and *Dream Man*, have been produced in cities across America, as well as in Düsseldorf, Edinburgh, and London. He was honored again with the LA Weekly Humanitarian Theater Award as a producer of the annual Southland Theater Artists Goodwill Event (STAGE) to benefit AIDS Project/Los Angeles. He produced and scripted *AIDS/US II*, and is currently at work on his new full-length play, *Queen of Angels*.

DAVID RAKOFF was born and raised in Canada. He attended Columbia University, where he majored in Japanese Studies. He lives in Brooklyn and works in New York City.

STEVEN SAYLOR is the creator of the ancient Roman sleuth Gordianus the Finder, hero of the novels *Roman Blood* and *Arms of Nemesis*, and of an ongoing series of short stories in *Ellery Queen's Mystery Magazine*. Writing as Aaron Travis, Saylor's erotic works include the novel *Slaves of the Empire* and *The Flesh Fables*, a collection of short stories. He lives in Berkeley, California, with his duly registered domestic partner and two cats.

DARRELL G. H. SCHRAMM has had articles and stories published in *The Advocate*, *San Francisco Review of Books*, *San Francisco Examiner*, *English Journal*, *South Dakota Review*, and others. His poems have appeared in a few dozen journals, including *Midwest Quarterly*, *Kansas Quarterly*, *Laurel Review*, *Midwest Poetry Review*, *Carolina Quarterly*, *Outlook*, etc. While he teaches composition and poetry at the University of San Francisco, he continues to think of himself as a Midwesterner from the Dakotas.

BOB SUMMER lives in Nashville, where he has chaired the Tennessee Arts Commission's literary panel and serves on the Tennessee Writers' Alliance's board of directors. His essay on Oak Ridge, Tennessee, appears in *Hometowns*: *Gay Men Write About Where They Belong*, and he regularly contributes book reviews, author interviews, and articles on the book industry to a variety of magazines and newspapers.

LAURENCE TATE lives in San Francisco and works at Project Inform. He has written articles for *Arrival*, *Body Politic*, and other publications and has an essay included in *Personal Dispatches*: *Writers Confront AIDS*.

CHRISTOPHER WITTKE is the Features Editor of *Gay Community News*, the Boston-based national lesbian and gay weekly. He has been a *GCN* collective member since 1985. His articles have also appeared in *In Touch*, *The Weekly News* (Miami), *Art Issues* (Los Angeles), and other periodicals. He lives with his lover, Sherman Hanke, and their many tropical fish.